THE IMMORTAL

BOOKS I & II

J. J. DEWEY

GREAT AD-VENTURES

P. O. Box 8011
Boise, Idaho 83707

GREAT AD-VENTURES

Great AD-Ventures; P. O. Box 8011; Boise, Idaho 83707

ISBN: 0-9665053-0-1

First Printing: June 1998
Second Printing: April 1999
Third Printing: Sept. 2000
Fourth Printing: October 2000
Fifth Printing: February 2001

Printed in USA

ᑕᕼᕮ IᗰᗰOᖇᑕᗩL

BOOK I

FOREWARD

"Peter seeing him (John) saith to Jesus, Lord, and what shall this man do?

Jesus saith unto him, If I will that he tarry till I come, what is that to thee? Follow thou me.

"Then went this saying abroad among the brethren, that that disciple should not die: yet Jesus said not unto him, He shall not die; but, if I will that he tarry till I come, what is that to thee?"
John 21:21-23

John, the Beloved, the Revelator, an Apostle of Jesus, perhaps the most mysterious man in history, comes alive in this book. Legend has it that John never died and still roams the earth as a teacher.

The contents of this first book and the additional series of books about The Immortal may or may not be true. It is up to the reader to decide. But whatever the opinion rendered, the story and teachings herein are worthy of serious consideration.

IMMORTAL COMMENTS

"This is the best esoteric novel - by someone still living - I've come across so far. The Celestine Prophecy was good, but this is even better - written on a deeper level." *Book Review by Joseph Polansky, Editor of DIAMOND FIRE*

"My God man, you are one heaven sent story teller... Whew..." *BT*

"I just wanted to let you know that your story is incredible! It has completely changed my life and even my religious views. I look forward to many more books with many more keys revealed." *DR*

"Just wanted to drop you a short note to tell you that I just got THE IMMORTAL and could not put it down. It is a fantastic book. I feel almost a sense of loss having finished it.." *CC*

"I have finished reading Book 2, and I am totally amazed by the claims you make; I am fully aware that such high levels of information could never be invented or brought up by the human brain for a fictional story. Congratulations, and please keep me informed of any future publications of yours, especially if it is Book 3!" *WL*

"I have just read your book. It affected me so much I went out and bought a Bible. I have never felt a need to learn about the Bible, or want to know more than that I was going to heaven (or so I supposed). But your book has so affected me that I am in. I felt an actual feeling inside my soul." *HL*

"Every chapter in your book spoke to me of the lessons I have learned over 30+ years of practicing medicine & developing a Complementary Medical approach to healing." *W.S., MD*

"As soon as I started to read it I felt a touch of the Spirit of God that dwells within me and knew what you had written was the truth." *MM*

"I just finished reading your book but now I have a hard time believing that all of it was fiction. When is the next book coming out?" *EF*

"I've recently finished reading The Immortal - Thank You! I've already told dozens and dozens of people, "If you read only one book this year, consider having it be The Immortal." And everyone that I've spoken with has had as enthusiastic response as I have and eagerly await both the newsletter and next book." *Diane*

THE IMMORTAL

BOOK I

THE IMMORTAL
BOOK I
By
J. J. Dewey

CHAPTER ONE
Elizabeth

I have always wanted to be a writer, but never seemed to find the time to carry out my dream. Ironically, this time in my life is the most difficult of all to begin such a project as this, but it is something I must do. I have a story to tell that is difficult to believe so I am writing it as fiction. It is too unbelievable to present as a true story. Nevertheless, I do maintain that the principles taught herein are true and that many readers will have this verified by their hearts and souls.

I'd like to start with John, but that probably wouldn't work. I must tell you about Elizabeth and something about myself before you can begin to understand.

There's not a lot to tell about me. I am average or below average in a number of ways. If there is anything out of the ordinary about me it's probably the fact that I am quite curious in nature. I have thought quite a bit about why things are the way they are. I've always asked myself a lot of unanswerable questions, like: Who or what is God? Is there life after death? What will it be like? What is the purpose of life? Questions - that seem to have no answers.

I met Elizabeth about ten years ago. I was 43 years old and Elizabeth was several years younger. I was just getting my feet wet in real estate after failing in several business ventures. Both Elizabeth and I had been previously married. But since we got along great together after experiencing difficult relationships with others we both felt like we had finally mastered the art of marriage to the extent we half-heartedly considered giving seminars on the subject.

Leaving my children with my previous wife was one of the most difficult decisions of my life, but the situation was not one of those win-win possibilities. It was lose-lose. The fact that I lost so much in my relationship with my children and they lost in their relationship with me made it all the more important to me that my relationship with Elizabeth would somehow be worth the great sacrifice.

Let's move on here. I know a lot of you have gone through difficult marriages and wish you could have your life with your children to live over again. But there is something else I also know. I know that all of you have the desire within your hearts to meet the love of your life and to fall in love and stay in love. I know that few of you have found the quality of love you are looking for.

Well, this is one area where my life was not exactly average. I found the love of my life. I found even more than I was looking for. I found Elizabeth.

After my divorce I starting teaching several classes in the local community adult education programs. It had long been a hobby of mine to study graphology, or how character is revealed through handwriting. Then, after years of dabbling, I became pretty good at it so I volunteered my services.

I thank God every day that I studied handwriting analysis because without it I may not have recognized Elizabeth.

At the end of my first class I had everyone in the class hand in samples of his or her handwriting. Then I proceeded to demonstrate that I was truly accurate by analyzing each of them. Now, this has nothing to do with psychic powers. Instead, it is an analytical way of discerning character.

There were about twenty in the class and I thought that I had analyzed everyone when Elizabeth stood up.

"You haven't analyzed me yet," she said.

"I'm sorry," I said. "Did you hand in a sample?"

"Yes, I did."

I picked up the pile of samples and handed them to her and said: "See if yours is one of these."

She looked through them. "Here it is," she said, handing it to me. "It seemed to have been stuck to another sample."

I looked at the handwriting. I did a double take. Through the years I had not only formulated an image of what I was looking for in the ideal mate, but I had also formulated what my ideal mate's handwriting should look like. After many years and thousands of handwriting samples I finally found one that looked like the image I had conjectured.

I probably embarrassed Elizabeth when I blurted out her qualities. Her handwriting showed that she was very intelligent, passionate: objective, yet caring; focused, yet curious; loving, yet having good common sense.

After telling her about a dozen positive characteristics I put the sample down and took a good look at her. The first thing I noticed was her very attractive almost sparkling face with darting intelligent eyes that seemed to focus with great attention from time to time. There was an honesty in her eyes that revealed her mood at the moment. I have since come to call them smiling eyes because when she is happy the sparkle in her eyes makes her feelings so obvious.

Physically she was about 5'3", light brown hair, great figure and with looks enough to generate an attractive pull in any male.

I somehow felt deep within myself that I would marry her. I tried to momentarily dismiss the feeling, but it stayed with me throughout the week. Then, after the next class, I accosted her and asked her to join me for coffee and the rest is history.

I could easily write a book about our relationship and how it developed, but that is not the grand purpose of this book, as you will soon see. What you need to understand at this time is that we fell as much in love as is possible for us mortals to do. Think of your favorite love story and multiply the emotions times ten and that was us. I felt fulfilled and secure for the first time in my life. It seemed that nothing could go wrong.

Until that fateful day...

I remember the day very clearly. I was in the family room reading a book and Elizabeth was fixing us an evening cup of coffee. The moment came as she was walking down the stairs, bringing my cup to me just as she did each evening.

But this time she fell down the stairs, knocking herself into a semi conscious state.

I ran to her, holding her as she revived and lifted her up.

"I can't stand up." she said.

"Sure you can, sweetheart. You just had a bad fall. Just rest a minute."

She rested a while, but still could not stand.

I rushed her to the emergency room. The doctor told me that they needed to run some tests.

Finally, after three weeks of testing, we discovered the problem. She had multiple sclerosis. My heart sunk as I asked the doctor how serious it was and how long she had to live.

"It varies with each person," he said. "Some go quickly, other hang on for years. I must warn you, however, it appears that the disease is progressing quickly with your wife. I would guess that she has somewhere around a year or two to live. You never know, though. She could linger on for ten years or more, but you must prepare yourself for the worst.

"Right now she can't even walk. She may get some of her strength back, but then will probably lose it again. It's like moving one step forward and two steps back. Sooner or later the disease gets you.

"The problem now is with her legs, but later it will be other parts of her body. Near the end she'll probably lose her sight, and even her ability to speak and feed herself. I hope you love her a lot because she's going to be very dependent on you."

"I'll be there for her," I said with tears in my eyes. "We'll do whatever it takes. Somehow we'll beat it."

"Just be prepared to deal with it. Don't get your hopes too high. It can be frustrating for both of you. Just be thankful that you have a year or two of sharing left. Many people I deal with have their loved ones taken suddenly and wish they could just have five minutes with them to say good-bye. You have time for a long loving good-bye. I would advise you to make the most of it."

"I appreciate the advice doctor, but don't take our hope away. There has to be a way to beat this."

"I understand your feelings," he said patiently. "But my experience tells me that I must do what I can to prepare you for the real world."

"I see your point," I said, "but I refuse to give up hope no matter what the odds are. I've always believed that all things are possible.

"I'm here to help however I can," the doctor said quietly.

The next year was rather discouraging. The doctor was proven to be entirely correct. Elizabeth got one step better and two steps worse. She got some strength back in her legs but later lost all strength in her legs plus some of her vision. During that year we tried every medicine, every health food, every herb that had any chance of working, but her health seemed unrelated to anything that we tried. She finally reached a point where she was confined to a wheelchair and was barely able to feed herself because of her shaking limbs. Fortunately, she still had her mental capacities, but the doctor warned me that even that could go next. At this point he told me that she seemed to be deteriorating and could go fairly quickly. She could go in six months or possibly linger on for years.

One night, as we lay in bed together and I held her in my arms, I thought of the years we spent together. In my mind's eye I visualized her being vibrant as she was when we first met and as she is now. I felt very sad. Why did this have to happen to the most wonderful woman I have ever met?

As I contemplated the situation I said a prayer from deep within my heart.

"Why God does something like this happen to such a wonderful person as my wife? You would think you'd have to be a serial killer to deserve such punishment, but Elizabeth has never hurt anyone. Maybe some very minor things, but nothing to deserve such pain. If this is a punishment it seems unjust and out of proportion.

"Even ministers these days are saying that life is unfair. If You are truly God, then one of Your main attributes should be fairness and justice. Where is fairness and justice in this situation? I ask not for myself, but for the woman I love. Surely there is an answer somewhere, somehow, someplace..."

This was a sort of basic prayer I thought within my heart several times daily ever since Elizabeth became ill. However, on this particular night I said it with great emotion and cried myself to sleep with my thoughts.

That night I fell into a very sound, profound yet peaceful sleep. Then in the morning something quite unusual happened. I was at that point where you are between being asleep and awake. I know there have been several times when I have been at this stage that I was not sure if I was dreaming or not. This was one of those times.

This was the first time I heard the bells; gentle, penetrating, familiar, soft, yet very real bells.

At the time I heard them I was sure I was hearing real bells, perhaps ringing somewhere outside my bedroom window, but then I roused myself and rose up in my bed and the sound disappeared. I was not sure if I really heard them or if I was dreaming. Then I settled back into sleep and I heard the bells again. I roused myself and the sound again went silent. Then this process was repeated for a third time.

One experience like this I could have shrugged off, but a three-time repetition got me thinking that there was some significance here.

Then the next morning I heard the bells again.

And again the next morning.

Finally, I felt I had to mention it to Elizabeth. I told her the story and she said, "The only thing I can suggest is that it must be some type of message or sign intended just for you. I was sleeping next to you each of these past three mornings and I heard no bells."

"But if it is some type of message intended just for me, what good is it? I've thought and thought about it and I can't see any hidden meaning in bells ringing."

"Have you heard bells in real life that sound anything like these?" she asked.

"Well, they sound something like Christmas bells and they seem very familiar. Christmas is just a few weeks away. Could it have something to do with that?"

"Who knows?" she shrugged. "Maybe you're just thinking too much about Christmas. How about taking your mind off the bells by doing some grocery shopping for me. Get a pen and I'll give you the list."

CHAPTER TWO
The Mystery of the Bells

Since Elizabeth became ill I did most of our shopping and must admit I got pretty good at it. I clipped coupons, checked for sales, compared store brands with national brands and much more. I got to the point where I somewhat enjoyed shopping and would probably still do most of it even if Elizabeth was healed.

As I drove up to Albertsons supermarket at 16th and State Street in our fair city of Boise, Idaho I noticed for the first time that Christmas decorations were up and Christmas trees were for sale. I wasn't sure if decorations were just put up or if this was the first time I had noticed. It seemed like Thanksgiving had just ended and it was too early to even think about Christmas. I felt a little like Scrooge as I got out of my car thinking about all the presents I had to buy compared to how few I would receive. I remember thinking as I entered the building how it would be a lot better if Christmas came once every five years...

Then, as I opened the door, all thoughts left me... I heard the bells! They were the same bells I heard in my quasi sleep, but this time I was sure that I was awake and the bells were real. I retreated back out the door and turned around. To my surprise I saw a bell ringer for the Salvation Army!

I was amazed that I did not connect the bells I heard in my sleep with those of the bell ringers. Somehow I did not remember them sounding like the bells I heard in front of me. The sound of these bells seemed to be so pure, sweet and almost holy. Perhaps I had just never listened to them before.

The bell ringer was a good-looking older man around sixty, clean shaven with dark hair and simply dressed. Some of the bell ringers look like they could have been taken from a homeless shelter, but this one did not give that impression. He was a far cry from any executive look but also gave the impression that he would never be down and out. If I were to guess his vocation by his looks I would guess that he was a high school teacher or maybe even a real estate salesman like myself.

After looking his direction for about thirty seconds he caught my eye and said: "Merry Christmas."

"Merry Christmas," I said as I retreated back into the store in a state of bewilderment.

As I went through my wife's shopping list I tried to find meaning in it all.

I heard bells on my awakening three days in a row and now I heard the same bells here at the grocery store by a Salvation Army bell ringer. At the time I heard the bells I was thinking like Scrooge about Christmas. Maybe I was being taught some supernatural lesson like in the movie. Perhaps I was being told that I should donate to the poor.

Financially, I was feeling like one of the poor myself, for I had gone heavily into debt and had no extra money because of Elizabeth's illness. Nevertheless, perhaps I was supposed to take my mind off my own concerns and think of others who have problems.

By the time I had finished shopping, I had decided to give the bell ringer a donation on the way out. It wasn't much, but maybe it was what I was supposed to do.

As I passed by the pot I dropped in a five dollar bill. The bell ringer looked me in the eye and said: "Thanks. Have a Merry Christmas."

There was something about the look in his eyes that disturbed me. He seemed to have large eyes with large pupils and the look about him reinforced the idea of a teacher in my mind. There was something about his look that made me feel that he knew things that I did not. I had never felt that way about a stranger before, but that is how I felt about this man.

I got in the car and started driving home and passed another store that appeared to have a bell ringer. I parked again and walked toward the bells and stopped in front of the man. I was stunned. These bells sounded similar, but not exactly like the first bell ringer or those heard in my dream state.

This piqued my curiosity, so for the next couple of hours I drove all over town and visited every bell ringer I could find. Each one of them sounded similar to the second bell ringer. Only the first bell ringer created a sound like the bells that I remember hearing in my sleep. Then I began to wonder if my mind was playing tricks on me. Maybe I just thought those first bells were like those in my dream state.

Elizabeth was upset that I was gone so long shopping and was worried about me. She quickly calmed down as I explained to her what happened. I ended with, "Maybe it was just my imagination that the first bell ringer sounded like the ones that I heard on waking."

"And maybe it isn't," she said. "Maybe it is a sign of some kind. Perhaps you were just supposed to remember the spirit of Christmas and give what you can afford and that's all there is to it."

"Maybe," I said, not convinced she was right.

I felt unsettled about any explanation we could arrive at about the bells. The next morning, as I lie between wakefulness and sleep, I became even more unsettled as I heard the bells again. This time I heard them resonate for a few seconds after I was fully awake. I knew now that the bells were not from my imagination. I also knew that the message of the bells was not resolved.

After I shared this with Elizabeth she said: "Your guess that you are supposed to have a more giving spirit may be correct. The last time you gave five dollars. That's probably about all we have given to the poor all year. Think about it. That's not much of a donation. I know we don't have much money, but we can do better than that."

"You're right," I said. "This time I will give fifty dollars. That's about all we can afford, but we can give that much."

I took off again to Albertsons at 16th Street and approached the bell ringer again. Again I heard the beautiful sound. They were definitely the same sound that I heard on waking. As I started to appreciate their beauty I felt my whole body and soul was resonating to the vibration of the bells. Somehow they made me feel whole, peaceful, strong, connected... It's difficult to give you the picture, but the effect was definite and strong. I put two twenties and a ten in the pot, looked at the bell ringer and said: "Merry Christmas."

"Your gift is greatly appreciated," said the bell ringer.

I started walking backward, catching the eye of the bell ringer for a few seconds before we disconnected. Again I felt unsettled as I drove home.

After I got home I told Elizabeth: "Giving the fifty dollars was a good thing to do, but I don't think it was the answer. Suppose that the answer has nothing to do with the bells, Christmas, the spirit of giving, but something else?"

"What else could it be?" she asked.

"Maybe it's got something to do with the man - the bell ringer."

"You said you felt he was different?"

"Yes. He was different...Maybe he knows something."

"If you hear the bells again then maybe you should check him out," she said.

CHAPTER THREE
The Bell Ringer

The next morning I heard the bells again. They continued to ring for several minutes after I was fully awake. This time I decided that I must talk to the bell ringer himself. I felt there was a possibility that he may somehow hold the keys to this mystery.

I drove over to Albertsons again and there he was, faithfully ringing his bell. I felt nervous about approaching him but forced myself onward.

I put a couple dollars in the pot and managed to say "How's it going today?"

"Fine," he replied.

"Has anyone commented that the sound of your bells seems to be different than the other bell ringers in town?"

"Several have commented," he smiled with noticeable pleasure in his eyes. "The reason my bell rings differently is that I have my own bell."

"I didn't know any bell ringers had their own bell."

"I've used this bell for a very long time. Here. Take a look at it." He put it in my hand.

It felt warm, almost tingly to my touch. I peered at it and said, "It looks like there are some ancient hand-carved hiero-glyphics on the surface." I looked closer. "This one here is inter-esting. It looks like a crop circle I remember seeing recently. Do you know what they mean?"

"The meanings are layered and are interpreted in levels. I understand several of the levels," he said.

After he said this I seemed to sense that my suspicion was correct, that there was something hidden about this man. I rang the bell gently against my ear. "It has the most beautiful sound I have ever heard," I said.

"Yes," said the man, smiling. "It really helps with the donations. Just because of that beautiful sound this location receives
over three times the donations of any other in town."

"Interesting," I said. "Has anyone told you they heard your
bells in their sleep?"

The man looked visibly shaken. "Not for a long time," he
said. "Why do you ask that?"

I told him my experience with the bells.

He smiled and said, "Then you are the one I have been
waiting for."

I stared at him wide-eyed. "You've been waiting for me? Why?
This is too weird to be true."

"If you think this is strange now, just wait a while. What is
your name, my old friend?"

"What do you mean by *old friend*?"

"I'll explain later when you are ready. Now tell me your name."

I figured what harm is there in telling him? "My name is J. J.
Dewey. My friends call me Joe."

"So the first J stands for Joe or is it Joseph?"

"On my birth certificate it is Joseph, but as you know almost
all Josephs call themselves Joe. Joseph seems a little pious.
About the only person who ever calls me that is my wife"

"It is good that you are not pious. Nevertheless, Joseph is a
beautiful and ancient name. Do you know what it means?"

"I think I read somewhere that it means *added* or *added
upon*."

"Whoever came up with that did not really understand the
Hebrew. In ancient days, when a father named his son Joseph he
did so with the understanding that his son will have great increase
- that whatever good that is in him will be amplified and eventually
bring forth an abundance of all the earth has to offer. Joseph of
the Bible who was sold into Egypt was the perfect example of this.
He increased in knowledge, virtue and eventually became the richest man on the earth."

"Sounds like a good destiny," I said. This man was unusually
knowledgeable for a bell ringer.

"Your second initial is J. What does that stand for?"

"John," I said.

"How appropriate! That is also my name. Do you know what
this name means?"

"I don't think so."

"This name comes from the Hebrew *Yowchanan*. Any dictionaries that define the word miss the full meaning. Basically, it implies that a man with this name will attract the attention of God to the extent that God will befriend him as an equal. Some say it means *favored of God*, but the meaning is more like *friend of God.*"

"So would you say that the apostle John is the great example of this since he was called the *beloved* of Jesus, or perhaps His best friend?" I asked.

John's eyes widened in surprise and he smiled. "He was an example perhaps. I don't know if I would call him a great one."

I pondered what he said. The comment seemed rather strange to me. Of course John the Beloved was a great example, I thought.

He shifted my attention again toward his bell. "See this symbol here," he said, holding up the bell.

I looked and answered, "You mean the two intertwined circles?"

"Yes."

"One has a dot in the middle," I remarked.

"That is my name." said John.

"So this symbol means John?"

"Yes and no," he said. "It identifies me and I am John, but it doesn't necessarily mean John."

"You seem to speak in riddles," I said.

"All teachers do at times," he said, smiling. "Did I hear right that your last name is Dewey?"

"Yes."

"Do you know what that means?"

"I'm not sure."

"The medieval Welsh altered the name of David, or the Greek *Dabeed*, to something like *Dawee* and finally to *Dewey*. Do you know the meaning of David, my old friend?"

I wondered again why he kept calling me old friend but I was too interested in the names to backtrack. "It seems like I remember learning back in Sunday School that it means *beloved.*"

"The standard meaning is close here. It means *beloved* as in the sense of a family member or close friend. King David of the Bible was called a man after God's own heart and God had compassion toward David in his weaknesses just as a Father would toward his own son"

"How do you know all of this? You almost sound like you know this from personal experience." This man was really arousing my curiosity.

"That doesn't matter right now," he replied. "The point is that you are blessed with three meaningful ancient names which will help you accomplish your mission."

"Mission?" I asked, startled. I would have walked away at that point if the man had not been so captivating.

"Your full name is strong with meaning. Put together, it goes something like this: *The desires of your heart will be amplified and fulfilled by attracting the attention of God or his servants.* If you use your power of increase for good, you will enter into the Kingdom of God and become part of the family of God."

"It's a good thing I didn't know the meaning of my name earlier - I might have gotten a big head," I laughed.

"You are far from being alone in having a beautiful meaning behind your name. Almost all names have a lot of beauty and meaning in them. It is sad that the ancient science of names and the power of their meaning has been lost to the world. But this loss is temporary. Mankind will soon learn the power of names again."

I studied this wise man closer. "You aren't just a bell ringer, are you? Who are you really?"

John sighed, looked heavenward for a moment and then looked at me. "I guess it's time to tell someone, but I can only tell you if you heard the bells as you were waking from sleep. You did hear them, didn't you?"

"Yes, I heard them loud and clear."

John shut his eyes for a few seconds as if he was reading a page from a book within his head. He opened them and said: "Yes. You did really hear them. I do not doubt you. This is a great day. Would you like to get a cup of coffee at Denny's when I finish my shift? It's only a few minutes away"

I didn't know if this guy was for real or not - *probably not*, I thought - but, like I said, I'm a very curious person. I replied, "I don't know why I find your words so fascinating. Yes, I would really like to talk more..."

CHAPTER FOUR
The First Communion

Drinking coffee at Denny's seemed to be a strange situation to have the greatest spiritual experience of my life, but that was where it happened.

After we received our coffee and exchanged several pleasantries about the Christmas season, I had to show my curiosity. "I'm full of questions. I want to know the meaning of the bells, who you are and what you mean by mission."

"One at a time," he smiled. "What do you want to know first?"

"Do you know why I heard the bells?"

"The bells were tuned to your vibration and I was calling for you. The spiritual law is that I could not come to you, but you had to respond and come to me. You heard the bells and came to me as I anticipated. That is all I will tell you right now."

"Well, I'll take any morsel I can get right now. Can you tell me who you are? Obviously, you're more than a bell ringer and I think more than any ordinary man..."

"If I just tell you outright you will not believe me," he said. "Hold your right hand up and let your fingertips touch mine."

I felt kind of weird doing this. I looked around and saw we were fairly secluded in a corner so I thought *what the heck* and put my fingertips next to his.

"Now look at me steady in the eyes," he said.

It seemed a strange thing to do, but everything about this man and events leading up to our encounter seemed strange, so I thought I had nothing to lose and looked him in the eyes as we touched fingertips. At first nothing seemed to happen.

"Keep looking," he said, "and free your mind from all thoughts."

As I cooperated with him I felt my mind begin to drift. I thought

15

we were having a Vulcan mind melding, for I sensed a merging of our two souls in a way difficult to explain.

He pulled away his fingers and asked: "Now you tell me... Who am I?"

I drew back in a start and exclaimed: "I know who you are. You're John!"

He smiled and said, "You've known all along my name is John."

"But you're not just any John. You are *the John*!"

"And which John is that?"

"You are John, the fisherman, the son of Zebedee, the apostle... the Beloved... How do I know this?"

"I transferred some of my memories to you. Do you believe them?"

"You're right. If you told me outright I might have thought you were a crackpot, but seeing your memories makes it hard to deny. A part of me believes what I received but another part says this is impossible. My mind has to make sense of all this. I have to ask a couple of more questions."

"Ask away."

"Two thousand years have passed since the days of the apostles. This means that either you are now an angel sent back to the earth or are a resurrected being... Or perhaps I am just dreaming all this."

"It is none of those things," he said.

"But what else could it be?" I asked.

"There is one more possibility that you missed. A hint is given in the Bible." He then reached into a bag he carried with him and pulled out a very old looking Bible. He found a passage, pointed to it and said: "Here. Read this...Verses 22 and 23 in the twenty-first chapter of John."

I picked up his Bible and looked at it. The print was very old. It seemed to be a King James translation, but the type was an old Roman style. "I suppose this is the very first King James Bible published," I said half joking.

He glanced back somewhat serious and said, "Not quite. The first edition was bulky and not practical to carry around. This is a later but still very old edition."

"Of course," I said, humoring myself. "Now which verses was it you wanted me to read?"

"Twenty-two and twenty three. Keep in mind Jesus and Peter were talking about the apostle John, who you now remember to be me."

I paused and read the verses: *Peter seeing him (John) saith to Jesus, Lord, and what shall this man do? Jesus saith unto him, If I will that he tarry till I come, what is that to thee? Follow thou me.*

'*Then went this saying abroad among the brethren, that that disciple should not die: yet Jesus said not unto him, He shall not die; but, if I will that he tarry till I come, what is that to thee?*"

"I remember this scripture," I said. "It is very mysterious. It seems to leave it up in the air as to whether John will die or not. I remember reading several legends that he was boiled in oil and still survived."

"That's not a legend. I was boiled in oil. In addition to that I have been crucified, tortured, stabbed, hung and shot several times."

"So, you went through all that and you never died?" I asked, amazed.

"Notice the careful wording of the scripture. It indicates that the will of Jesus is that I tarry until he comes again, yet he did not say that I shall not die. I have died several times, but was revived again and healed by God... something like the experience of Lazarus except when I was revived I was able to choose the age I was to be. I usually pick the early twenties."

"But now you look like you're around sixty. Is that the age you picked this time?"

"No, my friend. The last time I died I was revived looking about the age of twenty-one. That was back in 1944. Since that time I have been aging normally. My body presently has an age of about 71 years of age."

"You look good for seventy-one," I remarked with a smile.

"I've learned to take reasonable care of my body and have learned to overcome sickness. I have not been ill for about 1500 years, and even then I was careless and poisoned by an enemy, so I was not ill for normal reasons."

"So, how did you die in 1944?"

"I was hung with piano wire by a wayward brother."

"He must have been wayward all right. Who was this person?"

"Adolph Hitler."

"Hitler!" I exclaimed. After a moment of absorbing the moment I asked, "So were you in a concentration camp or something?"

"No." He paused a moment and continued, "I lived among the Germans and assisted in an attempt to overthrow the Nazis from within."

My eyes widened. "I remember reading about a rebellion against Hitler lead by a one-eyed, three-fingered man."

"That man was Claus Schenk Von Staufenberg who made a very brave effort to remove Hitler from power. I was there working with and encouraging the little band of conspirators, but not everything a disciple does succeeds. After Staufenberg failed in his attempt to kill Hitler everyone who even smelled like they didn't like Hitler was killed. I was unable to escape and was one of those rounded up and hung with piano wire because they couldn't find any regular rope."

"So, do you experience pain when you are killed?"

"When I am injured I feel what anyone else would feel, but have learned to neutralize discomfort by detaching myself from it."

"So when you die, and are revived, do you have the full memory of your past?"

"When I am revived I lose a lot of my memories, but then through contemplation I have learned to retrieve the important ones. That is an advantage I have over others, if you want to call it that. I have a memory that goes back 2000 years. If I were to write the story of my full life it would take many volumes."

"So, what have you been doing the past 50 years?"

"It's a long story, but I will give you a skeleton outline. After I was revived I saw that the next major threat was the Soviet Union and have spent most of my time there. I am not allowed to be a major player, however. My mission is to work with and inspire and teach people who can change the world in a positive direction. Therefore, in Russia I worked with those who sought freedom and democracy and encouraged them to forge ahead. The Christ told me that my work helped in the preparation for the falling of communism and the Berlin Wall.

"I also traveled to China and worked with the Christ to inspire the students at Tianamen Square, but as I told you, not everything I do succeeds immediately. Even though the attempt at democracy in China failed, we planted seeds that will materialize in the next attempt.

"We now are living in a time of great opportunity. The authority and tyranny that ruled Communism in the Soviet Union has basically come to an end. We still have China and Third World nations who will have nuclear weapons to worry about, but I saw a window of opportunity where I could take some time off and offer some pure spiritual teachings to the world. I have been looking forward to this for lifetimes. I just hope you are ready for what I have to give you, my friend."

"I've always been interested in philosophy", I said, "and the spiritual side of life. If you want to teach me, I'm a sponge waiting to be filled. I'm curious about one thing though. Why did you pick me?"

"Christ selected you. He tuned my bells to your vibration and sent me to Boise to send you the call."

"The call?"

"Yes. Before any great work is accomplished, there must first be a free will response to a spiritual call of some kind. You had to make a free will response to the bells you heard and seek me out as I sought you out. The disciple must meet the Teacher half way."

"So, this mission you have for me... Is that also based on my free will?"

"Of course. You can accept or reject it. Few disciples, however, reject a teaching mission. Instead, the problem is that most of them wind up messing it up by seeking glory for themselves instead of passing it along the chain that links us to the One God."

"And what is this chain?"

"Whenever true knowledge comes to the earth it comes through a chain of souls that are linked to the One Great Life. If you accept your mission, you are linked to me, I am linked to Christ, and Christ is linked to the entity he called *Father* in the New Testament. The Father is linked to God with such oneness that He is one with God and is God in every way that the average man can conceive. Any links higher than the Eternal Father are so far beyond us that it is futile for the average person to think about them."

"You mean there are lives higher than Jesus or the Father of Jesus?"

"It does not do a lot of good going into detail about this now, for it will offend some people as truth always does. I have been killed a number of times just because I was seen as a heretic."

John continued, "I will say this one thing. Imagine the consciousness of just one cell in your body. Next imagine the consciousness of all your cells put together, which consciousness is your own. The gap in consciousness between you and a cell is so great that communication on an individual basis is not practical. Yet, if you have a problem with your foot, which is composed of billions of cells, you will pay attention to healing it and in the process benefit not only the foot as a whole, but also the billions of individual cells within it.

"The One God governs over a large universe and right now this sector is a sore foot. You and I are cells that are working in conjunction with many other cells to heal the foot. That is all I will tell you about this at present. We must press on to your mission for I'm not sure how long I have with you."

"Why aren't you sure?"

"If a world crisis surfaces I may be called away from you."

"OK. I'll try to not distract you." I said. I was amazed at myself for being so believing for I am usually fairly skeptical of outlandish or unusual claims. But the reason I could not seem to question the validity of this man was that he seemed so familiar, like an old friend, and I could not deny the memories he planted in my mind. I had to ask, "What is my mission?"

"The first part of your mission is to teach the Keys."

"What are the Keys?"

"There are Twelve Keys of Knowledge, Twelve Keys of Understanding and Twelve Keys of Eternal Life. I am to teach them to you and you will teach them to others."

"Are you sure you've got the right guy?" I asked. "I've done a little teaching, but I'm no Moses."

"Moses didn't think he was a great teacher either, but he did OK."

"Well, I would refuse to teach anything that doesn't make sense to me," I said.

"That is exactly the quality we are looking for in a student," he said.

"I'll tell you what," I said. "Give me some of your teachings, I'll think them over and we'll go from there."

"At least you are willing to start the process," said John, "but I can only give you the keys one at a time."

"Well, I guess it wouldn't hurt to learn a couple of them and then if they make sense I could continue."

"A logical conclusion," stated John.

"So, when do we start?" I asked.

"How about now?" said John.

"Right now? I'm afraid I'm not prepared. I don't even have

anything with me to write on."

"This is not your standard method of teaching," he said. "You do not need any paper."

"What do I need then?"

"You need to use your understanding as you never have before..."

I was silent for a long 15 seconds in anticipation.

CHAPTER FIVE
Hints and the First Key

I gathered my forces and inquired, "So, how do we go about doing this?"

"If I were to just tell you the keys your understanding of them would be quite limited and you would not appreciate the depth of knowledge that lies behind them. Instead, we will use what is called the *Intuitive Principle.* I will give you pieces of information, or hints, and you contemplate where they are leading you and give me your intuitive feedback. Then I give you more hints until you come to an understanding of the principle. Sometimes that understanding comes gradually and other times it comes instantly in a flash of light."

"So, are you going to give me a hint now?"

"Yes. Your first hint is the question: WHO OR WHAT ARE YOU? Or if you put it in the first person you ask WHO OR WHAT AM I? Each time you are given a hint you are allowed to ask enough questions to get the direction of the hint settled in your mind so your intuition can foment. Do you have anything you want to ask?"

"I might as well take a stab at the answer. It seems easy enough. I am a human being."

"That is the definition of your physical presence, but the term *human being* is just a vibrating term that tells you nothing of what you are. Think again. WHO OR WHAT ARE YOU?"

Obviously, John was not going to let me off easy here so I reflected for a moment and replied, "If I recall correctly the scriptures tell us that we are supposed to be sons of God. Is that what we are?"

"It is true that you are a human being. You are also a son of

God as the scriptures teach. But just saying you are human or a son of God, Godlike or angelic means little. It is just an expression of words with little meaning to most. Let me ask you again... WHO OR WHAT ARE YOU, really?"

This sounded easy at first, but I was beginning to get the idea that this may be harder than I thought. I thought a moment of every teaching I could think of about whom I was and then responded. "Some say I am Spirit or Soul. Is that who I am?"

"And what is Spirit or Soul?" said John.

"Well, I guess it is me without my body. Perhaps that which continues after death."

"If I were to tell you that you are Spirit does that tell you anything about who or what you are?"

"Well, yes. I guess so."

"What does it tell you?"

"It tells me that I... that I'm.... that I'm, well, some type of spirit essence.."

"Didn't you learn in Basic English that you are not supposed to define a word with the word you are defining? You do not define red by saying it is red. You do not define spirit by saying it is spirit. Now let me repeat. If I say you are Spirit, what does it tell you?"

I was about to define Spirit by using the word *Spirit* again, but caught myself and thought a moment. "I guess if I am Spirit then I am not physical."

John then reached toward me and grabbed my wrist. "But I can feel your physical self. So are you really Spirit?"

"Well, I guess am a physical being with a spirit."

"Let me explain something that you must remember throughout this course. I will always speak to you precisely. I did not say that you have a spirit, but I asked you what it would mean if you were Spirit?"

"I guess it would mean that I am not physical."

"Progress at last!" said John. "But if you are not physical, then what is left?"

I thought a moment. "Spirit, I suppose."

John sighed. "Again I ask, what is Spirit?"

"I'm not exactly sure... Perhaps life, essence, vibration. It is what we are when we are not physical."

"But if you are Spirit it is also what you are when you are physical. If you are Spirit then you are always Spirit. Do you think you alter between being Spirit and not being Spirit?"

"I guess not."

"You now have food for thought. Think about this question for the next week. We will then meet in seven days and review your thoughts and give you more direction. Please repeat the question for me again."

"What is Spirit?"

"No, my friend. That followed the question. If you are to get the correct answer you must contemplate the correct question. What is the question?"

"Who am I?"

"Not quite. Think again. What is the question? Remember what I said about exact wording."

"Was it *What am I?*"

"Think again."

I thought back to the beginning. "Was it *WHO OR WHAT AM I?*"

"That is correct, my friend. Now contemplate that exact wording and the direction of our conversation during this next week. Make notes of what comes to your mind no matter how out of place or ridiculous the thoughts may seem. Also keep this thought in mind as we progress. Sometimes the hints will help you discover the direction you are not supposed to go, or wrong answers, so eventually only the way of truth is left."

"Interesting," I nodded in appreciation.

"Now let me ask again. If I were to tell you that you are Spirit, does that tell you anything about who or what you are?"

"I guess in reality it doesn't tell me a whole lot."

"You are correct. Even if the statement is true it means very little to you or anyone else in your present state of understanding. When and if you get the first principle you will at least have some understanding along with it."

"Fascinating." I felt like Spock on Star Trek observing an advanced alien race.

"Time is about up. I should be on my way."

"John. I have one more question."

"Yes..."

"Can I share what I have learned with my wife?"

"If you are successful you will share your knowledge with the world. Because the destiny of male and female is to become one, you should share all things with your trusted wife. But do not tell anyone else of your experience until the time is right or you will be cut off from further teachings. Here, let me get the tab."

"It seems strange to have John the Apostle buy me coffee. I would have thought someone of your status would just materialize what you need."

"How little do you realize the correct use of power, my friend. When in the world of man interacting with man, I must be as a man just as you are. You will learn more about power later." He shook my hand. "Good-bye for now."

"Where and when will I see you again?"

"I am working as a bell ringer seven days a week at Albertsons supermarket. I am easy to find. Come back in seven days, next Thursday, and we will continue class."

"OK. Sure," I said as I watched him pay for coffee and walk out the door. I half expected to blink my eyes and watch him disappear as he walked down the sidewalk, but he did not. He just looked like a normal older person strolling down the walk until he was out of sight.

CHAPTER SIX
The Beginning of Knowledge

After taking a few minutes to explain why I was late getting home I told Elizabeth the details of my conversations with John.

"I don't know.." she said. "It sounds pretty hard to believe. I think sometimes you are a little too eager to believe some of the weird stuff you get into. I mean - look at it from my point of view. One moment this man was just a bell ringer for the Salvation Army and the next minute he has you believing he's the Apostle John from the time of Christ. You told me not to tell anyone about this. You don't have to worry about that. I'm afraid if I did that they would put you away. Then I'd have nobody to take care of me during my last few months on this earth."

"I know it sounds crazy," I said, shaking my head, "and there is no way he could have convinced me in so short of time, but when he put his hand next to mine and looked at me it was like he and I were one person. For an instant I saw his thoughts, his purity and his memories from the days of Jesus. There was something so real about it that it is impossible to describe. After the thought transfer I am more positive that he is the Apostle John than I am sure of being here in this house at this moment. It sounds crazy, but you've got to trust me on this."

"I trust you more than anyone I know, but you sometimes make mistakes and your judgment is not always perfect. I trust your sincerity one hundred per cent, but you are not infallible."

"But you know I've never lied to you. I'm telling you John put his thoughts and some of his memories in my mind as clear as day."

"But I wasn't there. Maybe he's some master hypnotist of some kind, with perhaps an evil design."

26

"I can't blame you for doubting. I probably would too if you came home telling me a story like this."

"I'm not saying that your story about John is not true. I'm just not convinced. I'll tell you what would convince me though."

"What's that?"

"Do you remember reading in the New Testament that Jesus gave his disciples the same power to do miracles that he did? If I remember right they did some of the same amazing healings that Jesus did."

"You're right. I even have some of John's memories planted in me of some great miracles that are not even in the Bible. I have the recollection of John walking on water, and another time of putting out a great fire by his word and saving many lives... Then again he brought back a friend from the dead even as Jesus did with Lazarus."

Elizabeth's eyes brightened. "So, he should have no problem healing me then, should he?"

"I know he could. He spoke about the correct use of power, though, as if I did not understand it. Maybe healing you is something he is not allowed to do for some reason. During World War II he was strung up with piano wire and unable to save himself."

"But on other occasions he was able to use the power of God to help."

"Yes. That's true. I just don't want to get our hopes up here, but you're right. We may just have the greatest miracle man walking the earth right here in our midst. He may not only hold the keys of knowledge, but he may hold the keys to you being whole again."

"There's only one way to find out. You've got to ask him. If he heals me then I'll know for sure that he is the apostle."

"Well, I don't think I'd be struck down for asking. It's worth a try, but he told me to come back in a week to continue the lesson."

"Did he tell you that you couldn't talk to him for a week?"

"No."

"Since the man drank coffee at Denny's, he probably also eats. Why don't you go see him tomorrow and invite him over for dinner? We could ask him then."

"It's worth a try," I said.

That night I was lucky if I got two hours sleep. I had never felt such restless anticipation.

The next morning I took a little shopping trip. Sure enough, there he was, ringing his bell near the entrance of Albertsons. As

I approached our eyes met. He smiled a brief fatherly smile at me.

"I had to come to the store to get a couple of things," I said. It wasn't really a lie. There were a couple of things I needed.

John's countenance became more serious. "I suppose you have to do all the shopping since your wife is unable to."

"How did you know about my wife?"

"Not only did I give you some of my memories, but I caught a glimpse at some of yours. You love your wife very much don't you?"

"Yes. Very much."

"I was in your situation almost two thousand years ago. My wife became deathly ill and I had to watch her waste away. There was nothing I could do. It still bothers me, even after all this time."

"You mean you performed all those miracles and you couldn't heal your own wife?" I felt a sinking feeling that he may not be able to help Elizabeth.

"Yes. Through me God healed hundreds of people I didn't even know, but the woman I loved was beyond my power."

"It almost sounds like God is cruel," I said bitterly.

"Not really," John said with understanding and empathy. "There is always love if we see the big picture. All pain and all illness exists to either guide or teach us. If we do not learn the lesson from the disease then the disease will either continue or change form until we die. Even though my wife was a great lady she was also stubborn. She was unable to accept the change necessary to be healed. In some ways I think I suffered more than she did."

"I know the feeling," I said softly.

"Many of the people that Jesus and the disciples healed got their illnesses back because they did not make the necessary corrections in their lives. Some of these people turned into our enemies and sought our lives. Others were permanently healed and were faithful to the end."

John paused and looked at me with great earnestness: "You've come to ask me to heal your wife, haven't you?"

I was amazed by his perception, but then replied, "Yes. Is it possible? She is supposed to be incurable."

"Remember what the Master said. *All things are possible.*"

"Will you do it then?"

"I will let you know what I can do after I meet her. I sense she wants to meet me, to know if I am for real."

"She asked me to invite you over for dinner. How about tonight?"

"Can you pick me up here about six?"

"I'll be here."

John was waiting for me at six. After getting in the car I said, "You know I have a million questions for you."

"That is a good sign," he said. "The asking of questions is the beginning of knowledge. You'd be surprised how many people would have no questions even if God himself were to appeared to them."

"You're kidding! If a source of knowledge like you is available, then you would think the average guy would be spilling over, asking all kinds of things."

"Many people are afraid of the truth, even among those who claim to be seekers and teachers. When you come face to face with undeniable truth, you must either conform to it or live your life as a hypocrite. Because people resist change they resist truth. That is why few people have more than two or three questions they would ask, even if they knew for sure they could get correct answers."

"I must not be average. I must have hundreds of questions!"

"That's the way it is. You are either afraid of truth and do not want to know more than your comfort zone will allow, or you are open to truth and change and your range of inquiry is infinite."

"Since it is good that I have questions, will you answer them?"

"You can ask anything you want. I will either answer your questions or I will not. It is that simple. Some things you are meant to discover on your own. Others are hidden from you for a purpose. Certain other mysteries you are meant to discover at a certain time and in a certain place."

"Let's start with this. You do eat, don't you, since you're coming to dinner?"

"Yes," John laughed. "I live each rejuvenated life as an ordinary mortal. I am as dependent on food as you are."

"Are you a vegetarian or do you live on a special diet?"

"In ideal circumstances I would be a vegetarian but right now I try to eat a common sense diet. I do what is necessary to keep my vehicle strong and vital."

"Your vehicle?"

"Yes. I was referring to my body."

"Ah, well, since the Bible says you were a fisherman I thought we would serve you salmon. Does that sound OK?"

"Salmon is good," he smiled.

As we walked in the house Elizabeth was waiting in her wheelchair in the dining room. "So this must be the mystery man." She had a friendly, yet skeptical look in her eye.

John met her hand with a shake and said: "And you are Elizabeth - a woman of grace, strength and beauty. Do I look familiar to you?"

Elizabeth looked puzzled: "I'm not sure. Why?"

"As we talk, it will seem to you that you know me." He looked toward the kitchen. "Is there anything I can do to help with the meal?"

"Can you make a salad?" I asked.

"My specialty," he said proudly.

"Good. I'll put you to work while I sizzle the salmon steaks."

CHAPTER SEVEN
Questions

As John and I were preparing dinner, Elizabeth was sitting in her wheelchair at the dining room table. I sensed that she was uncomfortable with the idea that we were having company and that she was unable to do anything to help. She was getting to the point that if she got any worse she would have to have someone stay with her all the time. She was still insisting that I go out and work my normal schedule and that she could take care of herself, but I was beginning to feel uneasy about her.

I looked her direction. "Sweetie...Do you have any questions you want to ask John?"

"You guys go ahead and finish putting the meal on and I'll let John have it then."

I looked at John. "Do you drink wine?"

"A little now and then."

"How about some Gewurztraminer? It's our favorite for special occasions."

"You have good taste."

"I was a little nervous in offering it to you. After all, your contemporary, John the Baptist, was supposed to eat nothing but locusts and honey."

"But when he was in prison he ate whatever they gave him. Every food, every element in the universe is good and beneficial if taken in the right portions, in the right combinations, and bad when the limit is crossed. Quinine is a good example. It has been added in minute amounts to drinks for many years, but is deadly if any substantial amount were taken.

"Research now shows that moderate amounts of alcohol have a beneficial effect on the heart. Even cigarettes if taken in small doses, like just two or three a week, could have a beneficial stimulation to the system for some. The trouble with them is that very few people have the self control to limit their intake on these and other habit-forming substances."

"How about pot? How is that beneficial?"

"Pot, as you call it, is a medicine and should be administered by a knowledgeable healer. It should not be used on a regular basis without the advice of a physician or spiritual teacher. Overuse can have the negative effect of weakening the power of the will and delaying the correct use of the energy centers in the head. Extreme overuse can cause physical and other problems."

"Interesting," I said. John and I took the food to the table. "Looks like we are about ready to dine. Elizabeth tells me that I make the best salmon steaks there are."

"Looks as good as anything the French can dream up," John said. "And salmon is very good for Elizabeth's diet."

"Let me propose a toast," I said as I raised my glass. "May the truth always prevail."

"A great toast," John replied, smiling "That is not the first time I have heard you propose it, nor will it be the last." He saw a question mark in my eyes. "Don't ask me to explain that remark yet...May the truth always prevail," he said.

John and I drank deeply. I always filled Elizabeth's wineglass about half full so she could drink with her shaking hands. Still, she spilled a couple of drops. "Excuse me," she said, wiping herself with a napkin.

"No problem," said John. "Didn't you promise to interrogate me?"

"Yes, I do have some questions."

"This may be somewhat of a special occasion." John interrupted. "This is the first time I have opened myself up to questions with knowledge of my identity on the table for several hundred years."

Elizabeth set her fork down and wiped her mouth. "So, you really think you are John the Beloved? Tell me in your own words who you are. This is such a fantastic claim I want to hear it from your own mouth."

John leaned forward and looked at Elizabeth thoughtfully. "The Beloved was a term originated by one of my students and for some reason it stuck and I was called the *disciple that Jesus loved* in the final edition of the Gospel of John. I did not feel at the time that I deserved any such title. In many ways, back then I was somewhat immature and fell short as a disciple of the Master. All of us betrayed Him in some degree. Someday I will tell you why Jesus chose me to wander the earth until He comes again. In a way, it has been a great honor, and has had many rewards, yet in another way it has been very difficult."

"What do you mean you all betrayed Him in some degree?" asked Elizabeth. "I thought you were all holy men."

"Jesus was the only holy man among us and even that was not obvious until one looked below the surface. The disciples were much more ordinary than any of the churches would ever want you to believe. The twelve apostles were not much more out of the ordinary than a group of salesmen at a convention. The only thing we had in common was a desire to learn the deeper mysteries. We were also attracted to the power Jesus had and wanted Him to share it with us, but our motives were not entirely pure.

"At one point we let jealousy overcome us and accused Jesus of being a glory seeker. We told him that He needed to let us do and take credit for some of the miracles so He would be forced to stay humble. Now I see on reflection that it was we who needed to be humbled. He was just doing the job He came to do and it attracted attention. At the time we felt like we deserved attention just as much as Jesus did and we wanted our share."

"Well, if you are the Apostle and this is true, why are you telling us? I would think you would want to keep anything negative about your history under your hat." Elizabeth said matter-of-factly.

"That was our basic attitude when we related the story of the gospel to students that was finally written down in permanent form. We were somewhat defensive when the story of how we deserted Jesus on the night of his arrest kept surfacing. None of the eleven remaining apostles wanted that to go in a permanent record, but the truth was out about it shortly after the resurrection and there was no suppressing it. Peter suffered the most, however, because Jesus actually predicted he would deny him three times before the cock would crow. Many ignorant people thought he did not deserve to be a leader because of this act and some who were jealous of his position even crowed like a rooster when he walked by to remind him of his mistake. Peter suffered great pain because of his error yet he also performed the greatest of miracles among us.

John continued, "To answer your question *why do I reveal*

my past weakness? For two reasons. Joseph will write about our conversations, and in this round I must reveal the truth about the humanity of the little group who followed the Master. In the past we tried to portray ourselves as greater than we were. Secondly, I want you to realize that I am just a human being like yourselves. I have many answers, but not all the answers. I have some power available, but not all power. I would rather give you more than you expect rather than less."

I asked John if he wanted more salmon and he happily accepted. My interest in John increased by the minute.

"So, how would you rate yourself now?" Elizabeth asked. "Have you made some progress?"

"I appreciate that question. Yes, I have made a lot of progress. Back in those days I was like a kid in a candy store. Now I'm more like the father who had too much candy as a kid deciding how much candy my own child should have. My perspective and judgment is much improved. Even so, I cannot just blurt out the few mysteries of the universe that I know. Higher knowledge cannot just be poured into you like placing data into a computer. To be fully understood it must be verified through a person's own soul.

"And what is the difference between lower and higher knowledge?" Elizabeth. asked

"Lower knowledge deals with facts and can be used as soon as it is memorized, like how to spell certain words or the multiplication tables. Seven times seven is forty-nine. As soon as anyone memorizes this he can use it in the practical world.

"Higher knowledge deals with principles and requires a certain attuning with the spiritual self to be able to apply it. For instance, anyone can learn how to write down musical notes, but to compose a beautiful and original melody requires an attuning with music itself. Anyone can memorize a scale of notes but only the person who is in tune with music can come close to understanding the principle behind music and write original scores.

"So the first key which is WHO OR WHAT AM I? cannot just be told to us," Elizabeth concluded.

"That is correct. You must tune into it to understand the meaning. My job is to merely guide you in the right direction. I am like the person coaching the songwriter. I could say to such a person: *That doesn't even sound like music. Try again;* or, *that sounds beautiful and stirs my soul. Keep on writing.* I will know within myself when you have reached the required level of understanding."

"Interesting," said Elizabeth. (I was just sitting back relaxing and enjoying Elizabeth giving John an interrogation.) "Now I have some real questions for you," she mused.

"Ask on," John replied, obviously pleased with Elizabeth's curiosity.

Elizabeth reached into the pocket of her skirt and pulled out a list. "Here they are:

"One: What is the meaning of life? Two: Where did we come from? Why are we here and where are we going? Three: How much of the Bible is really true? Four: Is there a true church? And if there is, which one is it? Five: Is there reincarnation? Six: Is Christ really coming again? If so, when? Seven: When did the universe begin and when will it end? Eight: Who or what is God and why is He not doing something constructive on the earth today? It looks to me like He doesn't care much about starving children, for instance. Nine: Does this earth have any future awaiting it or is there going to be some dark apocalypse where life as we know it will cease to exist? Ten: Why does God allow suffering, disease and untimely death? What father would let his children suffer as some of us have to? If God is really a loving God it just doesn't make sense. Take me, for instance. I know I'm not perfect, but there are a lot of rapists and murderers out there who are in much better physical shape than I am. Why am I punished and not them?"

John smiled. "That's an impressive list of questions. Did you think them up yourself?" he asked.

"My husband and I thought them up last night when we sort of brainstormed."

"For several reasons I will only give you so much at a time. I will take one question from you tonight. Pick the one that means the most to you."

"I think you know which one that is," Elizabeth said evenly.

"That could be." John said. "Nevertheless, you must clearly state your question."

"Why is that?" she protested.

"There is a principle governing the transmission of higher principles. Have you heard the statement by Jesus in the Bible where he says: *Ask and you shall receive?*"

"I believe so."

"If you want to know any mystery, you must ask and know what you are asking. The one being asked must know what is being asked, and the one who is asking must be willing to receive if the answer is given."

"And if I reject the answer?"

"Then it will be as if the question was never asked," John replied.

"I'm not sure if you are really John the Beloved, but at least you are unusual... How do I know if I am ready for the answer?"

"When you are ready to consider anything, no matter how crazy it sounds," said John.

"So the answer to number ten could be that God is really a spoiled cosmic brat who is torturing us like a kid who sticks pins in bees and pulls wings off flies?"

"You never know," John said wryly.

"OK. I will not guarantee I am ready, but here's the question. It's number ten."

"Articulate the question," said John.

"OK. I'll repeat it." Elizabeth shifted in her wheelchair. "Why does God allow suffering, disease and untimely death? Why do some innocent children die? Why do some of us suffer with painful disease and others who deserve to suffer seem to be vibrant and healthy?"

"I'll answer at least part of your question," said John "In particular, you want to know why you suffer with such a dread disease when you have been basically a good person and do not deserve such pain. You wonder why your life will seemingly be cut short while other people can gracefully grow old with their partners. Is that what you want to know?"

"Basically, yes."

"I will give you a partial answer now and more later when you have additional pieces to the puzzle. Can you accept this?"

"I suppose so. Go ahead. Show me what you've got."

I smiled at Elizabeth's spunkiness and looked at John with great anticipation for the answer.

CHAPTER EIGHT
The Answer

John took a breath, leaned back in his chair, and said: "By the way, that's about the best salmon I've had in a thousand years. Good wine too. Reminds me of some good German ones back in the 30's. I appreciate your hospitality."

"Thanks. That means a lot coming from you," I beamed.

"Now on to the question," said John. "The question Elizabeth asked is not usually of great concern for a person who is healthy, active and gliding along in life. But sooner or later every soul in his or her progress reaches some type of life crisis or problem and looks to the skies at some invisible being and demands: *Why me God???* Or it may be *Why my wife?* or *Why my child?* or *Why my parents?* He wants to know why this suffering seems to single him out and not others who seem to richly deserve it. He hears that God is love, but if He is loving, then why would He allow this?"

John paused a moment then continued: "If and when you finish the 36 principles the answer to this will be fairly clear in your mind. For instance, when you understand who and what God is, it will be a great help, but for now we will stick to the basics."

"There are great truths hidden in some of the maxims of this world. For instance you have heard the phrase *no pain, no gain?"*

We both nodded.

"This statement is as good as scripture. Do you think there has ever been an Olympic champion who got where he was without a great deal of pain? How about a successful businessperson, an inventor, a great actor? They have all had to go through painful experiences or make painful sacrifices. But in the end the pain produced gain.

"Now an interesting point here is that these successful individuals volunteered for the pain because they had faith the pain would produce gain. The runner painfully pushes his body because he believes it will result in a stronger body and eventually the joy of accomplishment and victory.

"Let us imagine that various parts of your body had their own life and consciousness. See your lungs as one entity, your heart as another, your muscles still another and your brain as a fourth entity. You are the whole person and are in charge of the general decision making as to what is good for the whole. Let us say that the brain wants to read a book, the muscles want to sleep because they are tired, the lungs want some fresh air and the heart wants some romance. The problem is they cannot do all of these things - they can only do one of them. Who gets to decide? If the brain decides all the time the whole body will spend all of its time reading and will never get fresh air for the lungs. If the heart forces the body to spend all free time in romance then the brain will be bored to death. It is fortunate that decision making is turned over to you - the whole person running the body. You make decisions for the body by taking the whole into consideration. Your decisions may not be perfect, but they are much better for the whole than if power were turned over to a part."

"So are you saying that I am a part of a greater whole and that this greater whole is making me suffer for some greater benefit of something greater than myself?" Elizabeth. asked

"That is part of the answer," John nodded. "Now to visualize more clearly, let us suppose that you decide that you are going to be a champion long distance runner. When you start your training no one of these four lives I mentioned will be happy. During running practice the brain will have too much blood rushing through it to even be able to think. The lungs will feel like they are on fire and ready to explode. The muscles will ache and feel as if they cannot go on, and the heart will pump like crazy thinking it is being tortured. All these little lives are shouting out the question, *Why is this happening to us? What is the purpose of it all?*

"Then comes the time months later that the body is in perfect tune and ready for the competition. What do these little lives feel about being pushed now? The brain notices that it gets more oxygen and thinks and functions much better. The lungs are happy they have to breathe about half the frequency as they used to and breathing is much easier. The muscles are aware that the weight of the body seems much lighter and they no longer need so much rest. Finally, the heart, like the lungs, seems to be able to rest more and does not have to beat as often or with as much effort as it used to. In the end they all think the same thought: *We've been through a lot of pain, and we didn't like it at the time, but now life seems easier, fuller and more rewarding.*

"Now," said John, moving his chair closer to the table, "we'll move this analogy closer to home. It may seem to us that we are the highest lives in the universe and that what we do only affects ourselves. But it does not. Each of us has invisible links to family, friends, city, state and every other life on this planet and even the universe. These are all various higher bodies in which we interact and produce effect. We are linked to these other lives through the Holy Spirit who is the final judge as to circumstances that will be brought into play which will benefit the whole."

Elizabeth wheeled back from the table, "So, you are telling me that the Spirit of God decided to make me ill to benefit the whole in some way?" Elizabeth asked angrily. "Well, I don't think my illness is benefiting anyone or anything. In fact, it is keeping me from doing many good things I have always wanted to do." She looked ready to leave the room.

"It may seem that way," John replied softly and patiently. "But for greater understanding, you must realize that there are two of you who are undergoing a painful experience here. In some ways your husband suffers more pain than you do. When a loved one is suffering through what appears to be no fault of his own and you can do nothing about it, that helplessness is very painful. Believe me, I know. I was in Joseph's situation long ago."

After a long pause Elizabeth sighed, her eyes slightly tearful, "You're probably right. He also has to work much harder than he used to in able to take care of everything. Now I even have him doing housework. Believe me, that is proof he loves me. Then I probably bring him additional pain by complaining too much..."

"You don't complain as much when you are ill as others do when they are well," I assured her.

"Actually," said John, "the analogy so far applies more to Joseph than it does to you. Like the story of the four little lives, Joseph, through no fault of his own, found himself married to a person with an incurable disease. He is like all of us to some degree or another. We find ourselves in situations that we had seemingly little if any power in creating, and once there we just have to deal with it the best we can. Like the brain, he had to forego pleasant studies. Like the lungs, he had to work harder to supply oxygen or money to keep everything running smooth. Like the muscles, he had to be more active and take on a larger load. Like the heart, he had to put romance on the back burner and concentrate on just keeping your relationship alive by pumping harder to keep life-giving energy circulating between the both of you. Later, just like the four little lives, Joseph will find that he has more freedom, power and strength than he ever had before."

"That's all very interesting," said Elizabeth, shaking her head, "but I'm still in the dark as to why I have to suffer this disease. Don't tell me that it is just so my husband can have a growing experience."

"Not at all," John replied. "However, that may be part of the reason the Spirit sent a charge of energy that caused Joseph to fall in love with you and marry you. But the benefits of your disease for Joseph are merely side benefits that we all pick up on the road of life if we handle our situations correctly as they come up."

"You've gone all around my question but haven't answered me yet. Why don't you just blurt it out and tell me," Elizabeth pleaded, her voice shaking.

John looked into Elizabeth's eyes and replied softly and slowly, "Whenever you meet a true spiritual teacher worth his salt he will rarely answer you outright. Instead, he circles around the core thought so when the answer is finally manifested it will be understood. Now that is what I am about to do. Why do bad things, such as your illness, happen to good people?

"As I said before, you are a part of a greater whole that is joined together by the Holy Spirit. Each person in an individual life has one major lesson he is supposed to learn, one ability or talent he is to develop and one quality he is supposed to enhance. This triangle of learning is never easy and is always a struggle. For instance, if a certain person was born with the natural ability to play the piano the lesson would generally not be directly connected with it because internally this is something that is already mastered. Instead, the piano may be a distraction to tempt him away from his real lesson, which may be in an opposite direction such as heavy construction. If he is driven by his soul to become a famous musician the lesson could be connected with the fame and not the talent itself."

Elizabeth interrupted, "From the time I was young I had a gift for drawing. I never took any classes, but I could draw most anything in moments and it would look great. Just as I was think-

THE ANSWER   41

ing of developing this talent more fully I got this disease. Now my hands shake too much to be able to draw."

"This ability that you naturally had was your temptress to lead you astray from your true calling to improve yourself and to be more useful to the whole, thus becoming a whole-ly (holy) person."

"So what am I supposed to learn?" Elizabeth asked.

"As I said, the thing you are supposed to learn is something you are usually not very talented in and naturally resist to some degree. When the degree of resistance becomes too great and you are not hearing or seeing the messages that the Spirit is sending you, then the message must be sent more strongly. If it is resisted again you may be sent a life-threatening illness such as yours which forces you to look upward and shout out *why me God?*"

"I've done that before," said Elizabeth. "So what am I resisting?"

"Think," John suggested. "Think of situations you may not like that seem to keep repeating themselves, forcing you to do or work at something you don't particularly want to do."

"I know what mine is," I spoke up. "I've always enjoyed doing creative things, especially writing of all types and I've always been forced into situations where I have no time for creative endeavors and always wind up doing something in sales or business to make the money I need. I used to hate sales and business, but now I'm becoming good at it. I appreciate business and sales talent as much or more than I do an artist."

"And that is why you are healthy," said John. "You eventually gave in to the forces pushing you toward your lesson and are making progress. As long as you are making progress in your lesson your soul does not have to send you great pain to move you ahead."

"So what is Elizabeth resisting?" I asked again.

"She must examine the experiences of her life, look within, touch bases with the *still, small voice,* find out what she has avoided doing, and do it."

"How will I know when I have found it?"

"It will feel very right and good when you finally yield to it," said John.

"So what is the lesson of her disease?" I asked.

"Every disease is a teacher," said John. You must look at the disease, see where it is located and the effect it is having in order to discern its lesson. For instance, heart disease must be trying to teach us something connected with the heart. The heart is the seat of spiritual love. If it is time for you to learn the value and expression of love - which is an octave higher than passionate love or possessive love - and you resist, then the heart becomes weak as a message to you that your expression of love is weaker than it should be."

"But I've had some friends with heart problems and they seemed like pretty nice people," Elizabeth exclaimed. "On the other hand, I've known some cruel people who seem to not know what love is at all, yet have healthy hearts. How do you explain that?"

"The cruel people you mention are not yet ready to learn about spiritual love so their souls do not even attempt to teach them by bringing them pain in that direction. Maybe the cruel person needs to start with a simpler lesson. Perhaps he is just supposed to learn the value of giving and receiving affection. Maybe he is suffering through tremendous pain and rejection because he is not getting any affection from anyone. Maybe this rejection just about drives him crazy until finally he yields and gives in to it. For him that is a big step, but for us we wonder why anyone would have a problem with it."

"So what's the lesson of cancer?" I asked, becoming even more interested.

"Ah, cancer," said John. "Many great souls have died of this, one of the most painful of all teachers.

"All disease falls into two categories. First is congestion. This is caused by holding in too much, such as in suppression or denial. The second is inflammation. This is caused by not holding in enough and releasing more energy than you take in. Cancer is caused by congestion. The person holds in or suppresses energy or feelings that need to be released, and this holding in produces a growth which is symbolic of the unreleased desire or feeling.

"Let us suppose that you see yourself as a nice person and find yourself in contact with a rough individual who hurts your feelings. You have three choices. First, you can hurt his feelings right back; second, you can release your hurt by telling that person how he made you feel; or third, you can be a nice person and avoid conflict by pretending that everything is OK.

"This third alternative that many take is by far the worst choice. First, it encourages the rude person to continue in his behavior, and second, it is a deception that the Spirit of Truth will not allow to forever remain in an evolving soul. People think the most frequent lie is *The check is in the mail.* But in reality it is the communication which says: *I'm fine. You did not hurt me*, which is the biggest lie.

"Lesser souls are allowed to lie and get away with it. Like children they get away with certain things because of their lack of understanding. But when a person reaches a certain stage of progression, this greatest lie is no longer tolerated and the lesson must be learned.

"Cancer is caused by many types of suppression. Hurt feelings, as I said, is a big one, denial of feeling is another, and lack of sexual fulfillment due to lack of communication, miscommunication or guilt is another. All involve deception of some type."

"You're circling around the answer again," said Elizabeth. "I can see that this method of teaching does have the effect of stimulating interest. Now I'm more curious than ever about what you will say about my illness."

"That is as it should be," John smiled. "Every disease has both physical and spiritual ingredients affecting the problem. For instance, people think that contact with germs produce certain illnesses, yet two people can inhale the same germs and one can get sick and the other one not be affected. Perhaps the one who did not become ill was in better physical shape, but more often than not he was in more harmony with his soul in that area where the disease has a lesson to teach.

"Multiple Sclerosis was very rare before a hundred years ago and even today rarely occurs in the less civilized societies. Part of the reason for this is our overprocessed and depleted foods. Another is the chemicals and poisons that civilization is currently exposed to. You have heard the theory that mercury fillings can bring on MS and there is a grain of truth to this, but Joseph has more mercury in his mouth than you have, yet is unaffected. The difference lies in the spiritual reason.

"The seat of the problem lies in the brain and the nervous system. In MS there is a loss of a fatty protective layer between the brain and the nerves, causing a malfunction or loss of communication between the brain and the all-important nervous system.

"Spiritually, our nervous system needs a certain amount of protection from our thoughts, brain activity and our fears, which our brains and feelings tend to amplify."

"MS is basically caused by failure to correctly direct thoughts and fears into their right place. The patient must realize that un-checked fears and thoughts can run rampant and destroy the pro-tective layer over the nerves. When unchecked thoughts and fears interact directly on the nervous system a physical correspondence can take place and the person can become ill."

"So I did not get MS because I somehow do not let my thoughts and fears affect my nervous system?" I asked.

"You create the protection you need by shifting your atten-tion from destructive thoughts and fears. This shifting of attention gives your nervous system its needed rest. On the other hand, Elizabeth suppresses unwanted thoughts and fears. This gives her the appearance of resting the nerves, but its effect is oppo-site. Instead, she has another deception producing a destructive effect. By deceiving herself and pretending certain thoughts and fears do not exist, a dangerous situation is created and we have another disease of congestion as a result."

"So what thoughts and fears do I pretend do not exist?" asked Elizabeth, leaning forward.

"Unfortunately, it would not be right for me to fully explain that to you at this time. I can teach you around a principle, but you must do a certain amount of soul searching yourself or you will be denied a great growing experience." He paused a moment and said: "Here, let me touch your forehead."

John reached across the table and touched her forehead with the fingertips of his right hand. "Let the energy flow for a moment" he said, closing his eyes. He took a long, slow breath, and exhaled softly and evenly.

We were all silent for a short time.

"There," said John. "You will feel stronger for a few days. I do this for you to give you faith that you can be healed."

"I do feel stronger!" Elizabeth said, obviously surprised. She looked at John with great emotion in her eyes. "If you are really John the Beloved, can you just heal me like people were healed by Jesus?"

John paused in thought of his past. "Many healings were permitted at that time because it was extremely important as a witness to the Son of God. The good that resulted outweighed the bad, but there were some problems for those who were healed who were not ready. It is also very important that you be healed so you can help Joseph with the work he has to do, but the prob-lem is that you will need the benefits of the knowledge and ability gained from the healing to fulfill your own mission correctly."

"Does this mean I can be healed?" she asked eagerly.

"Definitely, but both you and your husband must do your part. You are in a race against time. You must achieve healing while your brain-body interactions are still intact, or it could be too late. If you and Joseph can solve the first three keys of knowledge before this happens you will be healed. On the other hand, you may be healed early through correct action, thought and faith."

"Doesn't telling her something like that increase fears and unwanted thoughts?" I asked. "Won't such stress make things worse?"

"If handled correctly it will force her to deal with her thoughts and fears so she will learn to put them in their right place," John answered, standing up to leave. "This is as far as we can go now. It has been a pleasure."

As I was opening the door for John to leave I asked, "How did you know I have more mercury fillings than Elizabeth?"

"You will find out at the right time," he smiled.

"Let me drive you home," I offered.

"That's all right. It's a nice night for a walk."

"But it must be five miles to wherever you live."

"It doesn't matter. Walking and arranging your thoughts is a very healthy thing." As he walked into the night he reminded me of Kane in the Kung Fu series. This time I thought he did disappear in the distance, but I wasn't sure. After all it was fairly dark.

CHAPTER NINE
Who Are We, Really?

I shut the door behind me and walked over to Elizabeth. "What do you think?" I asked.

"He's interesting," she said. I could see from the light in her eyes - something I haven't seen in a long while - that hope had returned.

"Do you think he's for real?" I asked carefully.

"I don't know for sure. Something about him is very convincing."

"A scripture about Jesus comes to my mind," I said, clearing off the table. "It says *He taught as one having authority, not one of the scribes.* John seems to teach with an authority or knowledge behind what he says unlike any teacher I have ever heard."

"It goes beyond that," added Elizabeth. "I definitely felt something when he touched me. I swear I think I can stand up." She nudged forward in her chair. "Take my hand," she commanded.

"You aren't going to try to get up are you?" I said walking toward her.

"I feel like I can stand. Pull me up," she insisted.

"I don't know," I said giving her a fairly limp hand.

She grabbed and pulled. Her pull made me pull back until she was standing upright.

"I don't believe it!" I exclaimed. "You haven't stood in months."

"I think I can walk!' she exclaimed as she took a step. Then she took another, letting go of my hand. Next she walked slowly across the room and rested against the wall. She radiated like an Olympic winner at the finish line.

"It's a miracle," I shouted.

"John said I would have increased strength for a couple days,"

Elizabeth cautioned, walking back and forth slowly across the room. "Since this is temporary, I think we should go for a walk while I have the strength."

"Do you think you can?"

"There's one way to find out," she said. "Get our coats and let's breathe some fresh air."

Sometimes there was no way of saying no to Elizabeth. I had to at least humor her. I got the coats. "Why are you so determined to take a walk?" I asked.

"There was something in John's voice as he was leaving. Remember what he said - something like walking helps you to arrange your thoughts. He said something about putting my thoughts and fears in their right place so they would no longer be destructive."

Then Elizabeth took my arm and walked out the door and down the steps with a strength and determination that amazed me. Soon, we were walking down the street at a brisker pace than I had thought possible. "Let's head toward the foothills where we used to go," she suggested in a childlike voice.

I couldn't discourage her at this point. We lived only a few blocks from some beautiful foothills that we haven't been able to explore since the illness. We headed toward them and to my pleasant surprise Elizabeth seemed to have the strength to continue.

"It's so good to be able to walk again," she breathed in deeply. "I have never felt so good in my life. Even the air feels like it is charged with life."

"Just think of all the walks we could have taken together but didn't," I said. "You know I've never thought of it before, but I can see how walks can take your mind off your troubles. Just look at the beauty of this place! How can a person be fearful or worrisome while walking through them?"

"I think I can see how John was right," said Elizabeth. "For several years before my illness, and perhaps even more so after my illness, I have had my attention on my problems and my fears. Even when I seemed to be taking it easy my concerns were still there gnawing at me. If my brain has needed a rest I can see how it didn't get it. On the other hand, it seems as if your brain doesn't get any rest either."

"You can't always tell what is going on inside by looking or even living with someone," I replied. "I think I am successful at keeping unwanted fears and thoughts from affecting me continuously. Even when I have little time or am under a lot of pressure, I set aside periods of time where my undesirable thoughts and fears are diverted. They are not suppressed, but sort of like in hibernation." Then it was like a light was turned on in my head. "Perhaps it would be more accurate to say it's like I have created a place for them and have put them there. That's kind of the way John put it, isn't it?"

"Yes," she nodded. "He said something about sending our thoughts and fears to their right place. That's a little the way I feel now, like my unwanted thoughts and fears are in storage behind some locked doors somewhere. Right now, while we are walking through these beautiful hills they have no power over me. This is the first time since my illness I can remember feeling this way."

"Maybe this means that you are healed," I said hopefully. It was too good to be true, I thought, but miracles do happen.

"I don't know. John said I would have added strength for a few days. It's like some other will besides my own is keeping those symbolic doors locked and making me safe for a period of time. He said I could be healed if we solved the first three keys. Maybe we should take this quiz program of his seriously. You said something about the importance of getting the question right. Tell me the exact wording again." We sat down on some rocks to rest.

"It was not just WHO AM I? but WHO OR WHAT AM I?"

"And what answers did you give him that he said were not correct?"

"He didn't quite say they were not correct but implied that my answers didn't mean anything. Apparently there's some core answer I'm supposed to come up with."

"Tell me the answers you gave him that were not it."

"First I said I was a human being."

"Well, when I look at your office I sometimes wonder about that," she smiled.

"You are feeling better, aren't you?" I quipped

"What else did you say?"

"I said a spirit, a soul, a son of God. None of these were it."

"Well, you would think our essence would be some type of spirit or spiritual. Why did he say this was not it?"

"He said that saying I am spirit does not mean anything. He asked me to define spirit and I couldn't say anything intelligent."

"So he wants you to say something definite about who you are, and if you do not know what spirit is, it means nothing to say you are spirit?"

"I think it's something like that," I answered.

"Have you done any more thinking about who or what you are?"

"Some."

"What have you come up with?"

"Not much. How about you? Can you come up with anything?"

"Well. I always find it's good to just rattle off whatever comes to mind, make a list and see if anything makes any sense."

"I've pretty much rattled off my list," I said. "Let's go through your list, perhaps from a woman's perspective."

"Smart man. Turn it over to a woman when you reach an impasse."

"OK. Let's see what you've got."

"WHO or WHAT AM I? Let's see." Elizabeth stood up and we started walking again. "In addition to what you've said I could add that I am my thoughts, my feelings, my personality... I am what I look like. I am female. Did you know that many women define who they are by their home? That the home is an extension of themselves?"

"I think you mentioned it to me. Your list sounds as good as mine. Somehow I don't think we have the answer though. Let's write our thoughts down when we get home and I'll present them to John in our next session."

"I guess that's about all we can do."

"There's one more thing I think I will do."

"What's that?" she asked.

"I'm going to have breakfast with Wayne tomorrow. He's been a good friend for years and an amateur philosopher. I think I will ask him the question."

Elizabeth glanced at me anxiously. "Didn't you say John told you not to tell anyone about this yet?"

"He told me not to tell anyone about him. He didn't put any restrictions on how I can come up with the answers."

"Well, don't do anything to screw this up," she said, squeezing my arm. "He said if we master the first three principles I will be healed."

"John said to listen to his exact words and his exact words did not forbid me from tossing this by Wayne."

"We haven't done that great so far. Maybe Wayne will give us an idea or two."

The next morning I met Wayne at our favorite cafe. Wayne was an old friend about my age who had his own business. He ran a yard care business and did a little of everything for his customers - pruning, mowing, pest control and so on. He looked like a regular homespun guy and usually wore a cowboy hat. You would never think by looking at him that he spent any time thinking about the meaning of life. But he loved to get together with me for breakfast at least once a week and just talk about philosophy, religion, the new age, politics, meaning of life or whatever. We both had respect for each other as two thinkers who looked a little deeper into the meaning of things than the average person. This morning I was hoping he would be at his philosophical best.

"How's your week been?" I asked him as the waitress seated us.

"You don't want to know," he said with a painful expression on his face.

Even though Wayne was a great philosopher he had not quite perfected the art of distilling his intelligence to the point of running his business smoothly. It seemed like every time we got together he had a horror story of some costly action one of his employees took. Several months ago one ran off with about $10,000 worth of tools just a couple days after Wayne bailed him out of jail. Just last week one of them showed up on his doorstep with his wife and kids because they were evicted. The reason? He spent his rent money on drugs. Wayne was beside himself on that one.

Even though I felt bad that my good friend had so many business problems I was always curious about what happened this time. I could never just let it slide. "OK Wayne. Tell me the story."

"I drew Skip a diagram - a map of the yard so there would be no mistake. Last time he told me that I wasn't clear enough, so this time I drew him a damn map!" Wayne almost spitted out.

"Wasn't Skip the one who pruned the wrong tree of some fussy customer?" I asked.

"Yep. He promised it wouldn't happen again as long as I was clear with him so I drew him a diagram of the yard with an X marking the spot where the birch tree was located. The instructions were simple. Take out the birch tree where X marks the spot."

"And he took out the tree from somewhere else?" I guessed.

Wayne shook his head and gritted his teeth. "The stupid son of a bitch took out a birch tree from the east side of the lawn, not the west side where I had the X."

"So there were birch trees on both sides of the lawn?"

"Yes, but I had the X marked on the West side."

"If your diagram was not clearly marked maybe he looked at it upside down and thought east was west." Good old Wayne doesn't get mad when I analyze his problems like Elizabeth does sometimes.

"That's what he claims, but only an idiot would have read the map that way. I had the roses marked on the West side by the correct birch. That was just one of the ways he should have chosen the right tree."

I thought to myself that I might have turned the map upside down had I been an employee, but my friend was aggravated enough without me adding fuel to the fire. "So what's the owner going to do?" I asked.

"We had to go back and take out the right tree for free and plant him three new trees and he still isn't happy. He's talking about taking us to court, but I think he just wants to blackmail us for all he can get. The last time I talked to him he said that if we mowed his lawn for free for all of next year he may not take legal action. I felt like telling him to take a hike, but I suppose we'll wind up mowing his lawn. That damn Skip! You'd think a guy could read a diagram."

"Maybe next time you ought to actually show him the right tree in person," I offered gingerly.

"I don't have time to hold everyone's hand," Wayne said, shaking his head.

Then at least you'd better mark East, West, North and South on your diagrams."

"Hell, that wouldn't do any good. Some of these guys don't know which way is up, let alone where West is." Wayne took a big gulp of water.

This conversation seemed to end where it does each week. Wayne had a major problem with one of his guys and there was no way to prevent it and there is no way to prevent it from reoccurring. I was glad I was not asking him for business advice. Philosophy yes, Wayne was as good as anyone I knew, but business did not seem to be his talent. Nevertheless, I did admire him for keeping at it despite all the setbacks. He did seem to be getting a little more savvy in the real world.

"I have a philosophical question for you," I said, changing the subject.

"Anything to get my mind off my guys," he said. "I told you I didn't want to talk about my problems."

"OK. Here's the situation." I bent forward and asked in softer tones so as not to be overheard. "Let's say that you have a vision and God appears to you."

"What does he or she look like?" Wayne asked with a smirk.

"It doesn't matter. Just suppose God appears to you and offers you a deal."

"What kind of deal?" Wayne seemed to be shifting his attention from his problems to his philosophical mode.

I thought carefully. I couldn't tell him about John. "Let's say that God tells you that if you can answer one simple question He will give you three wishes."

"I could use three wishes. I would take a stab at it. Why not? What's the question?"

"Here's the question: WHO OR WHAT ARE YOU?" Now here is what the answer is not. It is not a human being, a son of God, a spirit or soul. So if God says that none of these common answers are correct, what could it be?"

"This is an odd line of questioning for you," Wayne said, looking at me suspiciously. "Are you sure you didn't get hit on the head and see the Big Guy?"

"No. Nothing like that." I tried to sound nonchalant, but I didn't know whether or not Wayne guessed something was up. "Just been doing some thinking. I want your serious answer here. How would you answer the question?"

"OK. I'll play along. Not son of God, not human, not spirit, not soul. Well, Jesus said something interesting about who we are that is in none of those categories."

"That might be helpful. What did he say?"

"He said we are gods."

"That sounds like Mormon teachings." I've studied quite a bit about different religious teachings and so has Wayne.

"Yes, the Mormons have a slant in that direction, but in addition to them there are billions of people on earth with some type of belief that man is a god of some sort. Most of the Christians believe this doctrine is heresy however."

"But you are telling me that Jesus actually said it in the Bible? How does the actual wording go?"

Wayne took a sip of coffee and leaned forward. "I remember clearly three words he said. *It was Ye are gods.*"

"Jesus called us Gods?" I asked in hushed tones. I remember the Bible calling us Sons of God, but Gods? Do you remember where that scripture is?"

"I'm pretty sure it's in the gospel of John."

"John?" I sputtered, spilling several drops of coffee on my lap.

"Careful there," Wayne grinned. "Are you sure you didn't have some vision or something? You look pale." He looked carefully at my face.

"Here lately I'm not sure of anything," I said lamely "You really think Jesus said that in the book of John?"

"Like I said, I'm pretty sure. John the Beloved himself recorded that. He was definitely the best New Testament author. Keep in mind though that most Christians don't think he was seriously telling us we are gods."

"So, what do you think? Do you think we're gods?"

"Look at it this way," said Wayne. "God is supposed to be everywhere, right?"

"That's what they say."

"You occupy some of that space they call everywhere, don't you?"

"Yes."

"So, is God in the space you occupy?"

"If He is everywhere, then the answer is yes."

"That means that God is in you."

"Yes again."

"So would God be in your heart, brain, liver and even your cells?"

"Well, they are all part of everywhere. If God is omnipresent then I guess He would be in every atom of my body." I was catching on to Wayne's reasoning.

"So if God is in every atom of your body you are made of God. It follows then that you are God. If it's in you through and through, then it's you."

"So, do you think that is true? Do you really think we are Gods?"

"Hell, I don't know," Wayne said, leaning back in his seat. "I'm not even one hundred percent sure that there is a God. Sometimes I'm not even sure I am here on earth. Maybe everything is just a great dream and when we wake up there's nothing there. Or maybe when we wake up we are in some place that makes sense. Better yet, maybe we'll wake up on a south sea island full of beautiful girls to take care of our every need." Wayne grinned at this thought. Poor guy hadn't had a girlfriend in a long time.

"Very interesting thinking, but that scripture you mentioned interests me the most. I'm going to look it up when I get home," I said excitedly. "I faintly remember reading it, but never thought of it in the context that we could actually be gods." I couldn't wait to get home!

"Don't take it too seriously and expect me to worship you," Wayne smiled.

I cut our conversation short and sped home and started researching the book of John. Finally I found the scripture in chapter ten:

John 10:34 Jesus answered them, Is it not written in your law, I said, Ye are gods?

John 10:35 If he called them gods, unto whom the word of God came, and the scripture cannot be broken;

John 10:36 Say ye of him, whom the Father hath sanctified, and sent into the world, Thou blasphemest; because I said, I am the Son of God?

After a little research I realized that the "law" that Jesus mentioned was the book of Psalms. Jesus seemed to be saying that those who received the law of God or scriptures were called gods. Just maybe...maybe that was the answer. We are more than human. We are gods. I will admit however d, it seemed odd to think of myself as a god, but apparently the answer that John wanted was not just your standard Sunday school formula.

I took the Bible in my hand and found Elizabeth in the family room, "Sweetie. I think I may have the answer."

She looked up. "Don't tell me Wayne came up with something for you?"

"Actually, he did. It's a bit off the wall, but it just may be what we're looking for."

"OK. Let me have it."

"We are gods!" I exclaimed. I could hardly contain my excitement.

She didn't look impressed. "Wayne would come up with something like that," she said, looking back down at the book in her lap.

"Wayne didn't really think of it. Look here in the Bible." I moved toward her. "Jesus said it. If Jesus said it then that's got to be who we are."

"Let me read it for myself," Elizabeth said, taking the Bible out of my hands. She read the whole chapter.

"I remember this scripture" she said after a while. "I was

having an argument with a Mormon once and he quoted this and told me that our destiny was to be gods. I was a little rattled and called the Bible Answer Man on a radio station."

"What did he say?" I asked curiously. I didn't know she called radio stations about philosophical questions.

"He said we misread the scripture, that the original Psalm was making fun of man because of his frailties. It is a little bit like one person putting down another by saying, *You think you're hot stuff don't you?* The one guy doesn't really think the other is hot stuff. He's just making fun."

"So, this scripture is explained away with the idea that God is making fun of us?"

"That's basically what most people I have talked to seem to think."

"Let me have that Bible again," I said. I carefully read over Psalms eighty-two and John chapter ten. "I don't know. I've read it over carefully and I think Jesus was really saying that we are gods. "Look", I said, kneeling beside her. "He used the statement as a defense for saying He was the Son of God. In other words, If those who received the law are gods, then why make a big deal out of a statement from Jesus that He is the Son of God?"

Elizabeth looked up at me and smiled. "You realize, don't you, that there is one way to find out.

It dawned on me. "Yes. Yes," I said, "we can ask a man who knew Jesus personally. In fact, he's the man who wrote the scripture!" I laughed. This was unreal!

"He should be working at his bell ringing job right now," said Elizabeth. "Why don't you go ask him?"

CHAPTER TEN
The Dream

I drove over to Albertsons to seek out John again and ask him the two thousand year-old question.

I drove around the corner and saw the now-familiar sight of the bell ringer. I parked, got out of the car and headed toward him. "John!" I said.

The bell ringer turned. It was not the same bells, nor was it the same John.

"Where's John?" I asked.

"Who's John?" replied the man, a fairly scruffy-looking guy about twenty years younger than John.

"He's the guy who was working here before you."

"Oh, that guy. I'm not sure. He had to go out of town."

"When will he be back?"

"I don't know. People come and go at this job. Chances are he'll never be back."

"Is there anyone who would know?"

"You might check with the regional office."

I went home and made several phone calls and finally found someone who remembered John. He had basically the same story: John was out of town for an indefinite period and wasn't sure when he would be back. He said he hoped John would come back soon because he was their best fund-raiser.

This was an event I never expected. Even though I had only known John a few days it already seemed as if he was an old friend who would always be there when I needed him. It was almost as if he was a genie who belonged to me... as if he had not yet granted my three wishes and had no right to take any time off until I had my way with him.

"Damn!" I said to Elizabeth when I returned home. "John is gone and they don't know when he will be back."

"Do you know where he lives?"

"You know, I never even thought to ask him. Who knows? Maybe he's just sitting in some small apartment in the North End watching TV and drinking a beer." John was certainly a man of surprises.

"But didn't they say he was out of town? If he is a real apostle I don't think he would lie."

"Well, maybe he hasn't left yet. Maybe if we knew where he lived we could catch him before he left."

"Didn't he say he would give you more hints in a week? A week from your first encounter is next Thursday. If he is truly a man of his word he will be back by then."

"That's five days away. I wanted to talk to him today. I can't believe it. I feel more restless about seeing John again than I did about you when we fell in love. I never thought that could happen with another woman let alone a man." My heart ached with disappointment.

I realized I had made a statement that may have hurt Elizabeth and turned to her. "I'm sorry. You know you're the most important person in my life. It's just that I felt such spiritual love and power coming from John. It seemed so familiar and so good and now it's gone."

"I know," Elizabeth reassured me. "I probably would be upset too, but I feel the same way. As soon as you said he was gone I also felt a void and that extra strength that came through him is fading. I don't think I can get up again."

I didn't want to see her get weak again. I grabbed her hand hoping she could keep her strength until she was healed. "Here. Let me pull you up. You must keep faith in yourself that you can be well."

I pulled on her, but she was unable to stand more than a few seconds. She was very shaky and unable to walk. I helped her back into her wheelchair. I noticed a tear falling down her cheek as she said, "It was good to feel well for a day, but I'm losing strength fast. I think I'll soon be back to my normal weak self."

"John said that this short-term miracle was to give you faith that you can be healed. Even though it is passing maybe we should be thankful that we had the opportunity to see that miracles are still possible."

"Perhaps," she said. "But instead of faith I feel afraid. I'm afraid that we will never see John again. I don't know why. I feel kind of a sinking feeling."

"I feel the same feeling," I agreed. "For some reason I feel a great void of energy. I hope nothing has happened to him."

"If anyone can take care of himself I'm sure a two thousand year-old man can," said Elizabeth.

"It's probably just us. We'll just have to live this next week with the belief that we will see him again no later than Thursday."

"You're right," said Elizabeth. We will have to do everything possible to solve the first key. We need to at least show him that we have made the greatest possible effort."

"Yes, but I think I've done about all I can do at this point. The best that I can come up with is that we must be gods like Jesus said in the scripture."

"There is one other person you can call. Why don't you call your friend Lance in California and run by him the same question as you did Wayne?"

Yes, I thought. It would be interesting to get Lance's input. We had a long history together. We were business partners for a while and shared many good times together. We had also spent countless hours talking philosophy together. He moved to Los Angeles several years ago after he got thoroughly ingrained in the New Age movement. He has researched numerous groups and studied their philosophy. It's quite possible that he has come up with some interesting interpretations to John's first key.

"That's a good idea," I said to Elizabeth. "It wouldn't hurt to get his opinion. I don't think there is any new age group that he hasn't looked into."

Late that evening I finally caught Lance in. "How's things in the big city?" I asked.

"Exciting things are happening," he said. "Too bad you aren't here. I'm giving a seminar this weekend. You ought to come down some time and check out what I'm doing."

"Maybe after Elizabeth gets better," I said.

"How's she doing?" he said.

"She's having her ups and downs," I replied.

"Give her my best," he said. "Guess what my seminar is on."

"Knowing you, it could be anything."

"I call it *Ye are Gods: A Synthesis of the New Age and the Bible.*"

I almost dropped the phone. "What made you pick that topic?"

I asked.

"Well, as you know, just about all the New Agers down here think man is some type of god who has forgotten who he is... that we just have to remember."

"Is that what you think?" I asked hopefully.

"Yes, the idea is basically true. But what's interesting is that I have been running into these religious types lately who've been quoting the Bible at me right and left. They say the idea that man can become a god is Lucifer's first great lie. These guys really got under my skin so I started studying the Bible again to see if it was as backward as these guys make it sound. And guess what I found?"

"I'm sure it's interesting," I quipped.

"Interesting? Listen, the Bible teaches out the ying yang that humans are really gods."

"You mean like the Mormons teach?"

"Not really. The Mormons are in kindergarten on this and seem to be embarrassed to talk about this doctrine anymore. The Bible doesn't tell us that we are going to be gods in some far off future, but that we are gods in the here and now - very similar to many new age teachings. The thing that gets me is that most New Agers think anyone who believes in the Bible or studies it is back in the Stone Age. And Bible believers think that New Agers are worshippers of the devil himself. My studies reveal a harmony between the New Age philosophies and the Bible and no one seems to see it, so I thought I would give some lectures on the subject and see how much interest is out there."

"So if someone asked you who or what we are, would you answer that we are gods?"

"That's what Jesus said in the Good Book. That's also what every teacher that's into the New Age or philosophy around here thinks," he said.

I reflected a moment. "What if God himself appeared to you and told you that was the wrong answer and that you were supposed to guess again. What would you say?"

"I never thought about it being the wrong answer. It makes too much sense," he replied confidently.

"But just suppose it was wrong. Is there anything else you would guess?"

"What else could it be?" he asked. "In the beginning there was only God and He created the universe out of Himself. That means you are made out of God and you are a part of God. If you are one with the God consciousness, then you are God just as much as Jesus was. After all, He even said in the Book of John that we are supposed to be one with God just as He was."

"You're right. John did say that."

"Yes. Of all the writers of the scriptures, I think John was the greatest."

"I'll tell John that the next time I see him," I quipped.

"Funny," Lance said, not suspecting the truth behind my humor. "What did you call for anyway?"

"To ask you a question, but you already answered it."

"That's the way it happens when you're in tune with the universe, buddy" he said, sounding very pleased with himself.

We spent a few more minutes talking about family, friends and business ideas before we said our good-byes. He ended it with his favorite phrase, "Have a powerful day!" I related the conversation to Elizabeth.

"This sounds like the first insight," said Elizabeth.

"What do you mean first insight?" I asked.

"I thought you read the Celestine Prophecy. This book talks about insights that will transform humanity. The first one says that we are to pay attention to coincidences, that they will lead us to paths we are to follow."

"Yes, I do remember reading that now. It is a pretty fantastic coincidence that both Wayne and Lance had the same answer. It's especially interesting that Lance answered my question even before I asked it. Do you think that is some kind of sign?"

"It sounds like it could be."

"Let's suppose it is a sign then. That means we're supposed to think in the direction of us being gods. If I tell John the answer is that I am a god or God, could that be enough or are we supposed to think deeper?"

"Who knows?" Elizabeth shrugged. "The question I have is that if I am a god, why can't I snap my fingers and just make myself well?"

"Good question. But from what I've read about it in New Age books, the reason is that we are basically gods who have forgotten we are gods. Because we have all power as gods and we believe we are frail humans, this belief makes us frail humans. When we drop this false belief then the god within us will be revealed."

"So, all I have to do is drop my false belief and I can have power to heal myself?"

"That's the basic teaching of the present-day gurus."

"It sounds too simple."

"It does," I agreed, "but simple things are often the truest."

That evening when I went to bed I felt very restless. I felt a vacuum ever since I learned that John was out of town, but as I lay on my bed that night I felt even more depleted of energy. I felt as if I was fading in and out of reality. Finally I fell asleep and had an unusual dream. Now, in my experience some dreams are just dreams, but every now and then one comes along that seems very real and you think there must be a reality behind it. This was one of those dreams.

I found myself in a room surrounded by these floating evil-looking entities. Their faces were contorted and snarling at me as if they wanted to do me harm. I looked for a way of escape and found a door. I ran through the door and found a saintly-looking man in a rocking chair looking at me with a benevolent look on his face. I turned around and noticed that the evil spirits did not follow me into the room and it seemed that the kindly man was some-how protecting me from them.

I walked toward the man and asked, "Who are you?"

He looked back at me and I heard an authoritative voice projected toward me which said, "This is my beloved apostle - John."

I looked at the benevolent-looking man with a start. He looked nothing like my bell-ringing friend who I thought was the apostle John. This man had long sandy hair, a beard, and of fairly heavy build. John was fairly thin, no beard and black hair with touches of white. John's complexion was also darker than this man. This person in front of me was definitely a different person than the bell ringer I knew as John. Now this voice I was hearing, which sounded very authoritative, was telling me that this other man was John the Beloved. The voice sounded a bit like James Earl Jones when he says "THIS IS CNN", like you would imagine the voice of God to be. Because of the general situation the strong impression came to my mind that it must be the voice of the God or Christ himself.

I ventured forth a question. "Who is the other John - the Bell Ringer?"

The authoritative voice answered back, "The impostor you met has been an enemy from the beginning. He is a prince of evil and deceit who will lead all who believe him into the abyss and destruction. Beware of evil that has the appearance of good. Beware of all those who teach that men are gods. I alone am

God." His voice echoed until I woke up from the dream with a start and lay in my bed in contemplation.

John did indeed seem sincere and appeared to be a true teacher, but it never occurred to me to think he was some kind of evil incarnate. Now this voice that seemed to be the voice of God showed me what may be the true John the Beloved and the one who I thought was the true apostle may not be an apostle at all, but some kind of evil incarnate sent to lead me to... what? The voice said *the abyss and destruction*. That must be some type of hell, I thought.

It seemed to me that if the voice was correct I would be destroyed. If John-the-bell -ringer was right, I would go on to learn the Keys of Knowledge. I didn't like my choice. If John-the-bell-ringer was wrong, I may suffer some type of eternal punishment or destruction... But if the dream was wrong, I could go on to learn the keys of knowledge from John.

As this thought crossed my mind I found it interesting that I had fear of the voice of God in the dream. I feared it was right but did not want it to be right. I remembered the feelings of love I had when John-the-bell-ringer was in my presence, especially when he sent me his memories and later taught my wife. Then I thought of how I felt when I saw the supposed John the Beloved in the dream. The evil spirits in the dream did not follow me into the room where John was, and it seemed peaceful when I entered into the presence of John in the dream. But that peace was different from the peace I felt in the presence of the bell ringer. In that John's presence, I felt a peace that penetrated me to the core, perhaps the "peace that passeth all understanding." But in the presence of John in the dream, the peace was like the peace you have when a baby stops crying. It seems peaceful because of the lack of disturbance, not because of any inner feeling.

Next I contemplated the voice of Jesus or God I thought I heard. The feeling from the voice seemed to penetrate my outer body and tried to work its way into my heart, but the sound of the bells I heard from John seem to penetrate my deepest heart center or soul and radiated to permeate my whole being.

I again contemplated the two Johns and concluded the major difference between them is that one created the feeling of fear and dread in me, and the other a feeling of love and peace.

I thought long and hard within myself as I had a feeling that I was supposed to make a choice of some kind. After a period of absolute stillness I thought within myself, "If I have to choose, I will choose the John whose bells, thoughts and words touched my very soul."

Immediately, as instantly as one can imagine, I sensed a presence beside my bed. It was a presence of tremendous evil, of that I was sure. The vibration was so terrible and overwhelming that I felt like running, but somehow I knew within myself, as if I had been sent some type of revelation directly to my brain, that this powerful entity from the abyss was the one who had given me the dream and was the one who was the owner of the authoritative voice. I somehow knew that he did not know that I knew he was there. He seemed to be standing by my bedside, waiting to see if I would fall for the illusion he had created for me in the dream. I knew the truth was now revealed to me because I chose John-the-Bell-Ringer, that he was indeed John the Beloved, apostle of Jesus. My choice was true. If I had chosen the other John, I would have chosen an agent of the dark side.

I lay completely still for another few moments, holding my breath. I sensed the being was watching me, waiting for a response. I felt a fear beyond anything I had felt before. I somehow feared this being had power to destroy me if I did not please him. I spent several more minutes quieting the fear and told myself I would put myself in the hands of the true God, whoever and whatever that would be. Somehow I felt I must confront this personage who was waiting for a response. "Oh God," I prayed within myself with sincerity I had never had before, "what shall I do?"

Immediately I felt another presence. It seemed very familiar. Somehow I knew it was the presence of the real John, the real Beloved. "Oh John, are you there?" I asked silently. "What shall I do?"

An inner voice that I knew without a doubt came from John said these words: "Laugh at him."

I almost broke my silence with astonishment at that answer. It was totally unexpected. Here was perhaps the devil himself at my bedside, the most terrifying creature one can imagine, and I am supposed to laugh at him! I had to take a few more minutes to absorb that one. Finally I asked silently again, "Are you sure I'm supposed to laugh at this thing?

No answer.

Then I thought within myself. "Hey! What gives here? I want some reassurance. He might take me to some fire and brimstone if I laugh at him. Give me a sign that this is the correct thing to do, that I will be safe."

Nothing.

"John!" I shouted with a silent scream. "I need to know that I did not imagine I heard you. Please, give me reassurance just this one time!"

Still nothing.

For some reason, I thought I must go with what I had received. I reflected on the voice of John. It seemed very real, more real than anything I have ever felt. My mind just had a hard time accepting it. I had to go with that which was most real to my soul, I thought, and decided to obey and laugh at the intruder who I sensed was getting very impatient.

I took a moment, gathered my courage and lifted myself up in my bed and looked in the direction of the presence. I thought of Steven Wright (my favorite comic), let out a laugh as if I just heard a good new joke, and said out loud, "Great try you son-of-a-bitch, but your little trick didn't work! I do find it very funny though." And I laughed some more.

My laughter was stopped in its tracks by a negative force more powerful than anything I have ever felt. It was like a whirl-wind of negative energy that made me think of the Tasmanian Devil in the Bugs Bunny show, except I was terrified rather than entertained. I feared this thing was going to destroy my body and soul within the next two seconds.

Suddenly, with swiftness faster than light, the entire presence left the room, and a fire came down from some heavenly sphere and completely engulfed everything that was me. I was both on fire and feeling the "peace that passed understanding" all at one moment. I knew that only God could produce such a feeling. The feelings I had in the dream did not compare within a millionth of a degree to that of the fire and the peace that surrounded me at that moment.

As I was enjoying this great bliss Elizabeth turned to me sleepily. "Did I hear you laugh?"

I laughed again with joy that I could not hold back. "Yes, my sweet, you did hear me laugh. I feel too great not to laugh."

"Well, could you laugh more quietly?" she asked, somewhat irritated, and rolled over to go back to sleep.

"OK." I smiled. "I will laugh more quietly." Then I laughed what I have since called a quiet, heavenly laugh as I drifted into the most peaceful sleep I had ever experienced in my life.

CHAPTER ELEVEN
Reunion

It was a long wait until next Thursday. I had a million questions to ask John, but the most important thing to me was just to see him again. I wanted to share my dream with him, even though I assumed he knew the story. Now the problem was that I wasn't sure how to contact him. Just before noon on Thursday I went to Albertsons to see if he was working there again. I was disappointed to find that same substitute there again. Of course, the substitute did not know anything about when John may come back.

I went back home and had lunch with Elizabeth and shared my frustration with her.

"Are you sure you heard John right, that you would see him in a week?"

"I'm sure," I said. "But who knows what all things a 2000 year old man must attend to. Maybe he had to go to Bosnia or something."

"Even so, if he is a man of his word he should contact you today, shouldn't he?

"You would think so. Who knows! Maybe I'm not good student material and he gave up on me."

"I don't think so," Elizabeth assured me "From that dream you told me about, it sounded like you passed some type of test."

"Maybe so," I said. "I suppose I'd better get back to work. I' have to go show a house."

After showing my client the house I drove back to Albertsons and several other bell ringer locations. I looked everywhere I could think of just on the off chance that John was somewhere in the area. Finally, when my workday was done, I headed home with the thought that contact was John's responsibility. "If it happens, it happens," I thought.

Elizabeth and I spent a quiet evening together. Finally, she broke the ice. "Have you done any more thinking about the first key?"

"I've done a lot of thinking, but don't think I can go much further until John tells me about the man-God idea."

"What if he says that we're not gods? You've covered about everything else. What's left?"

"I don't know. Maybe we're just animals," I said sarcastically.

"You may be just joking," said Elizabeth, "but I guess we have to be open to anything."

"I guess," I agreed.

We went to bed just before eleven (which was quite early for me) and I lay on the bed trying to drift off to sleep, disappointed that I had not seen or heard anything from John.

Then, as I drifted off to sleep, I heard bells.

Bells?

I woke up suddenly. "I heard bells!" I exclaimed to Elizabeth. She woke up. "Bells? It must be John."

"Yes. It must be John. But now I'm awake, I can't hear them."

"You always hear them when you're close to sleep. Try going back to sleep."

"You're right. I'll try that," I said. I tried to go back to sleep, but sleep had fled from me. After a moment I said, "I couldn't sleep right now if my life depended on it."

Elizabeth sighed. "Why don't you just try laying still and tuning in. Maybe John will send you something."

"I'll try," I said. I laid still and tried to tune into my inner self. At first nothing happened, then faintly I heard the bells again. I somehow knew I was supposed to focus on the sound and did so. As I focused, the sound became clearer and an image of John formed within my mind. I saw him drinking a cup of coffee at Denny's at the exact same seat where we talked before. Somehow I knew he was there waiting for me.

"He's at Denny's!" I exclaimed as I rose up out of bed and headed for my clothes.

"Denny's?" Elizabeth asked sleepily.

"Denny's," I said firmly. "I'm going there now. I may be a while, so don't worry about me."

Elizabeth turned to me and asked, "Sweetheart?"

"Yes?"

"Tell John thank you for giving me faith again. Even though I've lost that extra strength, I now have hope I can be healed."

"I'll tell him," I said.

In a few minutes I was in my car approaching Denny's. I found myself wondering if there was something special about Denny's or if it was just a convenient place. Oh, well, that question was far down the list. As I walked into the restaurant I noticed the time on the wall clock was about one minute to midnight. I hurriedly walked to the corner where we met before and there he was drinking coffee looking exactly like I saw in my mind a few moments before.

"John," I said reaching out my hand. "I've never been so glad to see anyone before!"

John smiled as I sat down. "Not every beginning student feels that way," he said. "Are you sure I am not a prince of evil and deceit bent on leading you to some eternal hell?"

"You know all about the dream then?"

"Yes. It was not unexpected. He pulls a similar trick on any student I have that shows promise."

"He? Who is he?"

"Who do you think?"

"Well, I do know this. Whoever he is was capable of disguising himself as an agent of God; yet, when I sensed his true nature, it was an evil vibration beyond anything I have imagined. If there is a devil, this has got to be him."

John smiled. "In the days of Jesus we didn't use the silly-sounding word *devil*. We called him *The Adversary*. The word *Satan* in the Hebrew text means *adversary*. Today we would call someone like Hitler, Saddam Hussein or a terrorist an adversary or enemy, but it would sound silly to call them devils. We didn't use bogeyman-like words, fluffy words or fairy tale-like words back then. We were dealing with real energies, real beings and real situations. The religious authorities of that day were the ones who feared illusionary bogeymen."

I nodded. "I could certainly tell that being was an adversary. I knew he wanted to destroy me when he learned I saw his real self."

"He still wants to destroy you. You really made him mad when you laughed at him." John laughed.

"You told me to do it!" I exclaimed. "I didn't realize I was just making him mad. That's all I need - an enemy of immense power from the underworld." I frowned. John paused a moment and studied my face.

"As long as you side with light and truth he will be your mortal enemy with all the force he has available." Then, grinning, he said, "I figure you might as well get a dig in when you can."

"That doesn't sound like turning the other cheek," I countered.

"As Solomon said, there is a time and place for everything. Through his control of agents here on earth he has had me killed and tortured about twenty times. The last time I was hung by piano wire and the first time I was boiled in oil. That alone should be enough to deserve the reward of laughing at his defeat. You'll never realize the joy you gave me when you followed my instructions."

"I think we really pissed him off all right," I laughed nervously.

"That's an unpious term," John scolded, "but I couldn't express it better."

I took a sip of coffee. "It still makes me nervous. He might try to take it out on me." God, as if I didn't have enough problems in my life!

"From the moment you saw through the illusion and passed the test you became a mortal enemy. But don't worry. He cannot harm you if you follow the light of truth and the Holy Spirit within you. At present you are following the highest you know and you are completely protected. But there are energy points in time and space like acupuncture points on the body. When one of those points is arrived at, it provides an opportunity for both good and evil. For instance, the other night you had a visit from a strong evil force and also a powerful good force. The fire you felt was what we used to call the *baptism of fire*. If you go forward you must risk the chance of going backwards."

"What would have happened if I had fallen for the illusion?"

"I would have kept my word and saw you today, but because you would not have felt the spiritual fire you would have rejected me and the knowledge I have for you."

"Would I have been some servant of evil then?"

"Not in the sense you are thinking," John replied. "That would only happen if you have very selfish intent within your heart. What he seeks to do with basically good people is to neutralize them. After they are neutralized he generally leaves them alone and goes on to other work. Only if a person sinks to great illusion and selfishness can he then be of conscious use to the Dark Brothers."

"Who is this *Adversary* and who are the *Dark Brothers*?"

"They are just like you and me," John replied. "They are brothers of ours, but very wayward brothers. As you know, there must be opposition in all things. If there is an appearance of a positive force, then that appearance can only be held if there exists the appearance of a negative force."

"Why do you use the term *appearance*?"

"Because positive and negative is real to you in this world, but in a higher reality there is only one energy and that is God. It is important for teaching sake that we always deal with the reality we are in. If you try to solve the riddles of a higher reality before you understand your own, you can get caught in an illusion that will cause you to wind up far behind the simple realist."

I nodded. "I do notice that many intelligent dreamers do not seem to accomplish anything, whereas the dull-witted plodder often achieves a surprising amount."

"Your statement deserves to be reflected upon," he said evenly. I must have hit upon something important to my progression.

"So are these Dark Brothers burning in Hell like the preachers tell us?"

"They live in a world with no glory but the illusion of glory. To understand what that means you must solve a future key." He shifted in his seat and clasped his hands. "Let me put it this way. All of us have a spark of divinity within us. As you follow this spark, your glory, light, truth and power of love is increased. There are certain very selfish individuals who through conscious effort shut themselves completely off from soul contact. After this they completely deny all things that are good and true. Because they are conscious beings with no true spiritual contact their consciousness creates a world that is complete illusion, with no real light or glory. They believe that the true spiritual plane created by God is illusion and that they have discovered or created the only true reality. Because this false belief is so real there is no escape, and all that makes them personalities is in a state of death or disintegration. This drawn-out death often takes many years, but after it happens the spark that is their true self will continue, and the person will be re-created in a future opportunity on an earth that does not even exist yet."

"Heavy doctrine," I replied. "Does that mean there is no burning in Hell?"

"There is in a sense," he replied. "When one has rejected light, surrounds himself with illusion and then comes into contact with real light, it produces a spiritual pain something like a fire. Why do you think the Adversary fled so quickly when the Spirit descended upon you the other night? The light and fire of the Spirit was painful to him beyond anything you can imagine. Even though he wanted more than anything to destroy you he was forced to instantly leave."

"It was the most sudden exit I've ever seen," I nodded.

John continued. "When people die and go to the next world they reside with others who have a similar light to their own. Many are disappointed when they realize how little light they have followed on this earth and desire to go higher. This desire takes them near the presence of a greater light and it is very painful to them. They want to move toward the light but the approach is painful like a fire, so they are in hell two different ways. They have to live with others who are of lesser light and not very pleasant company, and secondly, a desire to escape leads them to a fiery pain."

"Are they stuck in that situation forever?"

"No. A way is made for their progress, but we could spend days on this subject. Let us move on." John nodded to a waitress passing by for more coffee.

"I have one more question first," I pursued after she left.

"Go ahead."

"Where have you been? I didn't expect you to disappear like you did."

John frowned. "Actually, I didn't expect it either, but my Master needed me."

"And that would be...?"

"Who do you think?"

"Jesus?" I asked in wonderment.

"Jesus' is the modern pronunciation of the name he went by two thousand years ago in Palestine. Of course, the preachers of this age have become attached to it, but those within His inner circle just call Him "The Christ" when making a reference to Him. When I get the opportunity to speak to Him on a personality level as I am with you I just call Him *Joshua*. The original pronunciation of the name Jesus was something like *Yay-soose*, but that name is pretty obsolete now. He decided a couple hundred years ago to use Joshua, the English translation of the Hebrew equivalent of Jesus, because it is still a name in common use."

"Joshua Christ," I smiled. "That will take some getting used to."

"He wouldn't think of using the name Jesus except for purposes of identification. Every time He hears one of the preachers speak or shout the name in that religious twang He cringes."

"You know, I always wondered what Jesus thought about how the preachers massacre his name."

John reflected a moment: "There are many mysteries to be revealed which are associated with Jesus, as you call him, and the Christ. I know Him by two of His names and He has a third which only He knows."

"What's the other name that you know?"

"I couldn't tell you that without His permission," he replied softly.

"What's the purpose of having more than one name?"

"I cannot tell you at present. That knowledge is contained in one of the keys you will learn in the future. I can tell you a little about the term *The Christ*. It is not part of His name, but is the name of an office. The most enlightened teacher, associated with mankind, on the planet has this office and is called *The Christ*. Joshua will not always hold this office. In about another thousand years He will leave this solar system and the position of The Christ will be taken over by a close disciple. The title Christ without the article *the* is used by many disciples who share what has been called the *Christ consciousness*. I am one who is free to use the name of Christ for myself as long as the one being communicated to does not mistake me for the master teacher. Those who bear the name of Christ are not permitted to knowingly deceive, and the wrong use of the title could produce deception. Self-deception, however, will often occur because of wrong interpretation of doctrine transmitted by the teachers."

"So, why were you called away so suddenly?" I probed.

"There was an emergency," John looked serious.

"Can you tell me anything about it?"

"Not a lot. I can tell you that a situation developed where some terrorists had an opportunity to obtain nuclear weapons that would have been planted in Washington DC. This event was not in the plan and had to be prevented."

"What did you do to prevent it?"

"Even if I could tell you I do not have time to go into it. Joshua needed my assistance and fortunately I was there to help. It was at great sacrifice that I was able to make this appointment with you. There are still some details I have to return to attend to."

"Is saving the world from nuclear attack something you do often?" I quipped.

"The last time we had a crisis like this was back in the early eighties when scientists were working on the neutron bomb. It's perfection would have been too great a temptation for any nation at this time, and this weapon and several others had to be contained."

"So, do you control men's minds to avoid catastrophes?"

"The Disciples of Christ, or the Brotherhood of Light, never force men's minds. We are obligated to honor free will. The Dark Brothers, on the other hand, will use force whenever they feel the need and have the opportunity. They often find that all they have to do is create a little illusion to have their way with the masses."

John paused a moment. "You've done a good job sidetracking me, but we need to get on with your education. Do you at least remember the question I posed to you last week?"

"I think I got that anyway. It is WHO OR WHAT AM I?"

"I am pleased you remembered the exact wording. Now can you give me your answer?"

"Well," I said nervously, "with a little help from my friends and the Gospel of John, which I assume you wrote, I concluded that men are gods."

"So are you God with a capital G or a god with a small G?"

I stumbled for a moment. "Well... the Mormons say we are becoming a god with a small G and the New Agers say we are God with a big G."

"What do you say?"

"Well," I stumbled again, clearing my throat, "if I am one with God, then I must be God with a big G." It sounds weird to say that, but that's my answer."

"Are you confident in that answer?"

"Sort of."

"What makes you *sort of* confident?"

"I've had several coincidences pointing me in that direction. I figured they must have happened for a reason."

"So you had some signs leading you toward the answer?" John smiled.

"I guess you could say that," I replied.

"Have you read what the Master said about signs?"

"I think he said several things, didn't he?"

John got out his old Bible again and turned to Matthew chapter sixteen. "Read verse four," he said, pushing the book toward me.

I carefully held the old book and read: "A wicked and adulterous generation seeketh after a sign..."

I just about dropped the book. "I remember reading this scripture, but I never thought about it in the context that is now entering my head. I thought the answer may be that I am God because of signs, but Jesus said the wicked seek signs."

"You were not actively seeking a sign," John assured me, "but several appeared to you and you thought they meant something."

"So are you telling me they didn't mean anything?" I asked, somewhat disappointed.

"It is true that there is a reason or a cause behind each happening," John replied, "but when people see coincidences they often read much more into them than should be. Suppose you roll dice hundreds of times. Sooner or later you will roll *seven* three times in a row. Does that have any deep meaning or did it happen just because you rolled the dice many times and the law of averages tells us you will eventually roll three sevens?"

"So, you're saying that coincidences just happen now and then?"

"Generally, that is the case, but then every once in a while coincidences are contrived by a higher power. But what usually happens when a coincidence happens to a superstitious person, much more will be read into it than is based in reality."

"So the fact that both Wayne, Lance and that Dark Brother mentioned man and gods was just coincidence and means nothing?"

"Not entirely," John replied. "You, Wayne, and Lance have been friends for many years and as such tune into each other's frequency and share many of the same thoughts. This greatly increases the chances that you will all come up with similar conclusions on various ideas. What happened with you three was not nearly as much of a coincidence as you thought. You were looking for an answer and you were happy that something finally seemed to jump out at you. It was no coincidence, however, that the Dark Brother jumped on this. It served his purpose."

"So, what about the answer, then," I asked. "Is it right or wrong?"

"Let's regress just a moment," John said, putting his fingers together. "Why do you suppose Joshua said a wicked and adulterous generation seeks for a sign? Now in reality wicked means *mislead.* So how is one misdirected who seeks for a sign?"

"I've never thought of looking for a sign in a negative light. Most people see signs as a positive thing." John was silent, evidently waiting for a concise answer. I continued, "OK, let me see. If we use a sign to guide our lives then we are using something outside of ourselves. Perhaps we are supposed to look within."

John smiled. "There is hope for you yet. I think your light is increasing. Now what is adulterous about seeking a sign for guidance?"

"That's a tough one. I don't see a lot of relation there."

"There is a lot of correspondence here, said John. "Answer me this: What is adultery?"

"It's where a person betrays his marriage partner and has a sexual relationship with someone else" I replied.

"And who is your spiritual marriage partner supposed to be?"

"You mean someone other than my physical wife?"

"Yes."

"Could it be God?"

"You are correct. This is taught throughout the scriptures. The Israelites are called the *Bride of Jehovah* throughout the Old Testament and the Church is called the *Bride of Christ* in the New. Both Israel and the Church are symbols of those who have the light of the Spirit of God within them. So how does a bride of Christ or God commit adultery?"

"Perhaps by leaving God and leaning on or uniting with someone else, or another God."

"Very close," said John. "The brother of light senses the Spirit of God within himself and has made a commitment to follow it and be one with it, similar to a marriage relationship. If he actively seeks a sign outside of himself for his main source of guidance, this causes a shift of attention away from the Spirit. So his God becomes a false God outside of himself and the inner God is ignored and betrayed. He has committed adultery against his only true source of guidance, which places a black wall between his personality self and the God within."

"Fascinating," I said, feeling like Spock again. "So the New Agers, who are always teaching about the God within - yet at the same time are always seeking coincidences and signs - are really teaching one thing and doing another?"

"They are not alone," John smiled. "On the other side of the spectrum, the very religious also seek for signs rather than an answer from God through prayer as they claim to teach."

"So, are we to look within for all answers?"

"Not exactly. That would mean the outside world has no meaning or purpose. The purpose of the outside world is to stimulate with experience and the purpose of the inner is to verify. Without the outer world there is nothing to verify, and without the inner there is no source to find the point of truth that exists in all things."

"It would appear to me, then, the religious fundamentalists look without for their answers and the New Agers try to look within; but both are concentrating too much on one side of the pendulum," I said.

"Another good answer," John said smiling "Now, you're going to want me to tell you if you have the right answer."

"I've been very curious all week." I leaned forward eagerly.

"Let's get another cup of coffee and we'll explore your thoughts."

CHAPTER TWELVE
GODS-R-US

John took a sip of fresh coffee and said, "Now, tell me your answer."

"I figure this has to be a good answer because it is a direct quote from Jesus, or Joshua as you now call him, and it was written by you in the book of John chapter ten. There Jesus said, *Ye are gods*."

John smiled and said, "So what is the answer to the question - WHO OR WHAT ARE YOU?"

"I guess men are gods." I replied tepidly.

"I keep telling you to listen to the precise words I say. The question is WHO OR WHAT ARE YOU? not *what are humans?* Now think over the question and answer again."

"Well, I guess I am God or a god," I said.

"Which one is it. Are you God or a god?"

I didn't think the answer would be that awkward. I tried again. "The Mormons say *a god* and the New Agers say just *God*."

"And what do you say?"

"I guess I am God," I said, feeling a little strange.

"Should I worship you then?" John grinned.

"No! Of course not!" I exclaimed.

"Then are you sure you are God?"

"I'm not sure," I replied weakly. "Maybe I am just a god."

"So you are a god then," John smiled again with that look in his eye that revealed he knew things that were beyond my grasp. "Then you must have great power. Why don't you levitate that waitress over there and show me your power? Or better still, why don't you snap your fingers and heal your wife?"

His latter words reached the core of my being. There was

nothing that revealed my powerlessness more than the fact that I had been unable to help my own wife. "What a fool I am," I thought to myself. "If I am God or a god, then I should be able to heal my wife." I cast my eyes to the floor with great emotion. I felt like I was nobody, let alone a god.

John looked n my eyes with compassion. "I didn't mean to hurt your feelings; I just wanted to get your attention."

"You got it all right," I said. "Boy, do I feel like a fool. I'm no more a god than that ashtray over there. If I was God's little toe I would have healed Elizabeth. I seem to do nothing for her, and I feel like nothing." I felt more emotional than I had in years.

"Don't let emotion take your eyes away from the truth," John said softly. "A true seeker must be part Spock, part Captain Kirk, with a dash of Bones."

I started to laugh.

"Glad I cheered you up. What's funny?"

"I just had an image of John the Revelator watching Star Trek. It just struck me as very humorous - comparable to Jesus singing a rap song." It's funny how you can sometimes switch from one emotion to another when something strikes you right.

John looked a little perplexed for the first time since I had met him. "I'll have to ask Joshua if he's done any rap lately," he quipped. "Now getting back to the subject. You must be part Spock and part Captain Kirk here to find truth. Emotion often turns the truth upside down."

"So, was my answer about being God right or wrong?"

"It was not the correct answer."

"So we are not really gods then?"

John paused and said, "Was your answer about being human the correct answer?"

"You said no."

"But are you human?"

"Yes.... So are you saying my answer may be true, but the wrong answer?"

"Exactly. We are called human beings, but since a human doesn't know who he is, then naming yourself human doesn't really bring you any knowledge about yourself, does it?"

"I guess not."

"If I say you are God and you do not know what or who God is, then that does not bring you an increase in knowledge, does it?"

"No."

"You don't really know any more about who you are than you did before I told you that you are God."

"I think I see what you're getting at. You're saying I must answer the question with something that really tells me about who I am. If I say I am flesh and I don't know the difference between flesh and silicone then I might as well say I am silicone. My answer means nothing if I don't know what flesh is."

"That is good, my friend. I may use your example with my next student. Yes, your answer must mean something. Saying that you are human, God or a son of God may all be true, but if you cannot explain what the terms mean, then they are just labels without meaning and true knowledge."

Frustrated that I still didn't know the answer, I stated, "Before we go on, I would like you to explain the scripture in John chapter ten. There is a big dispute among Bible believers as to whether Jesus is really telling us that we are gods."

"What conclusion did you come to?"

"It sounds like Jesus is really telling us that we are gods."

"You are correct. I was actually in His presence several times when He used this argument. After He obtained a certain amount of notoriety in Jerusalem He was often approached by religious authorities who had heard their followers express the belief that He was either the Messiah, a god, Son of God or an ancient prophet brought back from the dead or reborn. They would often speak to Him with venom, saying something like, *Who do you think you are, the son of God?*

"Then He would answer something like this: *And what if I did say I am a son of God? Why do you think that is a big deal when your own law of God in the Psalms and writings of Moses calls you gods? If those who merely received the scriptures are called gods, why do you think it would be a major claim for me to say I am a son of God?*

"Here, let's turn to Psalms." John opened his old Bible to Psalms. "The first verse of the chapter in question reads: *God standeth in the congregation of the mighty; he judgeth AMONG THE GODS.* Who are the gods that He judges among? It tells us in verse six which reads, *I have said Ye are gods; and all of you children of the most High.*

"Here we are told that the gods that God judges among are the ones who received the scriptures as Jesus said. In fact, there are numerous instances in the writings of Moses where the people who judged among the people were called gods. In the Bibles today these are usually translated incorrectly, but if you use any Hebrew Concordance from a regular Christian bookstore you can prove to yourself that the judges were really called gods time and time again. I'll write down these references so you can look them up."

John scribbled down some references and handed them to me. It read Exodus 21:6; Exodus 22:8-9. "Now, everywhere the word *judges* is mentioned in these scriptures it comes from the Hebrew ELOHIYM, which is the same word used for the God who created heaven and earth. Interestingly, they translated it correctly in the King James Version in Exodus twenty-two verse twenty-eight."

He handed it to me and I read: *"Thou shalt not revile the gods, nor curse the ruler of the people."*

John offered an interpretation: "The ruler of the people was Moses, and the gods were Moses and the judges. This is why David in Psalms called God *as one who judges among the gods."*

I added, "The Fundamentalist Christians think Psalms 82:7 refutes the idea that men are gods. Here, I'll read it: *But ye shall die like men, and fall like one of the princes.* Because this comes right after the *ye are gods* statement, they say the *ye are gods* is a mockery."

"What does it sound like to you?"

"It sounds to me David was saying they were gods who were behaving like they were just men."

"That is correct. Now turn to Exodus chapter four verse sixteen and read."

I read, *"And he shall be thy spokesman unto the people: and he shall be, even he shall be to thee instead of a mouth, and thou shalt be to him instead of God."*

John explained, "Here it is talking about the calling of Aaron to be a spokesman for Moses. However the translation is poor concerning Moses; the Hebrew reads: *Thou shall be a god to him (Aaron)."*

"I can see why your life is in danger from life to life." I remarked. "I'll bet you really make some religious people nervous when you talk the scriptures."

John smiled, "Unrealized truth clearly presented can cause a great disturbance. The master at that was Joshua, or Jesus. The Bible does not do justice at relating how angry he made the religious authorities of his time."

"I can imagine," I nodded. "So, from our conversation so far, it sounds as if you're telling me we are gods just as the scriptures say, but just accepting that does not really tell us who we are, so it is not the answer to your question."

"That is correct. You are both God and a god, and from another prospective, you are becoming a god, but none of these statements mean more than just words to those who quote them. I will give you a hint that will help you realize more of what God is. Read First Corinthians chapter twelve and tell me next week what you come up with. Here, I'll write that down next to the other references."

"I notice you quote a lot from the Bible," I remarked while he wrote. "What do you think of the other scriptures and philosophies of the world?"

"I use the Bible often with you because it carries much weight in this part of the world. There is some truth in all scriptures and all philosophies of the world. I am familiar with many of them and have taught with many of them. Now, getting back to the subject, do you have any other ideas about WHO OR WHAT YOU ARE before I give you your next hint?"

I thought for a moment. "So, basically all my answers are correct, but they just don't mean anything. I am a human, I am spirit, I am soul, I am a son of God and I am even a god or maybe even God in some esoteric way, but none of these statements communicate more than a vague idea. Is this correct?"

"That is exactly correct. Can you think of an answer to the question that does mean something to you?"

"I don't know if I can give you anything intelligent right now. Why don't you give me my next hint and I'll think about it during the next week?"

"All right, my friend. Here it is. To better understand who and what you are it is helpful to know what you are not. I think you have already concluded that you are not your body, that the body is merely a vehicle for that which is the real you."

"Yes, I have pretty much accepted that."

"Just like you have a car which is a vehicle that takes you places, with the real you inside the car, so do you have a body, which is not the real you, which is a vehicle that takes you places. The real you directs the vehicle. What many do not realize is that the real you has other vehicles besides your physical body.

There are two other things you are not: You are not your emotions and you are not your mind. Instead, these are two other vehicles you use to take you places.

The question remains: If you are not your body, your emotions or your mind - what remains? WHO OR WHAT ARE YOU?"

"That's interesting," I mused. "Many lay philosophers like myself are aware that we are not our bodies, but most see our feelings and thoughts as part of our eternal nature. But you say they are not a part of our real selves, but just vehicles?"

"That is correct," John replied. "Contemplate this and the scriptures I gave you and we'll meet back here at Denny's next week at midnight."

"Are you going back to your bell ringing job?" I asked.

"I may have to skip it for the rest of the season," he said. "Joshua needs my help to place some safeguards on some terrorism that has potential to hinder the purpose of God on earth. Whatever you see happening the next few years, I want you to know it would have been a lot worse without our intervention. Hopefully, we can get things taken care of the next few weeks. Don't ask me any questions about it. There is little I can reveal at present."

"Sounds like you're a spiritual James Bond," I said smiling.

John returned a light smile.

"Elizabeth told me to tell you she appreciates the fact you gave her hope."

"How is she doing?"

"She had her strength back for a short time, but now she is like she was before or perhaps worse."

"Ask her this for me," said John. "Ask her if she has discovered her fears and thoughts she has been hiding from herself, and has she learned to put them in their right place?"

"I'll ask her,' I said.

John arose as if he were ready to go. He pulled a red handkerchief out of his pocket and handed it to me. "Tell her to rub this on her forehead three times a day. It will give her additional strength and make life more bearable for her for the next week. However, you must return it to me next week."

"I'll do it," I nodded, taking the handkerchief from his hand. "Do you have to go now?"

"I'm afraid so." We paid and walked out the door. As we were walking down the street he said, "Your car is the other direction."

"I know, but I'm curious. Where are you going and how are you going to get there?"

"I'm going to the Middle East. The exact point I will not say.

How? You may ask. Let us go behind that tree and I will show you."

I walked with him behind a tree where we were out of sight from passers by. He stood perfectly still, closed his eyes, bowed his head slightly and whispered a word ever so softly. In an instant he was gone. He didn't fade away like some ghost in the movies, but he was just instantly gone.

I wasn't sure which word he uttered, he said it so softly, but it seemed like it was "Joshua".

CHAPTER THIRTEEN
Hidden Fears

On my way home I found myself thinking there was now no way I could doubt that John was a mystical being. I was already very convinced of his reality because of the power of his teachings and the internal spiritual feelings he generated. But when you see someone just disappear before your eyes like that it brings home a realization of a higher reality that is just undeniable.

After I arrived home I tried getting into bed without disturbing Elizabeth, but without success.

"Honey, it's after three. I was worried that you and John ran off together."

"Not a chance. You're lucky he had to go. I could have talked to him for days without sleeping. I hope you've gotten some sleep since I've left."

She was silent. That meant that she never slept. "I wish you'd listen to me about your rest," I said. "You've been awake all this time haven't you?"

"How do you expect me to sleep when you're out there having high spiritual drama?"

"I've got to admit, I couldn't have slept either."

"So did you have the right answer? Are we gods or what?"

I rehearsed to her the dialog that occurred between John and I.

"Let me get this right," she said. "Everything everyone thinks we are is not what we really are because they are just phrases that don't tell us anything. We are also not our bodies, feelings or thoughts. There doesn't seem to be much left for us to be. Maybe we are just blobs of nothing."

"That sounds about as good of an answer as any the way I

feel right now," I said, somewhat frustrated.

"Let me try out that handkerchief," she said.

I retrieved it and handed it to her. "He said to rub it on your forehead and it would give you strength. I know it sounds crazy, but after what I have experienced with John so far I'm willing to try anything."

She took it and placed it on her forehead. Then she rubbed it back and forth with her hand seemingly growing steadier. Finally a smile graced her face as if she were experiencing pleasure. She looked at me and said, "Sweetheart, make love to me."

I do believe I was more surprised at this request than John's disappearance. She hadn't shown any interest in lovemaking for some time because of her illness. "Are you sure?" I asked.

"Very sure," she said with a very sensual voice.

We made love immediately with more feelings of pleasure and sensuality - and on the other extreme - more spiritual feelings than I had ever felt in lovemaking. The only way I could describe the feeling was as a union that belonged to the gods and not humankind.

Afterwards we were lying together in silence, contemplating the experience. "If I never get better," Elizabeth said softly, "this moment is worth a lifetime. How many live a whole lifetime in good health and never have one moment as we have just had."

"Very well said. But of course, no one else is married to you."

We embraced and fell asleep in each other's arms.

We both arose the next morning after just a couple of hours sleep, but we both felt refreshed. Elizabeth seemed to have her strength back again and insisted she make breakfast. After we sat down together she asked, "So have you done any thinking about who or what you are?"

"A little."

"So, if we are not just a blob of nothing, what are we?"

"I've been thinking of it this way. If my body is taken away I may still have feelings and thoughts. If my body and emotions were taken away then I have thoughts, but if all three were taken away I would still be something. I've been imagining stepping aside from my vehicles and visualizing what is there. I know and feel there is something there, the driver of the vehicles. Some type of livingness."

"Maybe you are just life itself," she said.

"I know what John would say if I said that. He would ask, *What is life?*"

"And the answer to that has baffled philosophers for ages," she said.

"Maybe we ought to start with the easy stuff," I said. "John told me to ask you if you have discovered the thoughts and fears you have been hiding from yourself and if you have learned to put them in their right place.

"I must be hiding them wee for I'm not sure what they would be."

"Have you thought about them at all?"

"What's there to think about? I think I'm pretty open about my thoughts and fears. Actually, I don't have many fears outside of becoming incapacitated with this disease."

"I've thought a little about it. If you are hiding certain thoughts and fears, perhaps they are especially hidden from yourself as you said. So if you try to look for them they are hard to find because you yourself have hidden them from yourself."

"So you're saying I've hidden them so well that I can't find them?"

"Maybe it's something like this: Let's say you have an extra twenty dollars and hide it in a cookie jar. For some reason you forget about hiding it there. Then some time later you need the twenty and it does not occur to you to look anywhere for it because you cannot even remember that it ever existed. Perhaps you haven't seriously looked for these hidden thoughts and fears because you do not believe they exist. But just as the twenty dollars still exists in the cookie jar whether you believe it or not, so does your hidden thoughts and fears exist, waiting to be found."

"You've been spending too much time with John. You're sounding just like him."

"Thanks for the compliment, but I've known you a long time and I sense that you have a reluctance to find these hidden fears."

"If they are hidden and I don't know they exist, then they don't have power to hurt me. Why should I go looking for trouble?"

"You may not have been looking for trouble. In fact, you have probably been trying to avoid it. Nevertheless, trouble has found you. If John is right, you must realize you have to let down the barriers and find what you have hidden."

Elizabeth looked like she wanted to hit me. "So if you know me so well, you tell me what I'm hiding."

"I don't know if I can find it for you or not. I think only you can recognize them when found, but maybe I can encourage you and push you in the right direction."

"So push me then, I've drawn a blank here."

"I have a feeling you have some residual fears that are connected to your early religious upbringing."

"That's silly. My religious beliefs have changed drastically over the years. Just like I no longer fear the bogeyman I also no longer fear the fire and brimstone teachings of the old time religion."

"You say that, but is it possible that you almost put too much emphasis on the idea that you're not afraid of a burning hell and that guilt is beyond you?"

"I think the idea that God would send you to a burning Hell is ridiculous. A loving God would not do that."

"Logically, that's true, but things you were taught as a child may have had a much more powerful effect than you may admit. Weren't your parents very religious fundamentalist Baptists?"

"Yes, I had to go to church every Sunday no matter what."

"I remember you said that your dad's favorite preacher was this hellfire-and-damnation guy who loved to shout out the punishments of God. You said he portrayed all humans as terrible sinners who are going to suffer unimaginable pain and suffering if they don't follow the Bible and the line of virtue one hundred percent."

"Yeah, I cringe at the memory of that guy", Elizabeth replied. "Dad made all of us sit in the front row and listen to that horrible diatribe. At the dinner table during the week he would talk about the sermon and how it applies in our lives. When I got interested in boys Dad really hammered virtue into me. He made me feel that if I ever slipped and had sex before marriage I was going to burn in Hell forever."

I paused a moment and said evenly, "And those old teachings don't bother you any more?"

Elizabeth sniffed. "Of course not. Like I said, I've put them behind me like the bogeyman."

"I don't think you've put them entirely behind you. For one thing I can tell the memory of those days still bothers you"

"Everybody has painful memories they don't like to think of," Elizabeth said, wheeling her chair out of the kitchen.

I decided to change the subject for the moment. Elizabeth was getting pretty defensive. I stood in front of her. "Your mother was a perfectionist, wasn't she? Didn't she put a lot of pressure on you to be the perfect child?"

Elizabeth lowered her eyes. "When I was little I tried to never do anything to disappoint my folks - like I never misbehaved or talked back to them. I remember even apologizing to them in little notes I wrote for not being better in some way... But when I got older and more independent and started dating, they both seemed disappointed in me."

"Disappointed how?" I asked.

"I don't know how to describe it... like, their innocent little girl, their perfect child, grew up and innocence was lost. I did feel sexual guilt I guess. My mom gave me the third degree after every date and my dad wasn't comfortable being physically affectionate anymore. I really felt their discomfort with my sexuality. Maybe I was feeling their sexual guilt instead of my own." Elizabeth added after a pause, "It seemed like I couldn't do anything right."

"Did you ever feel like they didn't love you for who you really were, or that their love was conditional on you conforming to their idea of perfection?"

Elizabeth's eyes moistened. "Yes" she replied softly. "And I never measured up no matter how hard I tried. They never got to know me as a person and after a while, I didn't want them to. I got a little rebellious - did my share of sewing wild oats - and I'm sure they didn't want to know about that side of me either. It would have killed them, I think."

"That may be it!" I exclaimed, kneeling in front of Elizabeth. "If your folks knew who you really were, the real you, you think it would have killed them. So you punished yourself by suppressing the real you...by killing the real you."

Elizabeth looked a little pale. "You need to get to work. We can talk about this later."

"Work can wait", I replied. "Do you see now how there might be some connection between this fear of discovery, your suppression of the truth, your guilt and your disease today?"

"Um-m-m, maybe," Elizabeth frowned. "I think I've worked through my stuff pretty well, though. I'm my own person now; I don't need my parents approval anymore."

"But you need your own", I said gently, taking her hand. As I got up I said, "I think we need to explore it. I'll go to work now but I want you to promise me something. Promise me that you'll think about the guilt you may still feel about those days and the fear of not measuring up to your parent's standards for you."

"What good does it do? " Elizabeth looked up at me angrily. "It doesn't change anything."

"No, but facing your fears can change you," I said, squeezing her shoulder . "Will you try, please? It may heal your disease."

"I'll see what I can do, but I think it will do more harm than good."

"Trust me on this one. I think this is the right direction."

I kissed her good-bye and put on my coat, hoping I was right.

CHAPTER FOURTEEN
What We Are Not

The next couple of days were fairly ordinary. I got the feeling Elizabeth didn't want me to press her further about any hidden guilt so I laid low in that area. In fact, it seemed as if there was a distance between us that didn't exist before our conversation, and I did not seem to know how to close the gap.

I did quite a bit of thinking on who or what I was and was looking forward to my weekly breakfast with Wayne. Maybe bouncing a few things off of him again would bring some additional light.

This week I suggested we meet at Denny's and was fortunate enough to get the same booth that John and I had been sitting at. If Wayne only knew who was sitting in his seat a few days ago, I thought to myself.

Wayne started the conversation.

"Why were you so adamant that we meet at Denny's? We sometimes come here when nothing else is open, but not for our weekly discussion."

"I just like Denny's better than I used to," I replied nonchalantly.

"OHHH..KAY," Wayne said with a facial expression that told me he wasn't quite satisfied with my answer. He continued: "So did you look up that scripture where Jesus says we are gods?"

"Yes, it was quite interesting. I also found another scripture that sort of tells what God is and goes along with what you said last week." I pulled out a Bible and turned to the First Corinthians chapter twelve that John suggested I study.

Wayne looked a little startled. "I don't recall you ever carrying around a Bible in public places before."

"I never realized there was so much interesting stuff in it," I said. "I wanted to read you something interesting I found. Here let me read you this from Paul's writings. In First Corinthians chapter twelve, Paul starts out talking about the gifts of the Spirit. Then concerning these gifts and powers he says: *But all these worketh that one and the selfsame Spirit, dividing to every man severally as he will. Now there are diversities of gifts, but the same Spirit. And there are diversities of administrations, but the same Lord. And there are diversities of operations, but it is THE SAME GOD THAT WORKETH ALL IN ALL. But the manifestation of the Spirit is given to EVERY MAN to profit withal... For as THE BODY IS ONE AND HATH MANY MEMBERS, and all the members of that ONE BODY, being MANY, are ONE body, SO ALSO IS CHRIST. For by ONE SPIRIT we are all baptized into ONE body, whether we be Jews or Gentiles, whether we be bond or free; and have been all made to drink into ONE SPIRIT. For the body is not one member, but MANY ...Now Ye are the body of Christ, and members in particular. "* I looked up. "So what do you get from this?" I asked Wayne.

"Hand me that Bible a minute." Wayne took it and spent several minutes perusing the chapter. "It's funny," he said. "I've read the New Testament a couple times, but I seemed to have glossed over this. There's a lot of deep meaning here."

"That's what I thought too," I agreed. "Tell me how you interpret it."

"I could probably spend about a hour."

"I'll tell you what," I said. "Let's go through the part that I read verse by verse. It starts out *But all these worketh that one and the selfsame Spirit, dividing to every man severally as he will.* So what's your interpretation here?" I asked.

Wayne said, "It tells us that God has one Spirit and that every man has a portion of it."

"But what I find interesting is the word dividing. The Spirit is divided to every man," I said.

"So, you think maybe the one omnipresent God divides Himself to every life form? That's another way of saying what I did last week. If God is omnipresent, He is everywhere. In one sense He is divided into each and every form and another sense just one great life."

"That kind of makes sense." Then I read on: *"Now there are diversities of gifts, but the same Spirit. And there are diversities of administrations, but the same Lord. And there are diversities of operations, but it is THE SAME GOD THAT WORKETH ALL IN ALL. But the manifestation of the Spirit is given to EVERY MAN to profit withal...* This merely emphasizes what we've been saying. Basically there is one Spirit of God working through every man."

"But would that include evil men, and of course murderers, child beaters, rapists and so on? It does say that the Spirit works through every man," he said.

"I think Christians think *every man* means every Christian."

"But it doesn't say *every Christian*. It says *every man*. Actually, if God is omnipresent, the Spirit would have to be in every person, even in every form."

"That's true. But let's stick to Paul here. He definitely says the Spirit is in every man so I guess that would have to include evil men."

Wayne stared at me a moment. "So, how could an evil man have the Spirit of God in him and still be evil? Is God then evil?"

"Maybe the Spirit is in all men, even evil men, but the evil and violent people ignore that Spirit. Maybe we all ignore it to a certain degree."

"That's a possibility," Wayne said after a moment.

I continued. "I find this next verse interesting: *For as THE BODY IS ONE, AND HATH MANY MEMBERS, and all the members of that ONE BODY, being MANY, are ONE body, SO ALSO IS CHRIST.* What I find fascinating here is if we substitute the word *God* for *Christ*, we have a description of what God is."

"So you're saying that God is like a giant body and each life is a member of that body. I've thought of something like that before. Like, I'm just one of millions of cells in some great life much higher than myself."

"Let's say you are the mouth of the body of God and you say *I am God.* Are you telling the truth or not?"

"Well, my mouth says *I am Wayne* and it is telling the truth as I command it to. It is enough of a part of me to say it is me."

"So, if we are a cell in the body of God we are not incorrect in saying we are Gods. Do you think this is what Jesus meant when He said *ye are gods*?'" I asked.

"Probably. Even though the people who were called gods were far from perfect, they still compose a part of His life."

I looked at my Bible again. "This is verified by the last verse I read you: *For by ONE SPIRIT we are all baptized into ONE body, whether we be Jews or Gentiles, whether we be bond or free; and have been all made to drink into ONE SPIRIT. For the body is not one member, but MANY. Now Ye are the body of Christ, and members in particular.* This goes along with what we're saying. The body which is God is not one, but many. I find it fascinating the Bible verifies this thought you have had all along. We are a cell in the body of a being much greater than we are. What is really interesting is the Bible seems to indicate we can say we are that greater life which is God."

"Heavy stuff," Wayne quipped. "What have you been doing lately, reading some off-the-wall books?"

"Actually, I've been reading the Bible a lot lately."

"Feel a need to save the soul?" Wayne joked.

"All kidding aside, I have found some fascinating things in here. For one thing, did you know that the judges in the time of Moses were called gods?"

"I don't remember reading about that in the Bible."

"You don't because it's not translated correctly. In several verses the Hebrew translation reads *gods* and not *judges* as most Bibles translate it. Even Moses was called a god."

"Sounds like the Bible is a New Age book," said Wayne.

"The more I read it, the more it seems to support New Age philosophy rather than standard Christian dogma."

"Yet if you quote a scripture to a New Ager, he acts like you're in the dark ages, like you're a stupid hick that hasn't been enlightened. It's kind of ironical. The Bible has a lot of light that the orthodox Christians don't see and that the New Agers won't even look at."

I thought I would change the subject a bit: "Remember the question I asked last week WHO or WHAT ARE WE?' Now the best answer we've been able to come up with so far is we are gods. And what are we as gods? We are a part of the body of the one God. By identifying with the body we can legitimately say then that we are gods. But the problem is, even though this seems to tell us much, it also tells us little. Like, what is the one God anyway? One may answer life, but what is life? The problem I have here is all the mysteries of the universe are reduced to words, and the meaning of the final words are also mysteries. Therefore, saying we are gods or life means nothing if we don't know what God or life is."

Wayne grinned. "So, you're pretty much saying what I have believed most of my life. In the end, we know nothing for sure, so we should believe nothing for sure."

I frowned. Wayne sure could be a cynic. "I'm beginning to see why you have believed that way, except I have to go with an inward belief I have. That is, when we don't know a thing for sure it is because we are either deluded or don't have all the facts. Obviously, God and life are something. We just don't have all the details as to what they are," I said.

"How about love? Do you think that can also be defined?"

"I think if we understood love completely, we could pinpoint a definition. The trouble with love is everyone has a different idea as to what it is. The parent may think love is not giving the kid candy and the kid may think love is in the giving of the candy."

"So we have a similar problem with God, life and who we are. Everyone has a different idea."

"I think it's a little like guessing how many beans are in a jar," I said. "Everyone has a different idea as to the number, but when the logical process of counting is applied, an exact number is discovered. After this number is found, there is only one answer. All other answers are illusions. One of my favorite quotes is from the book A COURSE IN MIRACLES which says *the truth is true and nothing else is true*. When the true number of beans is found, nothing else is true. When we discover who we are for sure that will be true and nothing else will be true."

"But there can be more than one way to describe the truth," said Wayne.

"How's that?" I motioned the waitress for more coffee.

"Let's say there are is thousand beans in a jar."

"Yes. There's not 1001 or 1002, but only a thousand."

"That's true, but another way of describing the number is ten times one hundred or ten times ten times ten. There are numerous different ways to say the number *one thousand.*"

"That's a good point, but you will still have the truth as long as you are arriving at the correct number. The number one thousand is still constant though whether it is spoken in English, Spanish or as ten times one hundred. The definite number does not change, only the way it is described.   The trouble in philosophy is that people describe the number one thousand and they may make it sound like two thousand. But thinking there is two thousand beans in the jar does not add a thousand beans. The jar still only contains one thousand no matter how fancy your language is."

"You've hit on the concept that explains why very few people think alike."

"Yet, people would think alike if they could see through the fog that hides and distorts the true number of beans in the jar."

"I guess I could buy that," said Wayne.

"So, if we could see the true answer to WHO OR WHAT WE ARE, then it would probably make enough sense that we could become one in thought."

"That's true if we could both see without distortion, or pre-conceived notions."

"Let's say, then, the fact we are gods is not the answer because god is just a word for us that tells us little. Let's also say we are not our bodies because our bodies are just vehicles in use by the driver, which is our true selves. What is left?"

"Most philosophers agree we are not our bodies," said Wayne. "Without our bodies some say we are spirits or souls."

"But these are just words again. People are still not sure what spirit or soul is. Let's say you had an out-of-body experience and were floating above your body. What are you in this state that you can pinpoint?"

"Assuming that such an experience is real, I guess I am still thinking and feeling and have some type of consciousness."

"Let's suppose your feelings are not a part of your true self, but a vehicle like your body. Suppose you are now separated from them - what is now left?"

"Thought and consciousness, I guess," said Wayne.

"Now suppose your thoughts are not a part of your true self and you are separated from them. What is left?"

"Where did you get this stuff?" Wayne asked, confused. "Our feelings and thoughts probably survive death, assuming there is an afterlife."

"Even so, assume they are just vehicles and you are separated from them. What is left?"

Wayne sat back and stretched. "This is an unusual line of thought for you. OK. Let's see. I guess all that would be left would be life, consciousness, perhaps awareness. On the other hand, without thoughts and feelings you may be just a blob of nothing. It's hard to say."

I leaned forward. "I kind of thought that when this idea first came to me, but then I experimented. I spent some time meditating and cleared myself of all thoughts and detached myself from all my feelings, but I found that something in me was still there. I still had life and consciousness."

"Well, maybe you were thinking and feeling and didn't know it."

"Why don't you try it? When I did it I felt more alive than ever."

"See, you said you felt alive. You were still feeling."

"But it was a higher octave of feeling. It was not feeling in the normal emotional sense. I use the word feeling because I don't think we have a word for what I sensed," I said.

"So if I play your game here, our true selves must be some type of consciousness that can take in and use data, and uses emotion and the thinking process like you and I use a computer."

"You came to basically the same conclusion I did. If you had to make a guess, would you say we are consciousness?"

"Life, consciousness, awareness, spirit... Who knows? You're likely to go crazy if you think about it too much. I think I'll stick to being a god. It seems simpler and more fun." Wayne picked up his empty cup and turned around. "And if I were a god, I'd make more coffee materialize right now. Waitress!"

The waitress responded and brought some coffee. "Well", I grinned, "you got more coffee in about thirty seconds. That must be pretty close to being a god."

"I wish," he said. "I'll tell you this. I don't know where you're getting this stuff, but I'm looking forward to seeing what you come up with next week."

"So am I," I smiled. "I don't know what is coming yet, but I guarantee it will be interesting."

CHAPTER FIFTEEN
The Name of God

The rest of the week passed rather uneventfully. I didn't seem to be looking forward to my weekly meeting with John as much as usual because I knew I would have to give the handkerchief back. During the week Elizabeth didn't let it out of her sight. She had it in her possession at all times. It seemed to work for her though. She had most of her strength back and we went for short walks each day. In addition to this she did most of the housework and cooking. I was beginning to feel like we were a normal married couple again, except it was now Thursday and I had to deliver the handkerchief back to John.

That evening Elizabeth went to bed early. At about eleven I went upstairs to see her and observed her lying peacefully asleep with the handkerchief clutched in her right hand.

I nudged her. "Sweetie," I said. "It's time for me to take the handkerchief."

She squeezed it tighter. "No," she said. "It gives me strength."

"I think it's much better if we give it back than if we keep it."

"Ask John if I can keep it a while longer."

I paused and took a deep breath. "OK. I'll ask him, but I need to take it back."

"Let me keep it while you're gone."

"John made a point that I'm supposed to listen to his exact words. I think I should take it back, but I'll ask him if you can have it a while longer."

I almost thought I felt strength withdraw from Elizabeth as I took the handkerchief. I felt like a heel, but I thought it was the best thing to do. I kissed her good-bye and went out into the garage and seated myself in the car. Just as I reached to put the key in the ignition I felt a tingling feeling throughout my body.

The next thing I knew, I found myself sitting on the floor of a sparsely furnished room. I looked around and saw John sitting on a chair drinking a cup of tea next to a dining table. "Why don't you come over here and join me," he smiled.

I got up and walked toward him, somewhat disoriented

"Cup of tea?" asked John

"Sure. Why not," I said. I looked out the window. The sun was in the East. It looked like morning wherever I was. "Where am I and why is the sun up? Isn't it eleven o'clock at night?"

"Here, drink this," said John pushing a cup of tea my direction. I took it, sat down and started sipping. "Wow, this really has a zing. What is it?"

"I'm not sure, really. Joshua made it. There are several combinations that He likes."

"Joshua?? You mean Jesus?"

"That's the man."

"He was here?" I couldn't believe my ears!

"Just a few minutes ago."

"Can I meet Him?"

"That's not on the agenda yet."

"Are you telling me Jesus was here a few minutes ago making and drinking tea like a regular guy?"

"That's exactly what He did." John looked like he was having fun with this.

"But isn't He ascended into heaven or wandering around in the next world somewhere?"

John laughed, "You still have a lot to learn, my friend. But enough small talk. I am pressed for time and we need to get started."

"You never told me where I am and why it's morning."

John studied me for a second. "You are in Tel Aviv and it is eight twenty in the morning here."

I stared at him. "I'll tell you this," I said in amazement, "if I was not a believer before, I am now." I glanced out the window again. We seemed to be in the midst of the city center most of the way up a fairly tall building.

John looked at me in earnest. "As you know when we started this relationship, I shared some of my memories with you. Would you mind if I shared some of yours?"

I noticed John asked if he could share my memories. I thought about the request a few seconds. "That would be fine, but there are some embarrassing things that are now floating around my mind I would just as soon not share."

"Don't worry about it," John smiled. "I will only tune into the memories associated with our relationship and the teachings. A true teacher will only tune into memories that are released through free will. Now hold up your hand." Our right hands touched fingers and I felt a slight tingle.

John sat back in his chair and smiled. "So far so good."

"What do you mean?" I asked.

"You've been tempted to tell Wayne about me, but you have resisted. It's a good thing. Those who cannot keep a secret are usually revealed at this point. You shared discussions on the first key with him, but I did not forbid that."

"Was that all right then?" I asked eagerly.

"It was more than all right. This type of sharing will prepare you for your mission. You will be doing much of it in the future if you are faithful to the inner voice."

"You keep talking about a mission. Can you tell me more about it?"

"If you are faithful, your mission will embrace several areas. One will be the teaching of the keys. Any more I can say would merely be a distraction at present. Now we must move ahead. In your own words tell me WHO OR WHAT ARE YOU?"

I took a deep breath. "OK, here's my thoughts. If I am not my body, mind or emotions and if all the other terms I've passed by you do not have enough meaning, I guess all that is left is consciousness itself. I am consciousness."

"Do you know what consciousness is?"

"Consciousness is livingness. Life."

"And what is life?"

"An awareness."

"An awareness of what?"

"An awareness of whatever is out there?"

"How about things that are inside yourself? Is consciousness awareness of that too?"

I thought a moment. "I suppose," I said.

"So consciousness is awareness of things outside and inside self."

"I think so," I said unsure of myself.

"So the real you is like a camera that takes snapshots of what is outside and inside of itself?"

"I'm not sure," I replied weakly.

"That just doesn't feel right, does it?"

"No it seems silly when you think about it. We've got to be something more profound than a camera," I said.

"Again you found something that you are not. A camera is something a living thing uses, but it is another type of vehicle that is in use by the real Self."

I thought silently for a few seconds. "I think I'm at a dead end here. I have passed by you every thing that a human being has ever considered that he was and not one of them is the right answer."

John smiled. "If the answer was obvious you would not need a teacher. A true spiritual teacher does not show up to teach maxims that are readily available in the books of the world. There are hundreds of books in print dealing with the divinity in man or the idea that humans are gods. Then there are many others dealing with the standard spiritual ideas. Joshua and those working directly with Him only present a teaching when it is either something not yet clearly revealed to humanity or an aspect of an old teaching that is not understood in today's world. There are many teachings that have never been revealed, and there are yet many others that have been revealed in the past but have been lost for a number of reasons. The time is coming soon when all the old truths will be restored and many new ones will be revealed."

"Are the keys a new revelation or lost knowledge restored?"

"A little of both. Most will be new knowledge to seekers; but there are several of them that are openly taught in the world today, but the full meaning is not understood. Each key has points of enlightenment the seekers of the world need to tune in to. To solve each of them you must not only come up with the right answer, but you must demonstrate right understanding. I see from your memories you have been doing some thinking about the nature of God as described in Corinthians."

"Yes. Do I need to run my thoughts by you or can you read it from my memories?"

John closed his eyes for a moment and said: "Your memories give me the general idea of what you have come up with. You are on the right track and we'll talk more about who or what God is later. We are short on time right now, however, so we must move on. Continue to contemplate the mystery of godliness to prepare your mind for the future. Meanwhile are you ready for your next hint?"

"Yes. I am really curious because I've reached a dead end

here. I can't imagine what the next hint will be."

"The next hint revolves around the mystery of God that you have been contemplating. I'm sure you remember the story of Moses."

"Well, I've seen the Ten Commandments and I've read the Bible story," I said.

"Do you remember what Moses did during the second forty years of his life?"

"He was chased out of Egypt and became a sheepherder in the desert. If I remember right he was around eighty when he freed the Israelites, so I guess he was a regular guy most of the time during the second forty years. We don't know much about that period of his life."

"No part of any person's life is lost. All is eventually retrievable. Not much is written of this time period because it was a time of preparation. He found his father-in-law Jethro to be a wise man with teachings that had been passed down for many generations and learned a lot from him and the brotherhood of which he was a member. One of the major points of discussion Moses had with his little conclave over the years was about the nature of God. One of the great mysteries that was discussed at that time was whether or not God had a name and if he did, what it would be."

John continued, "The reason the name of God was such a big item then was that it was a tradition among the Hebrews and many other ancient peoples to attach great meaning to a person's name. In that period a lot of thought went into naming a child because it was believed that the name was connected to or would determine the child's destiny.

"For instance, Abraham meant *father of a multitude* and that was what he became. David meant *beloved* and David was the *beloved of God*. The name *Joseph* means *the person will have increase* and Joseph - who was sold into Egypt - became the world's richest man and also had a very great posterity.

"Because of this great interest in names, one of the greatest mysteries to Moses was the name of God itself. If one were to discover the name of God, he would hold the key as to what type of being He really is."

I nodded. John took a sip of his tea. "During this forty-year time period, Moses spent many a day tending sheep alone with his thoughts, questioning many of the mysteries of the time. The prime mystery that was in the front of his mind was the mystery of the name of God. He contemplated and wondered about this over and over.

"Finally came the experience of the burning bush where he entered into the presence of God and received that rare chance to ask any question he wanted. Do you remember what that question was?"

"Yes.' I replied. "He asked God what his name was. You know, I kind of wondered why he asked that question, but now it makes sense."

"Do you remember what the answer was?"

"God said I AM THAT I AM."

"What kind of name is that?" John asked.

"I don't know for sure. I always thought it was kind of a strange answer. I guess God is just saying that He just IS."

"Was God saying He has no name?" John asked.

"I'm not sure. It sounds like it. I have heard some say that His name is just I AM."

"If you were Moses and God gave you that answer to your question, would that satisfy your curiosity?"

"Hm-m-m, not really."

"If you were Moses what would have been your response?"

"I would have asked, *What kind of name is I AM THAT I AM?*"

"Moses was an intelligent man. Why do you suppose he did not ask for some type of clarification to a weak answer to a question he had been contemplating for forty years?"

I thought a moment. "I haven't thought about it that way, but you're right. I just figured it was one of the Mysteries."

"There are two possibilities. First, perhaps Moses was not the curious after all, or second he was satisfied with the answer. Which do you think it is?" John asked.

"You said Moses thought about this question for forty years so he had to be curious, but I cannot see why he would have been satisfied with the answer."

"You're right," John said nodding. "Moses was too curious to let a partial answer pass by. Let us say that Moses was satisfied with the answer. How could this have occurred?"

"Maybe he understood the answer better than I do."

"That is correct. However, he did understand the answer better than you do not because he was smarter, but because he heard a different answer than is presented in the various translations of the Bible."

John pulled out his old Bible again and opened it to Exodus chapter three and asked me to read verse 14. I read the words: *And God said unto Moses, I AM THAT I AM: and he said, Thus shalt thou say unto the children of Israel, I AM hath sent me unto you.*

"This is pretty much the standard translation in most Bibles, but it is a very bad one and most honest Hebrew scholars know this. In the Hebrew it reads: *I Am Becoming that which I Am Becoming. Go say to the children of Israel that He who Is Becoming has sent you.*

"The ancient Hebrew is much different from the English you are used to. It always had gaps in it that were to be filled by either the obvious or by the intuition. Now let me tell you plainly the answer that Moses heard. As you remember, Moses asked God what His name was. To this question God said: *You ask for my name so you will know who or what I am. This I cannot give you because I Am Becoming that which I decide to Become. Go tell the children of Israel that He who is Becoming has sent you.* John paused a moment. "Now tell me how you think Moses understood this answer."

"I think you've turned on a light in my head," I said excitedly. "Here's the way I see it. As you said, in that age, a name revealed the core essence of who the individual was and Moses was expecting an answer like this from God. In other words, he thought he might get an answer like *I am the great and powerful one*, or something like that. Instead, God told him that He cannot give Moses a standard name because He is in the process of becoming whatever it is that He wants to become. Thus any name given to Him at one time may not apply at a future time."

"Great answer! Perhaps we have the right man for the job after all," John smiled. "Your answer is right on track. God is always changing the image that He presents to the various parts of the world at different times in history. For instance, in the time of Moses He presented an image of the all-powerful ruler who is to obeyed at all costs. Then in the time of Christ this changed to the all-forgiving God of Love who sacrificed His only Son. This was a definite change in the presentation of God that is not acknowledged by most Christians. Also, God is presented to the world in different ways in many other religions that had an inspired beginning. Notice that each religion has a different name for God. This is because the name has a particularly important message for their consciousness that will help their particular group or race progress.

"God has many names because He is many things to many people in many times. Thus He could not give Moses any ultimate name because He becomes what He decides to become to the consciousness of any group or individual."

I nodded, but a thought struck me. "But isn't there a scripture that says God does not change? It sounds like He, in fact, is in a constant state of change."

John nodded. "When the prophets wrote about the changelessness of God they were telling the people that the words of God are 100 per cent dependable - that He does not promise the people one thing today and break it tomorrow. They were not saying He does not change in any way. I tried to make this clear in my own Book of Revelations. I talked about God revealing a new name, that He will create a new heaven and new earth, and that He will make all things new. Look at the earth and the universe around you, which is God's Body. It is all in a state of change or becoming new or renewed. Everything is changing. Because God is everything and everything changes, then God changes."

"Speaking of new, this is certainly a new teaching. I have never heard anything like this in any church."

John's countenance became serious. "The religions of the world do not believe in new things. They will always resist any new teaching and attempt to preserve the old, even if it is scientifically proven to be incorrect, as in the days the church persecuted Galileo for merely revealing what his eyes saw through a telescope."

"I've come to that conclusion myself. That's why I don't attend any church even though I basically believe the scriptures."

"That is also one of the reasons you were chosen. Anyone whose mind is fixed in a dogma is not usable to us as a world teacher. It may seem hard for you to accept but if the standard believer who is fixed in a dogma were to have experienced all that you have with me and were to have heard what you have just heard, I would be rejected as an agent of the devil."

"Even if he were transported halfway around the world in an instant?" I asked.

"The closed-mindedness of those stuck in religious dogma is beyond belief," said John, shaking his head. "This was demonstrated by Joshua when He raised Lazarus from the dead after he was three days in the grave. Instead of converting the religious leaders, it just inflamed them and hastened the crucifixion. The leaders also knew without doubt that Christ was raised from the dead, for He appeared to them after the resurrection so they would be without excuse. Even this did not convert them and they fought all the harder against His followers. When the average person has his mind centered on a belief, only the destruction of the world created by that belief will change him. That can happen by an inner or outer collapse."

"I've never thought of it that way, but I can certainly see that you are correct. I don't mean to change the subject, but what is my hint for this week?"

"What we have talked about is the hint," John said evenly.

I thought a moment, recalling the Bible verses. "Can't you give me something more direct?" I pleaded.

"I have given you much food for thought. Contemplate in particular what we have talked about concerning Moses and God."

I thought for a moment. "I have a couple other questions."

"Ask away. I have a few minutes."

"You said you have been killed a number of times, even once under Hitler. How could this happen to you when you have power to disappear? Look what you did to me. You teleported me half way across the globe."

John smiled. "Intelligent question, my friend. There are certain laws and principles in place that regulate how an evolving humanity can be assisted. The higher they evolve on the spiritual ladder, the more directly they can be worked with by the Brotherhood of Light. When a member of the Brotherhood decides to work directly with the people, he must be subject to the same personal limitations the general populace has. Thus, when I directly worked with Staufenberg in Nazi Germany, I became subject to the same perils he was. The only way I can be invulnerable to death is to work at arm's length through a disciple like yourself. If I were to work side by side with you, there would be so much controversy stirred up because of the nature of the work that we would both be killed before the work was done. There is another factor. In past ages I could move from one part of the world to another and no one would be the wiser. With today's communications systems, once my picture appears in a National Enquirer or the Star, any hope of anonymity is over. So taking all things into consideration, we have decided it best to work through an apparently ordinary mortal such as yourself."

"You mean I am just apparently ordinary?" I asked with interest.

"Joshua sees much more potential in you than you might guess," John said with a smile. "Even though your life has seemed fairly ordinary, you have had many experiences which have prepared you to be a teacher. You, in turn, will find others who will become major players in this part of history. Some of these would have just lived ordinary lives if not for the great opportunity you will present. Great opportunity brings forth greatness of the human spirit."

Wow, this gave me a lot to think about, but I couldn't remember having many experiences that would lead me to teaching "Sounds overwhelming. So what are you doing here in Tel Aviv?"

"We have a disciple like yourself here and several other middle eastern countries. Their primary purpose is not to teach, but to influence political leaders on the path to peace. Believe me, we have a difficult task, particularly since the Dark Brothers also have their disciples carefully placed. I thought I could spend some time relaxing in Boise and teach you at my leisure, but we seem to have a lot of crisis coming up lately that have to be dealt with. One major problem is the proliferation of nuclear weapons to third world countries that would not hesitate to use them. This is a much greater threat than your leaders realize and needs to be dealt with. This is all I have time to tell you about this at present."

Realizing my time was short, I reluctantly pulled the handkerchief out of my jacket pocket and handed it to John. "My wife appreciates the relief. Is it possible the can keep the handkerchief a while longer?"

John replied softly, "Believe me, I feel for her and also you, but the natural laws must be allowed to flow. She's got to be on her own with her struggle. Let me warn you it will be more difficult than you expect the next few weeks, but the end will be good if you both follow the highest you know."

"That's encouraging, I guess," I said without confidence. Elizabeth will be so disappointed, I thought.

John patted my back. "Time to send you back. Perhaps we can spend more time together next week."

The next thing I knew I was back in the front seat of my car. I got out and walked into my home in somewhat of a daze. It was several hours before I got around to going to bed.

CHAPTER SIXTEEN
Becoming

After getting to bed so late, I was hoping to be able to sleep in, but was awakened by Elizabeth shaking my shoulder.

"My legs! I can't move my legs at all!"

"Maybe they're just asleep," I said, half asleep myself.

"No. No. It's worse than it was before. I can barely move them at all now. Help me!"

I hated feeling so powerless, but helped her up into her wheelchair.

"Look! " she cried "My legs are now totally useless. Even at their worst they had some strength, but now it's worse than ever. Did you bring that handkerchief back?"

"Honey, John said I couldn't..."

"What kind of man is this guy? He gives me a gift and takes it away. Now I'm worse than I was. I wish I had never even seen John." Elizabeth sobbed bitterly.

I knelt in front of her and took her hand firmly. "Don't say that, sweetie. Because of John you now know for sure it is possible to be healed. He said if I solved the first three keys, you would be healed. We must look forward to that time."

She gathered her composure for a moment and asked, "So, did you get the first one yet?"

"Not yet, but I'm getting closer."

"Maybe you are and just maybe this is some cosmic joke and there is no answer. Maybe we are nothing and going nowhere," she said, starting to cry again.

I hugged her for a moment and then lifted her chin and looked deeply into her eyes. "I know there is an answer. I will find it."

Elizabeth turned her head away. "So consciousness is not

the answer?"

"No."

"So try *nothing* next time. That will be as good as anything. You've guessed everything else we could be."

I was startled with her coldness. "I've never seen you so negative."

"Negative? You don't know negative," she said bitterly. "Call Doctor Kovorkian and I'll show you negative!"

I felt a terrible feeling in the pit of my stomach as she said that. I felt like running out of her presence as far as I could. It was as if it was not her who was talking, but some hateful being. Nevertheless, I knew I had to override that feeling and show her all the love I could.

"You'll get your legs back. This is just a temporary thing," I tried to assure her. "We'll take you to the doctor. Maybe he can give you something."

"The doctor never helps. I'm staying right here."

"I'll call your mom and she can come over while I show some homes."

"I'm not helpless. Just go and I'll take care of myself." Elizabeth wheeled herself out of the bedroom toward the kitchen.

I called her mother anyway to keep an eye on her when I had to be out. There was a certain amount of work I had to do to survive financially, and I spent all the time I could with Elizabeth, but nothing I could do or say seemed to help. She was in the darkest spirits I had ever seen her in. It was almost as if she were turning into another person. Realizing she may not have much time left, I thought every spare moment about the newest hints and the first key. I came up with a few ideas and thought I would share them with Wayne during our next breakfast.

When Sunday came, Elizabeth was still in a negative state and didn't even want me to have breakfast with Wayne. I assured her I needed someone to bounce ideas off of and of the importance of solving the keys, but she seemed to act as if I were wasting my time. She was generally very supportive and this resistance did not seem like her. I went to see Wayne despite her comments.

"I see we're back to our regular eating place," said Wayne. "How was your week?"

"It was the best of times and the worst of times," I said with a forced smile.

"I've had a few weeks like that," he said. "So have you decided that we are consciousness or have you come up with some even heavier thought?"

"I've concluded that the core of our being is not consciousness, but uses consciousness. Consciousness is like a camera and our true self is like the one who takes the pictures."

"So who or what is the one who takes the pictures?" Wayne asked.

"I'm not sure yet. You know the philosopher Descartes tried to discover what there was in man that he could call real and he came up with the phrase *I think, therefore, I am.*"

"Yes," Wayne agreed. "If I remember right, the famous Latin phrase was *cogito ergo sum*. Descartes, using the process of elimination, concluded that the only thing he knew for sure was that he was thinking, therefore he had to exist. That was one of the few things I learned in college. I think it's interesting that both Descartes and God reduced our essence to the phrase I AM. Maybe we just are and it's a great mystery we will never know or understand."

"Funny you should say that. I've been studying the words of God to Moses and the phrase *I AM that I AM* is a mistranslation. The literal translation according to scholars is *I am becoming that I am becoming. Go tell the children of Israel that He who is becoming has sent you.* Taking this into consideration, it seems that the essence of God which may be our own essence also has something to do with the process of becoming."

"So maybe Descartes should have said *I think, therefore I am becoming.*"

"That probably would have been more accurate," I said, "but I think there is some mystery behind all this that we just haven't seen yet. We have an essence that is becoming, changing or evolving, but I don't think I've found it yet."

"I doubt if we ever will," said Wayne. "We just are. Any more than that would be just about impossible for us to find out."

"It can't be impossible!" I said with greater volume and emotion than I had anticipated.

Wayne looked startled. "Whatever you say, buddy. You feel pretty strong about this quest of yours, don't you?"

"I suppose. I didn't mean to startle you. I kind of feel under a lot of pressure. Elizabeth is quite a bit worse again, my finances for helping her are limited and my emotions are on edge."

"I feel for you and her. Want me to drop by some evening this week and see if I can cheer her up?"

"It might not hurt, but call first. She's been kind of withdrawn lately. She acts like she doesn't want to see anyone."

"Sometimes it's good to have company, even when you're not in the mood."

"I agree. Now getting back to our main line of thought." I said, leaning forward. "What do you think it is that is in us that is becoming? It can't just be called I AM. There's got to be a name for it."

"If I didn't know you better, I would say you're becoming obsessed here with this idea. Here we're talking about a crisis with your wife and you switch the topic back to philosophy. It seems kind of strange."

"You're right, it does seem strange, but I have a good reason for it." I paused for a moment to think of a good reason that would not be a lie. "Elizabeth is very interested in my finding the answer. I think it will lift her spirits if I can come up with something good."

Wayne didn't looked convinced. "That's an odd way to lift someone's spirits."

I paused. I really hated holding out on Wayne. "We've been friends a long time," I finally said. "Could you just trust me on this? It would mean a lot to me and possibly to Elizabeth."

Wayne looked me in the eye. "I've known you a long time. I think there's something you're not telling me here, but if it's important, I'll just play along."

"There is something I can't tell you. All I can tell you right now is that it is important that I find the answer to this question."

"Now you've really got me curious." Wayne leaned forward and lowered his voice. "Come on. You can tell me. You tell me everything."

"I'll tell you as soon as I can, but just not now."

Wayne leaned back. "OK. I'll let you off the hook for now, but I'll expect the juicy details soon. Why do I keep getting the feeling that you think you've had some vision or something?"

I tried to smile nonchalantly. "Who knows? Now I want you to wrack that brain of yours and tell me if you have any deeper thoughts on this subject."

"Answer me this then. Do you really think we are capable of getting the right answer?"

"You know I've never lied to you. I will tell you this. I happen to know that we are capable of getting the answer."

"You think so," Wayne said looking at me squarely.

"I told you I know so," I said with emphasis.

"OK," said Wayne. "We'll proceed on the assumption you are correct here and that we can really go where no man has gone before. Perhaps a key here is God really said to Moses he is becoming rather than he just is. Becoming implies action, movement, evolution, whereas I AM implies a static, unchangeable state. Now all religions that I know of think that God is perfect and does not change, but I AM BECOMING implies a God who is changing and moving toward a higher state. That means He isn't perfect, because if He were, He wouldn't have to evolve any further. Maybe humans are gods, as some teach, for the very reason that we are imperfect and that we are also in a constant state of change and evolution. Maybe the perfection of God is just some hocus pocus passed down through the ages and is completely false. Maybe God is trapped in this universe and is just trying to find his way home like the song says."

A light went off in my head. "Good Wayne! I don't know if you're right, but at least you're leading us into new territory. Now let's assume that you're on the right track about what God is. If we are truly gods, then who or what would we be?"

"That's a hard one. Maybe we're movement or action," said Wayne.

"You know, that could be it. Everything else that people think we are is just a vehicle or instrument that we use, but action or movement is not a vehicle. You know, as scientists investigate the atomic world they find only motion, but have not found anything they consider solid. When you think of it, everything is made of wavelengths in motion, therefore the answer may be motion."

"That's true. Without motion on the atomic level there would be no life, or form, as we know it."

I reached in my pocket for money to pay for my breakfast. "I think we're on the right track. I feel it in my gut. Thanks for your help Wayne. Sorry to cut our breakfast short, but I've got to go." I stood up, ready to leave.

"Why do I get the feeling we'll be talking about this again?" Wayne mused as we walked toward the cashier..

"You're probably right, my friend. You're probably right."

CHAPTER SEVENTEEN
The Attack Of Darkness

I had a feeling I should not leave Elizabeth alone for long and I should return as soon as possible. I found that my hunch was right when I returned home and found her wheelchair was empty.

"Elizabeth!" I shouted

There was no answer.

I started searching all the rooms in the house. Finally I heard a whimpering coming from the bathroom. I ran inside and found Elizabeth in a corner with a look of terror on her face with tears drying on her cheeks.

"Sweetheart, what happened? How did you even get in here with no wheelchair."

"I needed you and you were gone. I told you that I didn't want you to go."

"Here, let me help you back into your wheelchair and we'll talk." I lifted her up and carried her back to her chair. She was clinging to me very tightly, softly crying. "There. Now I'll make you a cup of tea and we'll talk."

I made us both some herb tea and sat down facing her across the table. "OK. Now tell me what happened."

She looked at me and suddenly a look of terror took over her face like I had never seen before. She screamed "It's him!" and started wheeling away from me as fast as she could.

I ran after her and caught her and forced her to look at me again. "Look at me! It's me. No one else."

"I saw his face. Your face became his face!"

"Whose face?" I asked with no small amount of frustration.

"When you left I felt tired and fell asleep in my chair. I dreamed

111

I was at this flea market where there were all kinds of people hacking their wares. I was in my wheelchair, but managed to wheel my way around from booth to booth until I came to one that seemed to me manned by John. I thought it odd that he was wearing dark sunglasses and I wheeled my way closer and saw that he was selling all kinds of scarves and fine handkerchiefs. As soon as he noticed me he said: *I know what you want.* He picked up an old wooden box and opened it up and pulled out the old red handkerchief.

"*Can I have it?*" I pleaded.

"*Of course you can have it my dear. Here, grab hold.*'

"He dangled the handkerchief in front of me and I grabbed an end and immediately I felt my strength returning, but was puzzled by the fact that John held on to the other end. *Are you going to let me have it?*" I asked?

"*On just one condition*', John said.

"*And that would be?*"

"*Look into my eyes for six seconds.*"

"It seemed like an odd request to me and something about him seemed unlike John. His voice, the sunglasses, the request - it seemed really strange. Nevertheless, I wanted the handkerchief and his request seemed harmless so I agreed.

"Then he said, *After you have looked into my eyes for six seconds you can have the handkerchief.* He took off his sunglasses and to my horror I saw that his eyes had no pupils or iris. They were entirely white. I was surprised, but I really wanted the handkerchief so I looked back at him. Suddenly, I felt the most evil feeling anyone can imagine. Then I felt myself paralyzed as I felt my very life force being sucked from my body. I wanted to turn away, but couldn't. I somehow sensed when the six seconds were up, I would be doomed to death, extinction, Hell...who knows what."

"So, did you look at him for the six seconds?" I asked, anxious to hear her answer.

"In a way the few seconds I did look seemed like an eternity, but somehow internally I seemed to sense the true passing of seconds. During the first three seconds the man's face changed and I saw that this person was not John. He was an older effeminate-looking man with white hair. Right around the fifth second he smiled. It was a smile I never want to see again. It made an evil shiver go all the way through me. The smile seemed as if it belonged to serial killer who is watching his victim die and enjoying the moment of death. At that instant I cried out to God in my heart to give me strength, and just before the sixth second I received power to turn away and instantly woke up."

I gave her a hug and said, "My poor sweetheart. What a terrible experience."

"That's not all," Elizabeth continued. "After I woke up I realized it seemed real but consoled myself in the fact that it was just a dream. But then to my side I sensed that same awful presence, similar to what happened to you. I tried to wheel myself away from it but it felt like the brake was on. Somehow I fell out of my chair and found myself crawling away. I turned and looked toward the presence again and saw a faint outline of the white-haired man and heard his words in a whisper. *You are dead anyway, why not give your life to me.*"

"I shouted, *NO!*"

"Then he said something very strange. *Tell your husband I know who I AM. I AM THAT I AM. I AM SELF. I, the self, is all that matters.* Then he disappeared, but I still felt his presence and crawled into the bathroom where you found me."

"Is his presence still here?" I asked.

"I felt it again when I saw his face instead of yours, but it seems to be gone now."

"It's funny that I felt his presence before, but not now," I said. "Maybe evil must be revealed as well as good."

"I'm just glad you're here," Elizabeth said with a weak smile. "I never want you to leave me again."

I hugged her again. "You would think going through this disease would be plenty for your share of pain in life without having to go through something like this."

"I'll tell you this." she said with a deep sigh. "I thought I knew what fear was when I found out that I had an incurable disease, but that was nothing compared to the shear terror I felt today. It was as if my soul was at stake, in addition to my life." Elizabeth was still shaking, and I continued to hold her close.

"I know," I nodded. "I felt that presence. You really do have to experience it to understand the feelings it can generate." I took a deep breath and let Elizabeth go. "I think it's time we finished that cup of tea."

We seated ourselves around the table again after micro waving the tea so it was hot again and resumed our conversation. I asked, "This entity made an interesting statement about who he thinks we are. Now how did he word that?"

"He said to tell you *I AM. I AM THAT I AM. I AM SELF. I,*

the self, is all that matters."

I replied, "What I find interesting here is that John said that *I AM THAT I AM* is a mistranslation. It's interesting to compare the two translations. *I am* implies a static condition and is another way of saying self. *I AM BECOMING* implies an evolving condition that involves looking outside of self. In a weird way this makes a lot of sense to me. To the good guys out there, self is not the ultimate, but what the self evolves into in connection with all other selves is the thing. But to the bad guys all there is self, so every goal they have is to only benefit the self as they see it."

"Why do you suppose his eyes had only whites?" Elizabeth asked, calmer now, but I could tell the memory of the event was still horrifying to her.

"I'm not sure. Maybe it's a symbol of their blindness."

"So do you think the New Agers are wrong when they tell us to look to the self for everything?"

"Maybe they just don't have the whole truth. On the other hand, the Christians could be equally as wrong for stressing the translation I AM instead of I AM BECOMING. It seems that both the New Agers and the Christians may have inadvertently put undue attention on the self."

"The funny thing is that this evil entity may have helped us rather than hindered," said Elizabeth, stirring her tea. "Is it possible that when all is said and done we are just individual selves?"

"In some way we are individual selves and for the Dark Brothers that's where it ends. Thus, all they do is for selfish ends. But the keynote of the Brothers of Light is unselfishness. Therefore, they see something beyond self or greater than self. Somehow, I feel that the word *BECOMING* is a key one here. Perhaps self is meaningless to those in the light because they are in a state of evolution. Therefore the self tomorrow would be a different self than the self today."

"And, by contrast, the unevolving self would be the same tomorrow as it is today," Elizabeth added.

"And the fascinating thing to me is that this is one of the main perceptions that people have of God - that He is the same yesterday, today and forever. When you think of it, this concept would make for a very boring God, wouldn't it?" I mused.

"Maybe that's one of the reasons I turned off religion so much. I always relished new experiences and everything about religion seems to be centered around keeping things the way they are now and not rocking the boat with any changes." She paused and finished her tea, then asked, "So what did you and Wayne come up with about the first key?"

"It seems that everything we've come up with that we could possibly be so far is a vehicle of some kind. Even consciousness itself is like a camera our real self uses. So we finally came up with something that John can't say is a vehicle."

"And what would that be?"

"Everything is created by vibration, action or motion, so that has to be what we are."

"Sounds like a strange answer to me."

"But think about it. If everything was still, there would be no interplay; and if even the vibrations that make the atom were stilled, there would be nothing to exist. We must be composed of some type of vibration in motion; and if it ceased to exist, then we would cease to exist. Therefore, we must be composed of movement itself. That would explain why we are becoming."

"Maybe, and it is a good thought, but it doesn't feel right to me," Elizabeth said frowning.

"It may not be right, but it's the best I can come up with at the moment. I have a feeling that we're getting close. I think the next hint will tell the tale."

"I hope so," Elizabeth sighed. "I don't know how much longer my strength can hold out."

I took Elizabeth's hand. "You'll make it, Sweetie. When we solve the third key John is committed to healing you."

"If you could solve even the first one I would be encouraged," she said. "It appears that you're trying to find an answer that has eluded the best philosophers in history. What makes you think that you can go beyond anything that has ever been done?"

"No one else had the apostle John to help them, " I said softly.

"But John's been wandering the earth for two thousand years. Maybe they have had his help. Maybe this will be harder than you think."

Good point I thought to myself as I tried to assure her that we will solve the keys.

CHAPTER EIGHTEEN
Dark Brothers Revealed

The next Thursday evening, as Elizabeth and I were sitting down for dinner and I was wondering how I was going to contact John this week, I heard a knock on the door. To my surprise it was John!

"I hope I'm not imposing," he said.

"No... No, come on in. Sweetie, look who's here!"

Elizabeth looked pleasantly surprised. "Come have some dinner with us."

"You might talk me into it," John smiled.

"Hope you don't mind Sloppy Joes," I said.

"If it tastes as good as it smells I won't mind at all."

We all sat down to dinner and told him what happened to Elizabeth.

"I knew they were going to try something like this," John said frowning.

"What would have happened after the six seconds if she didn't break it off?" I asked.

"This adversary would have stolen your life force to enhance his own vitality. Without assistance from the Brothers of Light you would have died within a few days."

Elizabeth looked horrified. "What are these guys, some type of spiritual vampires?" I asked, looking at her reaction, then to John.

"That's exactly what they are," he said. "You will find that many stories and fables from your culture contain some seeds of truth. According to stories, a vampire will steal blood from his victim to give himself a renewal of life. Theoretically, he could live forever if he could have an endless supply of victims. These dark brothers do not take your blood, but they do take your life force, which corresponds to the physical power of blood. This stolen life force allows them to continue their existence."

"What do they do then, spend their time preying on helpless victims like Elizabeth?" I asked, taking Elizabeth's hand.

"He attacked Elizabeth because he was trying to get to you and put an end to our work. Taking her life force would have been a bonus. Actually they get most of their energy by working through agents on the earth."

"What do you mean by agents?" Elizabeth asked.

"Just as you will soon be an agent for the Brotherhood of Light so also are there agents on the earth for the adversaries of light, or the Dark Brotherhood. The enlightened brothers feed the multitudes of those who are open to the Spirit and give out an increase of energy, but the Dark Brothers steal energy by feeding off the multitudes and are only interested in helping themselves."

John continued, "When you are in the presence of a dark agent you will often feel a drain of energy that is unexplainable. Sometimes you will feel weak and even have to sit down. A person under his influence will often not think clearly and be literally unable to speak anything but approving words."

"You know," I interrupted, "I've felt that way several times in my life, but I can't say that the people that made me feel that way were dark agents. One was a religious leader of high acclaim, another was a government official and the other was a head of a corporation. They all had impeccable reputations."

"Did you notice they all seemed to be surrounded with an unusual aura of authority?"

I thought of them a moment. "Yes. I particularly remember the authority around the religious leader. I remember that I disagreed with him and couldn't bring myself to vocalize it. At the time I couldn't understand why I didn't say anything."

John smiled knowingly. "They have to shut down your resistance before they can steal your energy. When you yield to their illusionary authority you virtually become a subject and a source of their power, but their power is not real because it is stolen. When humanity wakes up and reclaims their power, the power of the Dark Brothers will instantly vanish and the adversaries will be bound for over one thousand years as predicted."

"So how does one free himself from their control?" Elizabeth asked.

"The illusion of authority is what gives them power. They

had power to shut you up because there was a part of you that yielded to that authority. You can easily neutralize any dark agent by completely releasing yourself from all his so-called authority and recognizing only one authority. Do you know what that is?"

"God?"

"And where do you find God?"

"Within, I guess."

"Yes. The Master said *The kingdom of God is within you*. If you subject yourself spiritually to any person outside you, you are in danger of losing the true light and being subject to a false one."

"Does that mean that in a perfect world we shouldn't have leaders or civil authorities?"

"Not at all. The structure of society could not stand without leaders, bosses, and some civil authorities. You can support a boss, mayor, local police and others and yet give all your spiritual allegiance to God within yourself. Only a few can perceive the difference between cooperating with authority for the good of the whole and yielding your power to an authority. You only learn this completely when you successfully neutralize a dark agent. Then the seeker understands. You have successfully accomplished this when you neutralized the Dark Brother who appeared to you." John laughed wryly. "Believe me, you really caught him off guard by laughing at him. He's still reeling from that encounter. It's one reason why he attacked your wife." John focused his gaze on me. "Did you notice who he pretended to be?"

"Yes, he pretended he was you," I replied.

"Why do you suppose he did that?"

"Was it because you are the greatest spiritual authority in our lives?"

"Yes, and this is unfortunate. Elizabeth has given me too much of her power and this created an opportunity for the Dark Brothers to attack. You must remember this: A door must be open before they can come in. When you learn to keep all the doors shut they will be unable to touch you on the spiritual and energy levels."

"His eyes were terrible," Elizabeth grimaced. "They were white with no pupils or iris."

"The reason his eyes appeared white is because they were turned inward toward self. This is a symbol of their utter selfishness. Their eyes can appear normal when they desire, but when they attempt to commit the ultimate act of selfishness, which is to take another's life force and use it as their own, they turn their eyes inward to the self. This aids them in siphoning off your energy for their terrible use. Thus if you ever see or dream of an entity who only shows the whites of his eyes, avoid looking at him as you would the Medusa."

"Do the agents of the Dark Brothers on the physical plane have this power to steal life force?" I asked.

"The uninitiated agents on the earth do not have power to kill with negative energy, but do have power to steal enough to make you weak. Then there are a handful of Dark initiates on the physical plane who have greater power. The advanced Dark Brothers are in another astral sphere such as the one you just encountered. Generally you will only encounter them if you pose a real threat to their plans."

John continued, "These agents of the Dark Brotherhood are often given material success and prestige in return for transferring energy to the Dark Brothers. Even though they are dedicated to selfishness there are still some obvious reasons to assist each other. The Overlords in the unseen world find certain agents useful, and they know they must give them a few crumbs to get their cooperation; and when they are no longer useful, they no longer get the crumbs. On the other hand, the Brotherhood of Light is dedicated to their disciples as well as mankind, and are ever vigilant to lend a helping hand. We are not quite as all powerful as many assume; however, and are limited in a number of ways in the amount we can assist. You are fortunate that I have freed myself sufficiently to teach you."

"We are both honored to have you," I said, getting a nod of agreement from Elizabeth. "So I take it that many of our leaders in high authority, position and influence are really Dark Agents."

"Yes. Many of them are. Most of them are not aware they are agents transmitting dark energy, but a handful of the most dangerous are completely aware. Then too we must remember that all leaders are not dark agents. There are always a handful who are sincerely doing their best to serve. Even in this latter category many are following deceptive paths and their good intentions are thus neutralized."

"Are you saying," Elizabeth interjected, "that I would not have been in danger if I had not given you too much power?"

"That is exactly true," said John.

"How then can we learn from you if we don't recognize you as an authority?"

"The key," said John "is to realize there is only one authority.

That authority is the Holy Spirit and can only be contacted from within. Nevertheless, all humans are interconnected by the Spirit. The only authority that I have is through the Spirit. When I speak truth and you are focused on the Spirit within, you will feel a confirmation within. When you then feel that confirmation, you will accept my words not because you see me as an authority, but because of confirmation through your personal authority.

"You were deceived by the Dark Brother because you were accepting my words and actions without checking with the Spirit within. The healing power of the handkerchief convinced you that you just had to accept me no matter what. This is the great error beginning disciples always make. Even if I am right all the time, you must still check; for there may come a time that he who you think is me is not me after all, just as happened with your deception. Thus, giving your power even to a true servant may open the door for a Dark Brother to trick you."

"These Dark Brothers don't make a lot of sense to me," Elizabeth said, shaking her head. "I don't understand why they are so destructive."

"The main difference between the Light and Dark Brothers is one sees in the light and the other feels in the darkness," John replied.

I thought about this statement and asked, "Is this another way of saying one uses his mind to perceive the truth and the other uses emotion to cover the truth?"

John smiled. "Exactly, my friend. Imagine two groups of people trying to find their way home. One travels by night and the other in the light of day. Which one would have the easiest time?"

"The one traveling by day, of course," I answered.

"All intelligent lives seek God at one time or another. Even the Dark Brothers have gone through what both sides call the *long dark night of the soul*; but in that night they did not find Him, so they created God after their image and thus established a system where God is not found in the Universal Spirit, but in external forms. Thus, you see why the Dark Brothers convinced the Israelites to build the golden calf as a source of external power.

"All but a very few have their golden calf, which steals their power. But the glitter of gold must eventually yield to the pure white light of Mount Sinai that reveals the way home.

"There is much yet to be revealed about light and darkness. One may see correctly at one time and be deceived at another. To stay in the light requires eternal vigilance. I will reveal more to you about this from time to time."

John sipped his coffee, "My time is short so we need to get on with our lesson. Have you discovered who or what you are yet?"

"I think I have either found the truth or am close to it," I said, leaning toward John. "When scientists examine matter they say that they cannot find proof that solid particles exist. All they can seem to find on the smallest level is wavelengths in motion. If all these wavelengths were to be stilled, the universe would virtually disappear. If the motion of the wavelengths that make me would be stilled, then I would probably cease to exist. Therefore, the real me has to be motion or action of some kind."

"That's very good," said John. "Coming to this point is a milestone, but you are not there yet. Answer me this: What is it that is in motion and what is the force creating the motion?"

I thought a moment. "If there is no such thing as solid matter then nothing is in motion, if that is possible. I guess the force propelling the wavelengths is pure energy."

"But," said John, "if there is no solid matter, then nothing is in motion, as you say.   Therefore, does it not stand to reason that energy is not required for motion since nothing is really in motion?"

"Maybe I was right after all," Elizabeth chuckled. "I said half joking that we were nothing and perhaps I was right."

"As far as the material plane goes, you are correct," said John. "But from the greater reality you are a great something. That something which creates all motion in the universe is the great mystery. Energy is not the answer because in reality there is really nothing solid in motion.

"Now I will give you two major hints. First, in my hand I have a pen. Now I will take this pen and throw it on that sofa over there."

John threw the pen on the sofa.

"Now, what made that pen fly over to the sofa?"

"Obviously you did," I said

"And who or what am I? And don't say *John*."

"So the real you threw that pen?"

"Yes. That which is the real me made the pen move. This is the first major hint. The second one is a parable. Do you both have a few minutes while I relate it to you?"

"We're not going anywhere on a bet," I said.

CHAPTER NINETEEN
The Parable

John continued. "Listen carefully to this parable and write it down in your own words after I leave. You will publish it later and it will be an inspiration to many. If you sense the Spirit in the words you will guess where it originated."

"On a certain night Jim, Mike, Ron and Dave died. Shortly thereafter they all found themselves walking on a beaten path. It seemed right to follow the path. Finally they came to a dividing point. One path veered to the left; the other to the right. They stood a moment, pondering what to do, when suddenly a man in white appeared and gave them instructions.

"Welcome, my friends', he said. 'You are approaching your new home and I am here to instruct you as much as is permitted. You notice there are two paths before you: One of them takes you to Heaven, a place more beautiful than you can imagine. The other takes you to Hell, a land full of darkness, despair and wretched individuals. All I can tell you at this point is you are to choose a path, but once you reach your destination you cannot turn back. Once you get to Heaven you will stay there, or once you get to Hell you will stay there. One more word I can say. Do not be frightened, for that reward you get in the end will be that which you deserve. Go forth confident that if you have led a just life, you will reap as you have sowed. You must proceed one at a time and each walk the path alone.'

"After saying this the man disappeared. The four were astonished at this somewhat random method of reaching Heaven or Hell. Finally, they decided they must go forward and drew straws to determine who would go first. Jim got the first opportunity and chose the path on the right. He thought that perhaps this

would lead to heaven because the "right" is always associated with "good." But as he proceeded he heard the fierce sound of wild animals, clouds seemed to hide the sun and the earth seemed to shake. He became very frightened and thought, 'Maybe I have chosen the wrong path.' He turned around, went back to the beginning and told the others of his experience. Then he decided to try the left hand path. As he ventured forth he saw more ominous signs. He kept wondering how far he could go before he could not turn back, and with each step he became more and more frightened until he was forced to retreat back to the beginning.

"Seeing that Jim could not make a firm decision as to which path to take, Ron and Dave suggested Mike now take his turn. Mike, however, was paralyzed with fear for, according to Jim's story, neither path sounded very heavenly. 'I'm going to think about it a while', he said. 'Someone else can take a turn.'

"It was now Ron's turn and he said, 'I'm picking the right-hand path and not turning back.' He followed through with his decision, and went past the sound of wild animals and through the darkness and storm clouds until he found himself in a place of unspeakable beauty and peace. He assumed he was in Heaven and rested there.

"It was now Dave's turn to move onward. Jim said he thought he heard a wild animal eating Ron and a chill of concern spread through them all. Dave was not sure he was making the right decision, for he chose the path on the left. He thought within himself: 'No matter what happens I'll go forward on this path and make the best of it.'

"As he proceeded, things went from bad to worse. There were horrific shrieks from wild animals and storm clouds with fierce thunderbolts were everywhere. Still, he proceeded until he reached a sign that said 'Hell". Behind him, the path disappeared and there was no retreat. Before him was a depressing place dark and stormy, full of inhabitants living in run- down shacks. The people lived in constant fear of attacks from the animals and roaming gangs which stole whatever they could get their hands on. Everywhere he went he was told this was a land cursed by the devil, and that things are going to get worse for all eternity.

"Dave thought long and hard within himself. 'I promised myself I would not retreat from this path and make the best of it. I refuse to listen to these voices of doom. Within myself there is no Hell and my conscience is clear, so why should there be Hell on the outside?"

"From that point on, Dave went forth in confidence and taught the people they did not have to live in the run-down shacks, and that they could change their circumstances so they would not have to live in fear. He also questioned their belief the land was cursed by the devil. A handful of people took hope and listened, but the rest were afraid and even looked upon Dave as an enemy, fearing he would make things even worse than they were.

"Dave gathered the people who would listen. They refused to accept the slum they were given as a final resting place and made blueprints of new beautiful homes. The best land they could find was an uninhabited swamp. They drained it and built their homes and a beautiful city with teeming gardens and landscapes. The gangs did not bother them, for the inhabitants supported and protected each other. The wild animals became friends, for the people nurtured them. Even the dark clouds and storms began to subside and bright, sunny days became a common sight.

"The people who were against Dave saw what had been accomplished and they took courage; one by one, other parts of Hell became transformed into beautiful cities and landscapes. After a period of time there was nothing but beauty and peace as far as the eye could see.

"Dave surveyed the now-beautiful land and came to a realization: One more thing needs to be done. He walked over to the original entrance and found that old sign which read 'Hell', tore it down, and replaced it with one that said 'Heaven'. As he did, another path with a fork in it appeared and so did the man in white. His look caught Dave's eye and he said, 'I think you know what you must do'.

"Dave looked back and said, 'I see I must choose again'.

"'Correct'. said the man.

"Before I proceed, can you tell me the fate of the other three?'

"The man answered: 'Ron is in a city that resembles the place you have created. He has one regret: he wishes he had a part in creating it. When that desire becomes strong enough he will be given another path to choose and will wind up in a place called 'Hell'. as you did, and be given an opportunity to build Heaven.

"Jim and Mike are still paralyzed with fear, afraid to make a decision. They are the ones who are truly in Hell, yet sooner or later they must proceed onward.

"And what lies ahead for me?' asked Dave.

"The unknown', said the man.

"The statement made Dave afraid, yet excited at the same time. And with no hesitation, he proceeded on the path leaning to the right."

No one spoke for a moment. "That's a beautiful story," Elizabeth said, her eyes glistening through tears. "I'd better help my husband remember it."

"That's an excellent thought," said John. "Now the first step to solving the first key is to find the first keyword. The first keyword is the title of the parable and also the power that put the pen in motion. The second stage of the first key is in your understanding. You must show a degree of comprehension about the key."

Suddenly it seemed as if a light turned on in my head. "I have the word!" I exclaimed. "I can't believe I never thought of it before, but I'm sure I am right this time."

"You'll have to wait another week to give it to me," said John.

"You don't know what you ask here," I said. "Now that I have the word I want to talk about it."

"If you are correct you will gain much by contemplating the full meaning of the word and principle during the next week."

"I feel strongly in my bones I am correct. I am just anxious to be verified."

"A week is a very short period," John said patiently.

"Where will we meet next Thursday?" I asked anxiously.

"Denny's, unless there is a change of plans. There, we will discuss the beginning of your mission."

"Now you're making my wait worse than ever. You've mentioned a mission before. Exactly what do you have in mind for me?" I asked anxiously.

"It is more what Joshua has in mind. He has a plan to reveal new teachings to the world, and you, my friend, are a part of that plan."

"Now you really have me stimulated! Why don't you just stay here for three days and answer all my questions?" I felt like a kid on Christmas Eve begging to open presents early.

"At this moment, my time available is limited. Maybe we can spend three days together when Joshua can let me go for a while. In the meantime, happy contemplating until next week." John started walking toward the front door.

"Let me ask you one more question before you go," I requested.

"Go ahead," said John, turning around.

"The Dark Brothers attacking me is one thing, but picking on my wife seems really unfair. Is there anything we can do to protect her until we learn more about protecting ourselves?"

"It is not only your wife you have to be concerned about. There will be many others - who will seek the teachings of light and you will be assisting - who the Dark Ones will seek to distract and pull down to their level of selfishness. There is something that you, your wife and others who come forward can do to keep your minds steady in the Light. Of course, the greatest protection is found in becoming one with the Spirit and being true to the inner voice, but few have achieved that to the desired degree. There is a special prayer which has been passed down that will give aspiring disciples protection. We didn't plan to release it just yet, but perhaps it would be appropriate to give it to you now." John surveyed the room for a moment. "I need a moment of privacy. May I use your bathroom?"

"Sure. Down the hall and to the left," I instructed, curious.

When John went into the bathroom, I couldn't help but move closer to the door and stare at the crack under the door. I faintly heard some voices and couldn't tell if it was just John or John and someone else. It also seemed like the light coming from under the door intensified. When the voices ceased I backed off and soon John came out.

John looked quite pleased and stated, "Today may seem like an ordinary day, but in reality this day marks the beginning of the end for our Dark Brothers. Their power will end, not because we will destroy them, but because the pure in heart will no longer give their power over to them and thus the innocent will be protected. When the Dark Brothers are denied the source of power that does not belong to them they will destroy themselves. Tell me, have you heard of *the Song of the 144,000?*"

"If I remember right, it comes from the Book of Revelations. The Jehovah Witnesses use that number all the time."

"Find me a Bible and we'll read about it." John commanded.

I hurriedly got a Bible and gave it to John. He turned to Revelations chapter fourteen and read:

Rev 14:1 And I looked, and, lo, a Lamb stood on the mount Sion, and with him an hundred forty and four thousand, having his Father's name written in their foreheads.

Rev 14:2 And I heard a voice from heaven, as the voice of many waters, and as the voice of a great thunder: and I heard the voice of harpers harping with their harps:

Rev 14:3 And they sung as it were a new song before the throne, and before the four beasts, and the elders: and no man could learn that song but the hundred and forty and four thousand, which were redeemed from the earth.

Rev 14:4 These are they which were not defiled with women; for they are virgins. These are they which follow the Lamb whithersoever he goeth. These were redeemed from among men, being the first fruits unto God and to the Lamb.

Rev 14:5 And in their mouth was found no guile: for they are without fault before the throne of God."

John closed the book thoughtfully and looked at Elizabeth and me. "I wrote this in symbolic language nearly two thousand years ago. It sounds like the song will be sung by heavenly beings flying around the throne of God, but in reality anyone here on earth who recognizes the Spirit of God flowing through him is very close to the throne of God . It may sound like the song will be sung by virgin men but they will be both men and women who are pure in heart. Many have also thought the number 144,000 is a limiting number, but in reality it is the number of one great symbolic choir, one of many that will eventually come from this small planet. Also, the song will not be sung, in the ordinary sense, on the physical plane but by souls of aspiring disciples. It is to be spoken out loud and registered by the spirit within. When the words are registered by the soul a beautiful song is sent to God, and, in return, the seeker will receive spiritual protection and assistance."

CHAPTER TWENTY
Song of the 144,000

"So, are you going to teach us the song then?" I asked eagerly.

"Yes," John replied. "Get a pen and paper and write down the words precisely as I tell them to you. This is one teaching you are not to put in your own words, but must be exactly memorized."

I got the materials and prepared to write. "I'm ready," I said, poised for revelation.

John began by closing his eyes for a moment. Then he opened them and slowly spoke these beautiful words:

"We thank you Father that you have revealed to us your protective universal light; that within this light is complete protection from all destructive forces; that the Holy Spirit of Your Presence permeates us in this light, and wherever we will the light to descend."

John paused a moment and closed his eyes. As Elizabeth and I looked on in wonder, we became aware of a white light, ever so softly at first, growing in radiance about an arm's reach from John's body until we could hardly gaze upon it. Then, a few seconds later, we noticed a radiant light beginning to manifest and dance around our own bodies. After about another minute the three of us were like three glowing suns of light.

Then John spoke again:

"We thank you Father that you fill us with your protective fires of Love; that within this love is complete protection from all destructive thoughts and feelings; that the consciousness of Christ is lifted up in us in this love, and wherever we will the love to be enflamed."

John was silent again, and after a few seconds we noticed bright yellow, pink and magenta color added to his aura of light. Shortly thereafter, we noticed it in our own spheres of light. Then we felt the fire of tremendous love. It was a love and fire that permeated to the very soul and was very delicious to the spiritual taste, something beyond our power to put in words. Somehow Elizabeth and I both sensed we were all feeling it together; and even though we had not felt this intensity before, it seemed very natural and welcome.

Then, just as we were enjoying the greatest experience of our lives, John opened his eyes and spoke again:

"We thank you Father that you are in us and we are in you; that through us Your Will is sent forth on wings of power; that Your Purpose is accomplished on earth as it is in heaven; that through us Your Light and Love and Power is manifest to all the Sons and Daughters of Mankind."

This time, a deep violet with edges of gold manifested in his aura and again spread to our own light. In addition to feeling the Presence of Spirit and great Love, we now felt a sense of enormous Power that was overwhelming. If we had any doubts about the existence of a Supreme Being before, they vanished when we felt such a great manifestation. The sense of power seemed so great it felt as if the one who possessed it could snap his fingers and make the world disappear if desired. It was indeed a humbling experience.

John stretched both hands outward, and the light seemed to circulate around the three of us as if we were one life. Then he said quietly, "Ask yourself... When you are in this state is it even possible to feel any fear? Can you sense it would be impossible for the Dark Ones to disturb this peace?"

I looked at Elizabeth. "The way I feel right now, I can't even imagine anything negative existing, let alone fear it." Elizabeth nodded, smiling, in agreement. She seemed unable to speak.

John lowered his arms and the light began to fade, but even when it was gone we continued to feel a great peace within us. After a moment John spoke again, "You, my friends, have just heard the Song of the 144,000 before the throne of God. There are already groups of 144,000 singing the song on the spiritual planes, but this is the beginning of the spiritual song upon the earth. Soon, it will be on earth as it is in heaven; and there will be 144,000 and more who will feel the Light and Love and Power of the Father-Mother God and allow themselves to be a note played within the music of the spheres."

After contemplating this beautiful vision I asked, "Are we supposed to say this song or prayer on a regular basis?"

"Yes," said John. "Say it together at least once a day and say it as an individual at least once a day. Each time you say it, however, visualize all those who can sing the song of the soul as if they were in your presence and enjoying the light and love and power you have felt here tonight. As each new person learns the song the whole will be strengthened and energized."

John paused and continued, "My time is short and I will teach you more later on this subject."

We said our good-byes and again watched John walk off into the darkness.

That night Elizabeth and I said the song together before going to bed. We didn't see a visible light or feel the fire as we did when John said it, but we felt a peaceful feeling... and Elizabeth was able to fall into a deep sleep without fear of another dark attack.

CHAPTER TWENTY-ONE
The Mission

For the next three days we recited the song faithfully several times a day; then on the fourth day we seemed to get distracted and didn't think to say it. We didn't suffer any obvious attack, but I did notice that Elizabeth seemed more negative about her illness. In addition, we got into several arguments which seemed to take us out of the spiritual mood. During the fifth day there seemed to be a cloud hanging over us. At bedtime neither of us felt like saying the song, but I felt it was important so I prodded Elizabeth into saying it along with me.

After we finished Elizabeth said: "I think we slipped out of harmony with our souls. I didn't realize it until now. Let's say it again."

We said it again and this time we felt a return to the great peace we previously felt. As we were basking in the peace I said: "This song really does have a positive effect. We must remember to say it every day whether we feel like it or not."

Elizabeth agreed and we made a mental commitment to remember to say the song each day.

Outside of the two days we did not say the song, the week went pretty well. In fact it seemed to go better than usual. I sold two homes without the usual problems and went through what was supposed to be a difficult closing without a hitch. Elizabeth also seemed to have more physical strength and, except for the two negative days, her attitude was much improved.

Wayne and I were too busy for our weekly breakfast. In my spare time that week I thought much about what my mission was supposed to be and formulated a number of questions for John. From the little John told me, I knew I was supposed to somehow present his teachings and the keys of knowledge to the world, but I hadn't taken that thought too seriously yet since I had not even completed the first key myself. Yet he told me he was going to talk about my mission during our next meeting. I was indeed curious about that.

This time, when Thursday night arrived, Elizabeth and I said the song together. We both felt a great peace and neither of us was concerned about her staying alone for a couple hours.

As I got into my car to go to Denny's I found myself half expecting to be whisked away to who-knows-where, but nothing happened. Without incident I drove to Denny's, went inside, and found John drinking coffee and reading the local newspaper in our regular booth.

As I sat down John looked up and smiled, "I see you have been saying the song," he said.

"How can you tell?" John was always a surprise to me.

"I see it, as I just told you."

"What do you mean you see it?"

"When I sang the song for you what did you see?" John asked.

"I saw beautiful lights dancing around you."

"So you saw me singing the song?"

"Yes, I suppose so."

"Did you not also feel me singing the song?"

"Yes, we felt the most wonderful feelings one can imagine."

"And you also heard me utter the words, did you not?"

"Of course."

"The true singing of the Song of the 144,000 is accomplished on three levels: the physical, emotional and mental planes, which opens the door of the spiritual. You have been singing the song recently and I can see your light and feel your peace. Thus, I see that you have been singing the song."

"Could you explain more about what you mean by singing on three levels?"

John paused and said, "If a person merely memorizes the words and repeats them only on the physical plane, he is not truly singing the song. The vibrations of words only being uttered cause very little result. In addition to saying the words one must feel and think the words. In a sense you become the Word which is God. The final thing you must always do is to sing the song as if you are in the presence of all others who are also in the great choir. When you do this you open the door to the spiritual energy and become a true singer of the song; you not only help yourself, but you also assist all others who also know and use the song. There is a strong interplay and sharing of energy that is available to those who have the Father's name written in their foreheads."

"I have a question," I said. "When you sang the song we saw a visible light around us, but when Elizabeth and I did it we didn't see a light. How come?"

"You did not see a light, but I did. When I saw you walking toward this booth you were glowing like an angel. You saw the light in my presence for two reasons: I have had more practice singing the song than you and the light was thus more intense: second, your spiritual sight was more sensitive that night. If you develop your spiritual sight you will be able to see the light each time you correctly sing the song. You will sing this song in groups in the future and some will see the light and others will not. Everyone, however, will feel some type of effect. Those who are not ready will feel a negative effect and will drop out of the choir and not sing it again until they are more prepared."

"What's the main determination as to whether a person is ready?" I asked.

"Each person will be his own judge. But if one is not ready he will not benefit and thus will not even attempt to sing the song on a regular basis."

"It seems odd to say we are singing a song when we are not singing in the normal sense."

"From a higher point of view there is not a lot of difference in beauty between speaking and singing. The beauty of the song of the soul far eclipses the most beautiful singing on the earth. Thus you will find some of the most spiritual people on the planet often do not have a good physical singing voice. This is because they have put so much attention on the inner beauty. On the other hand, there are a handful of spiritual people who have also cultivated a good singing voice, so you can't really judge the spiritual evolution of a person by the sound of his physical voice."

"What a relief!" I joked. "I'd probably go to Hell if I was judged by the way I sing."

"Actually you sing very well. If you were to listen to your whole self, you would see it." John smiled.

"This is news to me," I said. "I've never thought of myself as being a good singer any way you look at it."

John took a sip of coffee and asked. "Do you think you have the first key word?"

"Yes. I really think I do."

"Let me have it then."

I told him the word that came to me last week.

"Are you sure that is correct?" he asked.

"Reasonably sure, yes."

"You must learn to trust the inner voice. When you are in tune with it, there will not be doubt. What does your inner Self say? Do you have the right word or not?"

"I'm real sure, but I wouldn't bet my life on it."

"There will come times when you must bet your life and more on your inner voice. You must learn to register it and then trust it with all you have. That is the only way to completely free yourself of the influence of the Dark Brothers and all negative energy. Now look deep within yourself and answer. Have you found the right key word? Yes or no?"

I tried to tune into that still small voice, but the more I tried to receive the more I doubted myself. Was I imagining the confirmation because that's what I wanted or was I getting a real answer? "I think I have the right answer, but to be honest I don't know for sure."

"It is good that you are honest, but to complete your mission you must learn to hear the inner voice and trust it. The question is this: Is the key word you thought you received confirmed by your inner voice or not?"

John sat up straighter and leaned forward. "If you cannot give me the correct answer in the next few minutes then our relationship is at an end and you will not see me again in this life."

I was stunned by his words and I felt myself flush. "What? After all that I have gone through you would just cast me aside if I cannot give you the correct answer here and now?" I couldn't believe his words!

John studied my face for a moment. "I would not cast you aside, but if you cannot receive and trust the inner voice of the Spirit after all that you have gone through, I must find someone else for the job. It is nothing personal, but I have a job to do and I must have someone who trusts the still small voice. Now I will give you a moment of silence, then give me the answer."

John was silent and I tried to tune into the voice, but seemed to get nothing. John's statement unnerved me, but I tried to focus. After a moment of frustration on my part John asked "What is your answer?"

I was angry with myself because my moment of contemplation gave me nothing. I decided to guess. "Yes. I have the right answer. I'll go with it."

"Did your inner voice confirm that to you?" John asked.

I paused a moment in fear. I never wanted to lie so much in my life, but if I told John I received something it would be a lie, and he would probably know it. I painfully told him the truth. "I tried to get a confirmation, but I drew a blank. Have I failed?"

"Not yet. Now take a couple minutes and contemplate. Are you sure you have the right key word? Do you have confirmation from the soul and do you trust it? Your next answer will be final. I'm going to the rest room. When I return I expect your answer."

"Take your time," I said to John as he walked off.

I had never felt under pressure like this before. In the past when I wanted some inner guidance I always tried to be in a situation where there were no distractions, but this seemed impossible. Nevertheless, I tried to clear myself and hear my inner voice. "I think I have the key word. Is it correct? God help me. Please tell me if it is correct!"

There was no answer. Nothing. I had never drawn such a blank in my life. Here I was, with perhaps the greatest opportunity a man has had for two thousand years, and I was going to let it slip through my fingers. In addition to that, I would probably lose Elizabeth because I would never receive the first three principles. I almost started to cry, but held back the tears and forced myself to continue. John would be coming back any minute.

I sat back in my seat, closed my eyes, and thought back to last Thursday night when John taught us the parable and song and when the key word came to me. For a moment I relived those few glorious moments.

In an instant I realized I had the answer John wanted. At that exact moment John came out of the bathroom.

He casually sat down in the booth and took another sip of coffee and asked, "Do you have a confirmed answer?"

"Yes. I do."

"What is it, my friend?"

"I did not get confirmation tonight because I already received confirmation at the time I received the key word. At the moment I received it, I was completely sure, but during the week my trust wavered and I doubted myself. When I let my mind go back to that moment last week, I realized anew I had definitely received the correct key word. My answer is yes. I am sure the key word is right and it was confirmed by my inner self."

"No doubts, then?" he said.

"I am now sure," I said firmly.

"What if I were to tell you that you are wrong?"

I felt a shiver of fear go through me for a second, but then gathered my composure. "I would say that you are wrong, because I know what the inner voice confirmed to me, and even God cannot take that away."

For the first time since I had known him John looked visibly affected. His eyes became moist as he grabbed my right hand with both of his,. and said, "The long famine of truth is over my brother. You are ready to assist in bringing a great light to the earth. Welcome to the Brotherhood."

John and I sat there in silence holding hands for what seemed to be an hour, but I knew it was less than a moment. During that interlude I did not have to ask him if the key word was correct. I knew it was. During this time something else happened. I saw the story of John's life over the past two thousand years. I was amazed beyond words at the struggles he went through to help mankind. But what affected me the most was that time and time again, his work met with failure because of lack of cooperation from those whom he had taught. Sometimes those who were supposed to be working for the Brotherhood of Light were just sluggish; other times they sought for their own glory; sometimes they were paralyzed with fear; then, sadly, there were other times when the workers of light lost their light and moved to the side of darkness and sought to destroy all things that bring freedom and light to mankind.

Then, once every several hundred years I saw that John had a faithful co-worker or two, and his heart was gladdened and his hope in mankind renewed. After that I felt overwhelming emotion over the hope and expectation that John had for me. At that instant I broke off contact.

"You expect more out of me than I expect from myself. I don't want to let you down as others have done."

"Never, never let fear of failure prevent you from taking action. Remember the lesson of the parable. Always take action on the highest you know and you will learn from your mistakes and eventually meet with success."

I waited for the lump in my throat to go down and said, "One thing that bothers me is that as great of a teacher and human being as you are, you have still met with failure time and time again over the past two thousand years. Do you really believe we can succeed this time?"

"The past two thousand years has been a time of training and preparation for the Workers of Light. We are now on the cusp of a new age and a new energy. The keynote for the past two thousand years has been sacrifice beginning with the sacrifice of Christ. Now we are entering a grand new period where we can enjoy the fruits of the sacrifice. The new keynote is service. Perhaps the greatest phrase ever recorded from Joshua is that the greatest in the kingdom of heaven shall be the greatest servant. The greatest among the Brotherhood of Light are those with the greatest capacity and willingness to serve.

"We seemed to fail a lot the past two thousand years because we were learning and demonstrating sacrifice, but now it is decreed we will learn and demonstrate service. In order to serve we must succeed; therefore, it is our destiny we will succeed this time around. There will be setbacks here and there, but our ultimate success is as good as guaranteed." John smiled at me as if I was part of this success.

"So, I take it I have passed some type of test here?" I asked.

"Yes, you have. More important than learning the keys is learning to trust what the Spirit confirms to you. When you are given a confirmation, you are not usually given another one until you are faithful to what you have already been given. Last Thursday you were given a confirmation of the key word and you were tempted to doubt it. Therefore, when you tried to get confirmation again it did not come. Doubt throws up a wall between you and your soul. You did exactly the right thing when you went back to the point of reception and reviewed it. You did the same thing when the Dark Brother tried to deceive you; you thought back to what the true voice of the Spirit was like and compared it to your dream. This is a process few have mastered. Almost everyone wants confirmation of truth again and again instead of trusting confirmation they have already received. If you cannot trust confirmation you received yesterday, how do we know you will trust renewed confirmation today?"

John continued. "The true disciple will not look for new confirmations again and again. He will find them naturally when he lives by the highest light he has already received.

John leaned forward and lowered his voice after our waitress finished filling our coffee cups. "Let me repeat myself. This is perhaps the most important advice you will ever receive: Always live by the highest light you have already received. If you do, you will receive more, worlds without end. If you do not, your progression will come to an end and cannot proceed until you go back, review the last light you have received, and then live your life according to the standard of that light."

I thought a moment. "I've always tried to do that, but did not realize the full implications of that standard until now. So tell me. Am I done with the first key or what?"

"You have found the first key word. Now your next step is to understand the key itself. During the next week I want you to think about why this particular word is a key of knowledge and why it identifies the core of your existence. Why is it the cause of all motion in the universe from a planet to a pen to an atom?"

"I feel privileged to continue this after the scare you gave me." I said, laughing with relief.

John smiled reassuringly. "Not as bad as the scare you gave me. I would probably feel worse losing a student with the mission you are supposed to have than you would have in losing the opportunity. After all, I have much more knowledge of the implications of it all than you."

"So you were supposed to tell me more about this mission..." I urged.

"Yes," he said. "There are several stages and all will not be revealed at once. We want you to concentrate on the work at hand rather than some future event that seems impossible at the moment."

"What then is the first stage?"

"The first stage is for you to write several books giving out new teachings and keys to the world."

I scratched my head. "I don't think you understand how busy I am. To pay all my bills including Elizabeth's medical expenses I now work 7 days a week, often 12-16 hours a day. I not only have to work like crazy to make money, but I have to do all the work around the house since Elizabeth's illness. I would be happy to do whatever you ask if you would materialize a few gold bars so my hands could be free."

John smiled. "I remember those few sweet years with the Master - how we would often give Him replies like that. Do you know what He usually said back to us?"

"What?"

"Oh ye of little faith."

I chuckled. "Well with me it should be *Oh ye of little time.* There are only so many hours in a day."

"Are you telling me it impossible for you to find time to write a book?"

I reflected a moment. Oh, what the hell. "All right. Nothing is impossible. I'll find some way."

"Let's look at the practical possibilities first. Can you mortgage your house to free up some money which would free up some time?"

I frowned. "Are you kidding? I'm mortgaged to the hilt!"

"How about friends or relatives. Will any of them help?"

"Most of them already think I'm too far out. No. None of them would loan me money to write a book. I'd have to lie to them and I know you don't want that."

"Dealing with the material side of life is something that even the highest teachers have a problem with," said John, frowning. "But especially in this age we recognize that it is a necessity. All you need to do is find time to write your first book or two. Now because of certain spiritual laws we cannot just materialize you bars of gold or other wealth, but we do believe that many people will be interested in the teachings and be willing to buy the books. When this happens, you will have enough coming in to free your hands so you can spend full time as a student, teacher and writer."

I took a long sip of coffee. "Maybe I could stay up an extra hour or two each evening until I get the book done. I'll find a way to do it. I must warn you I have been planning on doing some writing for years and have just not been able to find the time, but I know this is important. When am I supposed to start?"

"Right away."

"But I haven't even completed the first key."

"You don't have to. The first book will tell about your encounter with me and your experiences and what you have learned up to this moment. You are not to reveal the first key word in the first book. One reason is you are to give many copies of the first book free by making it available on the Internet or any other way you can come up with. There, seekers can download copies and get a feel for what is to come. If they are then interested, they can either purchase a hard copy or future books you write. This will supply you with money to free your hands and begin other projects we have in mind for you."

"So I am supposed to start writing right away and write everything exactly as it has happened? The trouble with that idea is no one will believe it. They'll think the book is the work of an illusionary dreamer."

"Actually, you are more correct than you realize. We have

made two previous attempts to put out advanced teachings to the world in a straightforward method and both failed miserably. We found that new age gurus who just made everything up from their subconscious had more success than did our two disciples. An additional problem was our disciples were so honest and straightforward they were boring."

"I'm sure you're not asking me to be dishonest."

"Far from it. Even Joshua would fall from the light if he asked you to do that."

"So what are you asking?"

"We are asking you to write a book of fiction," John replied.

"Fiction? But none of these fantastic things that has transpired is fiction." I exclaimed.

"No. But some of them are too unbelievable for you to write and there are other things that lack a certain glamour necessary to attract an audience. Therefore, we want you to create any characters or events you want to make the book interesting. Since you will publish the book as fiction you will not be dishonest in creating any characters, situations or events necessary to make an interesting story. There is one criteria, however, that you must adhere to."

"What is that?" I asked.

"The whole purpose of your writings will be to present teachings important for the coming age of peace. Therefore, you are under strict command to not alter any teachings you receive from me or any other future spiritual teacher. You are to present them as clearly and as honestly as you are capable. Even though you will publish the writings as fiction there are many who will sense the teachings themselves are true and many will want to know more."

"The most unbelievable part of this whole adventure is you," I smiled. "Should I tell the whole story about you?"

"We are leaving that up to you. You will probably have to alter me to some degree, or possibly many degrees. If necessary you can say you met Hercules, or the moon goddess, whatever you think will make a good story. Just be true to the teachings you have received.

"You and the Christ are much wiser than me. Why are you leaving such an important assignment up to me?"

"Teachings to humanity must come through humanity, through ordinary mortals such as yourself. Every time we have broken that rule in the history of the world it has always ended in disaster."

"I thought you spiritual teachers were infallible. It sounds like even the Christ can make a mistake."

"True perfection consists in having the ability to complete a task successfully. When one is in the process of completing a work there will always be mistakes, but that does not prevent the end product from being perfect. Look at this world and the inhabitants on it. There is much imperfection here created by God himself, but the end result of it all will be a perfection beyond imagination."

'Hm-m-m, interesting.' I thought. "So you are forced to rely on a mere mortal such as myself to get the word out?"

"Yes. The closest I can come to you is as a teacher, and even then you must be an active participant in asking questions and finding answers. You have to really want to know each step of the way as you progress."

"Well, I must admit I have a strong motive since the life of my wife depends on it."

John smiled, "I believe you would pursue the truth with a vengeance even if her life did not depend on it."

"Perhaps. I guess we'll find out when she is healed."

"I have faith you will help her achieve that healing. Just remember to always follow the highest you know. This principle also encompasses the area of healing. In fact, she is now anxiously awaiting your return. You need to go home so she can peacefully sleep."

"You're probably right." I said. "I'll try to get my first chapter done for our meeting next week."

"Do not bring it to me until the book is done," John said.

"Why is that?"

"The less influence I have the more powerful it will be even if it is written in your weakness. I will read it when you are finished, but I will be constrained from editing it."

"Won't you be able to give me your opinion at least?"

"I will tell you whether I enjoyed it or not. When you are done we will see how much more I can reveal." He got up to leave and said, "We'd better call it a day here."

"Will I see you next week?" I asked hopefully.

"We'll just meet here at Denny's again unless you hear otherwise."

"I look forward to it."

John turned back to face me. "There is just one thing I ask

as you begin this task."
    "What's that?" I asked.
    "Write a good book. Try to not embarrass me."
    "I'll make you larger than life," I replied, smiling.

THE IMMORTAL

BOOK II

THE IMMORTAL
BOOK TWO

CHAPTER ONE
The New Jerusalem

Elizabeth had her ups and downs over the next week. Overall it was a rather uneventful time. I seemed to pick up a strange vibration or feeling during this period, however. I felt a cloud was hanging over the whole planet. In the past there were times my wife and I seemed to be under some type of attack, but for some reason this time, I felt as if the whole planet was under a cloud.

Elizabeth and I repeated the *Song of the 144,000* several times a day and we felt some comfort, but something still seemed amiss. Since we didn't know what to do, we just kept on living life as usual. I was looking forward to seeing John, hoping that he could verify the reality of my feelings.

When Thursday arrived I found myself concerned for John's safety. I tried to put the thought aside. Surely John has some type of divine protection as long as he does not get directly involved with us regular mortals. After all, wasn't that the main reason he was teaching me so I could teach others? This was his method of not becoming vulnerable so he could finish his job as a teacher.

Ever since that time I was teleported to Israel from my car, I have approached starting it with some anxiety. As I got in my car that evening to drive to Denny's I felt a little nervous as I started the car, but nothing happened. I drove to Denny's and found our favorite booth and waited. After about an hour I noticed the time was a quarter to twelve. I began to worry John would not show. I felt restless just sitting there so I got up and went outside. As I was pacing back and forth near the front door I thought of the time I witnessed John disappear from my sight. I gazed at the spot in which I saw it happen and experienced a sad longing to see him again.

I looked at my watch. It was now five minutes to twelve. I thought to myself about how adamant John was about keeping his word. If he did not show up by twelve o'clock I would know something was wrong. I found myself unconsciously saying a prayer within myself, "Please let John be OK and let him show himself to me..."

I opened my eyes and there he was in front of me. He stretched his right hand toward me and said, "Go home and go to sleep."

I reached my hand toward him and it passed right through him and he disappeared from my sight.

I should have been used to being surprised by this man by now, but I was so disoriented that I was several blocks away from Denny's before I realized that I did not pay for my coffee. I backtracked, paid my bill, and left for home.

Upon arriving and (as quietly as possible) getting into bed, Elizabeth spoke softly, "You're home early. Is anything wrong?"

"I'm not sure," I replied. "You should be getting some rest."

"I never get any rest when I know you're off seeing John. So did you meet with him?"

"Sort of."

"Either you did or didn't. What happened?" Elizabeth asked impatiently.

"He appeared to me briefly as an apparition and told me to go home and go to sleep." I know I sounded vague, but I felt vague.

Elizabeth let out a short laugh. "I'm always telling you to get more sleep too. You've been looking tired lately."

"I don't think rest has anything to do with it. There's some reason he wants me to go to sleep."

Maybe you'll have some special dream," she said.

"Maybe," I said. "It makes me nervous thinking about it. I don't know if I can go to sleep."

"Well try and see what happens" she said, patting my back as I turned on my side.. "You need your sleep whether something happens or not."

"You're right. I'll see what I can do."

I laid still and tried to go to sleep for a few minutes without much luck. Usually if I feel anxiety like that it takes me several hours to drift off, but then I heard the bells again. I found them very soothing and was drawn to the lovely sound. The next thing I knew I was standing beside my bed viewing the bodies of two people I knew to be Elizabeth and me. Then I heard John's voice. "Come up here," he commanded.

Just thinking about being with John caused me to immediately shoot through the roof and I was whisked off to the portals of a most beautiful city, a beauty so rarefied that there is nothing I can say to do it justice. Actually, I could not yet see that it was a city. For some reason I just knew that it was a great city, a city beyond the imagination of men. What I saw was a large floating pyramid that had the appearance of being made of translucent gold. I stood in front of the middle of three great entrances on one of the sides. It was a large arched entrance like something out of Greek or Roman architecture with a large translucent circular pearl of light seeming to guard the entrance. I had heard the term "pearly gates" before, but never envisioned anything like this. As I looked up I saw an inscription written at the top of the arch, having the appearance of Hebrew. I found myself wondering what the meaning was and immediately the writing changed to English and it read JOSEPH. Wow, I thought. What a way to welcome me!

I somehow knew that John was inside the city waiting to meet me, but I found myself wanting to explore a little first; and as soon as I felt this desire welling inside me I started checking out the other entrances. The next entrance had another name written on it. Again it appeared to be in Hebrew, but as soon as I wondered about it, the name BENJAMIN appeared in English. Then something interesting occurred to me: the entrance called JOSEPH had nothing to do with me. Benjamin and Joseph are the names of two of the tribes of Israel. Since meeting John, I made some effort to study the Gospel of John and the Apocalypse - or the Book of Revelation - and the remembrance came to my mind of the holy city of the New Jerusalem that is supposed to be in heaven. I remembered the city had twelve entrances with a name of a tribe of Israel on each of the entrances. When that memory came to me I found myself moving from one entrance to the other and viewing the names all in English now. In addition to JOSEPH and BENJAMIN there was ZABULON, ISSACHAR, LEVI, SIMEON, MANASSES, NEPHTHALIM, ASER, GAD, REUBEN and JUDAH.

Under each of the twelve archways were twelve great foundation stones, each giving off a different hue. I felt the urge to touch them, even though they seemed to be miles away. As the thought came to me I immediately found myself with hands outstretched touching one of the stones that now seemed to be as large as a planet. The name PETER came with great power to my mind. Next I saw a glimpse into his life and how it ended with a sacrifice for the cause of truth. In another instant I found myself at the second foundation and the name JAMES came to me. I again saw his life briefly, ending with a sacrifice of his life. Then I touched the third and felt the name JOHN. Again, I saw numerous sacrifices that John had made for the cause of truth. At that time the words of the book of Revelation came to my mind, "And the wall of the city had twelve foundations, and in them the names of the twelve apostles of the Lamb" (Rev 21:14). Then I realized that the names of the other apostles were in the other stones. With this realization I saw the lives of all the apostles one by one. I saw that all of them were far from perfect, but they laid the foundation to a great work by the service they rendered and the sacrifice of their lives. I also realized that the names of the tribes of Israel and the names of the Twelve Apostles represented twenty-four principles and found myself wondering if there was a correspondence to the first twenty-four keys.

Somehow, I also realized this whole city represented the perfection the work of the Apostles, that on the earth only the bare essentials of the foundation are represented, and that a New Jerusalem will eventually exist on earth as it does in heaven.

I drew back a considerable distance with a thought and viewed the walls and foundations as a whole; they radiated light and a great heavenly fire, giving off more than a rainbow of colors. The colors seemed to ascend to the top of the pyramid and form an oval of white light, making the appearance of an all-seeing eye.

I felt it was time to go in and picked an entrance at random. As I started to pass through, a beautiful male and female pair with oriental features appeared to me and said, "This is not your entrance."

Then I went to the next gate and a dark-skinned couple likewise appeared and said the same thing. As I found myself wondering if they were of African descent I instantly saw their color change from black to the most beautiful and glistening white one can imagine. In this beautiful state all I could say about them was that they were human or perhaps angels or more; the differential of race could not even come to mind. Then I went to the next entrance and another couple appeared. This couple had the appearance of American Indians and said the same words and again had the same transformation into raceless beautiful angelic beings who glowed like the sun.

Somehow I now knew that my entrance was at the gate named JOSEPH, whether by design or coincidence, I did not know. As I approached, a Caucasian couple appeared and spoke, "Only the pure in heart may reside here. Have you examined your deepest thoughts and intentions?"

I was taken back for a moment and after a brief reflection I said, "I believe so. I only want to be of service to my fellow men and women."

The two stretched forth their hands and seemed to run them gradually from just below my navel to the top of my head. "You may pass," said one of them. The two beings merged into one and after a few seconds disappeared.

As I passed though the gate I found myself wondering how I even knew this was a city. Until now all I could see were the walls and foundations, and through the arches was nothing but light. But now that I was through the gates I expected to see a great city with streets of gold, as described in the scriptures. Instead I was surprised to find myself in a pleasant city park and noticed John sitting on a bench feeding some pigeons. He looked up, smiled and said, "Come over here."

I walked toward him and sat down. "So, is this the city of the New Jerusalem you wrote about?" I asked.

"This is the place," he smiled.

"But I don't see any city. All I see is a park - something like a city park on earth."

"Isn't this to your liking?" he asked.

"It's fine," I nodded, looking around. "Just not what I expected."

"What did you expect?"

"Didn't your vision indicate there were streets of gold or something like that?"

"Streets of gold... yes," he smiled. "How's this?"

In an instant we both were standing on a beautiful translucent golden street, and before us was a magnificent crystal castle that would put the Crystal Cathedral to shame. I had never imagined something so opulent and wonderful.

"Is this more like you were thinking?" John asked, amused

by my expression.

"Yes, I believe it is," I replied, trying not to sound awestruck.

"Then tell me, my friend. Where would you rather have our discussion?   In the park, or in this castle?"

I looked up at the beautiful building. My first and only inclination was to go in there, but as I thought about it a moment I became a little uncomfortable in choosing it; and for some reason I felt a lot more comfortable going back to the park. "It may seem crazy, but I think I would prefer to talk with you in the park."

I thought as much," said John. By the time he had finished the sentence we were both back on the park bench. There was no one else around. Just he and I and a few birds and squirrels.

I looked at him with wonder and said, "How is it I get the feeling you know better why I chose the park than I do?"

"You are probably right. I have a conscious recollection of dwelling in this city in my sleeping hours for almost 2000 years. I have introduced many to the translucent castle. Actually, it is a final test."

"A final test?" I asked perplexed.

"Yes. Every newcomer is introduced to the most opulent residence possible. He is also given all the servants he desires. If he then becomes comfortable with that situation and begins to feel he deserves more exaltation than those who are his servants, we know that his ego still needs work and he is sent to another place."

"Would that be Hell?" I asked.

"Actually, it is a heaven compared to earth life, but in a way it becomes a hell because of the stories that are spread there about the crystal castle and other mansions and how a person who lives in the castle is almost a God. The funny thing is that all the residents in the next level down are pained because they want something that the true residents here do not even care about."

"You mean they long for the great reward of opulence and that is not where the true happiness is?"

"Exactly," said John.

"So if the true reward is not a castle of translucent gold and many servants, then what is the true reward of the good guys?"

"It is written in my book of Revelations Chapter 22, verse 12."

Here we did not need a Bible. I saw the verse within my mind's eye. It spoke of the coming of Christ and said, "And, behold, I come quickly; and my reward is with me, to give every man according as his work shall be..."

"What do you think it means - that your reward is with Christ? Do you suppose He carries in His pocket a million castles and mansions to pass out?"

"It does sound rather ridiculous," I mused.

"Then what is it He has with Him to give as a reward?"

"Well, to be able to give it out to millions... it would have to be intangible," I replied.

"And what would that be?" he asked.

"I'm not sure. Would it be love?"

"It could be called that, but back on earth there are many interpretations of what love is. If you were to teach on earth that love is the great reward, it would mean something a little different to everyone."

"What is the reward then?" I asked, getting very curious.

"It is amazing how the truth of our questions is almost always right in front of us - or should I say within us. Close your eyes, be still for a moment, and tell me what you feel."

John closed his eyes and I followed suit. As I did so, I realized I had been feeling something different ever since I passed through the portal. I felt a very deep abiding peace that now seemed to intensify with my eyes closed and my attention focused. In addition, I felt a presence I can only describe as the Spirit of God. It was something like I felt the night John taught us the *Song of the 144,000*, but even more complete. As I put attention on the Presence the intensity grew. It continued to increase until I couldn't bear any more of it and I felt a fullness of joy within myself. I call it a *fullness* because I was full to the brim of the highest spiritual vibration one can imagine. I had all the joy and peace I could handle. One must feel it to accurately describe it.

I opened my eyes and so did John. I felt like crying, but held back. "Is there anything more desirable that what you just felt?" John asked softly.

"I cannot imagine anything I could want more," I replied. I continued to attempt to hold back the tears, but could not. I rarely cry, but the inner joy was too much for me.

"Would you rather live in the great castle with a thousand servants for a lifetime or have this feeling for five minutes?" he asked. I noticed some tears in John's eyes also. This amazed me since I thought he would be used to having this wonderful feeling, but on reflection I have concluded there is no getting used to it. It is always new and wonderful.

"There is no comparison. Nothing can compare to this," I said "I'm not sure what to call it except for a fullness of joy and happiness. I have never been that religious, but I can only say that we are basking in a Presence that can only be called God or the Spirit of God. Even though I have felt nothing like it before, it is very familiar and I know what it is. It's like... coming home." I felt close to tears again.

"It's familiar because you have felt it before and it's like coming home because it is home," John said calmly.

"When have I felt the Presence like this before?" I asked sensing that John was correct.

"We'll cover that in some detail a little later. Now it's about time to get to your lesson."

"Can I ask a couple of questions about this city first?" I asked anxiously.

"We have some time. Go ahead."

"What is the meaning of the twelve entrances and why could I only go through the one named JOSEPH?"

"There are twelve types of people upon the earth which belong to twelve different families of wavelengths, or vibrations, as some are prone to call them. To enter the city you have to have your vibration tuned to the Presence within the City or you will suffer excruciating pain. You had to enter through the correct tuning fork, so to speak. The different races you encountered symbolized the different types of people. Did you notice that they changed into glistening white beings and then the male and female merged into one? This symbolizes the oneness of all classes and types of people who submit to the higher intelligence of the Universal Spirit. The twelve entrances symbolize the uniqueness that each of us has as an individual entity."

"Is this city just for Christians? I would imagine a Hindu or Buddhist would not even recognize the names of the tribes of Israel."

"The mansions of God are not for just one belief system. The quality of a human being is created by how well he follows the highest knowledge of which he is aware. When a worthy Buddhist approaches the gates of the city, he sees a name that has an important meaning to him."

"So why are there two names, one above the portal and one below?"

"The one above represents the personality and the one on the foundation stone represents the soul, or the unseen part of the person. But the soul is also that upon which you as a personality are built, so to speak. It would be profitable for you to contemplate and eventually write about the meanings of the higher and lower names."

"Very interesting," I nodded. "Now, you call this a city but I haven't seen anyone but you. How many people live here and where are they?"

"The actual number is not to be revealed at this time, but believe me, it is a very large number for the inhabitants come from twelve different star systems." He stretched out his hand and a circular portal appeared and I saw into it like a three-dimensional television screen. I saw people living in all kinds of pleasant situations, but all of them lived in a state of equality, with each living in a unique situation geared to individual and group happiness. I saw places of great beauty, even more lovely than the crystal castle, but the beauty was not created or used as a reward but always benefiting some grand purpose and serving the enhancement of the whole rather than the individual. I wasn't able to look for long as John turned off whatever it was.

"One more question," I insisted.

"OK, one more before we begin," he sighed.

"I was amazed at the appearance of an eye at the top of the pyramid. It reminded me of the all-seeing eye on our dollar bills. Can you tell me something about it?"

"There are many mysteries connected with the city and the so-called *all-seeing eye*, but I will tell you just a few things. There are three major divisions within the city. The first two each have three subdivisions. The three plus three plus the one represented by the eye equals the seven of completion. You and I are now in the foundation level. The angels who greeted you are from the fifth level."

"As a person grows in knowledge and union, he can progress from one level to another until he reaches the eye of the portal which is both an eye and a portal. Actually, it is two eyes, each with two types of vision. One sees all things in connection with this universe and the other sees into the formless worlds. They then blend their seeing as one great eye and transmit the knowledge to the lesser lives who are ready to receive. The city itself is a living entity and the inhabitants are cells in its body. The great eye communes with millions of other cities of God, and when one reaches the sixth level of the city he achieves such a state of oneness that he shares the vision of the eye and discovers new worlds and universes beyond anything we can imagine at this level. When the seventh level is attained, he reaches the portal where the disciple can travel to other universes and assume challenges that we can only guess at."

I sat in silence for a moment contemplating the greatness of this knowledge. Finally, John said, "Now let's get back to the basics. I sensed you have the correct key word. Now you must state it to me and tell me what it means to you."

I found I had to adjust my attention for a moment. At that moment the keys seemed mundane, if that is possible. "OK. Let me gather my thoughts and I'll share them with you."

CHAPTER TWO
The Key Word

I thought a moment about the keys, but I found my curiosity interfering. "There is another question I must ask first," I said.

"OK," John sighed. "But we must move on soon. Our time is limited."

I contemplated a moment and asked, "I have always assumed the ultimate goal for humans was oneness and unity of some kind. I would like you to elaborate on the twelve entrances. Evidently, I was only able to go through the one in harmony with my vibration. What was the meaning of the different races at different entrances?"

John smiled. "One thing I like about you as a student is that you have good questions. You do not know how rare that is." John was silent a moment and answered, "A good question deserves a good answer. The purpose of the twelve entrances is the oneness that you mentioned. The main quality needed to dwell in this city is pureness of intent, or purity of heart as it is usually called. Pure intent, however, is far from the end of the spiritual journey. Take twelve people of great purity and put them to work on a project. Do you think all will agree as to the best way to accomplish it?"

"I think I see what you're getting at," I said. "Just because two people are good people doesn't make them agree on everything or see everything the same way."

"Exactly," said John. "Even though those on the first level are good, decent and unselfish people, they are far from the unity of vision symbolized by the all-seeing eye at the seventh level. The twelve different entrances represent, for want of a better word, twelve different thought patterns that humanity gravitates toward.

Each person of pure intent can be fairly united within his own pattern, but has great difficulty in harmonizing with another outside his pattern. That is part of the reason that a good Jew, for instance, can see eye to eye with another Jew of similar thought, but may feel the Hindu or Christian is mislead. His thought patterns will not let him see the beauty of other religions, patterns or philosophies."

"So are the twelve different groups manifested in different races?"

"A fairly high percentage of each race belongs to a certain pattern. For instance, about 85% of the American Indians are in the pattern of Manassah, around 60% of white Americans are of Joseph as you are, and about 75% of the Jews in Israel are of Judah. A person who seems to be out of sync with the general thought or attitudes of his group or race does not usually belong to the majority pattern. This is perhaps the most obvious today among the blacks. An African American today who goes against the regular pattern is often told that he is no longer black by his peers. A black person who is of the pattern of Joseph will especially experience this problem. He seems to be more white than black to his friends and, from a metaphysical point of view, he is. In fact, after a black person from the pattern of Joseph enters the city where the majority are of the white race, he will usually assume a Caucasian appearance so he will not be such a minority within his group."

"So, if I enter the city a black man, I can turn white if I want?" I asked in amazement.

"Yes," said John. "In fact, the reverse is often true. In this world, and in the higher ones, thought has power over form. A Caucasian who has a black pattern will often change his appearance to that race so he can feel more united with them. Union is a great desire of the twelve groups here and much of the work and effort on this level is in the interplay of the groups working toward oneness."

"So is this oneness achieved?"

"Eventually, all goals are achieved," said John. "When the second level is reached, the twelve merge into seven. In the third level the seven merge into four. At the fourth level the four merge into three. Then at the fifth level the three become two; and finally, at the sixth level the two become one."

"So what happens at the seventh level?" I asked

"The sixth level merges the thought patterns into unity, but a differentiation of the male-female energies still exist. At the seventh level male and female become one."

I let out a chuckle. "That makes sense. I always thought that understanding a female would be the last frontier."

John smiled. "How little you understand at this point. The understanding you have in mind is only a small part of this great unity which is beyond the comprehension of any mortal person."

John's answer sobered me up. I changed the subject. "So which level in the city have you attained?"

"I can only tell you I have gone beyond the first, but have not attained the seventh." John looked somewhat impatient as he added, "Now, is there anything else before we move on?"

"Just one more item. To what do I owe the pleasure of this location for a meeting rather than the fabulous Denny's?"

John reflected within himself for a moment and said, "During this past week did you feel anything unusual?"

I was surprised. "Yes, a very unusual feeling. It was as if there was a dark cloud hanging over not only myself, but the whole planet. I don't know if it was my imagination or what, but there seemed to be a dark fog everywhere."

"Because you are sensitive, you picked up on it," he nodded.

"Picked up on what?" I exclaimed.

"There are ebbs and flows in all things," John replied, "including the flow of spiritual energy both from the Light and Dark Side. At this point in time, the positive energies are such that an approximate 20-year window or weak point is exposed, and the Dark Brothers have taken full advantage of it. Their first step was to send a neutralizing energy through this wormhole. This does not hurt the Workers of Light, but it distracts them, giving the Dark Brothers an opportunity to pick certain areas of the earth to plant their ideas and promises of power to large egos. The problem is, during this window, the Dark Ones are able to keep some of their workings secret by sending a distracting energy so the Brotherhood of Light on the earth cannot attend to their full duty. For this reason, my stabilizing help was needed and I was unable to visit you in the physical body. But I did tell you we would meet, so I went out of my way here to fulfill my word."

John continued. "During one of these windows I mentioned, the Dark Ones found fertile soil in the minds of Hitler, Mussolini and Stalin, and planted the seeds necessary for their missions. Now in some ways we face an even more dangerous time. You would think the fall of communism and the Berlin Wall would make things safer. It is true that opportunities for advancement are open as never before, but the extra freedoms also open the door to the possibility of great evil. During this period of distraction, we believe the Dark Brothers are attempting to initiate a plan to spread the sale and development of nuclear and chemical weapons as far and as wide as they can. They will look for opportunity in any land where there is a lack of freedom in countries such as North Korea, China and the Middle East. In addition, the third world countries and terrorist groups are also a threat. They will also attempt to give new life to the Nazi party in Germany, but we do not believe this will be successful."

"It sounds to me as if they could create a situation that could destroy us all. Then we would all lose," I interjected.

John's countenance turned serious. "That's where you are in error, my friend. If mankind is completely destroyed, they win. That is what the leaders of the Dark Brothers want - the complete elimination of mankind on the earth. Their lower-end dupes working in physical bodies on the earth do not understand this."

I was stunned. His statement did not make sense to me. "But why?" I asked. "If they destroy everyone there will be no kingdom to rule."

"You are wrong again," he said. "If we are destroyed, there will arise another kingdom that is not human as we know it, one that the Dark Ones can completely control. I know you are curious, but I will have to delay more elaboration. You must ask me another time, for the full answer is very important knowledge that has been kept hidden from the earth."

"You're right. I am very curious. Are you sure you can't tell me now?"

"Yes. I am sure, but these keys will help to insure the survival of the species, so let us proceed. It is time for the first key word."

"All right," I said. "I believe I have the right word, but it does not make complete sense to me."

"The word," John commanded firmly.

"The key word and name of the parable you gave is *Decision*," I said resolutely.

John smiled widely. "That is correct. Now tell me, how does this answer the question WHO OR WHAT ARE YOU?"

"I have been thinking a lot about that," I replied. "What seems to be the answer does not satisfy me."

"And what seems to be the answer?"

"That who and what we are is the result of the combination of all the decisions that we have made."

John paused a moment and asked, "Do you think you are a different person today than you were twenty or thirty years ago?"

"Yes, I have changed a lot."

"So you agree that you are a different person today than you were back then?"

"Yes, of course. I think we all change with time."

"Then your answer is not entirely correct. It is indeed a point of truth that we are the result of our decisions, but this idea is common knowledge. We are looking deeper than that. Who and what you are today is the same as what you were twenty years ago and is the same as what I am. The answer is decision, but you do not understand it yet. Think on this throughout the next week and see if you can retrieve the answer."

"Now you have me mystified again and I think I am at another dead end," I exclaimed, exasperated. "Can you give me another hint?"

"Just one," said John. "Which do you like best - apples or pears?"

"About the same I guess."

"Good. Now imagine you are very hungry and before you is an apple and a pear; you are allowed to eat one of them but you must decide which one. You like apples and pears an equal amount. Think of the apple, then the pear, then the apple - as if your power of decision were fluctuating between the two. As your power of decision fluctuates, try to feel and sense this power operating within yourself. As you sense this power ask yourself. How am I DECISION? What does it mean? In your silence feel this life energy fluctuate back and forth between the apple and the pear and try to register in your conscious mind the magnitude of what you feel. Ask yourself again and again *How am I decision?*"

"Hm -m-m, that at least gives me something to go on," I said. "I hope I can come up with something." I wasn't sure exactly what John was getting at, but I trusted that contemplating his example as he instructed would get me closer to the answer.

"It is about time for me to return to my body. I am to assist Joshua in neutralizing the distraction of the Dark Brothers and we must attempt to discover where they have planted their mischief." John took a deep breath, "Ah, but it was nice to come here again and refresh my soul."

"How long have you been here?"

"About an hour by mortal standards, but the refreshment of being here for about an hour is worth a night's sleep. But you do not have to go. Why don't you finish the night here?"

"That sounds great to me. I would love to look around."

"I'm sorry, but that is not allowed. Even though your intentions are good, you are likely to write something which is forbidden. You cannot be allowed that temptation."

"So what am I supposed to do the next few hours?"

"Relax and soak in the energy and refresh your soul. Believe me, you will be glad you heeded my advice."

"So how am I supposed to do that?"

All of a sudden the scene changed to my bedroom, but without Elizabeth. John said, "This should be familiar to you. I recommend you just lie in this replica of your bed and just soak in the energy. You will need it. If I had time I would stay here with you."

"What if I get up and look around?" I asked, showing some mischievous curiosity.

"You will find nothing without a guide to reveal it," he replied firmly. "Again, I would suggest that you just relax, forget about the outer form world and let the inner prevail."

"I'll try," I sighed. "So... Are we on for next Thursday again?"

"We'll meet at Denny's unless something comes up again."

"I'll look forward to it," I said eagerly.

John smiled and stretched out his right hand. I stretched mine out and our fingertips touched. At that instant he disappeared. As he departed I felt a surge of spiritual energy go through me again and felt a combination of sadness and great joy at the same time. I knew and sensed again that John had a long history of sacrifice for the cause of humanity. I could feel his great love for people and that he was willing to do whatever was necessary to help the race we call mankind. Here was a man who has labored continuously for 2000 years with no record given him in our history books. Perhaps I could give him a little recognition in what I write, I thought.

After I adjusted myself to being alone, I lay down on the bed and tried to relax. It was easier than I thought. I found if I desired to feel relaxed, I felt relaxed. There was something about being in the New Jerusalem that seemed to amplify the power of thought and desire. I sensed my time would be well spent if I followed John's advice and sought refreshment, and this was where I set the direction of my thoughts. As I did this I felt that sense of joy and fullness I felt earlier with John. Instead of experiencing bore-dom, as I supposed, I found I was very happy to spend a couple of mortal hours in blissful silence just enjoying the presence and energy of the city.

I awoke too soon. I felt as if I could have stayed completely still within the city for days, perhaps months, perhaps forever. Whatever the case, it was better than any drug, and I left far too soon. I felt badly for John that his stay was much shorter than mine, but I found that John was right about the refreshment con-cept. I have never awakened feeling so energized in my life. The only negative effect was the lingering knowledge in the back of my mind that the Dark Brothers were hard at work plotting the de-struction of humanity. "What kind of kingdom did they have in mind if humanity was destroyed?" I wondered. A medieval pic-ture of devils and demons in Hell came into my mind, but I re-jected it. I intuitively sensed the answer was more than that... Much more.

CHAPTER THREE
An Attempt To Heal

That next morning would have been perfect had it not been for the nagging awareness that the Brothers of Light were having some major problems to deal with and that John, who I now considered a personal friend, was working at great sacrifice for the benefit of mankind. Somehow I was beginning to feel some type of spiritual link with him. I seemed to be experiencing some awareness of his consciousness and sensed he was having difficulty of some type. I also sensed a strong belief that the purpose he espoused would prevail.

I didn't have any pressing appointments so I stayed home that morning and told Elizabeth my experience.

After I finished she reflected a moment and said, "That's all very interesting, but don't you think it could have just been a dream?"

"I don't think so. I have had many dreams before, but none like this one. The experience was at least as real as I am experiencing talking to you this moment."

"OK. If it was real, then why didn't you guys take me along with you?"

"Well, that was not my choice, but if I had to guess, I would say it has something to do with me needing practice."

"What do you mean *practice*?"

"Remember John told us it would help to solidify the teachings in my mind if I explain them to you? By teaching you I am preparing myself to teach others in the future."

Elizabeth smiled. "Sounds like a lame excuse, but I'll play along for now. If you are supposed to be my teacher, how about coming up with something to help me overcome this disease? It sounds like you don't yet fully have the first key, and I don't want to wait here forever."

I took a deep breath. "I'm glad you brought that up. During my period of rest in the New Jerusalem I had a lot of interesting thoughts go through my mind. It was as if I saw things much more clearly when I contemplated there, and one of the things I thought about was your illness. I began to see we were putting too much weight on waiting for a miracle to happen when we solve the keys, and not doing enough to help ourselves now. I saw that the greatest miracles happen among the human kingdom after we do all we can with what we have. I saw that there are certain beings called Watchers (who some may also call angels) who watch various human groups. I noticed they rarely intervene for human good unless we do all we know first. I caught a glimpse of the suffering humans experience on the earth and I saw much of it happens because people just don't take the course of action they know within their hearts they are supposed to do.

"Then I saw something that is, unfortunately, a rare occasion. Among mankind there are individuals here and there who search their inner selves and follow the highest path they can perceive. I saw that these individuals had many things happen to them that seemed to be bad luck, but if they persevered and did everything within their power to press on to their goal, there were times the Watchers were moved, came forward, and assisted them with an unseen hand – and, in this case, the miraculous did happen. Sometimes it was an instantaneous healing, sometimes it was the right people showing up at the right time to help; other times, it was the removal of obstacles and sometimes it was even money. But I had a sense of inner joy that the faithful person received when he or she received the direct assistant of a Watcher. I saw that the joy came as a result of the person following through with the highest knowledge he could perceive. And that's what I want to talk with you about. We must now follow through with the highest knowledge we have about your disease."

"And what is that?" Elizabeth asked impatiently. "I suppose you want me to have my mercury fillings removed. Well, I've thought about it and I'm not convinced it will help. A handful of people seem to benefit, but others do not."

"That is a possibility," I said, "but that's not what I have in mind. The law I perceived is we must follow the highest we know. Now we do not know for sure about the mercury thing, but there is something that we do know for sure about."

Elizabeth scowled at me. "As far as this disease is concerned, I don't think there is anything I know for sure except that John does have the power to heal me. I just wish he would quit playing these games with me and just make me whole so I could get on with my life."

"But that's my whole point." I struggled to find the right wording so I would not offend her. "I saw the miracle will not happen unless we do all we can do first - that if John were to just heal you, he would be violating some type of higher law."

"Well, I've done all I can do, so I should be ready for healing, shouldn't I?" she asked defiantly.

"There is one thing we definitely know that we haven't done," I replied.

"And what is that?" she asked.

"John gave us some knowledge about MS and other diseases I felt was true and that we should follow. I think you felt it too, and I perceive you know within yourself that there is something you must do. There are fears and emotions within you that you are trying to pretend don't exist. This is a form of deception, and all deceptions must be dispelled to have perfect health."

Elizabeth sighed and shook her head. "Here we go again. How am I deceiving myself?"

"A while back we talked about your early upbringing and a fear of Hell, and you acted very evasive," I said. "I think it has something to do with that. Mentally, the traditional hellfire and brimstone doesn't make sense to you, but emotionally I think there are some residual fears there."

"I don't think so," she said.

"Don't you see? You're saying that because of denial. If you are really over your fears, then it won't bother you to face them, will it?"

"I'm not afraid to face them. There is nothing to face!" she insisted.

"I think you have two major fears," I insisted. "First, a fear of displeasing your parents. I think you carry this fear even when you are not in contact with them. The second fear is a fear of Hell, which is in connection with some ingrained guilt complex. Basically, I think you need to face the reasons for your guilt."

"But I don't have any guilt!" Elizabeth repeated. "I gave up guilt when I quit believing in a God that would damn us to hellfire and brimstone for eternity."

"I know you don't want to believe in a God like that, but I

think you still fear that such a God exists."

"And just what makes you say such a thing?" she challenged loudly.

I thought for a moment. This was a critical point in our discussions. I had to get through to Elizabeth on this. "Three things. When I was in the New Jerusalem in meditation it just came to me that I had to pursue this direction with you. Also, I think the Dark Brother who gave you such a bad time was able to obtain the power he did because of some fear or guilt you carry. Finally, John hinted your disease is caused by unexamined fears. I think you need to be honest here." I knelt down in front of her. "Do you still fear the damnation of Hell and a God of vengeance?"

Elizabeth looked uneasy. Tears came to her eyes. "What do you want me to do? Lie and say I am afraid when I am not?"

"Look, I know this is difficult for you," I said, putting my hands on her shoulders. "But just humor me for a moment. If you have blocked out fear and guilt, it would seem they don't exist even though they are still there lingering on the shelf doing damage. It's like heading for a cliff when you think you are seeing a straight road ahead. You have to see what is really there to avoid disaster. I feel impressed to tell you that you must see the true picture here to be healed."

"So how am I supposed to see or feel something I don't see or feel or don't even believe exists?"

"First, you have to be open to the possibility that some hidden guilt or fear is there. Can you be open to that?"

"No, I don't want to be open to it. I got rid of my guilt years ago and don't even want to think about bringing it back!" Elizabeth looked like she wanted to run away if she could.

"Don't you see? You've just stated the problem: you don't want to face these things. I think you've got to face them. Your life may depend on it."

"Why don't you just go face your fears first!" she shot back.

"Sweetie," I began softly. "I don't mean to agitate you, but I am not the one who is sick here. Don't you realize I am trying to help you because I love you and want to keep you here with me?"

"Of course I realize that, but I think you are as deceived as I am. You see guilt and fear that doesn't exist."

"OK. If guilt and fear doesn't exist in you, then you shouldn't be afraid to discuss them, should you?"

"I suppose not," she said defiantly, but more subdued than before.

"I was talking to your mother the other day about that preacher your dad used to take you to listen to. I believe they called him Reverend Bill. She said she had some tapes of his best sermons. I acted interested in hearing them and she loaned me a couple. I have them in the car now. How about if I go get them and we'll listen to one right now?"

Elizabeth looked startled. "I can't stand that man and do NOT want to hear his voice! Just give those tapes back to my mother."

"I thought you weren't afraid of facing your fears," I challenged.

"I'm not afraid of Reverend Bill... I just despise the man. When he died a few years ago I thought he was out of my life for good and now you try to bring him back."

"Elizabeth... Listen to what you are saying. You are afraid of the man! You need to face him one last time. If you were truly not afraid you would humor me and listen."

"Not liking something and fearing it are two different things," Elizabeth replied evenly.

"There's a lot of music I don't like, but it isn't painful to listen to. If you just do not like Reverend Bill, then I would venture to say that listening to him as a favor to me would be no big deal. If you refuse to listen to him, that convinces me that you're afraid." I knew this psychology would get to Elizabeth. She is always up to a challenge.

The look on her face convinced me I was right. "I'm not afraid! Bring in the damn tape and play it! Then I don't want to hear any more about this again."

Without further comment, I ran out to the car and got the tapes. This was one time I was glad she couldn't get up and run away. I knew I finally had her in a situation where the healing could begin.

As I put the tape in the recorder I noticed Elizabeth was trying to look away. I guess this must be what they mean by tough love, I said to myself as I pressed PLAY.

Elizabeth looked very uncomfortable as we listened to the preacher's introductory remarks. It wasn't long before he started laying it on thick.

"Do you think you can possibly escape the wrath of God and the hell that awaits you with the devil and his angels just by being what you think is a good person? I say unto you nay! Unless you are washed by the blood of Jesus and are accepted into his flock, you shall in no ways inherit the Kingdom of God.

"The devil is out there I tell you and he seeks to ensnare you. Do you feel lust for the opposite sex? Then you have sinned already and he who falls short of the glory of God will go to a place where the worm dieth not and his thirst is not quenched. You shall be burned with fire from the presence of the Lord."

He rambled on for several minutes in a similar vein, but then he said something that even made me cringe.

"Have you ever burned a finger on a hot stove?" he shouted "Of course you have. It hurts, doesn't it? Now, have you ever held your hand in a pot of boiling water? Probably not, but you can imagine how bad it would hurt. Now imagine how much worse it would feel to have your whole body roasted in burning lava.

"Now here on earth, if you jumped into molten lava the pain would all be over in a few seconds, but under God's punishment you burn and burn and burn for ever and ever and ever with no relief. If you are not open to God's great mercies and love here on the earth, God will have no mercy on you in Hell."

"Have you broken even one of the commandments? Then the Lake of Fire will be your fate if you do not receive the grace of God through the blood of Je-e-e-sus!"

I noticed Elizabeth was visibly disturbed. I couldn't blame her. This man's interpretation of the scriptures was outrageous. I turned the tape player off and put my arm around her. She started to gently cry and then wept profusely.

"This is it my dear," I tried to assure her, holding her closer. "This is a fear you need to face."

"Everyone has broken some commandments, haven't they?" she choked out, asking for reassurance.

"Of course, they have. I'm sure Reverend Bill has also," I replied softly.

"I-I tried to receive God's grace and forgiveness. I tried and I tried, but I still felt guilty. I was not sure I was forgiven so I told myself that Reverend Bill's God could not exist. I created a happier version of God, but something in me still feared this God of vengeance. I could never completely switch over to a God of Love... Oh, God! I can't believe these feelings still exist. I thought I buried them long ago."

"That's where the problem is, sweetheart. You buried those feelings. Now we are going to bring them to the surface and destroy them once and for all."

"But how?" she asked, reaching in her skirt for a tissue, and blew her nose. "I've tried everything to get rid of my guilt and fear. I thought they were gone, and now they are back again stronger than ever!"

I grabbed her firmly and looked her in the eyes. "I have something very important to tell you. I did go to the New Jerusalem and somehow during my meditation I tuned into the universal Spirit of God, as I had never done before. It was like certain knowledge was poured into me. There are now things I know for sure. Some of these things I thought I knew, but they were like theories then, and now it is like sure knowledge. One of those things is the Love of God.

"God would never send anyone to a fiery pit for eternity, especially for some small infraction by a sincere person such as yourself. Nevertheless, there is suffering both in this world and the next, and any suffering we endure we bring on ourselves. We must look within ourselves for the cause of any suffering we have and bring that cause to the surface and face it. Then we must harmonize our outer selves with our inner selves.

"The great truth I perceived is that God would never dream of punishing us as much as we punish ourselves. We treat ourselves so horrifically that no devil with a pitchfork is needed. Our own guilt is the sharp ends of the devil's pitchfork, our own resistance to accepting ourselves as part of the love of God is the fires of Hell, and our efforts to pretend that we don't feel the Spirit of God is the worm that dieth not. All the eternal punishments mentioned in the scriptures are descriptions of what we do to ourselves."

Elizabeth looked at me for a moment, not convinced my words were true. "Well, if God is truly Love, then why does He allow us to hurt ourselves so much?"

"Because to not allow it would take away from us what we are. Decision is the first key word and without the power of decision, which includes being responsible for the effects of our decisions, we would virtually cease to exist. According to John, we are even more than the results of our decisions. This power is somehow connected with the essence of our very being. Your power of decision leads you to the fear and guilt that caused your disease and now decision can lead you back to health. You've got to take your power back to yourself and not give it away to some hateful God." Wow! I said things I didn't even know that I knew. Somehow, teaching someone else brings forth knowledge from some deeper place than your conscious awareness, I thought to myself.

Elizabeth was startled too. "So when did you get so wise? You're beginning to sound like John."

I laughed, "This may sound crazy, but I was just thinking the same thing. It's like I'm tuning into his mind somehow and partaking of his wisdom. I don't know if I would have had the wherewithal to push you this far, but it's like I know where I am supposed to take you here."

"Well, she said, "so far you have managed to bring up a problem in my life I thought I had left far behind, and you've driven me to a very uncomfortable state of mind that makes me feel worse and not better. So what's the next step?"

"I'm not sure," I said. I really thought Elizabeth felt better, but I didn't want to push my luck.

"So what does John's mind say about it?" she quipped.

I wasn't sure if she was being serious here or not, but her statement changed the direction of my thought. For a few moments I felt very sure of the direction I had to take my wife, but then I seemed to doubt myself and lost the direction. I instinctively knew I could answer Elizabeth's question if I could tune into John's mind, the Spirit, or whatever it was that was guiding me.

"John's mind... Yes. Why not? Let me close my eyes and contemplate a moment." I closed my eyes for a moment and felt a warm vibration that reminded me of the New Jerusalem. Within seconds I knew the answer.

"The next step..." I said. "I know what it is and you won't like it."

"Why am I not surprised?" Elizabeth asked sarcastically.

"I wish I could have a pleasant surprise, but here goes: The first thing you must do is listen to this tape over and over until it doesn't bother you to hear it. You must be able to listen to anything Reverend Bill says and be no more affected than if you watched a Mickey Mouse cartoon."

Elizabeth squirmed a moment and frowned. "I don't know. The little I did listen to made me feel a lot worse, not better. I don't know if I can take anymore."

"You'll have to take even more than this tape. I have two more." I hoped I wasn't pushing too hard, too fast.

"Mom gave you three of those tapes? She must hate me!" Elizabeth started wheeling her chair out of the room.

I followed. "Actually, she thought it would do you some good to get some more religion. I believe she was right, but not in the way she thinks," I added quickly. "I'll tell you what. I think you've had enough for one day. Why don't you take it easy and relax today and plan on listening to the tapes tomorrow?" I asked hopefully, mentally crossing my fingers.

"And what makes you so confident I will do such a torturous thing?" she asked, almost playfully.

"Two things," I said. "First, I know you want to live, and second, if you check with your inner self you will know it is the right thing to do. Will you at least promise me you will think about it?"

"All right. I'll think about it. Now you had better get ready for work."

I approached her wheelchair, knelt beside her, embraced her lightly and looked into her eyes. "I know a door is opening for your healing and I want you to take it. I need you to take it. It will be like living in the New Jerusalem if you are well and healthy again." I felt a lump in my throat.

Elizabeth lovingly touched my faced and kissed me lightly. "I said I'll think about it. Now go to work."

CHAPTER FOUR
What We Are

I was pleased when I came home from work that evening and found that Elizabeth had already listened to all three tapes. Actually, she seemed quite pleased with herself. She explained to me that even though the experience was very uncomfortable it seemed right to her to take the chance. After all, she said, she had nothing to lose. I was happy to see her making some sort of positive attempt, right or wrong. I knew it would at least give her hope.

The next Sunday I had a long overdue breakfast date with Wayne. I was looking forward to running some things by him. I arrived a little early and after ordering a cup of coffee Wayne came in and plopped down, looking a little disturbed.

"Problem with your guys?" I asked.

"What don't I have a problem with?" he growled. He took off his cowboy hat and threw it beside him.

"Must have been one of those weeks," I ventured.

"I guess," he said. "I don't know if it's the moon, something in the air or what, but everything has gone wrong that could go wrong. I think I'll change my name to Murphy."

I thought back to John's statement that this was a period the Dark Brothers were preparing for their next assault. I wondered within myself if this was causing some type of disturbing vibration that filtered down to us ordinary mortals. "Actually," I said, "I have felt something odd myself. Maybe there is something in the air. So what happened this time?"

"It's that damn Jeff," he said.

"Wasn't he having some problem with the law?" I asked.

"Yeah. Then just a few days ago I spent $500 bailing him out

171

of jail. After that he swore that he's in my debt for life. Now guess what that son-of-a-bitch did yesterday?"

"What?" I asked, knowing the answer was not going to be good.

"The guy had the gall, after all I have done for him. He broke into my place and stole a stash I had of $5000 in cash and heaven knows what else!" Wayne pounded his fist on the table so hard it just about spilled my coffee. "He'd better pray the law finds him before I do!"

"I know you've had problems before with your guys running off with your stuff and I know you have a thing about not locking your doors. Don't tell me you're still leaving your place unlocked?"

"Well, I feel like I shouldn't have to lock my doors. I feel I should be able to live in a society where I can trust the people who associate with me."

"That's a fine ideal," I said, "but it's not always realistic."

"Realistic or not, life should be that way," he said, shaking his head.

"Maybe yes, maybe no," I said, "but you have to deal with the reality that not all people can be trusted. In fact, a large percentage of people cannot be trusted if the temptation is great enough. As your friend I can only insist that you start locking your doors."

"Even if I wanted to I can't because my guys need to get in the garage or house for tools and other stuff when I'm not there."

"Well, I'm sure you could devise some system that would cost much less than $5,000 for the inconvenience."

Wayne thought a moment, "Probably," he said. "But I'm too angry to think about it right now."

I paused a moment. I knew I was pushing my luck, but I had to ask. "What in the world were you doing with $5,000 in cash laying around loose in your house?"

"It wasn't laying around loose," he replied impatiently. "It was well hidden. I don't know how he found it. I always try to keep some cash around. You never know when you might need it."

Wayne was not a member of any group that I knew about, but he did have a lot of survivalist in him as well as a distrust of the powers that be. I could only imagine the reasons he wanted to keep a stash of money readily available. We tended to keep our conversations more on an intellectual basis and only delved so far into each other's personal lives.

"So... Outside of losing $5000, how was your week?"

Wayne glared at me. "Do you want me to stay calm enough to be civil here or not?"

From that statement I gathered there were other problems in his week that he just didn't want to discuss. I figured it was time to move on. "OK," I said. "Let's shift gears and talk of more pleasant things. I think I finally have the answer to WHO OR WHAT AM I?"

Wayne leaned back and motioned to the waitress for more coffee, "So you think you've come up with something better than all the great philosophers including Descartes?" I was amazed to see Wayne's countenance change from agitation to one of calmness almost instantly. He loves to talk about philosophy or anything that requires thought and analysis, and seems to go into a different mode whenever he is engaged. Whenever he enters what I call his *thoughtful mode*, he appears to be much more wise than he seems to be in his general everyday life. I would venture to guess that many of his own family are unaware of this thoughtful mode I had come to appreciate.

"At the risk of sounding like a giant ego, I do think I may have something that has eluded the philosophers of the past," I replied, wishing I could tell Wayne about John. I made a mental note to ask John if the time was right to tell others besides my wife about him.

"Well, I've known a lot of big egos that I don't think you could compete with," he quipped.

"Thanks for the vote of confidence," I said. "Descartes reduced our essence down to thought, but we already concluded that our minds are really just vehicles that are used by our real essence. Then we concluded that consciousness was above thought and finally that motion or action may be behind consciousness. But the key to it all is that which produces action. There is a power in us that is behind all motion that we initiate. What would you say that is?"

"I would say thought, but we've already covered that ground so I would guess you have something else for me," Wayne said dryly.

"Some actions follow a thinking process, but many others do not. We have numerous thoughtless actions, but all motion is the result of one great inner power we have. Here... I'll demonstrate it to you." I picked up a glass of water and moved it several inches. "Now, what made this glass move?"

"I think it was you," Wayne smiled.

"Of course, it was me," I said, "but what was it within me that caused the glass to move?"

"I don't know," he said. "You just decided to move the glass for some reason."

"That's it!" I said. "I can't believe you just got it off the cuff like that."

"What's it?" asked Wayne. "All I said was that you decided to move the glass. I wouldn't say that that is a profound statement."

"But it is profound," I insisted. "You just said the key word."

"Key word... What key word?"

"*Decide. Decision* is the key word as to what we are. We are decision. Every action that takes place is preceded by a deciding intelligence of some kind. I am an intelligence who just moved the glass because I decided to. A decider may use thought and emotion, but thought and emotion alone does not create motion. Thought and feeling with no decision is powerless."

"That's all well and good," said Wayne. "I can see we are the results of our decisions, but to say we are decision would not be technically correct."

"But somehow it is, Wayne. In some way the very power within us that makes decisions is what we are. Let's say you are deciding between bacon and eggs or pancakes when you have an equal desire for the two. Let your power of decision fluctuate between the two and you can feel that which is the real you, the power of decision at work."

"It won't work for me. I'd choose bacon and eggs over pancakes any day," Wayne quipped.

"Very funny. But you know what I mean. You have two things of equal desire. Let your attention shift back and forth - you can feel the inner power, the power that actually puts things in motion."

"Where are you getting this stuff?" Wayne asked, looking at me with deliberation. "Where's the old Joe who just wanted to know simple things like when time began or where God came from?"

"I'm the same guy. Just had a little change of direction."

"O-kay..," he reflected a moment leaning on his elbow. "I have a feeling you want to use my incredible mind power to delve further. Let's see what you've got here."

"You're right. I thought that maybe by putting our brains together we could take this a step further. Humor me a moment and assume that we are more than the results of our decisions, but somehow we are decision or the power of decision itself. If you knew this was a true statement, what would it mean to you?"

"Hmmm," reflected Wayne. "I've thought of myself as being thought, feeling, love, consciousness and even a part of God, but this is a new one. *I am decision*," Wayne mumbled to himself. He closed his eyes. "I am decision... I am decision," he repeated. "I like it," he said, opening his eyes widely. "It feels good. Isn't that close to what you said was the Hebrew reading of what God said to Moses? Didn't He tell Moses he was deciding or something like that?"

When Wayne said that, a light turned on in my head. "Wayne, you're a genius, I tell you. A genius!"

"Why of course I am," he smiled, flattered. "Now tell me why so I can brag about it."

"What God said to Moses was a major hint. Moses asked God what His name was and back in those days the name of a person revealed what was supposed to be a person's essence or true nature. So Moses was probably expecting something that described the typical human version of God. He probably would have been satisfied if God had told him that His name was THE HIGH AND MIGHTY ONE or THE ONE WHO HAS ALL KNOWL-EDGE AND WISDOM or something like that. The interesting thing is God did not give Moses any regular name. Instead He basically said I AM BECOMING THAT WHICH I DECIDE TO BECOME. He was telling Moses He was decision and that He couldn't give him any regular name because, as decision, He could decide to be different tomorrow than He is today. Because God makes different decisions about how He will manifest, He cannot give any name that will apply in all time periods, except for something like THE ETERNAL, which is what Moses finally decided to call Him."

"Very interesting. Glad I could help," said Wayne, looking pleased with himself.

"That's not all," I said, leaning closer. "Look at how God has manifested through the ages. In ancient times there were supposed to be many gods. Then in the days of Moses there was just one powerful God of vengeance. Later, in the days of Jesus, God was called Love."

"And that's just the Christian God, " Wayne added. "Suppose all the major religions are part of the plan of God. If this theory of yours is correct, then God has decided to manifest a little differently through each one. Perhaps He has many different identities in different places and ages."

"And that would make sense," I said, "because each different civilization or body of people may have to be presented with an interpretation of God which is comfortable within their belief system before they could accept any new and different teachings. The funny thing is, it may be the same God manifesting as He decides to manifest, and this decision would be made according to the circumstances of the people."

"Looks like we have the whole mystery of existence thing sewed up here," said Wayne. "The only trouble is, what are we going to tackle next?"

"There is a step further we can go here," I ventured. "Remember when we talked about the idea that we may be Gods?"

"Yes."

"We have just discovered a similarity between the description of the God of Moses and us mere mortals. Somehow we are both decision, or decision is somehow our highest essence."

"So, do you think this is the end of your strange quest to discover who or what we are?" asked Wayne.

"I'm not sure," I shrugged. "This talk with you has been very helpful, that's for sure, but I think there may be more to understand."

"I can think of things already," said Wayne. "Like, what was the first decision? Was there a time when decision did not exist? If there was such a time, then there was a time you did not exist or maybe God did not exist... A guy could go crazy thinking of these things. Maybe we ought to switch to politics for a while."

With that statement Wayne changed the course of the conversation to more mundane topics, but my mind was only partially present. I couldn't help but reflect constantly on the idea that God becomes who He decides to become and perhaps so do I. Do we obtain the power of God by magnifying our power of decision? I wondered to myself. Somehow I sensed that mankind had only a primitive understanding of what decision is and how it can be used. I began to greatly anticipate my next meeting with John.

CHAPTER FIVE
The Doctor

The next morning as I was preparing to leave for work I mentioned to Elizabeth, "Today is your doctor's appointment, isn't it?"

"Yes. Mom is coming to pick me up this afternoon."

"How are you feeling? Is there any difference since you have listened to the tapes?"

"I feel some stress from it. It's hard to tell if that's good or bad."

"What does your inner sense tell you?"

"I feel confused about it. A part of me tells me the discomfort is good, like the pain from a disinfectant put on a wound, but then another part of me tells me I am crazy for doing this, that it is only common sense to avoid pain."

"The first part of you is right," I said as I kissed her good bye.

"I hope you're right," she said. "If I get much worse I won't be able to stay home alone for any length of time."

"Meanwhile, if you have any problem of any kind, page me anytime and I'll be home in just a few minutes."

I had a weekly office meeting I had to attend and several appointments that forced me to be out of the home, so Elizabeth's mother had to take her to her appointment. Fortunately, I was in a job where I could do much of my work from my home. When I did have to be gone I tried to not be away more than three or four hours at a time. I used a dedicated home number, which was listed first in all my real estate advertising next to the office number so clients would call the home first. I also did a lot of my phone work and research from my home. Overall this worked out well. My broker wonders, though, why I am one of his best agents when I'm hardly ever in the office. It's no mystery if a person were to hang around our office for any length of time. Most agents just sit around drinking coffee, waiting for the phone to ring. I find I keep much busier than most of the other agents even though I use my home for my main office.

The positive aspect of this is I can keep a good eye on Elizabeth and be there to help her. The negative aspect is our bills are so high, I have to work like crazy day and night and she often feels lonely and ignored. Each day I try to set aside some time for each of us to give one hundred per cent attention to the other, but that precious time seems to be becoming less and less.

That afternoon I felt a "disturbance in the force," so to speak. Every once in a while I do pick up on Elizabeth's feelings, and this was one of those times. Unfortunately, I knew the news was not going to be good. I feared the doctor must have had some bad news for her. I rushed through my last appointment and hurried home as fast as I could.

As I arrived home I noticed Elizabeth's mother's car was in the driveway. Elizabeth's father died a few years ago leaving her mother, Leona, alone in a big house. Fortunately, she has a lot of time on her hands and is willing to help whenever Elizabeth needs her.

"Sweetie!" I called as I opened the door. "Is everything OK?"

Leona came in from the kitchen looking quite disturbed. "Oh, dear," she said. "Something is wrong and Elizabeth won't tell me what it is. I think the doctor told her some bad news but she's completely mum about it. Maybe you can find out what it is."

I walked into the dining room. Elizabeth was sipping tea at the table, looking very downcast. "What's the matter, sweetheart? What did the doctor tell you?"

"Everything's fine. Everything's just fine." she said in a flat tone that clearly revealed everything was not fine.

"I don't know what it is, but I think you need to unload something."

"Not with my mother here," she whispered.

I walked over to Leona and softly said, "I'll spend some time with her and see if I can cheer her up. Why don't you give us a call later tonight and see how she is."

"But maybe I should stay with her."

"I think it's best if she deals with us one at a time. If I can be alone with her I think I can find out what's wrong. Come back tomorrow and spend the whole afternoon if you want."

Leona reluctantly left. I hoped I had not hurt her feelings.

I turned to Elizabeth. "OK. I know there's something you need to tell me. What did the doctor tell you?"

"You don't want to know," her lips quivered.

I knelt beside her. "Listen, Sweetie. Whatever it is, we are going to beat this thing. You have a destiny left on this earth. Together we are going to do great things."

"Not if I kill myself." She started crying softly.

"What are you talking about? You are not going to kill yourself."

"That's not what Doctor Bernstein says!"

"This can't be true. Your doctor would never tell you that you are going to kill yourself even if he thought it was true."

"But he did. He told me I was killing myself," she sobbed.

"Now calm down," I said patiently, taking her hand. "Tell me exactly what he said."

"I told him about the tapes; I wanted to see what he thought. Then he asked me some questions and he became very agitated. He started going on about how stupid we were for swallowing this psychobabble treatment. He told me the trauma of bringing up these old feelings could kill me. He said you could be responsible for my early death."

"I can't believe this!" I said angrily. "Doctor Bernstein always seemed like a gentleman in the past and now he upsets you like this. Can't he see that what he just said to you is the thing having the real negative effect?"

"That's not the way he sees it," she said grimly. "He wants to see you privately tomorrow, and I don't think he has anything good to say to you."

"Why did you have to tell him about the tapes and the stress they produced in the first place?"

"He's our doctor," she said defensively. "I'm supposed to tell him everything good or bad that is relative to this disease. Maybe it's good that I did. Maybe we are being stupid here."

I grabbed Elizabeth's arm. "We're not being stupid. He might even do the same thing in our position. I wish you wouldn't have told him though. It sounds like he thinks we've gone over the edge. It's a good thing he doesn't know about John..."

Elizabeth's eyes looked down in a way that made me nervous. "Oh no, you didn't tell him about John, did you?" I asked, clutching her arm.

"I just mentioned we had a friend who was giving us advice."

"Please don't tell me you told the doctor that we have been talking to John the Revelator!" I repeated anxiously.

"Don't worry. I just told him that we had this wise friend," she answered evenly.

I sighed. "I hope so Sweetie. I hope so. If you give him any hint of what is really happening here he'll think we are stark raving mad. A little wild and crazy I can handle, but you can imagine what treatment a doctor may recommend for a person who talks with a 2000-year old man, let alone John the Revelator!" God, they could institutionalize Elizabeth!

"Don't worry about it," Elizabeth tried to reassure me. "Meanwhile, the doctor thinks I should avoid all unnecessary stress, so I think I should lay off the tapes for now."

I moved closer to Elizabeth. "That's the fearful side of your nature talking. Doctors aren't always right. You've got to look within yourself and trust your inner guidance. Ask yourself... What does the Spirit within you say?"

Elizabeth took a deep breath. "I don't know. I just feel confused right now. I want to coast a few days, so for now I'll follow his advice. I just want to rest for a while. I don't feel like solving problems." Elizabeth motioned for me to help her into her wheelchair.

I felt it wouldn't do any good to try to change her mind at that time. Perhaps I would talk to her again after my visit with her doctor.

The next day the doctor wanted to see me at two o'clock sharp. I juggled several appointments to make it on time. Then after going out of my way to meet him on time he made me wait a half-hour. Typical, I thought to myself.

Finally a nurse said, "Mr. Dewey? Doctor Bernstein will see you in the first room on the left."

As I walked in I noticed it was one of his regular examining rooms. There was an examining table in the middle of the room and two chairs next to the wall. In one of them was sitting Doctor Bernstein. "Have a chair," he said.

As I sat down facing him, I thought he reminded me of a chemistry professor I had in college. He was probably about 55, gray beard, balding and had an air of authority about him. As he looked at a yellow pad with some notes on it he said, "Thanks for coming in, Mr. Dewey." His tone had a sense of practiced courtesy.

"Whatever I can do to help," I said.

"I don't believe you've ever been in to see me as a patient. Who is your regular physician?"

I felt a little uneasy with this question because I wasn't sure how he would handle the answer. "I don't have a regular physician," I said.

"Do you not believe in doctors then?" he asked.

"Obviously I do. After all, you are my wife's regular physician."

"But that's your wife. I'm asking about you. When's the last time you saw a regular medical doctor?" he pried.

"Well let me see. I think it was about twenty years ago."

"Twenty years!" he exclaimed. He rose up, walked to the far wall, came back and sat back down in his chair and calmly asked again, "Now tell me, Mr. Dewey, why haven't you been to a doctor for twenty years?"

"I haven't needed one."

He let out a short laugh, paused a moment and asked, "I'm curious, Mr. Dewey, why did you see a doctor twenty years ago?"

"I had an accident and needed a bone set," I replied.

"Mr. Dewey, I'm certainly glad you had the sense to realize you needed more than a positive attitude to set a bone."

I was becoming a little irritated with his repetitive use of my name, as if it was his way of demonstrating his authority over me. After a pause he said, "Tell me, is that all you think doctors are good for?"

"Not really," I said. "I think it's important we have qualified physicians available when they are needed."

"But you just haven't needed one for twenty years?"

"No. Is that some type of crime?" I asked, my voice rising.

"No, Mr. Dewey. It is not a crime, but in my opinion it is personal neglect. Surely you have not been in perfect health for twenty years?"

"Well, I get a cold once in a while, but the last I heard you don't have a cure for that, so I've had no reason to see a physician."

"But, Mr. Dewey, don't you think it is wise to get a checkup now and then just to make sure everything is functioning correctly?"

"I'm not against getting checkups, but if I'm feeling good I just don't see the need."

He then gave me a look one would give an ignorant savage and said, "Mr. Dewey, did you attend high school?"

"Yes, of course," I replied, wondering why he was asking

this.

"Hmmm," he said raising his eyebrows. "And did you graduate?"

"Yes," I said, feeling uncomfortable with his direction.

"And did you go so far as to attend college?'

"Yes, I attended college. Where are you going with this?"

"Let me put it to you this way, Mr. Dewey. When I found out you deliberately convinced your wife her disease is her own fault and talked her into this program of psychological abuse, I thought perhaps you lacked an even basic education. To be frank, I am surprised to find you have graduated from high school, let alone attended college." Then he raised his voice with agitation. "How could someone with a basic education in this day and age fall for this crap? Don't you realize your wife has only a short time to live?" Then he rose and standing above me said in an even louder voice, "You can measure in months the time she has before she loses the few faculties she now has. Do you want to make things worse than they already are? Do you?"

"Of course not." I tried to stay calm, but I felt like a little kid being scolded for being naughty.

"Well, that's what you're about to do!" he shouted. "A high level of stress right now could accelerate her deterioration." He composed himself and sat back down and calmly asked, "Mr. Dewey, do you want to kill your wife?"

"I love my wife," I said, feeling even more agitated with this guy's rudeness.

"Well, that's what you're about to do if you persist with this idea that the disease is her own fault." He paused a moment and said, "Mr. Dewey, I know you're not smart enough to have concocted this torture system on your own. Tell me about this guru your wife mentioned to me. I think there may be legal procedures we can use to keep him from harming others."

This time I rose up. "I've had enough of your rudeness. Any stress I have put my wife through palls in comparison to what you have put her through. You should have seen her when she came home yesterday. She went to you full of hope and left full of despair. Who is doing the real damage here?"

The doctor's face turned white, as if he had never been talked to that way before. "Who do you think you are?" he shouted loud enough for the whole staff to hear. "I'll not have an uneducated idiot lecturing to me that way!"

"You won't, my friend. You are fired. We'll get another doctor, this time someone who really cares."

"I care. I care a lot!" he said again with a raised voice. "That's why I called you in here."

"Insulting me is not the way to show it," I said walking away.

"You can't fire me. Elizabeth has to."

"She fires you too," I replied over my shoulder.

"If anything happens to her I'll have charges brought against you. I'll see that you pay!"

"Give it your best shot," I replied on the way out. Then I paused, turned around and added, "One more thing, Doctor. With or without you, Elizabeth is going to make a full recovery. I suggest you become part of the solution, not part of the problem."

The doctor abruptly turned around and disappeared down the hall. He seemed to be too disgusted for any more exchange.

As I drove off feeling his seething emotion I was amazed at how quickly our previously amicably relationship came to an abrupt halt. Before this confrontation, I had no reason not to put our full trust in this guy. Now I almost thought I was dealing with the devil himself.

That evening I told Elizabeth what happened. She seemed alarmed and said, "You don't have the right to fire my doctor. He's not your doctor, he's my doctor."

"You're right, Sweetie. I just wanted to fire him as far as I had any authority. But I think we ought to look for another doctor. I've got a bad feeling about this guy."

"I don't understand," she said after a moment. "He's been my doctor since I've had this disease and he's always acted like a perfect gentleman. He's supposed to be as good as anyone in town for treating MS."

"But a good doctor is more than a person who just has good technical knowledge. A good doctor also instills hope, and if you have hope then even a fatal disease is less of an enemy."

"Yes, but you also like to know where you stand and I think he's been pretty honest in that regard," she said.

I took Elizabeth's hand. "I'll support you in whatever you decide here, but I think he will interrogate you every time you visit him in the future. He may even want to see you grovel in his presence before he will let you continue as a patient."

"You ought to know by now that I am not big on groveling. If he's as rude to me as he was to you then I'll drop him, good doctor or not," she said firmly.

"Whatever the case, I urge you to think about a change," I

pleaded.

"I'll see how my next visit goes, providing I can get in to see him," she said.

The next Thursday evening I was really looking forward to my visit with John. Despite all the other problems I had, I felt like the luckiest man in the world to be able to visit with this man. Just as I was preparing to leave to go to Denny's the doorbell rang. "Oh no," I thought to myself. "What a time for company. I've got to figure out some way to get rid of them quickly"

I walked to the door and opened it. I stepped back in surprise and delight. In the doorway was a kindly gentleman named John. He smiled. "You don't happen to have any left over salmon, do you?" he asked.

"No, but I'd be happy to run to the store and get some," I ventured.

"Not necessary," he said as he strolled through the door. "I would like a repeat performance of that dinner we had though. I can't seem to get that nice flavor out of my system."

"Whatever you want," I said. "I am your humble servant," I said playfully, bowing.

"You have it backwards," he said smiling. "That's my job. Haven't you read your Bible lately? If I am your teacher, then I am the servant."

"What part of the Bible are you referring to?" I asked.

"The words of the greatest teacher as recorded in Matthew 23:11, which reads: *But he that is greatest among you shall be your servant.* The gurus of this age have it backwards," he said. "They attempt to spread light and desire the reward of servitude for the favor. The true spiritual teacher only desires to serve, not to be served. Any service extracted from others is not due to the personality of the teacher, but is pointed toward the One Great Work."

"I can tell already I am going to enjoy this session," I said.

At that point Elizabeth wheeled toward the doorway. "I thought I heard a familiar voice. I've been feeling ignored by you, Mister Revelator," she teased.

"Well, you won't be ignored tonight," he smiled.

And we all gathered around the dining room table for what we knew would be an interesting visit.

CHAPTER SIX
The One and the Many

"What can I get for you to drink - coffee, glass of wine?

"What kind of herb teas do you have?" asked John.

We have several," I said. "I think we have some raspberry, chamomile, green tea and some kind of blend called Emperor's Choice."

"What's in the blend?" he asked.

"Let's see." I got up, grabbed the box and read off the ingredients. "This has cinnamon, blackberry leaves, eleuthero ginseng root, orange peel, roasted chicory root, rosehips, ginger root, lovage root, licorice root, natural flavors and panax ginseng."

"Sounds good," he said. "I'll have to try it."

"And what would you like, Sweetie?" I asked Elizabeth.

"Emperor's Choice sounds good to me," she said.

"I guess I'll join the crowd," I said. "Emperor's Choice it is."

As I hurriedly made the tea, Elizabeth told John about my confrontation with the doctor.

"Authorities must be dealt with wisely," he said. "If you let them know you are operating outside of the parameters of their approval, they will feel very threatened and seek to reaffirm their power over you in any way possible. This has changed little in the two thousand years of my memory. Reflecting on this situation will provide you with a major hint to the truth behind the *mark of the beast*. I'm amused at the way many believers are waiting for a great world dictator to appear to force the mark upon humanity when the mark is already here."

"Exactly what is the *beast* and the *mark*?" I asked.

"Maybe we had better set aside an evening to explain that," he replied. "When you write about it in your book I want you to convey it in a way that will be understood. I will tell you this; I have not read any religious literature that has interpreted it correctly."

"How about the number *666*?" asked Elizabeth. "I've heard a lot of different people are supposed to have this mark - everyone from the Pope to the President."

"That is also misunderstood," he said. "Actually, your doctor bears the number as well as most of the people on the planet." He paused a moment and sighed. "You would think after two thousand years someone would correctly interpret my writings. I suppose I shall have to do it myself. When it is revealed you will see it makes a lot of sense."

"So, since my doctor has the mark of the beast does that mean I should drop him?" Elizabeth asked.

"The next one will probably have the mark also. The important thing is to not provoke the beast. Do not tell any of the powers that be about me or any of my teachings. Joseph will eventually write about me as fiction, and part of it will be fiction, making the teachings more palatable and less threatening. Still, there will be many who will be disturbed. Let me stress here that it is extremely important you do not put me in a situation where the authorities become interested in me. If I am ever captured by them and interrogated, I become as vulnerable as you are."

"But you've transported me half way across the globe," I countered. "Couldn't you just escape if you had to?"

"Not necessarily," he answered. "In each life I can either work at a distance as a teacher or become directly involved with humanity. If I work at a distance, as I am with you, I can retain certain spiritual powers that you have witnessed. But if I become directly involved then I lose these higher powers. This is what happened in World War II. I felt the defeat of Hitler was so important that I worked directly with Stauffenberg as I mentioned earlier. The beast made sure I paid for it. As I told you earlier, I was strung up with piano wire for my effort."

"What a terrible thing," cringed Elizabeth.

"It could be even worse in this period," John added. "In the past I have been able to hide my identity, but in this age it would be more difficult. If the beast had me in his control in this life my fate would be worse than what Hitler dreamed up, probably electric shock treatment, drug therapy, or something like that."

"I didn't realize I was putting you in danger," Elizabeth said humbly. "I'll be careful from here on out."

"That would be much appreciated," said John. "You might

be interested in knowing that after Jesus was delivered to the authorities by Judas, He could not have escaped them if he wanted to."

"But I thought he could have called down legions of angels," I exclaimed.

"Technically He could have, but it would have been contrary to the laws that govern the Brotherhood. There was virtually no way out for Him except to drink the cup that was offered him."

"Interesting," I said. "Before we begin with the Keys, I have a short question. I have noticed lately that I seem to be tuning into your mind or aura or something. Sometimes I think it's my imagination and other times I am quite confident that I'm pulling things from your essence or something like that. Am I going crazy or is there something to it?"

"It is good you noticed this, my friend. You have a glimmer of the relationship I have with the Christ. Even at this moment I am embraced by His presence and am able to tune into His mind and heart. This is the fulfillment of His prediction I wrote about when He wanted his disciples to become one with Him as He is one with the Father.

Do you remember that great feeling you had in the New Jerusalem?" John asked me.

"How could I forget?" It was really great.

" I have that feeling right now because I am one with Christ. Now as you, Elizabeth and others become one with me, you also become one with Christ and the Father, and thus the resources and knowledge available to one become available to all. It is a little like a spiritual internet."

"You mean as a spiritual web surfer I can tune into you and access data from you? That's a fantastic thought!" I said, smiling.

"Unlike the limitations of the Web, you can access more than data. You can also access the feelings, love, judgment and wisdom of the one tuned in to. You always have the free will to accept or reject it. For instance, you tuned into the idea Elizabeth should listen to those tapes. You were not quite sure if that was your idea or my idea, were you?"

"No, I wasn't."

"But the decision on how to proceed was entirely yours, was it not?"

"Yes, it was."

John leaned forward. "Now I am going to tell you something I want you to always keep in your consciousness. The Brother hood of Light will never seek to take your power of choice, but will always seek to amplify it. The Dark Brothers, however, will seek to garner all power of choice for themselves and diminish this power in others. As you look among the leaders of humanity, you will see that most of them are willing to sacrifice free will for something that seems to be a good end. There are many others who will acquiesce free will because of a lack of values. There are a small number who have a true instinct of what freedom is and fight for it."

"But don't we have to give up some freedom for the common good?" Elizabeth asked. "For instance, I should not have the freedom to kill my next door neighbor because I want to."

"It is true that you should not kill your neighbor," John replied, "but the truth is you should have the freedom to make the attempt if you decide. The freedom to decide anything must not be infringed. Murder and other crimes are to be prevented not by taking away free will but by making just laws with consequences severe enough so that crimes like this will be discouraged. Eventually when humanity understands the laws of cause and effect, education will be the main deterrent against crime. Until that time civil law is essential.

"The point here," he continued "is that civil law governing crime will discourage negative choices, but it does not remove or diminish the power of choice."

"How can the power of decision be diminished then?" I asked.

"It is a very subtle thing," he answered. "And the sad thing is that choice is often diminished in the name of freedom or a good objective. The welfare programs of the nations are a good example. A certain helpfulness is a good thing, but placing a person on an assistance program that provides him with enough to survive on without having to make any choices causes the power of decision to atrophy within him; thus, his very power of livingness becomes diminished. Communism is another example. It embraces a good objective, which is equality, but attempts to force it upon the subjects. This removes the power of choice for the individual, who can no longer choose equality for himself. True equality can only exist in a state of freedom."

John continued. "Other things that take away freedom are group thought forms, hypnosis and illusion. These often do a great deal of harm in diminishing choice. For example, do the people of this country consider the right to vote a sacred duty, and would they not go down kicking and screaming if anyone taught they should not be able to cast this vote?"

"Yes," I said. "Even the man on the street values the right to vote."

"Yet, let us suppose you were a member of a group or religion that taught you that the entire system is evil and that it does not matter who is elected because it will soon be destroyed anyway. If you were to swallow this idea do you think you would vote?"

"I'd probably be discouraged from it," I concluded.

"That is true. Then after this idea is fixed in your mind for a while, the time comes when the decision to vote does not even occur to you. You have given up this freedom without feeling that you have given up anything. You have been deceived into diminishing your power of choice."

"There have been times when both candidates for office seem equally bad," said Elizabeth. "Should I still vote in that situation?"

"There is always more than one office to vote for and there are always some good candidates. Maybe you do not have a good choice for President, but there is a good candidate for the Senate, for example. On the other hand, just as there are no two snowflakes alike so are there no two candidates of equal value. Even when the choice is between two people of low value, one will be better than the other. You must use judgment to decide which one that will be."

"I've always voted all my life," she said, "but it has never made a difference. No election I have participated in was decided by one vote."

"Even if your vote did not alter the election, you still participated in a process which is held sacred by all the brotherhoods of light universally. And nothing is without effect. By refusing to participate in an election process that affects your life, your power of choice is diminished, but by your participation your power of decision is increased."

"Some intelligent people do not vote," I said, "because they believe the candidates on both sides are selected for us by the powers that be: bankers, a conspiracy, or some other thing."

"In some cases there may be a little truth to that, but these candidates still effect our lives and one candidate will still be more beneficial than the other. The choice to vote should always be exercised in good times and bad times, in season and out of season, when you make a difference and when you do not. Now the Dark Brothers always do everything in their power to influence candidates in tune with them to run for office. They influence through the power of the ego, and politics is certainly a playground for egos. Nevertheless, there are always a certain number running for office who are sincere in their intent. If good people do nothing, these people will never be given a chance."

"It seems to me that a lot of things about our government get worse no matter who we vote for," I said. "I would like to see a lot of things changed and I know the vote alone will not do it."

"That is true," John agreed. "Nevertheless, the sacredness of the vote should never be overlooked. This is a key power the people must always possess if the kingdom of God is to be established on the earth. As for making changes, if people realized the power of decision within them, this nation could be turned around tomorrow. Even if only twelve people in oneness used their power of decision for good, the power to change can be enormous. I would venture to say there are not even three mortal people on the earth who function in unity with a realization of their power to change the earth for good. The power of decision is indeed unappreciated, and thus we get to today's discussion. Have you received any further light on the subject?"

"I think so," I replied as I prepared another cup of tea. "In my talk with Wayne I realized that when God appeared to Moses He virtually told him His name was I AM BECOMING THAT WHICH I DECIDE TO BECOME. Now, since the name in those days revealed the essence of a person, this answer revealed that the essence of God is the power of decision. I thought this idea may be a key as to why men are called gods. If God is decision and we are also decision, this is a way we are like God."

"Very good reasoning!" John smiled. "This is indeed the power that links men and gods, and it can raise a person from the animal nature to great spiritual heights. Perhaps this concept will help you realize the answer to last week's question. Who and what you are is DECISION. Why is it you are called *decision*?"

"I guess something about my essence is governed by this power," I offered.

"It is much more than being governed by this power. You ARE this power. How many times do I have to tell you? You are DECISION. Did you practice the exercise of deciding between the apple and pear?"

"Yes, I played around with it."

"Did you tune into your essence as you felt your power of decision move your consciousness back and forth?"

"Yes, kind of."

"And how about you Elizabeth?" John asked, turning to Elizabeth.

"I tried it out. I seemed to sense something, but I'm not sure."

"Let's go a step further," said John. "We will repeat the emphasis, and let me stress in this exercise that you should see yourself as being very hungry. In fact, you are so hungry that you must have the apple or pear soon or you will die. The problem is that one of them is an illusionary hologram and one is real. The hologram is so realistic, it is impossible to tell the difference between the two; nevertheless, you think that if you study them closely enough you may be able to discern the real one. If you choose the hologram you will die, but if you choose the real fruit you will live. Now let your attention fluctuate between the two. It should become more riveting and bring you closer to your essence."

"Why do you call that essence *decision* rather than the power of decision?" I asked.

John reflected a moment and answered, "In the beginning was the ONE, and within the ONE resided the initiating Cause. The keyword representing this Cause must be discovered by you in a future key. Within the ONE resided Decision and the latent power of decision, and at the beginning of time the great Decider made the first decision for this creation. What do you think that first decision was?"

"Maybe He, She or It just decided to be," said Elizabeth.

John showed the first glimmer of surprise I had ever seen as his eyes widened. "That, my dear, is very very close. Very close. The first decision was to manifest. The second decision was to give itself the power to exercise a decision. This decision, interplaying with the power to exercise it created the wavelength represented by light (or intelligence), and love (or magnetism). Thus we have the Trinity of Power, Light and Love; or Father, Son and Holy Ghost. The wavelength created infinite space, which is the mind of God."

John continued, and as he did, his face seemed to become almost transparent and radiated a glow. "In order for the ONE to manifest, It had to become the MANY. To manifest, the ONE Decision reflected Itself from the Prime Cause. Because the Prime Cause is infinite, the reflection was infinite; and infinite points of Decision filled and created all space. Each point was in the image of the ONE and had all the potential of the ONE. In other words, each point was a Son of the ONE or a Son of God.

"The points gathered into groups of three and the THREE became ONE. The THREES who became ONE gathered again, this time into fours and the FOUR became ONE. The ONES gathered into fives and the FIVE became ONE. The ONES gathered once again into sixes and the SIX became ONE; and thus was created the foundations of the particles within the atoms that make up this universe. Finally, the ONES began gathering into sevens, producing the seven building blocks of all we see about us. I wrote about these seven as the seven creative Spirits before the throne of God; the ways we see them manifest is in the seven layers of electrons within the radioactive atoms, the seven chakras in the human body, and the seven notes in the musical scale."

After a short pause I asked, "So, have these seven become one?"

"This is the present in time and space on this world and all worlds," said John. "The seven are in the middle of the gathering process to become ONE."

"And what will happen then?" I asked. "Will we have eight notes on the musical scale?"

"In this sphere there will always be the SEVEN and the seven notes, but it will seem to be an eternity before the SEVEN become ONE. At that time, the solar systems, galaxies and the universe will reach a high state of evolution and will look nothing like they do today."

"So, will the seven which have become ONE gather again into EIGHT?" I asked, fascinated.

"Yes," he said, "and a billion years in our time will be less than a second in that higher sphere."

"So, will it ever end or are there gatherings to infinite numbers?"

"The Decision was to gather until twelve is reached, the number of perfection, which will be many eternities as far as human consciousness is concerned. This is why there is such great power in the gatherings of twelve and is why Jesus chose twelve disciples. This was one of the keys of their great power after the resurrection."

"So, when the twelve is reached and the final perfection achieved, will all things eventually end?" I asked again with great interest.

"The Many becoming Twelve and the Twelve becoming ONE are incorporated in the first great Decision. When the Twelve become the ONE, another great Decision will be made. Even the highest initiates do not have a clue what will be involved there. No living entity can yet conceive of the universe built on the EIGHT. We only know that it will exist trillions and trillions of years in the future.

"The interesting thing here is that we live at a very unique time. In the whole creation of things we live at the meridian of time. In fact the appearance of Christ in Jerusalem was calculated to be a midpoint of all time."

"But how can that be?" I asked. "If the universe of EIGHT will encompass more time than has ever been?"

"Time is even more relative than anything Einstein perceived. Time does not flow evenly for your consciousness, but moves forward in packaged units, so to speak. These units are around one sixteenth of a second and within that package of time are billions of years of passage within micro universes. The decision points within these realms have perfected themselves and have moved their consciousness up to our universe. Later when we have perfected this universe we will move our consciousness up to the universe of EIGHT. Because of relativity the conscious passage of time through each universe is the same. Thus we can truly say we are in the meridian of time."

"How could anyone even know such things as you tell us?" Elizabeth asked with wonder in her voice.

"Each of us is a reflection of the original Decision, and even within yourself are billions, even trillions of reflective Decision points. Within yourself is a virtual universe and you are a god to that universe, just as the originating God is a God to us. By observing that which is without and reflecting it off that which is within, you can eventually access all knowledge that is available in the universal mind of God."

"But you said that even the highest initiate does not have a clue about the kingdoms built on the number eight. If God is supposed to know everything, then could not that knowledge be accessed?" I asked, proud of myself for having asked a clever question.

"Who told you God knows all things?" John asked.

Elizabeth and I stared at him, startled, wondering if we heard him correctly. "Everybody believes that," Elizabeth pronounced. "God even knows when a sparrow falls to the ground. He is omniscient and omnipresent, isn't He?"

John paused. "God does know when a sparrow falls to the ground because God is reflected in the sparrow. This is what makes

Him omnipresent. In a way, the mind of God is like a great computer database. In this database resides the information about
the falling of the bird; but you, as a reflection of God, have no
reason to access that information and keep it on your current computer screen. Even so, all things that happen are potentially know-
able to the mind of God, but not in the consciousness of all the
reflections of God. However, the fall of the sparrow is an important event for the reflections within its little life."

John looked for comprehension in our faces and continued.
"In the beginning, the ONE decided on the gatherings unto the
number twelve. It knows the end from the beginning, and the
desired end will be achieved. That is a certainty based on the
Faith of God and all the reflections. However, that which happens
between the ONE and the TWELVE is a great mystery even to the
mind of God Himself. No life, including the One Initiator, knows
the details about the evolution of the EIGHT, let alone the final
TWELVE. We do, however, have some pretty good ideas about
the end product of the SEVEN."

"That's an amazing concept I haven't heard before," I exclaimed. "You are saying that there are things in the future that
even God does not know?"

"Yes, many things."

"So, is it then impossible to predict the future?" I asked.

"The future is foreseeable only insofar as certain points ahead
have been Decided by the mind of God," John replied. "For instance, the Christ predicted that He would come again because
He reached a Decision about it. He will make His presence felt
again on the earth, but the details as to how that would happen
were not pre-determined. At that time the prophecy could be fulfilled in one of several ways."

"So, have the details been worked out by now?" I asked.

"Many of them have," said John, "but everything is still not yet
set in stone. As I said before, we have made two previous attempts to make our basic preparatory teachings available to humanity and they have failed. You shall be the third attempt. If you
succeed in bringing these teachings to mankind, this will prepare
the world for a different and higher type of Second Coming than
will happen otherwise."

"Can you tell us about the various possibilities of His Coming?" I asked.

"Time prevents us from discussing this further tonight," he
said. "Now, we were speaking of the future. There are only two

ways for men, angels or gods to predict the future. The first is to gather all available data, analyze it and make an intelligent judgment as to what may happen. As one grows in intelligence, one can use this method with enough success to be considered a prophet. The second method is to achieve control of circumstances that will effect an event and then Decide that the event will occur. You can then predict that event with close to 100% predictability."

"Is 100% accuracy possible?" I asked.

"If time is not a factor you can be 100% accurate. For instance, we are sure that the TWELVE will gather into ONE, but if we tried to predict the date we would be off trillions of years. From our point of view there are Beings who have such great power that simple people on earth would call them the highest God. These Beings have made certain decisions which have set things in motion. When a spiritual person on the earth tunes into some of these decisions, he will then have the power to see certain events that will happen in the future, but the time frame is always difficult to pinpoint."

"It sounds like things are not as black or white as they teach in church," Elizabeth commented.

"Religious teachers on the earth are teaching with very limited knowledge," said John. "Yes, things are not as black and white as they seem, but shades of gray is not the correct term either. What seem to be shades of gray are caused by a recognition of incomplete knowledge; and when you have incomplete knowledge, you have to do a certain amount of guessing between the black and white, which is the gray area. Many people refuse to recognize they have incomplete knowledge and the black and white is the easy direction for them. Nevertheless, when the day comes you have complete knowledge on a subject, there are no shades of gray. For instance, two plus two equals four. You know all about it and no gray area is possible. But people who say God knows everything know nothing about God. They are really guessing that God knows everything."

"You know," I interjected, "I've always thought the regular religious view of God is very boring and undesirable. They say He knows everything and lives in ultimate perfection that cannot be improved. I would not want to be in that situation. There would be nothing to look forward to."

"That is an intelligent point," said John. "Such a state would be the worst hell one could imagine. For one thing, if there were ultimate perfection, no decisions would be required. If there were no decisions possible, there would be no life. The very life of God would die. Fortunately, we live in a universe where there is much uncertainty and many decisions are always required. It will be that way with periods of rest until the TWELVE become ONE. And even then, another great Decision will be made.

John continued, "In the beginning, when the decision to manifest occurred, the ONE and all the reflections experienced a great fear and trembling because of the uncertainties. This originating fear is woven into the fabric of the universe itself, and when it is conquered on one level it must then be faced on another. Uncertainty and fear of the unknown, simply put, is what keeps life interesting for all lives, great and small. It also forces us to use our life-expanding power of decision."

"Wow," Elizabeth exclaimed, stretching. "A person could go crazy just thinking about what you told us tonight. So tell me... are we ready to move on to the next key?"

"Not quite," said John. He looked at me closely and said, "Tell me, Joseph, your current understanding of the question WHO OR WHAT ARE YOU?"

Suddenly, I felt a little nervous. "OK," I said. "Let me see. The real me is not just the result of my decisions, but I am Decision, which is a reflection of God. The part of me that actually makes a decision is the real me. When I realize this, I am like God in the fact that I can then become what I decide to become."

John nodded, "You have an elementary understanding of it, but let me tell you this. Even the Christ himself is still learning greater realizations of himself as Decision. You have just opened the door. As you contemplate this key, many doors of knowledge will be open to you. You will never be done learning about it, just as the initiating Decider has not."

"It would seem there must be something that precedes the first Decision," I said.

"As I said earlier, there is one thing. There is a key word for the One Initiating Cause. This Word creates and makes decision possible. We could also say that you are this particular word, except you would not have guessed it. It will be revealed in a future key and will throw more light upon Decision. The understanding of Decision is the beginning of you knowing who and what you are."

"So are we ready to move on?" I asked.

"Not quite," said John. "There is a companion word to decision you must understand. This quality applied with decision produces consciousness as we know it and consciousness applied with decision in turn creates this power. It's a little like the chicken and the egg. Consciousness and this mysterious, but common word are co-equal and co-eternal. This is what I want you to consider for the next week: What is consciousness and how is it created? Keep in mind that without decision, there can be no such thing as consciousness or even life or motion. *Consciousness, life, and motion are created by decision and then applying this key word to that decision."*

"Then if I get the right word, will I be ready to move on?" I asked impatiently.

"I do not know," said John, sounding like Cain in Kung Fu.

"But if you do not know, who does?" I said, sounding a little exasperated.

"I was making a point," John smiled. "Exactly what you will experience and come up with next week is not 100% predicable. Because you are Decision, you are impossible to predict completely. You could decide to jump off a bridge tomorrow. Nevertheless, I anticipate that you could be ready to move on after next week."

"Great," I said. "At least I see a light at the end of the tunnel here."

John smiled. "I know you are anxious because you want to see your wife healed, but you must not hurry truth. The greatest revelations come to you in quiet moments of contemplation, and one of the greatest lessons a disciple can learn is to create those quiet moments for himself amidst the turmoil of everyday living. You cannot go off to a monastery, so create the monastery within you. If you can learn to do this in your stressful situation, you will have gained much."

John paused a moment, finished the tea in his cup, and then said to Elizabeth, "Now, in the time I have left I will answer your question. I sense there is something important for you to have answered, but first I think a refill on the tea would be in order."

Elizabeth looked startled that he read her mind, but I just smiled to myself, not surprised in the least. I got up and refilled all of our cups as we waited for Elizabeth to ask her question.

CHAPTER SEVEN
The Question

"I feel kind of strange asking a question," said Elizabeth. "You already knew I wanted to ask you something. I wouldn't be surprised if you knew what it was."

John looked at Elizabeth and said, "I could discern the question if I wanted to put attention on it, but there is something to be said about normal human exchange. It helps to crystallize thought in the minds of both parties if there is an honest communication. Go ahead. Ask your question."

"I have a question I know many people who have misfortune have. There are many people in the world who are good people who have diseases like I do, and many in even worse circumstances. Yet, some truly evil and undeserving people have perfect health and are even born into a life of wealth and ease. Then there are some innocent babies and children who suffer terrible disease and death, or a life of hunger and poverty, whereas others are born to a life of comfort and good health. My disease has caused me to reflect upon the unfairness of it all. Ministers say God will work it all out in His plan, but that does not satisfy me. It used to, but not after I got this illness. Now I feel I must find out the reason behind this unfair suffering."

John paused a moment and answered, "Have you heard the statement that has been circulating lately - that life isn't fair?"

"I've been hearing that a lot lately," I injected. "The funny thing is everyone used to insist God is just; therefore, life is fair. Then one day someone, I don't remember who, publicly stated that life is not fair and it just seemed to catch on. Now everyone is saying it."

"And why do you suppose everyone is saying that?" said

John.

"Because if we go by our current knowledge and observation, life is obviously unfair," said Elizabeth. "I don't know how many times I've looked up and asked the question *Why me?* But there never seems to be an answer." Her eyes became moist.

"Yet if God is truly just, does it not make sense that life would be fair? Indeed, if life isn't fair, then God isn't fair," John said.

"I've often thought that," I said. "If God is indeed just, then life would have to be ultimately fair. Even the Bible says that as *ye sow so shall ye reap.* I don't believe Elizabeth has sowed anything in this life but good. Even if she is in some denial, it still doesn't seem fair she should suffer the way she does."

John nodded slightly and said, "So, if Elizabeth has done nothing in this life to deserve such punishment and if a sick baby has done nothing to deserve the pain he receives, then when could they have done things that would cause these problems?"

"Well, if the cause was not in this life, then it has to happen before birth, either in some spiritual sphere or some previous life here on the earth," I said.

"And which do you think is the actual cause?" John asked.

"I tend to gravitate toward the belief in past lives," I said, "but there are several problems that keep me from embracing the doctrine wholeheartedly."

"And what are these problems?" John asked.

"I basically believe the Bible is an inspired work and my relationship with you has enhanced that belief. After all, you are proof that much of the New Testament is true. There is a statement in the book of Hebrews that says *it is given unto men once to die.* Now, if we die only once, then we would only be born once."

"And do you have any other barriers to a belief in multiple lives?" he asked.

"The other thing that bothers me," I said "is I have done a lot of reading of various books on religion, philosophy, the new age and so on, and have embraced a handful of books and teachers who I think are truly inspired to a degree. The weird thing is that two teachers who seem equally inspired disagree on reincarnation. Some seem to indicate it is true and the Bible and other good books seem to be against it. But I feel within me there is truth in the doctrines on both sides of the issue so I've always been unsettled about it."

"Have you ever participated in hypnotic regressions?" he asked.

"I have been interested in the subject ever since I heard about Bridie Murphy when I was young," I said. "I studied a little hypnosis and experimented on friends and had some fascinating regressions. Some very impressive past lives seem to surface. I have also talked to a number of people who have done regressions."

"Have you ever taken Elizabeth back to a past life?"

"Unfortunately, she does not seem to be a good subject for hypnosis."

"So what conclusion have you arrived at on the subject of past lives?"

"I am pretty much open to anything. The concept of past lives seems logical and fair but I have also considered that we have the memory of our ancestors imbedded within our DNA, and in regression we tune into some ancient memories recorded in our physical structure."

"But even if such a tuning in were possible, it would not rule out multiple lives," he said.

"Well, if there is reincarnation, I must have been pretty wicked in the past," said Elizabeth. "I must have tortured someone to death or something like that."

"Actually, you're not far from the truth," he said. "You were one of those who tortured confessions out of the Knights of the Temple during the Spanish Inquisition."

Elizabeth and I both dropped our jaws. "You've got to be kidding!" I exclaimed. This was the first time I seriously doubted John. "I cannot for the life of me imagine Elizabeth torturing anyone. She goes out of her way to avoid stepping on a bug."

"But she was under orders from the Pope. Do you realize what that meant to her internally?"

"It would put pressure on her, but I think she would have risen above it.," I said somewhat defensively. Elizabeth's eyes were glazed over at this point.

"But in that age she was a young man who was raised as one devoted to the Pope. To him, the Pope was the voice of God. Do you realize how many sincere believers in history have resisted that which they truly believed to be the voice of God?"

"Well, not too many I suppose."

"Less than that," said John. "The answer is virtually none."

"But aren't there many people every day who disobey God?" Elizabeth asked.

"It appears so," said John, "but these people you speak of do not really believe they are defying a real and living God. In that life you were under the sincere illusion that the Pope's words were God's words so you actually considered it an act of faith to obey. You felt that such obedience would insure a place in heaven and that disobedience would send you to Hell. This is a form of belief that is almost beyond human capacity to defy. The only way around it is to lose your faith or see through the illusion. Actually, the entity will lose his faith in numerous lifetimes before he finally sees through the illusion and gains a true and living faith."

"So, even though she was sincerely mislead, she still has to pay for her acts?" I asked.

"Cause and effect is a little like gravity," John replied. "Whether you fall off a cliff accidentally or jump off willingly, you are still subject to the law. The soul especially wants us to learn a lesson if we commit a harmful act under the orders of one who takes the place of God. We must all learn the lesson of Joan of Arc and listen to the inner voice rather than the outer authority."

John paused a moment. "Actually, all of us have had similar debts to pay off at one time or another. If any person thinks he is not capable of such atrocities in the right circumstances is fooling himself. Even those who crucified Jesus thought they were doing the will of God and considered themselves righteous for doing it"

"It may seem funny," said Elizabeth, "but I could see myself doing something like that if I thought God commanded it. But the weird thing is it feels good to me to know of a possible root cause of my disease. It somehow seems it may be a step toward healing."

"How right you are," said John. "Now in this life you are learning to search within. You have a sense there is some truth in my words. Something about them just feels right to you."

"It's strange, but you're right," she said. "So, I take this to mean there is such a thing as reincarnation?"

John looked toward the ceiling for a moment, as if he were searching for the right words, then said, "yes and no."

"How can the answer be yes and no?" I asked.

"You brought up an important point earlier," he said. "You mentioned that some inspired teachings seemed to favor reincarnation whereas others discouraged it. Have you ever considered that both groups of teachers were correct?"

"Not really," I said. "It would seem as if the principle is either true or false, not true and false. A yes and no answer seems to be impossible."

John paused a moment. "As the soul evolves and one travels into the light, at first things appear to clarify and concrete answers seem to appear. Then, as illusion is broken up, that which seemed to be clear becomes foggy again. Then when the fog clears, concrete answers on a higher level appear, but in time they too are broken up and rearranged. There are concrete points of truth in time and space, but we consistently add new points that change the image of the picture we see. Thus we can see why it is difficult for any two people to agree on ideology, for each sees an image around his limited understanding. Truth is not relative, but the image of truth we have in our minds is indeed relative to our understanding.

"Even so, the fact as to whether or not there is reincarnation is relative to what you think you are. If you think you are your body, emotions or even mind, there is no reincarnation, for after death these three parts of yourself are changed forever. Since few people know more than is represented by their body, feelings and mind - which is their whole personality - to them reincarnation does not exist.

"Then there are others in the East who see the body, emotions and mind as vehicles and the real part of ourselves as a part of God. For these people reincarnation is a reality because this real part of ourselves does continue to exist and gets recycled."

"So I take it this real part of ourselves, which seems to be that part of us that makes decisions, is reborn in both East and West," I added. "It's just that many religions in the West see humans as personalities rather than a part of divinity."

"That is correct," said John. "Religions in the West see survival after death as the survival of our personality makeup, whereas most of the cultures that believe in reincarnation - which is a majority of the world's population - see it more as survival of consciousness."

"So after I die and am reborn, am I still me or someone else?" asked Elizabeth.

"You will always be you, but not you as you are today," said John. "As you can guess in each life you will have a new physical body. Each physical body will have a certain influence on us because the form and make up of each one is unique. Even a plastic surgeon will testify that a simple nose job or something that alters physical beauty can change a person's personality. Doctors tell us that some of us have certain chemicals in the brain that can cause alcoholism or depression. The point is, the quality and type of your physical body definitely influences who you appear to be. If you and I were to change bodies we would both be under a different influence and act a little differently."

"So in each lifetime do our feelings also change?" I asked, becoming more interested.

"Our feelings, or our emotional body, undergoes the greatest change for the average person because the consciousness of the average person is centered in the emotional self."

"So what causes a change in our emotional self and how much change is involved?" I asked.

"Your emotional body not only changes between lives, but it changes some within one lifetime. For instance, twenty years ago your physical body looked different than it does now and it also influenced you a little differently. The same goes for your emotional self. If you think back to how your feelings responded to various situations you will realize that over the years you have changed some in that aspect as well.

"A larger change takes place between lives and especially during the period of gestation. Your emotional body undergoes an adjustment to prepare you for the new things you will learn and experience in your next life. This may cause a fairly dramatic change in your outward projection and may change you from an extrovert in one life to an introvert in another. Or it may change you from one who loves to associate with people to one who loves to tinker with things. Or, it could change your interest from a love of art to a love of business."

"So does the mind also undergo a change?" Elizabeth asked.

"In some people it does, but you may be surprised to learn that true mental energy is not awakened in most of humanity. That which most people call mind is really physical brain activity. True mind is much higher than that and is higher than the emotions; it controls and directs the feeling nature."

"Is that why so few people seem to be capable of arguing or debating in a logical manner?" I asked.

"Yes," John replied. "People of all stages of evolution argue and debate, but the majority with sleeping minds are limited to using their brains and feelings. If such a one has been taught and programmed well, he can put up a good argument until he matches wits with an awakened mind. Such an awakened person can confound the most highly educated with a minimum of facts, even on subjects on which he has little direct knowledge."

"So, how many people have awakened minds?" I asked.

"Only about ten per cent of humanity are awakening on a mental basis. Of that percentage only a very small number are close to being fully awake."

"Does this have anything to do with the fact that we only use less than ten percent of our brain?" asked Elizabeth.

"What you are referring to," said John, "is our brain again. It is true we do not use our brainpower to capacity, but the mind is another matter. Most of humanity use zero percent of that because it is sleeping and has not been awakened."

"How do you tell if your mind is awake?" she asked.

"The person with the unawakened mind will be limited in his personal philosophy and belief to what he feels and what he has been taught or what is recorded in his memory. The person with the awakened mind will not be so limited. He will be capable of putting several apparently unrelated facts together under what is called a *principle*. Using principles, he can arrive at new vistas of truth without the aid of the regular educational process. Sometimes these new truths will conform to his feelings and sometimes they do not. In either case, the awakened one will consider the new insights."

"Could you give us an example of something that would come from an awakened mind?" Elizabeth quizzed again.

"Einstein's theory of relativity is a famous example of a person associating numerous known facts and using principle to create a new conclusion. An example of intelligent brain activity by a sleeping mind could be that of a professor who does a lot of research and writes a textbook in his field. Even with an unawakened mind he could still write a definitive book that could achieve critical acclaim, but there would be no breakthrough of thought as happened with Einstein."

"So how does one awaken the mind?" I asked.

"There is no easy method," said John, "it happens gradually over a period of many lifetimes. About the best you can do in any lifetime is to listen to the highest part that resides within yourself and follow its direction. If you do, you will be working on your next step, whatever it is supposed to be. Now I will give you a piece of advice that will only make sense to those who are in the process of awakening the full personality: Practice putting two and two together and see what you come up with. This statement will have meaning to those who are ready."

"So, do those with active minds have changes from life to life?" I asked.

"Yes, they do," said John. "The change is sure but not as fast as the emotions. Such a change may cause a person like Einstein to switch his attention from physics to world peace."

"So Einstein could be out there today somewhere promoting world peace?" asked Elizabeth.

"It is a possibility," said John, "but because he is a true thinker he would be doing much more than mindless protesting. He would be thinking of some type of plan that would have a logical chance of succeeding. The interesting thing is, true thinkers have a diffi-cult enough time in science - which is supposed to recognize logi-cal thought - but if you try to apply thought to politics, religion or philosophy you find yourself up against an almost insurmountable force of unthinking emotional programming. This is why even the Brotherhood has failed twice in our presentation of the teachings of the coming age. As I told you, your mission will be to apply a new twist by presenting the teachings as fiction. People are less resistant to fiction, but those who are ready will recognize the teach-ings are at least inspired and will develop a great desire to know more. These few who do want to advance in knowledge will not be disappointed, for there is much awaiting them."

"Yes, I believe you said there were thirty-six keys altogether and I haven't even gotten through one yet. I hope I live long enough to get through them all," I said, shaking my head.

"There is also much knowledge that is not in the form of keys. There is an infinite amount for us to know. When the time is right I will take you on a tour from the atomic worlds to the edge of the universe. Such a vision brings true humility and a sense of the reality of our eternal progression. Saying there is no end to our learning and progression, and having a sense of its reality are two different things."

"I'll hold you to that statement." I said. "I've always had a lot of questions and thoughts about inner and outer space. Now let me see if I understand you correctly on reincarnation. The an-swer to it is yes and no. It is no because when we are reborn our vehicles that influence us are altered and the person who we seem to be is altered. So from this point of view we are not reborn. The answer is yes because that which is reborn is the true decision-maker, the real part of ourselves which never dies. Is this why inspired teachers of the past seemed to teach conflicting views on the doctrine?"

"That's exactly correct," said John. "It was an important part of the strategy of the Brotherhood to stress the one life throughout western civilization. One of the problems with the teaching of multiple lives is that it makes average people lazy. They do not give the present life a wholehearted effort because they think they will do it in the next one. You will note this plan is one of our great successes. Look at the degree of progress of those nations which believe in one life versus those who believe in reincarnation. You can see that the one life idea has motivated the West to make something of what they have, at least on a physical level."

"So would it be counterproductive to teach reincarnation in my writings?" I asked.

"No," said John. "Western civilization has reached a point where the truth will not significantly distract their progress any more. People are evolving enough to handle the truth with at least a degree of common sense. Besides, those who are not ready will reject your writings. It will take about two hundred years for the idea of multiple lives to completely saturate the West. Actually, the Brotherhood calls the concept the *doctrine of endless lives.*"

"Endless lives!" said Elizabeth. "I've read quite a bit about reincarnation and it seems most believers think we will live several lives as a human and then have a last life. Then after that we go to some eternal rest or nirvana."

"Last life..." John smiled. "The funny thing is, most people who believe in reincarnation think they are on their last life. How deceived they are."

"So there is no last life?" I asked.

"Yes and no," said John.

"Oh, here we go again," I said. "It would seem that there is either a last life or there is not."

"OK grasshopper, I will enlighten you here," John said with a twinkle in his eye. "There is a series of approximately one thousand lifetimes that you live and progress as a human, and after you complete that circle you live a last life of relative perfection as was demonstrated by the Christ and Buddha."

"And what is relative perfection?" I asked

"Perfection in the eyes of one is sin in the eyes of another," said John. "For instance, the perfection of Christ was seen as evil by the Jews who had him crucified. Relative perfection is judged by those who are in touch with the inner Spirit of God."

"So is this last life really a last life, then?"

"Not really," smiled John. "It is, however, the last life you have previously decided to participate in. Each human entity is committed to reach relative perfection. After this perfect life is reached, you are free to choose life or death."

"To choose life or death... What does that mean and why would someone choose death?" I asked.

"When you have mastered all things in the human experience the only reason to reincarnate as a regular human soul is for the sake of service. You gain little progress for yourself, but as a master teacher you are able to be a big help to others. In the Brotherhood this is called *choosing death*."

"So what happens when you choose life?" Elizabeth asked.

"When life is chosen the entity advances to a sphere where the beings are more gods than humans and he begins again as a student, but even his progression there is predicated upon the amount of service he has rendered to the human kingdom. This provides incentive for the beings of endless lives to serve on little planets like this one from time to time.

"So are Jesus and Buddha serving here so they can advance in other spheres?"

"That, plus the joy of service itself, is part of their incentive. In truth nothing would get done in this universe if there were not some benefit for self in connection to the whole. By contrast, the incentive of the Dark Brothers is the self only, with no connection to the whole. Self alone is all that matters to them. Each one of them sees himself as an isolated universe, an island unto himself.

"Earlier you mentioned to me that you have suffered death many times, but you get reassembled or something like that. I take it that is different from reincarnation?" I asked.

"Reassembled..." John smiled. "That is an interesting way to word it. Yes, what happens to me is different from reincarnation. The Christ had need of an assistant from the human kingdom who would have a continuous memory from His first coming to His second. With regular rebirth the memory is lost and what is sometimes retrieved is often inaccurate. After I am killed and then rejuvenated I can accurately recall my past memory after a period of reflection. I am an historian of sorts for the Brotherhood and have perhaps the only accurate written history of the past two thousand years."

"So was this position a reward you received for being faithful to Jesus?" I asked.

John chuckled to himself for a moment. "Reward!" he exclaimed. "No. I am afraid not. It was more like a punishment."

"Punishment!" both Elizabeth and I whispered together.

John reflected a moment, "Punishment may not be the right word. You know the feeling a father sometimes has when he wants to teach his child a lesson just to quiet him?"

"Kind of."

"It was something like that," John said.

"So you're saying that Jesus has made you wander the earth for two thousand years just to teach you a lesson?" I asked incredulously.

"I have been of some service which I think has been helpful, but the greatest benefit has been the lesson I have learned," John replied.

"And what is that?" I asked.

John paused reflectively and said, "Remember the old adage which says *be careful what you ask for, because you just may receive it?*"

"Yes."

"I believe I may be the one who initiated it. Turn the Bible to Mark chapter ten and read verses 35-41."

I opened the Bible and read the following:

10:35 And James and John, the sons of Zebedee, came unto him, saying, Master, we would that thou shouldest do for us whatsoever we shall desire.

Mark 10:36 And he said unto them, What would ye that I should do for you?

10:37 They said unto him, Grant unto us that we may sit, one on thy right hand, and the other on thy left hand, in thy glory.

Mark 10:38 But Jesus said unto them, Ye know not what ye ask: can ye drink of the cup that I drink of? and be baptized with the baptism that I am baptized with?

Mark 10:39 And they said unto him, We can. And Jesus said unto them, Ye shall indeed drink of the cup that I drink of; and with the baptism that I am baptized withal shall ye be baptized:

Mark 10:40 But to sit on my right hand and on my left hand is not mine to give; but it shall be given to them for whom it is prepared.

Mark 10:41 And when the ten heard it, they began to be much displeased with James and John.

"I see your request irritated the other ten apostles," I mused.

"It did indeed," John said. "They never got over it. It was an ignorant request at the time. James and I thought we were a step above the other ten and that we deserved special attention. I do not blame the others for feeling irritated on learning about our thoughts."

"So, I take it because of your request you have had to roam the earth for two thousand years, but how about James? Is he doing the same thing?"

"Once, when Joshua visited us after the resurrection, He called James and I aside and reminded us of our request. He then pointed out to us the difficulties of the path He was on and that His crucifixion should be just a forewarning of what we were in for if we wanted to follow through with a chance to be on His right hand. He then gave us a second chance to back out of the deal. James was smart enough to *smell the coffee*, so to speak, and opt out for the normal rebirth process, but not me. I thought I was a being of such superior attributes that I could follow any path the Master would take. I insisted I would drink of the same cup that He had. Joshua sighed and said He would grant my request."

"So are you glad you did it?" I asked.

"Yes and no," he said again with a smile. "If I had known at the time what I was in for, I would not have had the courage to go forth, but now that the worst is over I would not trade the experience for anything. The worst part has been the isolation. I could not really say I am lonely because I am always in contact with the group mind of the Brotherhood, but for two thousand years I have not been fully a master and I have not been fully human. A full sense of belonging is missing. But on the other hand, I have learned a lesson in humility and service that few Masters, gods or humans have experienced."

"It seems as if you have also gained tremendous knowledge and power," Elizabeth offered.

"That is true, but the price has been great," he said. "I would not recommend my path for the timid."

"So are you going to wander the earth forever or is your time about done?" I asked.

"It shall be as it is written in the Bible," he said. "I am to tarry on the earth until the Christ comes again. As I told you earlier, the fact of His coming is a sure thing and has been decided. Exactly when He will come is contingent on several preparatory events happening first. The keys I am releasing is a part of the necessary preparation, so I certainly hope you will write a successful book so the Coming can be expedited and I can finally be released from my impulsive commitment."

"When you are released what will happen to you then?" I asked.

"Then," sighed John, "then, I can die a normal death, go to the Spirit world, have a normal rest, and finally have a normal birth and life and the freedom to prove my worth as a regular human being again."

"I've never looked at being a regular human in that light before," I said. "I guess I should appreciate it."

"Yes...yes," said John, "you should appreciate it. Even though your lot seems difficult at times, you should be grateful for your life."

After a pause I said, "I realize that your time is limited here, so before you go, I would like you explain the scripture in Hebrews that seems to refute the idea of reincarnation."

"You have a deal," John said stretching. "I am getting tired of this tea, however. Hot chocolate sounds nice if you have it."

"I believe that can be arranged," I said as I rose from my chair, looking forward to more answers.

CHAPTER EIGHT
KRISIS

Elizabeth and I usually didn't drink much hot chocolate, but since John wanted it I made some for us all.

John took a sip. "You know, sometimes there's nothing like a good cup of hot chocolate in the evening during a good conversation. Let's see. You wanted to talk about that verse in Hebrews. I believe it is found in chapter nine verse 27. Would you like to read it?"

I opened the Bible and read, *"And as it is appointed unto men once to die, but after this the judgment."*

"That sounds pretty cut and dried, doesn't it?" said John. "If it is appointed for us to die only once then we could be born only once."

"That's the way it would seem," I said. "But I've learned to not accept things the way they seem since I met you."

"That's a good first step," smiled John. "The problem with this scripture is that it is not translated correctly and I'll prove it to you by letting you translate it yourself."

"That would be a miracle," I said. "Wouldn't I have to be a Greek scholar?"

"Not at all," said John. "I believe you have a Strong's Concordance. Will you get it for us?"

I fetched the concordance and laid it on the table before us.

"Now, look up the word *judgment*," he said. "Then find the reference number for Hebrews 9:27

I looked up the word and ran my finger down the references until I came to Hebrews 9:27. "What is the code number for the Greek word?" he asked.

"It looks like it is number 2920," I said.

"Now look up number 2920 in the Greek dictionary."

I turned to the Greek dictionary and read, "It says here that the word *judgment* comes from the Greek word KRISIS."

"Then in italics there it gives the core meaning for the word. Read that," John directed.

"It says *decision!*" I said with some disbelief.

"Does this knowledge put a different slant on the scripture?" he asked.

"Yes, it does," I said. "For instance after death our personality, as it was, ceases to exist, but that which we truly are, which is decision, remains."

"That's a good possibility," said John, "but now let's shed some more light on the word. The Greek word you read was KRISIS. What English word does that remind you of?"

"Crisis, I suppose, with a *c* instead of a *k*," I said.

"Yes. The English word crisis owes it's origin to this Greek word and is actually a much better interpretation of the Greek than our Bible scholars have done with it. How do you suppose a crisis and decision are related? What do you think Elizabeth?"

"Well, let me think..." she responded. "The Cuban missile crisis, for instance, forced President Kennedy to make some tough decisions. I would say that a crisis forces us into a situation where we have to make a decision of some sort."

"Very good," said John. "And when a crisis forces us into a decision, what is the hopeful result of that decision?"

"The decision should lead us out of the crisis to a better situation."

"Exactly right," said John. "So do you think it would be accurate to say that a crisis is a situation that causes us to make decisions that will hopefully correct a bad circumstance?"

"Sounds good to me," she said.

"For instance," he continued, "your disease is a crisis which is forcing you to make tough decisions, is it not?"

"That's certainly true," she said.

"Thus we arrive at the true original meaning of the Greek word KRISIS, which is a decision that brings correction. Now the irony is that when the true meaning of this word is understood, this scripture becomes proof that the principle of many lives is true instead of being ammunition against it."

"This is terrific," I said. "This scripture has bothered me all my life and now in just a minute you have clarified it for us."

"Let me tell you what was in Paul's mind when he wrote this. He knew that the injunction of the Brotherhood was to stress the importance of making the best of the current life so he wrote, *It is appointed unto men once to die.* Then he thought a moment how this idea was correct in the sense of the personality, but incorrect from a higher point of view so he added the final line so he wouldn't be judged as deceptive by future enlightened generations. He essentially wrote this: *but after this comes the decision that brings correction.* Actually, it could have been translated, *but after this comes reincarnation,* for the word KRISIS is as close to meaning reincarnation as any Biblical Greek word except maybe the word resurrection itself. Now read on in the concordance and you will find a list of four ways KRISIS is translated in the King James Bible."

"Let's see. It looks like the four words are accusation, condemnation, damnation and judgment." I said.

"Look up the word *damnation,*" he said.

I looked it up and said, "It looks like this word is translated from several Greek words."

"Find the number 2920 again. That will mean that it is translated from KRISIS."

"Here's one in your gospel of John."

"Good. Turn to that and read it."

I turned to John chapter five and read verses 28-29. *Marvel not at this: for the hour is coming, in the which all that are in the graves shall hear his voice, And shall come forth; they that have done good, unto the resurrection of life; and they that have done evil, unto the resurrection of **damnation**.*"

"Of all the mistranslations of my writings, this was the worst," he sighed. "The word *damnation* was deliberately thrown in to keep subjects afraid of going to Hell."

"So, what are the two resurrections?" I asked.

"The resurrection of life is interpreted on two levels," he said. "The first level was intended to place the goal before humanity of the final conquest of physical death, as has been demonstrated by Christ. Each of us will experience this when we have lived our life of relative perfection, our last required life. At this point we move on to eternal lives. Then, on another level, since this final life is so far away for most of us, I wanted to give more immediate hope with the idea that if we live a good life it will be much better for us in our next life, however people would interpret that. In the latter part of the scripture I was telling readers that if they do evil, they would be placed in situations where they would be forced to right the wrongs they have committed. That is the opposite of damnation. It is a situation that brings progression."

"Very interesting," I said. "You know what you ought to do is translate the Bible correctly into English so we could finally have a correct version."

"Many people would still get it wrong," he said. "From a higher point of view our system of word communication is primitive. Our communication can only be accurate and reliable when we are in harmony with the universal Spirit of God. When two or more people feel the Spirit together, as we felt in the New Jerusalem, the two then understand as one. This shall be one of the most important messages you will teach."

"When I begin this mission, as you call it, and start teaching do you think anyone will listen to me? It would seem that success would be much easier if you used someone like Billy Graham."

"Billy Graham is one of the few ministers who has sincere intent, but neither he or any of the other famous teachers is prepared to teach what is to come without altering it to fit their preconceived notions. After your book gets circulated people will begin to listen to what you say. Do you remember reading that Joshua told us He would be with us unto the end of the world?"

"I think so."

"Because of the oneness principle He has been with me the past two thousand years; and now through the power of the Spirit my presence will be with you, which also brings the Presence of Christ. As long as you tune into this Presence you will be able to speak the words of Christ, and when you do people will feel it in their hearts."

"Sounds better than selling real estate," I smiled.

John laughed softly and said, "One minute of communicating the words of Christ is worth a lifetime of preparation and struggle; the best part is this communion is available to all. The true principle of communion has been virtually lost because of the illusionary veil cast by the Dark Brothers."

"I have a question about the Book of Hebrews," said Elizabeth. "I read somewhere that scholars are not sure who wrote it. They say it got in the Bible because it just seemed inspired and some thought that Paul wrote it. Are you saying that Paul wrote it after all?"

"Yes and no," John smiled again as if he had one up on us.

"Now how in the world can this answer be yes and no?" she asked.

"Somewhere around the turn of the first century a disciple

who had a keen interest in Paul collected and made copies of everything he could find that Paul had written or said. He found there were about a half dozen fragments that would not make sense as books of scripture on their own, so he studied them carefully and compiled a coherent book around these writings. He compiled them into one book with some words of his own added for clarification, while staying as close as possible to Paul's original meanings. It was accepted as scripture by the early church because the authorities at that time knew they were teachings originated by Paul. But believe me, if Paul had compiled the book himself he would have put his name on it. He had a powerful ego. On the other hand, the humble disciple who did compile it was not sure if he did a good enough job for it to be worthy of Paul's name, and he did not feel it right to put his own name on it. Little did he realize how good of a job he did."

"Is there any question you cannot answer?" Elizabeth asked.

"You can answer any question I can when you learn to tune in or commune," he said. "When you do this, you can learn the answer to almost anything."

"Now, getting back to the subject," John continued, "the scripture in Hebrews is the only one that seems to make a case against reincarnation, whereas there are many scriptures that make a very strong case for it. Joshua did not teach it openly to the masses; nevertheless, many of them thought that He must be an ancient prophet born again, as evidenced in Matthew 16 verses 13 & 14."

I opened the Bible and read:

"Matt 16:13 When Jesus came into the coasts of Caesarea Philippi, he asked his disciples, saying, Whom do men say that I the Son of man am?

16:14 And they said, Some say that thou art John the Baptist: some, Elias; and others, Jeremias, or one of the prophets."

"Some thought Joshua may be one who was possessed of the spirit of John the Baptist. The name Elias is the Greek equivalent of the Hebrew *Elijah*. There were many who were thinking He was Elijah the prophet, Jeremiah, or some other Old Testament prophet returned again through reincarnation

John continued, "Whenever a significant teacher appeared in those days, those who followed the scriptures always considered that He might be Elijah. Just as in this day - where many are awaiting the Second Coming of Jesus - even so, in those days, they were awaiting the Second Coming of Elijah. Now read the last two verses of the Old Testament."

216THE IMMORTAL

I read Malachi 4:5-6. *"Behold, I will send you Elijah the prophet before the coming of the great and dreadful day of the Lord:*

And he shall turn the heart of the fathers to the children, and the heart of the children to their fathers, lest I come and smite the earth with a curse."

"Can you see why the believers at that time expected the return of Elijah in one form or another?" John asked.

"Yes. It says point blank that Elijah will return."

"Now read from Matthew 17 verses 10-13."

I read the following:

"Matt 17:10 And his disciples asked him, saying, Why then say the scribes that Elias must first come?

Matt 17:11 And Jesus answered and said unto them, Elias truly shall first come, and restore all things.

Matt 17:12 But I say unto you, That Elias is come already, and they knew him not, but have done unto him whatsoever they listed. Likewise shall also the Son of man suffer of them.

Matt 17:13 Then the disciples understood that he spake unto them of John the Baptist."

"Notice in verse ten that the scribes were teaching Elijah must come before the Messiah was to appear. They taught the doctrine because of that verse in Malachi we just read. Then Joshua acknowledged this was true and told us that Elijah will come before the great and dreadful day thousands of years in the future, but he had already come to prepare the way for the Messiah in that age. Then He told us point blank that John the Baptist fulfilled the prophecy of the coming of Elijah in that age - that John was Elijah born again."

"But didn't John the Baptist deny he was Elijah when he was once asked about it?" Elizabeth asked.

"Yes," said John. "The scripture records this correctly and John the Baptist did say he was not Elijah. He denied this for two reasons. The first is he suspected he was the return of Elijah, but he had no actual memory or proof. Even if he wanted to admit to it, he was not sure enough of the fact to state it. Second, if he had admitted he was Elijah, it would have put his life in even more danger than it already was, and he felt he may jeopardize his mission."

"That makes sense," I said. "But since Jesus actually said he was Elijah you would think the believers in this day would accept that as the final word."

"You would think so," John agreed.

"I have kind of a silly question," said Elizabeth. "Are we ever born again as animals, spiders or anything like that?"

John smiled knowingly again. "I know you're getting tired of this, but the answer is..."

"I suppose it's yes and no," I injected. "I've got to hear this one."

"The answer is no," he said, "when we consider the person as a whole. The human entity, which is you, always moves forward. Except in rare cases of the Dark Brothers, humans are always moving forward to a better, more refined human body with expanded light and consciousness.

"The answer is yes in the fact that within the universe of your being, every kind of living entity is represented. Some of this is obvious. The mineral kingdom, which does have a consciousness of its own, is represented in you by your teeth and skeletal structure. Your hair and fingernails are highly evolved parts of the vegetable kingdom. Then some believe that humans are merely highly evolved animals. A human as a unit is much more than an animal, but we do have animals in our nature. For instance, I think all of us at one time or another, when angered, have felt like a roaring lion out of control."

"I can identify with that," I said, "but where is the roaring lion? You've told us where the mineral and vegetable is, but I don't see where the animal is unless it's the body as a whole."

"They are represented by parts of the body not normally seen," he said. "Have you heard of the seven chakras, or energy centers?"

"Yes," I said. "I've read about them in various yoga and other books."

"And I also assume you have read about acupuncture points?"
"Yes."

"There are hundreds of smaller energy centers that compose these points. The five lower chakras and hundreds of the smaller energy points are actually little lives that were once animals and other little lives eons ago. These lives do not become human, but combine to create something greater than themselves. This is the true order of evolution. The subatomic particles unite to create atoms, atoms unite to create molecules, molecules unite to create cells, cells unite to create the vegetable kingdom, the essence of vegetable life unites to create animal, and animals and all the smaller lives unite in consciousness to create human.

Thus, you are a universe composed of millions of smaller lives including the animal. Because we are closest to the animals it is easiest to sense the animal within us.

"For instance, we speak of animal magnetism in relation to sexual attraction. When we get very angry or fearful in a danger-ous situation, our animal instincts may take over, without mental intervention. Many people are closer to their pets - are more in tune with them - than with their family or friends. My point is, if you pay attention you can sense the various animals within you. These lives, many many years ago, reached the highest point they could as animals and to go higher they had to become part of some-thing greater than themselves. The lion in you is still an animal, but shares your consciousness so he becomes more than a lion. You are like a god to him and give him commandments that he must obey so you can harness his life energy for good."

"That is a fantastic teaching," I said. "I've read a lot of books but have never read anything like that anywhere."

"That is one of the differences between a true and false teacher," said John. "The false teacher will rehash old material borrowed from others. He may change the vocabulary a little and claim he has something new, but in the end all he wants to pro-mote is his ego. The true spiritual teacher will seek to *make all things new*, as the scripture I wrote proclaims. Such a person will throw new light on old teachings and bring forth some new ones. You are right; the mystery behind our evolution has not yet been written, but this shall be the beginning of the great revelation. There is so much in store for the human race here, especially concern-ing future evolution, that it is mind-boggling, even to me."

"You mentioned that the lower five centers are animal enti-ties. What, then, are the highest two?" asked Elizabeth.

"Very insightful question," said John. "The sixth center - which is in the center of the forehead between the eyes - is sometimes called the third eye or the ajna center. It is only opened in those who have awakened the sleeping mind and is occupied by that being who has been traditionally called the *Guardian angel*. This is one or more fairly advanced beings from another plane of exist-ence who works to help you because you, in turn, supply him with power to advance to his next step. For those who have not yet awakened the mind but are pure in heart, these angels will some-times descend to the heart and throat centers when they sense they can be of assistance. They will do everything in their power to help you advance to the full use of this high ajna center. For them, residing there in full awareness is like worshipping God before His throne.

"How about the seventh center then?" I asked. "Who or what resides there?"

"The seventh center is often called the *thousand-pedaled lotus at the top of the head.* Each petal represents the imprint, energy and quality of one of your thousand lifetimes as a human, and this center does not function to a high degree until most of the petals are open. One who is called a Master works through this center after the entity has proven himself to be a useful servant. This Master is one who has finished his thousand lifetimes and is linked to a number of students whom he is helping. This is such a highly evolved entity that the average person would feel he met God if he met his Master."

"So, I take it your Master is Christ?" I asked.

"Yes. I receive from Him through my head center and you in turn are learning to receive from me through your head center."

"Are you a Master then?" I asked.

"Not yet," he replied. "But I am a disciple who is capable of being a transmitter for the Master to other disciples. As you and I become one with Christ, we also become one with each other."

"And how many Masters are there?" Elizabeth asked.

"There are just a handful on this little planet. I will give you more details on their numbers at a later time. My time left here tonight is limited. If you have any other important questions, now is the time to ask."

"I have something important to me," said Elizabeth.

"Go ahead."

"It sounds like I did a lot of damage and caused others a lot of pain in the Middle Ages and may have a lot of debt to pay off. It looks to me like I would have to suffer with MS or some other disease for several lifetimes to redeem myself here. Is there some other way besides extended suffering to pay the debt? Wasn't that what the sacrifice of Jesus was supposed to be about?"

"The mission of Joshua was not to take our responsibilities from us, but to remove the greatest hindrance in the way of paying off our debt to the whole. That hindrance is guilt. Guilt is a very negative force that creates tremendous harm in our personal lives and makes us feel unworthy to make any effort to make things right with our souls or our brothers. But as far as our debt goes, Joshua himself is quoted in the Bible as saying we will have to pay the *uttermost farthing.*"

"That doesn't sound very encouraging," I said.

"That was the bad news, but I also have good news for you," he said.

"Great. Let's hear the good news," said Elizabeth.

"There are other ways to pay a debt than extended suffering. Humankind's illusionary sense of guilt does everything possible to convince us that we can only pay off the debt that all of us internally sense, by a long and drawn out period of suffering. Joshua came to show us another way to pay what we owe.

John continued. "Perhaps an analogy will help. Let us suppose you were working for a wage of $5.00 an hour and ran up a bill of $1000. Under these circumstances you would have to work 200 hours to pay off the debt. But then let us imagine that by your ingenuity you discovered a method of making $20.00 an hour. How long would it take you to pay the debt then?"

"It would only take one quarter of the time or 50 hours," I said.

"Now let us suppose your boss gave you $1000 bonus because he thought you deserved it," he said. "Now how long would it take you to pay the debt?"

"It could be paid instantly," I said.

"Guilt makes the average person feel internally that the only way to pay off a debt is at the original rate of $5.00 an hour, but when Joshua came the first time, he did his best to show us our debts can be paid at an accelerated rate. One of the reasons all of the apostles except Judas were willing to serve to the death was that Joshua showed us the debts we had accumulated from past lives. After this revelation was given to us we were horrified and downcast at the amount of suffering it would take to balance our accounts. He then showed us the importance of our missions and that, if we successfully completed our jobs and took advantage of the great opportunity offered us, we could pay off the debt of many lifetimes by helping many people in one lifetime."

"So if Hitler decided to repent, so to speak, and pay the debt for killing six million Jews, he wouldn't have to die six million times. He could possibly come back and by some great work save the lives of six million people," I ventured.

"You are thinking in the right direction," John said. "Keep in mind here the payment must be in equal value to the debt, but not necessarily in equal kind. For instance, I may be able to pay off the $1000 debt in something besides money, but still an equivalent value. Perhaps I could give $1000 worth of labor, diamonds, food or some other commodity. Even so, if Hitler came back and discovered a cure for cancer or something similar, that may do the trick."

"So it's possible that Louis Pasture injured many people in a past life and his vaccine helped to redeem himself," Elizabeth added.

"Quite possible," said John. "Often those with a great debt who have turned to the light are driven to accomplish a great mission for a reason unknown to their conscious mind."

"I have always felt like I was supposed to do a significant service for humanity. Does this mean that I also have a large debt?" I asked with some nervousness.

"You still have some debt to pay," he said. "But your account is nothing like it was a couple thousand years ago. You have literally given your life numerous times for the cause of truth and thus you have had an enormous debt lifted from you. This is because your sacrifices have benefited many people over the years."

"It sounds like I was one bad dude many years ago," I quipped.

"Yes, in a galaxy far away," John smiled. I wasn't sure if his quote from Star Wars was humor or something more literal.

"So, what can I do to pay off my debt more quickly?" asked Elizabeth.

"If your soul sees you will truly use the opportunity in service, you can be released from this illness and go on to a more joyful work where you can pay off your debt more quickly."

"I'll be willing to do anything," she said. "Just tell me."

"Keep this in mind. If Joseph is successful at promoting these teachings it will help an untold number of people and will be more than enough to pay the debt for both of you. Then your illness will no longer be necessary. Joseph has been a little slack in starting the book. The first thing you can do is to keep him encouraged and motivated. I also want you to read through all of his writings and edit them. Also give him suggestions for improvement and clarification."

"I would be happy to do that except it's getting to the point where I have a hard time reading and my hands shake too bad to write legibly," Elizabeth said, looking down at her hands.

"You won't have these problems when you are helping on the book," he said. "When you are doing this your eyes will be perfect and your hands will not shake."

Elizabeth's countenance brightened. "In that case, I will encourage Joseph in a way that he has never been encouraged. So, are you ready to begin writing?" she asked, glaring in my direction.

"I've been doing a lot of thinking about the book and making notes on the computer, and I am just about ready to begin," I replied.

"He will begin tomorrow," said Elizabeth. "Won't you, dear?" She looked at me with a determination that I had not seen in her before.

"I'll see what I can do," I said.

She repeated, "You'll start tomorrow, won't you, dear?"

"OK. I'll start tomorrow," I said with a smile. There was no backing out now that Elizabeth was directly involved.

"All right. I have your word, and you gave it in front of the Apostle John and apparently within the hearing of Jesus himself. You'd better get something in writing tomorrow or you're going to be in big trouble," she said with mock anger in her voice.

I laughed. "Actually, I'm more afraid of you than I am Jesus. I can see that I had better get going here."

"I can see this young lady is going to be useful to us," John smiled.

"You don't know the half of it," I said. "Just wait until she gets well."

"John, there's something else I want to know," Elizabeth added. "Earlier you indicated to me that a cause of my disease was certain denials I have. Now you tell me that I owe debts from the past. What is the main cause here?"

"A disease or situation can have many ingredients that create it. It takes more than sugar to make a cookie. Your debt and your denials are interlinked. The debt must be paid and the denials faced. Working on improving your diet would not hurt either," he said.

"I feel strongly I need to know more about my life where I created this debt you talked about. Can you do something to help me remember?"

John looked at her with concern. "My dear, remember how I once asked Joshua to be on His right hand, but did not realize what I was chewing off? Your request might be like this - you might see more than you are ready to assimilate."

"I've got to know the truth about this even if it kills me," she said firmly. "I feel I must know."

"I'm not sure about this," John said. He rose up and placed

his right hand on her head and closed his eyes in silence for a moment. Then he sat back down. "The Christ has just probed your past, your current life force and communed with the highest part of you. He has told me to go ahead and bring forth the memory, but I warn you it will be startling; and Joseph, prepare your mind and heart. This will be difficult for her, but the end will be good."

I thought a moment and said, "If I trust you with my wife it means I trust you with everything."

"And I will trust my Master," said John.

"Hasn't He always pulled through for you in the past?" I asked.

"Yes," he said, "but not without putting me through some nerve-wracking experiences first."

"Let's get on with this before I lose my nerve and change my mind," Elizabeth urged.

With that John laid his hand on her forehead and whispered some phrases in a language I have never heard before; and then there was a period of dead silence. It probably lasted about 90 seconds, but it seemed like an hour.

Finally, Elizabeth broke the silence in dramatic fashion. She shoved herself away from John shouting at the top of her lungs "NO! NO! NO! NO! John...John, why didn't you tell me... Why didn't you tell me?"

"What is it sweetheart? What is it?" I asked, alarmed.

"I tortured and killed him. I killed him!" Elizabeth buried her face in her hands and cried profusely.

"Killed who?" I asked, looking at both of them several times. "Please tell me! Who was it?"

Elizabeth caught her breath and looked at John with a mixture of love, guilt and pity.

"I killed John. John the Beloved! He was a Knight of the Temple and I tortured and killed him for the Pope! How could I have been so deceived?" She cried for about five minutes while I knelt beside her with my arms around her.

CHAPTER NINE
Catharsis

After a few moments of gathering our wits, I looked at John and asked. "Is this true? Is it possible this harmless lady could have done something like this?"

John looked at me solemnly. "It is all true and more, my friend. Now ask her what she did to you."

As I looked in her direction Elizabeth pleaded, "These are terrible memories. Please make them go away."

"Now that you have retrieved them through your own request they have to be dealt with," John replied softly. "Tell Joseph what you remember about him. I know this is difficult, but you must face it."

Elizabeth put her head in her hands for a moment, took a deep breath, bravely lifted herself up and said to me. "I feel we have known each other for numerous lifetimes... Some time after I tortured John, you were brought to me and I had to obtain a confession of guilt from you or you would have to forfeit your life. They were hesitant, however, to have you die because the authorities believed you had knowledge of certain relics and writings from the time of Jesus and they wanted you to reveal what you knew before you were killed.

Elizabeth looked at John and then back at me with more sadness and pain than I have ever seen in her eyes.

"You proved to be an unwilling subject. Even after I had beaten your back, arms and legs, and crippled you for life, you told us nothing. Then came a time you and I were alone in the torture chamber. I felt sorry for you and did not relish the idea of hurting you further after you had already suffered so much. I also came to believe that if you had withstood us so far, death would be welcome and that the possibility of getting information from you was low. As I was contemplating these things you unexpectedly spoke to me."

(Joseph, speaking in past life, as recalled by Elizabeth) *"You are deceived, my friend. You think you are doing God's will, but you are doing the will of the Dark Ones. Did the real Jesus and the apostles bring pain and suffering or did they relieve pain and suffering? Did they force their will on others or did they offer all a choice to believe? You do not belong in this chamber of horrors. I see a spark of light in you that tells me you can see beyond this."*

(Elizabeth, quoting herself from the past) *"The Pope speaks the will of God and sometimes that will is difficult. Jesus had to go to the cross and Abraham had to sacrifice his son."*

(Joseph) *"But Jesus and Abraham did not receive such a commandment from any outward person, but from within themselves. And you forget that after Abraham passed his test he was told not to kill his son. A way of deliverance was revealed. Even so there is a way of deliverance prepared for you should you decide to accept it."*

(Elizabeth) *"I would say that you are the one who needs deliverance. All you have to do is tell us what you know if you want to live."*

(Joseph) *"And if I tell you what you want, can you swear in the name of Christ that my life will be spared?"*

(Elizabeth) *"It's your only chance for life."*

(Joseph) *"It's not a chance. If I revealed what I know there is no way I would be allowed to live. They haven't told you what they are looking for, have they?"*

(Elizabeth) *"I do not need to know. My superiors tell me you know what you are to tell us and that they will recognize the truth when you reveal it."*

(Joseph) *"There are certain responsibilities and knowledge I have that are even hidden from the Grand Master and I will reveal them to you if you will do something for me."*

(Elizabeth) *"What is that?"*

(Joseph) *"Find me the body of John who you just killed. Bring it here for me to see for myself and I will tell you all I know."*

(Elizabeth) *"Give me your word on that as a Christian and it shall be done."*

(Joseph) *"You have my word."*

(Elizabeth) *"I will have the body removed from the tomb and brought forth."*

Elizabeth continued. *"I then personally accompanied sev-*

eral soldiers and watched as the seal was broken and the tomb was opened. I was beside myself with terror when I saw it was empty. As I accused those in charge of slothfulness - that perhaps the Knights stole the body the situation of the empty tomb of Christ flashed before my mind. I tried to ignore the thought as I told the men it would probably be best if we did not mention the empty tomb to anyone. We would probably just be held in suspect by our own authorities. After this I hurried back to your chamber and visited with you alone."

(Joseph) *"I do not see the body of John."*

(Elizabeth) *"Someone stole it."*

(Joseph) *"But something in you knows that is not true, doesn't it? That tomb had an unbroken seal on it and witnesses saw the body placed in the tomb. Tell me, if you had lived in the time of Jesus would an empty tomb be evidence that you would just lightly cast aside?"*

(Elizabeth) *"Of course not! This is different. The knights are trying to trick us."*

(Joseph) *"But something in you knows that is not true."*

(Elizabeth) *"Then what is true?"*

(Joseph) *"The truth is that the one you seemed to kill was John the Apostle who was to live until the Second Coming of the Lord. His tomb was empty because the Christ has brought him back to life."*

(Elizabeth) *"That is blasphemy! If he has indeed come back to life let him show himself."*

(Joseph) *"He can't just yet. His memory has not yet fully returned."*

(Elizabeth) *"You speak in riddles to save your life."*

(Joseph) *"I do not seek to save my life in this broken condition, but I do seek to save yours. You must look within for your authority, not without. You have seen the empty tomb. Many others would believe if they saw such evidence. Ask the God you worship in prayer if what I tell you is true!"*

At this point John interrupted the story, stepped forward, and spoke to Elizabeth. "At that time you tried to ignore his advice, but that night something in you caused you to utter a silent prayer to show you the truth. At that moment you experienced the baptism of fire and you felt a spiritual witness that you could not deny. The next day you helped Joseph escape and in the next couple of months you nursed him back to health amidst great danger and peril. Joseph recovered enough so he could hobble along with a crutch, but for the rest of his life he was very dependent on you, just as you are now dependent on him in this life. You, on the other hand, became his disciple and he taught you many mysteries he had received from his association with me and his study of secret manuscripts."

"What horrible things I did in that life!" exclaimed Elizabeth. "I am suffering in this life as I made Joseph suffer in that awful past. I do not deserve to be healed." Elizabeth looked as if she was going to cry again.

"On the other hand," said John, "Joseph suffered in that past life to pay off an ancient debt that was greater than what you are working on now. And even my last two thousand years of service go to pay off crimes toward humanity that I do not like to remember to this day. You should rejoice that you and Joseph have a work to do together that will enable you to pay off your karma to the point where you can be permanently healed."

"But after regaining that memory I almost feel like I should die in pain and suffering as I made others do," Elizabeth exclaimed. "It seems strange now, but that's the way I feel."

"But now you have a choice," said John. "You can pay off your debt slowly by undergoing pain and suffering - which only benefits you - or you can assist in bringing light and love to many which will help others as well as lift your debt quickly. Which choice makes the most sense?"

"Bringing others light and love sounds the best, but I don't feel worthy of it," she said softly.

"You bring up an interesting point," said John. "How often the way of pain and guilt is chosen over the path of joy. From a higher point of view this choice is completely insane, but our feelings drive us on to strange paths. You must follow the common sense of your mind and choose the path of joy and peace. Joseph will encourage you, won't you Joseph?"

"I'll do everything in my power," I nodded. "But it seems that most people think the highest we can do is to follow our hearts. I find it interesting here that you tell Elizabeth to follow her mind."

John paused a moment and put his hand over his heart. "We should pay attention to our hearts, but not necessarily follow the feelings thereof. If heart is not tempered and guided by mind, then all types of complications arise in life. For instance, a good part of Elizabeth's pain and disease is caused by her following her feeling nature, which tells her she does not deserve joy and peace, but must suffer guilt, pain and disease. It takes the clear cold light of mind to guide us out of the hot flames of emotional entanglement."

"That makes sense when you think of it," I said.

"That's right - when you think of it," said John. "The Dark Brothers do everything in their power to get you to not think, to believe that the feelings and heart are higher than the mind. Once convinced of this idea, people can be controlled by them." He then looked at me intently and said, "Do you forgive Elizabeth for torturing you in that past life?"

"Of course I do," I replied. "There is really nothing to forgive because I don't even remember it."

"It would help," said John, "if you look at her now and just tell her you forgive her."

It felt kind of strange since I didn't have a memory of what I was supposed to be forgiving, but I looked at her and said, "I forgive you."

It had a powerful effect. She put her arms around me and cried. "Oh, my sweet husband, I am so sorry... I'm so sorry. I do not ever want to hurt you again."

Next she looked at John. "Do you forgive me John? I brought you so much pain and now the pain I feel must be as great as what I made you feel. Is it possible that you could forgive me?"

"The pain is not in my conscious thought," said John. "As Joseph said, there is nothing to forgive. The person who must forgive in this life is you. You must forgive yourself."

"Knowing what I now know, that is the hardest thing of all," she said.

"You must have faith in my words, for they are also the words of Christ," said John. He knelt down in front of her and said, "Look at me."

She brushed away her tears and looked into John's eyes as he said to her, "I forgive you, and all I ask in return is that you forgive yourself. Say it. Say *I forgive myself*."

She looked down and said, "I can't."

"Say it!" John said with a startling command.

Elizabeth looked up at John and gathered her strength and said softly, "I forgive myself."

"Say it again louder!"

"I forgive myself."

"Again louder!"

She said it again louder.

"Now shout it out and don't hold back."

"I forgive myself!" shouted Elizabeth in a voice that even made me step back.

That seemed to do something. She seemed so overcome with relief that she trembled for a moment. Then she looked up at John with tears streaming down her face. "I feel so overcome with joy I want to hug you!" she exclaimed.

John stood up, reached forth his hand, backed away and said, "I would welcome that. Come to me and give me a hug."

"I can't!" she said.

"You can," he said. "Stand up and walk toward me."

"I will fall!" she protested.

"You will not fall. Stand and walk toward me now!"

She seemed to take courage and stood up very shaky at first, but seemed to gather strength, then walked toward John. As she walked toward him, he continued to back up. "Surely you can walk forward as fast as I can go backwards," he said smiling.

After he said that Elizabeth seemed to be more stable and rushed toward John and fell into his arms. "Oh John, John am I really forgiven?" she cried.

He stood back again and said, "If you can stand on your own you are forgiven."

Again she seemed a little unsure of herself, but then gathered strength and walked back and forth across the room. She then grabbed hold of both John and I with both of her arms and hugged us both very tightly. "I love you guys more than I can express. I feel nothing but love at this moment. I want to experience this forever!"

John and I both hugged her back in a sort of group hug that lasted through several minutes of bliss for all of us.

CHAPTER TEN
Revelations

After a few moments of intense sharing that is difficult to describe in written word, John asked, "Elizabeth, would you like to finish the rest of our conversation sitting in a regular chair?"

"I would love that," she smiled, "but first there is nothing more I would like to do than to do something of some small service to you. Can I get you some more tea, chocolate or something else?"

"Actually, I'm starting to feel a little hungry," said John. "Some bacon and eggs with coffee sure sounds good."

"You got it!" she said. "I'll make bacon and eggs for all of us." She got up and gingerly went to the kitchen and went to work.

I was left wondering as to whether John was really hungry or if he just conjured up a good excuse to put Elizabeth into action with her newly-found strength. In the middle of this thought I smelled the sizzling of bacon and began getting very hungry and decided that the answer may be both. It wasn't long before we were sitting at the table eating one of the most satisfying meals I have ever had. After a little small talk I realized that our time with John was limited and pressed on with the questions.

"Elizabeth seems to be back to normal," I observed. "Is she healed or is this a temporary thing again?"

"There is usually more than one cause behind every major illness," said John. "What we have done with Elizabeth is discover the root cause of the debt she is paying off in this life and we have offered her an alternative choice of payment of that debt. If she makes a definite decision and feels comfortable taking this alternate path, her disease may be permanently lifted."

By this time I had learned to listen carefully to John's exact words so I asked, "I notice you use the word *may*. Does this mean she also may not be healed?"

"Good question," said John. "As you know there is another major factor involved here besides her debt, or karma, as it is called. This debt she had could have manifested as some other disease besides MS or she could have had a very disabling accident. The question left for her to deal with is why this debt manifested in her as MS. Why not something else? Or better still, why did she have to have any disease? Why not pay off the debt through the alternative of joyful service to mankind? After all, this type of repayment is much more beneficial to everyone involved than pain and suffering brought upon yourself."

"Apparently, " I mused, "the reason she has MS has something to do with guilt and the denial of guilt. Isn't that the reason she has to listen to those tapes - to bring the guilt to the surface?"

"Exactly," said John. "Because of this particular past life in the Middle Ages, where she also had an awakening to her soul, she has had a difficult time feeling worthy to enjoy life. She and millions of others feel an inward need to be punished and their own decisions, not an angry God, carries out the sentence."

"So what can we do to help Elizabeth eliminate the guilt once and for all?" I asked.

John looked at Elizabeth and said to her, "Conscious realization is the key, my dear. You must bring all possible guilt to the surface and destroy it with the conscious realization that you are paying off the debt another way, through joyful service. You must realize that this is a better way, that God, angels, men and women universally would rather have you serve and contribute than suffer. You must realize that guilt is caused by illusion and is the most powerful of tools in the hands of the Dark Ones."

"It's going to be difficult to deal with the memory you revived in me without feeling some guilt," Elizabeth replied. "It's also difficult to listen to those tapes without feeling guilt. I think Reverend Bill somehow brought a feeling of unworthiness to the surface that is connected with my past life mistakes."

"That may be true, but you must remember the old adage that *energy follows thought.* If you put your attention on the negative, guilt will surface again as well as your disease. The key is not to deny your feelings, but face them and then shift your attention to the positive. By doing this, your healing can be a permanent thing and you will be much more useful in the work you and Joseph have to do. But I must warn you. Remember the words of the Master after his healings: He said *Sin no more, lest a worse thing come upon you.* You must be careful to follow the highest possible good that comes from within yourself. If you reject it, suppress it, or deny it you will place yourself in grave danger."

"If anyone can live up to their highest good, it is Elizabeth," I said smiling.

"It is good you have confidence in her, but it is also important you both be eternally vigilant and hold your focus steady in the light. If either of you notice the other getting off track or sense a *disturbance in the force,* so to speak, you must gently and lovingly guide the other back on track. Now my time here is nearing an end. If you have any questions remaining you need to ask them now."

I felt a little uncomfortable with this thought, but because of time limitations I decided to change the subject and ask several remaining questions. "Apparently, Elizabeth was a man in that past life," I said. "Do we switch back and forth between the sexes?"

"Our incarnations are divided into three sections," he said. "The first are the *trial and error lives*, the second are the *learning lives* and the third are the *teaching lives*. The period we call your *trial and error lives* is a time you learn the basic lessons of living and you fluctuate cyclically between the sexes. Therefore, one must beware of how he treats his opposite, for he will receive the same treatment in return in a future life. Then, during your true *learning lives*, where you are a developing disciple, you will be assigned to the sex that will be most beneficial to your advancement and area of service. Finally, in the third period of progression called your *teaching or sending lives*, you will choose the sex, race and situation into which you will be born. If you think that the area of greatest opportunity is in being male, female, white, black or red, then you can choose your area of battle in your latter lives. Before that time, you are assigned your place of greatest learning by a higher intelligence."

"So what you are saying here is that the highly evolved souls and teachers of the race get to choose their situation?" I asked.

"That is correct," John answered.

"I must not be one of them," I said. "I think I would have chosen to be born rich."

"Don't be so sure," said John. "The teachers are often harder on themselves than God himself. Most of them are hesitant to be born rich out of concern about self-corruption. Many of them will place themselves in a situation where a great struggle of some kind will sharpen their edge. The important thing for most of them is an ultimate atmosphere of freedom. Before the Civil War here in America, few of the teachers were brave enough to incarnate as a slave, not because he was black, but because of the lack of opportunity. Now we live in an age where the blacks have a greatly increased opportunity as free men and women, and thus we have a much larger number of teachers incarnating into that race. There is a particularly great opportunity for the teachers of the black race and other minorities at the current moment. Of course, the Dark Brothers always have their counterparts planted in place and will seek to introduce slavery again, but on a different level."

"What do you mean by another level?" I asked

"Have you heard the statement *we make our own reality?*"

"Yes. I believe Jane Roberts coined that phrase," I answered.

"It is a statement worth contemplating," he said. "If we truly did just live through one incarnation, we could be justified in saying that life is not fair, that we are victims of circumstances or the random placement of God or chance in which we find ourselves; that reality makes us rather than us making reality. But that is not the way things are. In truth, your essence is Decision, and as Decision you have created the reality you find yourself in, whether good or bad. Slavery and victimization are always caused by the illusion that we have little or no control over the reality we see before us. If we believe we have no control, we acquiesce our real power, become subject to the decisions of others, and become like a leaf floating helplessly down a current of other people's decisions."

"So you are saying we become a slave when we allow our lives to be controlled by the decisions of others rather than our own?" Elizabeth asked.

"Basically," said John. "By allowing your life to be controlled by the decisions of others, you are put in the position of abdicating yourself from personal responsibility and placing all blame on the decision-makers in your life. Instead, you should be the main decision-maker in your own life, which then makes you responsible for your reality in the long run. All those who are in the third category of evolution and are the teachers of the race have the realization they are the masters of their reality. In fact, after one has lived through the required course of approximately 1000 lifetimes, he advances to a fourth category and becomes a master of reality as we understand the term; such high entities are often called Masters. Some even call them Gods."

"So I assume then that Jesus is a Master?" I asked.

"Yes, but He is not alone. There are a small group of others on this planet who have become Masters of Reality who work with Him."

"So did Jesus, or Joshua as you call him, live 1000 lives?"

"At least that many," said John. "I indicated this in my Book of Revelation chapter 19 verse 12. I stated that on the head of Christ were many crowns. Tell me: how do you suppose Christ received many crowns when he is only recorded as living to the age of 33?"

"Could the many crowns have something to do with many lifetimes?" I asked.

"Correct," he said. "Each crown here represents a life where a great victory was achieved. Now I want you to read the next quote from the Bible with your own eyes. Turn to the very last verse in my Gospel of John."

I turned to the last chapter in the book of John and read the last verse, *"And there are also many other things which Jesus did, the which, if they should be written every one, I suppose that even the world itself could not contain the books that should be written."*

John smiled as he asked, "How do you think Jesus did so many works that an unlimited number of books could be written about them?"

"Well, we only have a couple of small chapters written about His known life upon the earth. It sounds like you were referring here to His works and teachings of past lives."

"You are correct again," said John. "The history of the Christ did not begin in Jerusalem. He did reveal to us enough about His past lives for me to realize it would take many books to accurately record His true history. My awe over His history as He revealed it to us caused me to emphasize that even the world could not contain the books. This statement has meaning beyond what I have time to reveal at this moment. Do you have any other questions before I leave?"

"Who are the Knights of the Temple?" I asked.

"Their current name is the Knights Templars. In their early days they were called the Knights of the Temple."

"Yes. I think I have heard of the Knights Templars. What were the secrets I was hiding from the authorities in that life?"

"You were entrusted with some manuscripts containing secret teachings of Jesus about the Tree of Life. They told how it is to be created and the source of power. You also were entrusted with the certain artifacts from the days of Jesus. The authorities thought you had the actual cup used at the Last Supper and they knew about the bells. They wanted to get these from you and destroy all the sacred manuscripts."

"I've never heard any legends about bells," I said.

"They have been lost to history," said John, "but the bells they sought were twelve bells that belonged to the original twelve apostles. After my execution and temporary amnesia you became the caretaker for the twelve bells. The authorities got wind of this and suspected you knew about their location. Legend at that time had it that the ringing of the bells could bring the administration of angels, telepathic communication, and even bring the dead back to life."

"You mean I actually had these twelve bells?" I asked incredulously.

"For a time you did. I am the true caretaker of the bells, but when I saw my life was in danger I turned them over to you until I was able to return with my memory intact. Because you were not in a high position with the Knights, we assumed you would not be bothered by the authorities, but in this assumption I was in error. One of the Knights under torture revealed that you were my disciple and brought you under suspicion. Thus, you were eventually brought to the torture chamber."

"I can understand them wanting to get the artifacts, but why destroy valuable manuscripts?"

"Because the Order that creates the Tree of Life neutralizes the power of unjust authorities that rule the earth. They sense this and automatically seek to destroy this knowledge of life before it takes form."

"So will these ancient manuscripts be discovered again?"

"When the time is right they may come forth, but their physical presence has fulfilled their function. In that life as a Knight of the Temple, you spent half a lifetime memorizing and contemplating the writings, some of which were penned by Christ himself. You were so dedicated to this that you have literally become the manuscript. Through this past life and others you have incorporated within the memory of your soul all the ingredients necessary to recreate the Tree of Life in this age."

"But how can this do me much good when I cannot remember enough to know what you are talking about?" I asked.

"The memory can be retrieved through contemplation," he said. "Here is how you will do it. Ask yourself this question: how was both Jesus and the apostles able to have such great power to do miracles? Then read the entire New Testament, and the Book of Isaiah from the Old, paying particular attention to my writings with this question in your mind. Take note of interesting sections and reread them. During your reading, the principles will all eventually come back to you. As they do, you are to write down the thoughts that come to your mind. When you feel you have the Tree of Life principle crystallized in your mind, you are to give it a new name more in harmony with the thinking of this age."

"This is indeed a strange request. If it were coming from anyone but you, I would probably ignore it. After all, the New Testament is not the most exciting book in the world and I have never gotten any great revelation when I have read it in the past."

"This time will be different," smiled John. "Before you are done with this quest, you will find excitement you never dreamed of in Sunday school."

"Well, I must admit that I have been reading your writings and have found some interesting things," I agreed.

"There is more... Much more," said John. "Start at the beginning of Matthew and read through to Revelation. In the New Testament there are certain triggering or key phrases that are intended to activate the memory of certain disciples. When you sense you have hit upon a triggering sentence go back and study the context. It would also be helpful to commit the scripture to memory. As you do this the inside light will burn brighter and your stored understanding from the past will come to the surface."

"I can't believe you have me interested in wading through the Bible," I said.

John turned to Elizabeth. "I know we've put you through a lot of strain here. How are you handling it?"

"I'm feeling strong again like I did when you gave me that handkerchief," said Elizabeth. "But I'm a little nervous that my strength will go away again."

"It's good to be a little nervous," said John evenly.

"Is there anything you can tell me to help me keep my focus in the right direction so I don't lose my strength again?" asked Elizabeth.

"Remember the Oneness principle," John replied.

"Are you referring to the principle that links you with Christ?" I asked.

"Yes," said John. "The Oneness principle links all true members of the kingdom of God and makes all truth available that is sincerely sought. As I am one with Christ and Christ is one with God, you and Elizabeth and any other human can be one with me, which also makes them one with Christ and God. The main way to know you are headed the right direction is to check yourself regularly to see if you are experiencing the sensations of the soul."

"And what are the sensations of the soul?" asked Elizabeth.

"The main sensations to look for are a sense of inner peace, the feeling of love, and a value of things greater than the individual self. Notice, however, I say *inner peace*. If you keep your focus in the light you can experience inner peace amidst outer turmoil. Inner peace is a subtle thing. You can be in the process of losing it and not be aware of the change unless you are vigilant in paying attention. To understand my point, place yourself sometime in a room with a dimmer adjustment. Then dim the light slowly to half strength. After this is done quickly return the light to full strength. The sudden return to full strength is so obvious it is startling, but if you dimmed the light slowly you hardly noticed the difference. So it is with the light of the soul or spirit. If you take your attention off the light, the dimming begins slowly, and unless you are paying attention you will hardly notice that you are in danger of losing the light. But then if a teacher comes along and points you toward the light again you are surprised to learn of the darkness that you drifted toward. The student becomes amazed as to how far off center he was."

"Speaking of darkness," I said, "how is the struggle going with the Dark Brothers?"

"Things have returned to normal, but we have not been able to learn all their plans. Their main thrust is to create turbulence among the nations with nuclear & biological weapons using the less developed nations. We have already been able to thwart several attempts from our end, but the Brotherhood can only do so much. Humanity must wake up to the danger and create an international law to make weapons of mass destruction illegal. This cannot be done unilaterally by the United States, but must involve all the developed nations. The Dark Brothers are also following their usual course of attempting to put their people in positions of power and creating unrest among the nations. But take heart, for if the Disciples of Light do their job the new millennium can usher in an age of peace that mankind has desired for so many centuries.

"I have overstayed my allotted time." John sighed. "I must be on my way. Do not forget to contemplate the additional hints on the first key so you can finish it and move on."

"He's going to be a busy man," said Elizabeth. "He must finish the first key, start the book and read the New Testament. I think I'll need to use a cattle prod on him," she joked.

"Sometimes you just have to do whatever is necessary," John smiled.

"One more question," said Elizabeth. "How can I ever have the peace of God consistently now that I have this terrible memory?"

John looked in Elizabeth's eyes and spoke evenly. "You turned around in that life and did much to start the repayment by helping Joseph to escape and assisting him for years to come. Your suffering with this disease has done much to help you understand the suffering you caused. Now by assisting Joseph in the work to come you will do much to pay off your mistakes from this past life and a few others. Be of good cheer; your attunement with the peace of God is always determined by the present moment. I must go now."

"How is it determined by the present moment?" she asked.

"The *peace that passes all understanding* is not determined by our past or future, or even how good we have been in the past. If that were the case, none of us would have peace. The most holy peace comes when we focus correctly on our present purpose with a purity of heart. This does not lift our debts from us, but does release us from guilt and opens the door to the Divine Presence, which leads to the payment of all debt and the peace of everlasting joy."

After a moment John got up and walked toward the door.

"By the way," I said, breaking the peaceful moment. "I've been wanting to tell Wayne about you. Would that be all right?"

John seemed to pause a moment and said, "Have you heard the statement that when three or more people have a secret, it is no longer a secret?"

"I've heard something like that."

"There is a lot of truth to these words. When three or more people know something, word of it will usually leak out through some means. If you tell even one more person the truth about me, the chances are it will be the same as broadcasting it over the radio. It will be just as effective and much safer for me if you use some version of me as a fictional character in your book. Then you can talk about the book."

"That's all well and good, but even if I just write about your teachings and the events so far, I'll bet there are a lot of people who will think that I just couldn't have made this up," I countered.

"That is fine," said John. "It is in the plan that there will be many who will sense many underlying truths in what you write, and that your source of knowledge comes from beyond your normal capacity. Even many doubters will be convinced of this after several keys are revealed."

"Won't that bring risk to you?" I asked.

"Very little," said John. "Those who see the truth through the Inner Vision are the harmless ones and, unless they experience a change of course, they will seek to help, not hurt. You, however, must be wise in your presentation and teaching of the material because the way everything is being set up, you will be the focus of attention rather than myself. This makes it easier for me and harder for you, but it is the path we must take."

"And what makes you think I will not back down if the going gets rough?" I asked somewhat tongue-in-cheek.

"You have stood firm in past lives, my friend," he said. "I have no reason to doubt you now."

"Maybe someday I will believe in myself as much as you do," I said smiling.

"Someday you will," he smiled back.

"Do we meet at Denny's again?" I asked, realizing he needed to leave.

"It will be Denny's unless I notify you of a change of plans." John looked at me a moment and stated, "You haven't been saying the *Song of the 144,000* every day, have you?"

"We've been forgetting sometimes," I answered, blushing.

"It is important you say it daily." John then looked at Elizabeth and said, "Saying the Song daily will help you pass the three temptations which are to come."

"Which temptations are these?" asked Elizabeth.

"The temptations that will come to you before we meet again," he said. "You will be tempted to doubt the light you have received and revert to your illness again."

"If I have any say in the matter, this disease will never come back," she said matter-of-factly.

John didn't look convinced. "Remember my story about the dimming light. Be ever aware. It is so easy for the disciple to get caught off guard and think that everything is going fine when he is going backwards. Joseph will meet me alone next week and teach you what he receives. As he suspects, part of the reason for this is to give him practice in teaching. Then, if you pass your three temptations, I will meet with both of you the week after."

"I can't for the life of me imagine how I can be tempted to go back to the disease," she said.

"Illusion," said John.

"Illusion?" I asked.

"Always find the illusion," said John. "That is the key to turning the light back on to full intensity. And don't forget to use all your light to find the companion word to decision. Decision plus the mystery word equals consciousness; and consciousness plus decision equals this word."

John then took hold of our hands and led us in the Song. We were left with a powerful spiritual peace as he silently departed.

CHAPTER ELEVEN
The First Temptation

The next morning I overslept and on waking was surprised to find Elizabeth's side of the bed empty. I rose to the smell of coffee and hot cooking of some kind. I rushed out of the bedroom into the kitchen and found Elizabeth working over the stove making an omelet.

She smiled at me, looking proud of herself. "I hope you don't mind eggs two meals in a row, but it's all we have that looks edible."

"It's fine," I stumbled, "but you know I hardly ever eat breakfast."

"That's probably because I hardly ever make it. Now sit down. There's your coffee with cream in it just the way you like."

"Breakfast once in a while is OK, " I agreed "especially if I don't have to make it."

"I want you to start on your book tonight after your work is done. I don't care what time you finish your real estate. I want you to at least get started."

"I'll see what I can do," I said.

"I want you to promise me you will at least come up with a general outline and get something written down. You've never broken a promise to me so I want you to promise you will begin tonight."

"All right, " I said more firmly. "I've already spent some time making some notes but I'll begin in earnest tonight. By the way, aren't you supposed to go to the doctor today?"

"Yes, I called him a while back and smoothed things over with him. He wants to remain my doctor to neutralize your negative influence."

"I think the truth is the other way around. I need to remain your husband to neutralize his negative influence."

"Maybe so," she smiled, "but we certainly have a positive surprise in store for him this time, don't we?"

"Why don't you just call him and tell him you're healed and don't need him any more?" I asked.

"My healing is not a sure thing yet," she said, "so I think I should keep in touch with my doctor. But most importantly, I want to see the look on his face when he sees that I am well."

"Yes, I would like to see that too," I laughed, then sipped my coffee. "Isn't he aware of your temporary healing when you had that handkerchief?"

"I didn't go to see him during that period and I never told him about it. This time my healing may be permanent so I figure that I'll just go show off my radiant health."

"I wish I could go with you, but I've got a full day."

"Oh, guess who called just before you woke up?"

"I don't have a clue," I said.

"Lance," she said.

"You mean my old friend Lance from California?" I asked.

"The one and only," she said.

"Well, what did he say? Why didn't you wake me up?"

"You needed your beauty rest. He says he's arriving at the Boise airport at 9:20 Sunday morning and wants you to pick him up."

"Is he going to stay with us?"

"I guess so. He kind of invited himself and I didn't say no. It's either us or Wayne, and I know he would rather stay with us."

"Did he say anything else?"

"Yes, he did say one thing. After I told him you would pick him up he said he was bringing a friend."

"A friend. Who is this friend?"

"He said this guy is the most evolved person he has ever met, perhaps the highest being on the planet."

"And I suppose we can't miss meeting the most evolved being on the planet," I added sarcastically.

"Well, if you don't want Lance to bring this guy, you'd better call him now. It sounded like they were packing as we were talking on the phone."

"I doubt if Lance could ever conjure up someone more evolved than John, but I am curious to meet this guy. I'll just plan on picking them up at the airport."

Elizabeth sat down and poured us more coffee. "I want you to continue thinking about the final clues to the first key. I'm not sure if I will feel 100% healed until we get the third key because at that time we have John's word without qualification that I'll be healed."

"Actually, I no longer need any incentive to proceed with the keys. I find all this knowledge fascinating."

"Do you remember the main hint?" she asked.

"I think so," I said. "Decision plus the mystery word equals consciousness."

"That's only half of it," she grumbled. "If we're ever going to get to the third key I can see I have to get more involved here. The second half is *consciousness plus decision equals the key word*."

"I stand corrected," I said. It was at this point in time that I realized Elizabeth's healing not only helped her physically, but also seemed to restore her acute mental alertness. "Do you have any thoughts about the companion word?" I asked.

"I'm not sure," she said. "It almost makes your head spin when you think on our essence for a while. I can see how consciousness could not exist without decision, but it would seem there could be no decision without some type of consciousness. Maybe consciousness, decision and this second key word are interdependent somehow."

"That makes sense," I agreed. "But somehow our essence is more related to decision than consciousness. If decision comes before consciousness, then perhaps we decided to be conscious at some point."

"And maybe before that we even decided to decide," she added.

Something clicked inside me. I looked Elizabeth in the eyes and said, "You sound like John talking."

She looked a little startled. "I kind of do, don't I?" she smiled

"Do you think this is you talking, or do you seem to be picking up something?"

"Kind of both," she answered. "It seems to come from me, but then it seemed like I also picked it up. John said you picked up his thoughts when you were coaching me on the tapes. What did that feel like?"

"It's kind of like you said. It seemed like it was coming from me, but it also seemed to be above my regular knowledge, like I was receiving it."

"Then maybe I am picking up something from John," Elizabeth mused.

"Or through John," I added. "Let's try an experiment. Try to tune into John and see if you receive anything else."

"I'll give it a try," she said and was silent for a moment. "Here is something that seems to focus in my mind: *If we are one with John, we are also one with Christ and God, because John is one with all his brothers who came before him, who are one with Christ and God.*"

"That sure sounds like John," I said. "But, on the other hand, I know you're an intelligent student and you could have put that statement together from what John taught us."

"But something in you feels that it is John, doesn't it?" she asked.

"I think so," I said. "It's more than what you are saying. It's also what is registering inside."

"I think you hit on something," she said. "The words I just spoke do feel very good within myself."

"Do you seem to register anything else?" I asked.

She closed her eyes for a moment and said, "Yes. Yes - I have just received something wonderful. Even though it seems to be my thoughts, I'm sure my own intelligence did not come up with it."

"What is it?" I asked anxiously.

"I've been thinking nervously all morning that my new-found health is too good to be true. As I reflected on that thought just now something in me said these words. *There is nothing too good to be true. All truth in its purest form is good'.*"

I reflected for a moment on that statement. Then I said with some excitement, "That's John all right! I would bet on it."

"So, you don't think I could say something that good?" she poked at me playfully.

"Well, you're good," I said, "but you've never sounded like John before."

"Don't worry about getting in trouble with me," she said, reading my mind. "I'm in too good a mood to get upset today."

I went to work that day feeling very lighthearted and peaceful. This feeling continued until about three P.M. About that time I felt a very disturbing feeling register inside and I realized this was about the time period Elizabeth would be visiting with Dr. Bernstein. I became agitated with myself - thinking I should have gone with her to her appointment - and cut short my appointment and rushed over to the doctor's office. I walked in and asked the receptionist, "Is Elizabeth Dewey still here?"

"Oh, Elizabeth. Yes, she was here. One of our nurses just drove her home."

"What do you mean drove her home? Didn't she drive here by herself?"

"Yes, but Doctor Bernstein thought she was jumping the gun about a recovery and felt it was dangerous for her to drive."

"Where in the hell did he get that idea?" I asked, raising my voice.

The doctor must have heard me, for he appeared out of the hallway with a most serious look on his face and said, "Mr. Dewey, may I speak to you in private for a moment?"

He then ushered me into a private room and spoke in almost a whisper. "Mr. Dewey, I know you are encouraged by your wife's remission, but this happens regularly to victims of MS. The trouble is, this will only last a short period of time and then the disease is likely to come back again more ferocious than ever."

"She is not in remission. She has been healed just like I told you would happen," I countered, raising my voice.

"Now Mr. Dewey, I would appreciate it if you could keep your voice down this time. We do not want a repeat performance of the last visit."

"I wasn't the only one who raised his voice on the last visit," I argued. "Now let me repeat," I spoke in a controlled voice, imitating the doctor. "She is not in remission. She has been healed just like I told you would happen."

Damn it!" said the doctor, raising his own voice. "In my life of practice I must have seen 100 remissions, and time and time again people get their hopes up just to have them dashed to pieces. I do not want to see your wife suffer that devastation. I must protect her from that. Sometimes the remissions last only a few hours, sometimes a few days and once in a while a few months, but they always end; and to give a patient the false hope that the disease is gone is criminal. In fact, even as Elizabeth was here with me some of her symptoms returned and I had to have her driven home."

"Oh no," I exclaimed, standing up. "Are you telling me you sucked the hope out of her and made her weak again? You fool! You don't know what you have done!"

"If anyone is a fool it has to be you, Mr. Dewey. I suspect your blasted guru has something to do with this foolishness. Elizabeth wouldn't admit it but I could tell by her response that he had something to do with all of this. The man is headed for some serious legal trouble I tell you."

"And you're headed for some serious moral problems," I spat back. "Now you'll have to excuse me. I have to head home to see if I can undo the damage you have done."

"I don't usually lose my temper, but there is something about you that infuriates me," he said.

"Good!" I shot back as I walked out.

I then hurried home and was sickened as I opened the door to see Elizabeth in her wheel chair with a great cloud of sadness hanging over her. "Sweetie, I just came from the doctor. What happened? What did he do?"

"It was me. How stupid of me to think I could have any permanent healing!" she exclaimed, pointing to her legs. "Dr. Bernstein told me he has had at least a dozen patients in his career who were healed by various faith healers. They produce a hypnotic effect that works for a short term and then wears off. Then they are usually worse than ever. He must be right. John just hypnotized me and gave me some temporary strength. It didn't even last a day. I felt my strength evaporate as the doctor explained things to me. He brought me back to the real world. And I can't get those thoughts out of my mind about the Knights. I'm not even sure if they are real or what, but they really make me feel unworthy of being healed."

I sensed a tremendous depression looming over her that seemed impossible that morning. It was as if every Dark Brother in existence was pulling her down an abyss. I knew I had to do something but was not sure what. "Do you remember what you said to me this morning?" I asked, kneeling down in front of her.

"I said some words, that was all... just meaningless words."

"No... No, sweetheart. You said some wonderful words." I took her hands in mine. "It was like you had the voice of God. You said nothing is too good to be true, that all truth in its purest form is good. Do you remember saying that?"

"I don't think I said that," she said with her head down.

"Look at me!" I demanded.

"I don't want to. Just leave me alone," she said, pulling her hands away.

"I won't leave you alone... I'll never leave you alone. I love you damn it, and I am going to make sure that you do not leave me!" I grabbed her by the shoulders. "Do you hear me?"

After a moment Elizabeth said, taking my hands again, "Yes, I hear you my sweet husband. Why don't you just give up on me? I'm no better than those others who thought they were healed and were deceived."

"It's not a question of being better," I said. "It's a question of following the highest that you know. Remember John told us that you would have three temptations that would cause you to doubt the light you have received and revert to your illness again?"

"I'm not sure."

"You are sure. I know you remember. Remember how he said that saying the *Song of the 144,000* would help overcome the temptations?"

"Maybe."

"I think we should say it now together. Will you do that with me?"

"Why don't I just give in to this temptation?" she said. "Then I don't have to worry about the other two."

"And where will that leave us?" I said, deciding to speak from the hip. "That would mean you would die, I would be alone and the important work you are to assist in will not get done. Your feelings are telling you to give up, but you must shift your attention to your mind and when your feelings do not support you, just do the thing that makes the most sense. Think about it. Doesn't it make sense to do what is necessary to get well?"

Tears flowed down her cheeks as she said, "Right now the only reason I want to stay in this world is because I love you."

I was happy to hear her say this. At least this was something positive for her to feel. "And I want you to stay here because I love you. Now will you say the Song with me?"

"To be honest, I just don't feel like saying the Song."

"Remember, John said that to continue to say the Song we must stay focused on the Inner Light of the Spirit. Don't you see the doctor has shifted your attention - that you have taken your attention off the light and the radiance of it has dimmed? Focus on the light and you will feel like saying the Song."

"I'm not sure I know how."

"Try this. Repeat your words from this morning: *There is nothing too good to be true.*"

"I don't even feel like saying that," she said, shaking her head.

"Just say it as a favor to me then. *There is nothing too good to be true.*"

"There is nothing too good to be true," she said softly and quickly.

"Say it again, louder," I said, taking a clue from John.

"There is nothing too good to be true!" she said a little louder.

"Again!" I commanded. "Pretend I am John talking to you."

"There is nothing too good to be true!" she exclaimed in a fairly raised tone.

I smiled. "Now will you say the Song with me?"

"You're not going to give up are you?" she said, almost smiling.

"Never," I said, hugging her.

"OK. I think I can say it now."

We held hands and said the Song together three times, Finally, I sensed the dark cloud lift and we had a sense of peace together again. After this I felt impressed to follow John's example and I stood up and backed away from her a few steps. "Rise up and walk toward me and give me a hug," I demanded.

"Sweetie, I love you, but you're not John," Elizabeth said with a chuckle. "You don't have the same powers he does."

My first feeling was that she had caught me in some stupid scheme. Who did I think I was - that I thought I could do what John had done? Yet, there was something else in me that told me I had to try no matter what, even if I felt like a fraud in front of my wife. I searched for the right words and finally spoke with as much confidence as I could muster. "Maybe I do have the same powers because maybe this is John speaking instead of me. Maybe I am one with John and John is one with Christ and Christ is one with God. Maybe I speak the words of God and the words of God are telling you to receive strength and rise up, walk toward me and give me a hug."

My words seemed to have an effect. Elizabeth looked at me hopefully. "Do you really think John is with you?" she asked.

"I know God is with me and John is one with God." That was the best I could come up with that I knew was true. "Now rise up and come to me." I stretched forth my hand.

"I think I feel stronger," she said, and struggled to her feet. "I'm not sure if I can make it to you though.".

"Look at me and say *Nothing is too good to be true.*"

She gathered her composure, looked at me and firmly said, "Nothing is too good to be true."

"Keep saying it again and again," I said.

She said it over and over and started walking. I think I was more surprised than she was as she made it to my presence and fell into my arms.

I felt impressed to speak words of encouragement to her, "Sweetheart, I do believe that you have just passed your first temptation. Do you know what that means?"

"What?"

"It means you can be well again. Only if you fail will you get sick again!"

"Do you really think so?" she asked, eager for me to be right.

"I know so. Try walking around the room again," I said, praying within myself I was right.

She walked away from me, at first unsure of herself. But then on her own she started whispering to herself, "Nothing is too good to be true. Nothing is too good to be true. Nothing is too good to be true." As she said this, her strength seemed to increase until she turned and smiled at me and said, "I'm myself again - I am healed! Now I see that the doctor actually deceived me into being sick again. I think he meant well, but he just about brought me down to the depths of despair and death."

She then looked upward and shouted, "Thank you John wherever you are!"

"And thank God wherever You are," I affirmed with a sigh.

CHAPTER TWELVE
Brother Philo

After the second healing Elizabeth and I went for a walk again and enjoyed her new-found health once more. This time we hoped her healing was permanent. After coming back home she eagerly volunteered to make dinner again and I went into the family room and started typing away a brief outline of the book on my computer.

Later as we were eating dinner she asked, "What were you doing on your computer?"

"You made me promise I would start on the book today so I started writing down a few thoughts."

"Have you thought up a title yet?"

"I've got several ideas in mind."

"Like what?"

"Well, since John will be the central character of the book I thought the title ought to reflect something about him."

"The book will also be about his teachings. You could call it something like *The Keys of Knowledge*," she suggested.

"That's not a bad idea," I said.

"So what have you come up with?" she asked.

"I notice that many best selling books have short titles so I was thinking of calling it *The Beloved, The Immortal* or just *John*," I said.

"I like *The Immortal* best," she said.

"So do I and I also like your title. *The Keys of Knowledge* has a nice ring."

"The only trouble is," said Elizabeth, "I think my title would attract a more limited audience. I think a wide variety of people would wonder what *The Immortal* was about."

"Do you think *The Immortal* is appropriate? John tells us he does die and then is reassembled, or something like that."

"Yes. It's a little like the guy in the movie Highlander. He's called an Immortal even though he can be killed by losing his head."

"Yea, I wonder if John has an Achilles heel like that," I quipped.

"His only Achilles heel seems to be too much interference in the affairs of us regular mortals," she said.

"I hope so," I said. "The man has enough to worry about without having to deal with sword fights and losing his head."

"John may not literally be immortal yet," said Elizabeth, "but I say two thousand years is close enough. Let's go with *The Immortal*. It has a nice ring and I haven't seen any other book with that title."

"OK. So the title is settled. Now we just have several hundred pages of writing to take care of."

"Now that I am better you should have more time," she said, patting my hand.

"That will certainly help, but we've run up a lot of bills since you got sick. I'm still going to have to put in a lot of hours in real estate to make ends meet. Another problem I have is that the more I learn from John, the harder it is to keep my mind on such a mundane thing as making money. I'm beginning to appreciate the scripture that says you can't serve God and mammon."

"Yes, I've noticed that your sales drive has gone down lately. I thought it was because of me."

"Not at all," I said. "It's totally because of John. The last thing I want to think about is real estate when there are so many wonderful things to learn. We may have the greatest opportunity of anyone on the planet, and I have to go out and do boring work."

"Until you have a best selling book I think that a certain amount of boring work is going to be necessary," said Elizabeth. "I can see I'm going to have to help you stay focused if we're going to pay all our bills. Now I'm feeling better I can help you with some of your real estate research."

"I'm probably going to need it," I nodded.

"Now, tell me what you've come up with so far," she asked, leaning forward.

I then related to her the basic drift I had come up with for the book.

"So, you are going to change some things," she concluded.

"Some things," I said. "I think I have to make it commercial enough to really sell."

"But I think the way it really happened is more fascinating."

"Yes, but I studied fiction back in my college years and there are certain principles you must follow to create a book a publisher will accept."

"So, are you going to call yourself by your real name or something else?"

"I think I'll use my real name."

"I don't want you to use my real name." she said, shaking her head.

"Why not?"

"I'm not sure. I just feel kind of funny about it," she shrugged.

"Maybe it's good that we don't use your real name," I said after a moment's thought. "That way, it will later become obvious to readers that everything is not to be taken literally. Hopefully, they will realize they must read the writings in the light of the soul and discern the true principles and the meaning behind the events."

"I still like the real story, though," she frowned. "Maybe it's true that truth is stranger than fiction."

"I met a professional writer once who told me things that really occurred in his life were so difficult for readers to believe that his publisher made him rewrite them and tone them down a little. The funny thing was that his fiction was more believable than the truth. He said that unless a story is believable, you will lose your readers."

"I'm not sure our story is believable no matter how you write it," she chuckled.

"Well, we have to make our best effort," I said.

Elizabeth seemed to be in thought for a moment, then said, "Do you know why people are going to see a lot of truth to our story?"

"Why?'

"Because they will know you just couldn't have made up all these beautiful teachings John gave you. And we just have the tip of the iceberg. What we've received so far is good, but just imagine what people will think when you have published a half dozen books about John's teachings he has yet to give us."

"You're right. I have the feeling John has some things to tell us that has never entered into the hearts of men. People are either going to think these things are true, or that I have developed one whale of an imagination in my old age."

"It's going to indeed be interesting to see what people think," she agreed. She began clearing away the table to wash dishes.

"I'll tell you what," I said while helping her. "let's run the basic plot by Lance and his friend, and later Wayne and possibly others. Maybe that'll give us an idea of how well the book will be accepted."

"Good idea. Just don't tell them John is real."

Sunday morning I was a few minutes late getting to the airport and found Lance waiting for his luggage at baggage claim. Next to him was a tall man, about 6'2, with long light brown hair tied in a ponytail. I would guess he was somewhere in his late thirties or early forties. He was very tan, dressed in bleached and very worn Levis and a bright Hawaiian type shirt. He basically looked like a southern Californian. Lance's eyes lit up when he caught wind of my presence and exclaimed, shaking my hand, "Joe. Great to see you!"

"It's been too long," I said. "So, is this your friend you told me about?"

"It sure is! Allow me to introduce you to Brother Philo."

"Brother Philo?" I quizzed as I shook his hand. "Is Philo your first name or your last?"

"It's my first and last," he smiled. "I'm just Brother Philo."

"O-Kay," I said, somewhat amused. Lance surrounded himself with interesting friends. I paused a moment, turned to Lance and said, "So what have you been up to? Have you got that Center put together yet?"

"Everything is really coming together," he said brightly. "We are so close to making a big leap here, it's scary!"

Every time I meet Lance he sounds very upbeat as if he were on the verge of monumental success, and I could see this meeting would be no exception. Lance is in his early forties, a boyish-looking and charming character whose hair is a little lighter than Brother Philo's. He is about 5'11 and average weight. I always thought he missed his calling as an actor; he has the looks and the personality. Instead, he's spent the last dozen years promoting and searching for his brand of truth in various places around the country, finally settling in the Los Angeles area - which is, of course, the capital city of the planet as far as avant guard philosophy goes.

I met Lance about 15 years ago. We both worked at a health spa selling memberships. It turned out we had quite a lot of free time and some common interests, so we often spent hours talking about philosophy, new age thought, religion, the meaning of life and so on. Even though we only worked there for a short period of time our friendship continued. For several years we shared in a search for truth. We attended a number of different churches and checked out all the new age and metaphysical groups in the area. We didn't seem to find much besides platitudes. The best thing we found was in the written word.

We both combed through many books and shared and traded the most interesting. We concluded there was a certain amount of truth in many of the scriptures of the world including the Bible, but we felt that the religions of the world were just a preparatory thought to condition mankind for the real thing. We felt that many of the so-called channeled New Age books contained very little real truth, but now and then we came across one that really made us think. There were a few, out of the many that claimed to be revealed from a higher source, that we came to accept as teaching some higher truths.

Lance was very stimulated by some of the things we learned, and came to the conclusion that there must be much more truth than what we could dig up in our "backwoods" state of Idaho. He then liquidated all his assets and took off on a sort of Vision Quest. He spent time in Sante Fe, New Mexico: Sedona, Arizona; New York, San Francisco and finally settled in the City of Angels. He checked out dozens of New Age, metaphysical and offbeat religious groups. Time and time again he would give me a similar report when he called. He would say something like, "You know, I left Idaho in search of higher truth and the more I search, the more I conclude that nobody has any more truth than we do. These guys down here are just a bunch of large egos looking for an audience. I think we ought to start our own group."

While Lance got caught up in New Age thought, I got caught up in marriage and making a living. I continued my own search with the limited time I had and Lance continued his quest on a pretty much full-time basis. Over the years he has visited or called periodically and kept me informed about his progress. The past couple of years he has been trying to form a group that is a notch above the regular cult mentality, but he hasn't had much luck and is always on his last dollar. He tells me that the regular New Agers seem to want a standard guru to tell them what to do, even the ones who claim to not want leaders.

He's also has been talking about creating a Center for gathering New Age types, but has never pulled together the funding to fulfill his dream. Nevertheless, he continues to press forward with enthusiasm.

"So, did you stumble across some big bucks in the big city to create your Center?" I asked.

"It's as good as done," he replied. He turned to Philo and clapped him on the back. "Brother Philo here knows an unbelievable number of people, even a couple of movie stars. He thinks my idea of the Center is a great one and that getting funding will be no problem at all. There are people he can call on tomorrow that would give us the money."

"How long have you known this guy?" I whispered to him as we were walking out to the parking lot.

"Just a couple weeks, but that's enough. Believe me, this guy has a lot going for him. He not only knows rich people, but comes from a rich family and has traveled all over the world, including mystical places like Tibet and India."

"Really?" I said. "If Philo has all these resources, then why doesn't he build his own center?"

"Philo works behind the scenes on the spiritual plane," Lance stated matter-of-factly. "He helps others accomplish great works. He doesn't take credit himself, but is just interested in seeing greater light come to mankind."

Something in me registered a suspicion toward this guy but I thought I had to be fair here. It was possible that Lance had come across another exceptional being like John. "So what kind of things has Philo worked with in the past?" I asked.

Lance looked slightly disturbed and whispered, "When you're talking to him always call him Brother Philo."

"Is there some reason behind that?" I asked.

"Brother Philo is just the name he goes by and that's what he wants to be called," he said.

"Sounds more like something a born-again preacher might want to be called rather than a New Ager," I remarked.

"Maybe," said Lance, "but Brother Philo sees himself as a brother to all men and women, so I guess it makes sense. In answer to your question, Brother Philo has worked with many groups and individuals over the years. He may only look about forty, but I think he's really over 100 years old. Maybe much older than that."

I stared at Lance for a moment. "Has he told you he's over a hundred?"

"Not directly, but he's hinted at it. He's such a fantastic person that if he told me he was two hundred I would believe it."

Lance could be so gullible! "You were telling me about his

accomplishments," I said, wanting to hear more concrete information about this guy.

"Well, like I said, he doesn't take credit for what he has done, but he has been the force behind a half dozen environmental groups and dozens of study groups in various places across the country; and then in deep meditation he contacts world leaders and influences their decisions for good. He even used is powers to influence Gorbachev, Reagan and others to bring down the Berlin Wall."

I about dropped his duffel bag before I put it in the trunk of the car. "You don't usually believe such astounding claims. What makes you think this guy is telling you the truth?" I asked.

"The best answer I can give is to let you get to know him," he sniffed.

We all got in the car and drove home. Brother Philo was completely silent, apparently dozing lightly in the back seat, as Lance and I exchanged some small talk. I didn't tell Lance about Elizabeth's recovery. I thought I would let it be the pleasant surprise as indeed it was. As we entered our home Lance noticed Elizabeth setting the table for breakfast.

"Elizabeth!" he gasped. "You're up! You're walking! Where's your wheelchair?"

"I'm thinking of burning it," she said, laughing while they hugged.

"But you look like you're all better! What happened?"

"The doctor thinks she is having a remission," I injected flatly.

"But she looks so good," said Lance. "Like she's reborn or something. It looks like a miracle happened here. You're not holding back on me are you," he asked, clasping her shoulder.

"Well, I do believe God has healed me," said Elizabeth, beaming. "That's about all we can tell you."

"You mean there's more?" he said mockingly. "Come on. You can't hold out on your old friend. What happened here?"

Elizabeth looked in my direction, so I replied with deliberation. "We met this healer who helped us to understand the cause of her illness and helped her get better. The doctor thinks it is a remission, but we're hoping it's permanent."

"I'd like to meet this healer," said Lance.

"You have met him," Brother Philo injected.

Elizabeth looked startled. "You mean Lance has met John?" I could tell that she gave out John's name without thinking and didn't catch herself in time. I wasn't sure if that was all right or not.

Perhaps it would be, as long as we did not tell them who John was.

Lance turned to Philo and said. "So... have I met this John?"

Philo put his hands together in a prayerful manner, closed his eyes a few seconds, then opened them and said in all seriousness, "If you have met me, you have met John."

"Are you saying you are John?" asked Elizabeth with some nervousness.

He closed his eyes again for about 15 seconds and answered, "I am John, I am Jesus, I am Buddha, I am Patanjali, I am one with all the Healers."

I felt a disturbing inner feeling from this guy. He seemed so different from John, who I knew was a real spiritual teacher. The main immediate difference I noticed was that everything this guy seemed to do was to produce an effect - the way he spoke in such pious terms, putting his hands together as if being obviously prayerful, closing his eyes. John just seemed like a regular guy and did nothing for effect only. My inner self told me that this guy was definitely a phony, but my outer self told me that I must be open-minded and give this guy a chance to prove himself. What bothered me is that Philo's words sounded enough like John's that Elizabeth might believe him.

My fear was somewhat reinforced by Elizabeth's next statement, "So are you a part of the Brotherhood of Light?"

"So you know of the Brotherhood?" he asked, a little surprised.

"Some things," she said.

"Tell me something you know," he said.

I tried sending Elizabeth a mental message to not reveal too much. She answered. "I know that there is a Brotherhood of Light and then there are the Dark Brothers."

"Ahh. The illusion of good and evil," said Philo. "In the end, good and evil are seen as two parts of a whole. The Brotherhood is just the Brotherhood. They are neither good nor evil. They just are. You just are. I just am. I AM." He spoke I AM with the mannerism that he was saying something infinitely profound.

"So, do you see yourself as being one with the Brotherhood?" I asked.

Philo looked in the direction of the ceiling. "All who are one with the Higher Self are brothers and dwell in oneness."

"But I have had a definite experience where I have encountered a being from the invisible world that was definitely not good.

He was definitely evil and wanted to do me harm," Elizabeth countered.

Philo began pacing back and forth, his hands clasped behind his back. "There are lives in every plane who do not realize their connection with their source and seem to do harm. In reality, they are just mischievous children who have not found their way home. If one of them comes into your life experience you must ask yourself why you needed that experience."

"So, you are saying that if someone robs me it's because I need the experience?" I asked.

"Yes, and if the experience seems unpleasurable, you must ask yourself what there is in you that wants pain in your life rather than pleasure."

"Do you believe in karma then?" Elizabeth asked.

"Karma is for those who feel they need it. When you no longer need it, you do not have to suffer its consequences."

"So, if I kill someone and decide I don't have a need to pay for my crime, then I don't have to pay for my wrong doing?" I said, incredulous at his philosophy.

He reflected a second and replied slowly, "You bring to you what you think you need. If you feel you do not need punishment, then you will not draw it to you."

"So if he is not punished, how will he learn that it is wrong to kill?" Elizabeth asked.

"All souls progress toward the Light, and as we do, we just drop our harmful characteristics and keep the good. The old souls become part of the One Brotherhood. It does not matter what they have done in the past because it is the past and they live in the present. The Present is all there is."

"See. I told you this guy was great, didn't I?" Lance exclaimed, elbowing my arm. "He has an answer for everything."

"But having an answer and the right answer are two different things," I said, glaring at Philo.

"Well said," replied Philo, smiling. "It is understandable that you doubt my words. The idea that the earth was round and not flat was difficult to understand a few hundred years ago, but now it is impossible to see otherwise. If you will elevate yourself to the view of the Higher Self, you will see as I see."

I felt that I might offend my friend Lance if I replied with my true feelings at that time. Everything about this guy's manner was so phony and pious and revolting to me. I just hoped Elizabeth wasn't swallowing his illusionary thoughts.

We sat down to a late breakfast and reverted back to small talk. Lance and I caught each other up on the latest happenings in our lives. Elizabeth related some of her struggles with her disease and entertained Lance with her description of my encounters with the doctor. This time I could tell that she was trying to avoid mentioning John. Brother Philo did not seem to involve himself in our conversation. He ate slowly with no expression as if he heard none of the conversation that was going on.

Finally, after seeming oblivious to our words, he looked up at Elizabeth and spoke, "You seem concerned that your disease may come back. Perhaps you would find comfort if I sealed your wellness for you."

"Sealed her wellness? What in the world does that mean?" I asked with some noticeable distrust in my voice.

"Does wellness disturb you, my brother?" he asked. "Would you rather that I talk about disease and death?"

"Give the guy a chance," Elizabeth said, glancing at me. "There has to be many teachers in this world. Perhaps Brother Philo has something to offer here."

"Thank you," said Philo. "You are indeed a spiritual lady. Would you like me to check your wellness then?"

"What harm can it do? Go ahead," she responded.

"Let's go in the living room and have you sit in a chair," he said, pulling Elizabeth's chair from the table.

I felt uncomfortable as we proceeded with this. The guy was a little strange but my feelings went beyond that. I felt distrust for him beyond what seemed reasonable. If I were Spiderman I would say my spider sense was tingling.

We went into the living room and Elizabeth sat in a chair as we gathered around her. Philo stood in front of her and raised his hands toward the ceiling with his eyes closed and lowered them as he opened them. Then he moved his hands around a circumference about two feet from her body as if he were feeling something.

"He's feeling her aura," Lance explained, sensing our curiosity.

"This is an unusual subject," said Philo as he was methodically moving his hands through the air surrounding her. "I must make visible the invisible." He then stood back and held his arms open wide and stared at her.

"Good God!" he almost shouted. This was the first emotion, real or imagined that I had seen in the guy and it came as a surprise, especially to Elizabeth.

"What is it?" she gasped, getting up.

"Sit back down!" he commanded. "You have a great dagger planted right in the midst of your back. Remain still so I can focus on it."

"What do you mean dagger in her back?" I asked.

"It's not in her physical body, but in her spiritual, and it's been the cause of her ill health."

"But I'm better now," said Elizabeth. "If there was some sort of dagger in me surely it would be gone now."

"It has changed position recently," said Philo. "Unfortunately this will only give you temporary relief. When it adjusts to its new position you will be in a worse condition than you ever were."

"What shall I do then?" she asked with growing concern.

"A master physician must pull it out," he said.

"And that would be you, I assume," I said wryly.

"If Elizabeth wants me to remove the dagger I will," Philo replied, patting her shoulder.

There was silence for a few seconds.

"Would you like the dagger removed?" he asked Elizabeth.

"I suppose," she said nervously. "What harm can it do?"

"It shall be done," said Philo. He then grabbed what appeared to be an imaginary object from her back and dramatically pull it out. After he pulled it out he held the invisible object above his head and mumbled several sentences in some language I had never heard before. He then "raked" the "hole" left in her aura by the removed dagger and breathed out "Ah" in a long, drawn out phrase.

"What language did you just speak?" Lance asked.

"I spoke to the Guardian," he said. "The Guardian of the Soul. I asked him to take the dagger so it can't hurt Elizabeth again."

"So did he take it?" asked Lance.

"The Guardian fulfilled my request," Philo said with great seriousness.

"So who is this Guardian?" I asked.

"The Guardian is our Perfect Self who links us with the Brotherhood, and will lead us to peace, health and happiness," he said as he was slowly waving his hands over her invisible aura. "Now Elizabeth, stand and feel the power of the Guardian. Feel the Great Life that flows through you."

She stood up.

"How do you feel?" Lance asked.

"OK, I guess," she said.

"Walk back and forth across the room," said Philo.

Elizabeth walked back and forth across the room. After a moment she said, "I think I do feel better."

"You were already feeling great," I said. "Are you sure you are feeling even better?"

"I think so," she said. "I seem to feel lighter and have more energy." She looked at Philo. "Do you think this means that my disease will not come back?"

"It will not come back unless someone places another dagger in you," he said.

"How could that happen?" she asked.

"The first dagger was placed in you a couple of years ago by someone very close to you," he said. "Often, even those we love can create negativity which can materialize in the spiritual world as a dagger or other deadly object. It secures itself in our spiritual body and affects our physical."

"It sounds like you are insinuating I did it," I said, sounding visibly upset.

"I am sure she has many loved ones," he said. "I am not naming names, but she must discover the source of the dagger or another one could be placed in her. Negativity will rear its head again shortly. It is important that she recognize it and avoid it."

I was starting to feel even more negatively toward Philo. Lance seemed to sense it and injected, "Brother Philo and I have some visiting to do. I want to introduce him to several friends, but we'll be back around eight this evening. How about calling Wayne and inviting him over and we'll have some good conversation."

"I'm sure Wayne will find Philo an interesting piece of work," I said flatly.

"It's not like you to be sarcastic," Elizabeth said, frowning at me. She turned toward Philo and Lance. "We'll look forward to seeing you both again this evening."

In a few minutes they were both gone, but I couldn't shake the feeling that Philo was a complete phony and that Elizabeth was being taken in by him.

"That is a very interesting person," said Elizabeth right after I finished my thought. She continued talking, walking down the hall to the bedroom, "He's also very good looking. Maybe he missed his calling as a famous actor."

"I don't think so," I whispered to myself.

CHAPTER THIRTEEN
For the Love of Philo

A few minutes later, after Elizabeth came back to the kitchen, I broke the silence. "So do you think you felt any different or do you think that dagger thing just produced a psychological effect?"

"I seemed to feel lighter and a sense of well being after he pulled it out," she answered with some surprise in her voice.

"But you were already feeling better than you were in years. What bothers me is that there is no visible or noticeable effect of his so-called healing."

"What I don't understand," Elizabeth said, "is you almost seem eager to accept everything that John gives you, but you seem to immediately reject everything that Brother Philo says. John came to us and taught some profound things and we considered them. Now, another person comes along and says even more profound things. Shouldn't we consider his sayings with equal validity?"

"Well, clear from the beginning when John spoke to me, everything seemed to make sense and registered with my inner Soul, but this guy is the opposite. His words don't make sense to me and strike no chord with my soul."

Elizabeth's voice raised. "But isn't it possible you are just not listening to him with an open mind? There may be a lot of teachers out there like John. Maybe they are both part of the same Brotherhood."

"But their teachings on the brotherhood and many other things disagree. Philo teaches there is only one Brotherhood and John teaches about two."

"But maybe they are saying the same thing, but in a different way."

"I would say they are saying different things in different ways," I said firmly.

"You don't know that," she said flatly.

"I do know that. This guy is not from the same Brotherhood as John. All he did was a bunch of mumbo jumbo and produced no visible results. John performed actual miracles with you and me."

"But every time John has helped me I got sick again. Brother Philo says that removing this spiritual dagger can heal me permanently. I think it's worth a try. It can't do any harm."

I sighed in frustration. "But if this guy is from the Dark Brothers, it can do some harm."

"Don't you understand?" cried Elizabeth, rolling her eyes. "I want to stay better from now on and Brother Philo offers me some hope. Why do you want to take that away from me?"

"I'm only trying to help and protect you," I said a little softer.

"Well, you might have even been the one to cause all my problems," she shouted back. "You tell me I have fears and negativity that I am denying. Well how about you? Maybe you have some unconscious negativity that produced that dagger. Come to think of it, we did have some strong disagreements just before I got ill."

I couldn't believe I was hearing this from my wife. "Sweetie! Why are you saying this? We've had a few disagreements, but we have always resolved things. I'm only guilty of loving you like crazy since I met you!"

"But if I knew someone tortured me - like I did you - I don't know if I could live with them without holding some strong negative feelings."

"But I don't even remember that life, and even if I did I forgave you in that life when you became my disciple."

"But there could be something on the subconscious level, and beyond, that John remembers from that life, when I tortured and killed him. He may not have completely forgiven me. Maybe his stringing us along with these keys and giving me a false hope is his way of getting back at me. Maybe there is no final answer. Maybe this will just go on forever!" Elizabeth put her hands over her eyes and cried, her back turned to me.

I immediately put my hands on her shoulders and turned her to face me. "Sweetie, all the time of this illness you have been strong and positive. I've never seen you so negative. What's going on here?"

She stopped crying and seemed to get a hold on her emotions for a moment. "I felt something when Brother Philo pulled that dagger out of me. He might also be two thousand years old and as powerful as John. I have a chance at a permanent healing here and you're against it."

"He's not promising more than John. He's promising you an easier way than John. The easy way isn't usually the right way and it's often deceptive."

"Well, it won't do any harm to try it. I'm not going to let you stop me," she pronounced over her shoulder, walking out of the room.

She slammed the bathroom door and remained there for about forty-five minutes. She seemed distant from me the rest of the day. I have never felt more alone than I had at that time.

That evening around eight the doorbell rang. I opened the door to my old friend Wayne who I called and invited earlier in the day. He took off his cowboy hat and ambled in. "What's this you were telling me about this guru that Lance dug up who might be a couple hundred years old?"

"That's what he told me," I answered, shaking my head.

"Lance comes up with some weird stuff, but I didn't think he was that gullible," he said, plopping himself down in a chair.

"Neither did I," I agreed, thinking how Wayne would flip if I told him I knew a 2000 year old man. At least I had strong evidence to support my belief I thought.

"I'm looking forward to talking with this guy. I love putting know-it-alls in their place," he chucked, pulling off his boots.

"Take it easy on him for a while at least," I said, in a lowered tone of voice, looking toward the bedroom "Elizabeth has seemed to take a liking to him and is in a strange mood today."

"Well, she ought to be in a good mood if she's walking again like you say. I hope she can stay better this time."

At that point I told Wayne the details of our morning encounter and the removal of the dagger.

"Sounds like the guy is really full of hocus pocus to me," he agreed. "It's like he's trying to take credit for a miraculous recovery that has already occurred."

"That's what I thought," I agreed, nodding. "But this guy seems to have a hold on her that I've never seen happen before. Maybe they knew each other in a past life."

"Like I always say, anything is possible, but we only know a few things for sure."

At that moment the doorbell rang again. Elizabeth came out of the bedroom and joined us. As I answered it I was almost surprised to see Lance in a lighthearted mood accompanied by Philo still looking sober. Lance seems to have a talent to bring out the humor and lightness of any situation.

"What have you been up to?" I asked, inviting them in.

"We just got back from cruising in the park," said Lance, "and we met these two babes who we impressed to no end." Lance walked to the kitchen refrigerator and took 2 beers, handing one to Philo. He asked Elizabeth and I if we wanted a beer, but we declined.

Lance has been single for several years and is an endless flirt. He's had a number of girlfriends since his divorce, but the relationships have been short lived. Nevertheless, he is never deterred from his endless quest to find the perfect female, a quest he attacks with gusto.

"So, did you do all the impressing or did Brother Philo join in?" I asked jokingly.

"Are you kidding? We were a team like you wouldn't believe. I got the conversation going and Brother Philo impressed the hell out of them with his deep thoughts." Lance grinned at Brother Philo, who seemed a little dispassionate at the humor.

"Like what kind of deep thoughts?" Wayne asked.

"Oh, he said several things about relationships, but then when he started talking about sex, they really got interested."

"What did he say about sex?" asked Wayne.

"He told them how they could have a climax a hundred times more powerful than anything they have ever had before."

"I would be interested in hearing that line," Wayne quipped, who's also a single man.

"I'm not sure I want to know," I said

"Speak for yourself," said Elizabeth. "The majority rules here."

"Actually, it's not a line. This guy is for real," said Lance. "He told them about how two people during sex can meditate on their sacral or sexual center in connection with the rising of the Kundalini, and can have an experience that is mind-blowing beyond any drug."

"I've read that the stimulation of the Kundalini can be dangerous," I said, frowning.

"Not when you know what you are doing," said Philo in a more serious tone than Lance.

"So, tell us more about how to have this mind-blowing experience," Elizabeth asked.

"Telling you is of little value. I would have to show you," Philo replied, giving Elizabeth a very penetrating stare that flattered her, but made me uncomfortable.

"And by *showing,* I suppose this means you would have to have sex with the person to teach them," I said dryly.

"That is correct," said Philo in all seriousness.

"What did I tell you?" Lance laughed. "Is this guy a good partner in picking up girls or what? I'll tell you this. After Brother Philo finished telling the gals about how sex should be, they were more eager than you can believe to see us again."

"I guess Philo can't be all that bad if he can help you get a girlfriend," Wayne joked with Lance. "God knows you need one."

"Speak for yourself," said Lance. "And call him Brother Philo."

"Why the hell should I do that?" Wayne asked, who has a natural rejection of direction from most any source.

"Because that's the name he wants to be called by."

"As far as I'm concerned he's Philo, and that's probably not even his real name. Philo is all you're getting from me. That all right with you Philo?" Wayne asked, looking him in the eye.

Philo smiled in a patronizing manner. "Call me what you wish. How you honor the name given to me by the Guardian is a reflection of your Inner Self."

"Well, I happen to like that reflection, Mr. Philo," said Wayne.

"As you wish," said Philo, nodding.

Lance looked a little disturbed. "I don't know what the big deal is here," he said to Wayne. "Brother Philo makes one simple request and that is to be called Brother. I've introduced him to a lot of people in LA and they don't seem to have any resistance to the word. I'm not sure if the problem is that we're in the backward state of Idaho or if it's just you guys."

"It's probably both," said Wayne. "People in Idaho have more sense than people from California and we, or at least I, don't just call anyone brother. I don't just call anyone Father or Your Holiness either."

"I don't know if I would equate the word *brother* with Your Holiness," I said. "To me, it's more like someone wanting to be called Mister Bill instead of just Bill. It seems a little silly unless we are in some group that has some established protocol."

"I think you guys are making of big deal out of nothing here," said Elizabeth, exasperated. "If he wants to be called Brother Philo, let's just call him Brother Philo and move on."

"I don't think anyone is making a big deal," said Wayne. "I just don't want to be forced into calling someone Brother unless I have good reason to."

I was glad Wayne gave the rebuttal. I didn't want to offend Elizabeth by disagreeing with her in one of our few times we seemed to have an opposing view.

"OK," I said. "I think we have gone as far as we can on this subject. Whether Philo is called *brother* by us or not, we're curious about his views; and I know all of us love to talk philosophy, so this should be an interesting evening. I thought we'd start the ball rolling by telling you about a new project that I'm going to undertake with Elizabeth's help. I'm going to write a book."

"About time you did something worthwhile," Lance jested. "By the way, did you know that Brother Philo has written several books?"

"No we didn't know that," said Wayne expressing mock surprise. I sensed that Wayne felt a similar vibe from Philo that I did.

"What are your books about?" asked Elizabeth, ever the pleasant host.

"They are journals, really," said Philo. "I keep a journal of my thoughts on a regular basis, plus all the revelations I get from the Guardian."

"He's had a lot of different backers who want to publish them," Lance added, "but Brother Philo feels the time is not right."

"I think everyone has a book inside them," said Wayne. "I've started writing a book several times, but never finished one. So what's your book about, Brother Joseph?" he asked, turning to me.

I smiled at Wayne for calling me *brother* after giving Philo such a bad time. "You remember all those conversations we had about the question WHO or WHAT ARE WE?"

"Sure," Wayne answered.

"Well, I thought I would write a book about a guy - someone like me - who just happens to stumble across a teacher who has been roaming the earth since the days of Christ. This teacher has twelve Keys of Knowledge, but instead of just teaching, the guy he gives him hints that he has to solve. He goes through a great struggle before he gets the first key, which he must solve before he goes on to the second, and so on."

"So is Elizabeth going to be in the book?" asked Lance.

"Yes. She's going to be suffering from a disease when they meet the teacher, and the teacher will promise her a complete healing if the guy can solve the first three keys. This puts him under pressure to really make an effort." I paused a moment. "So what do you guys think of the basic idea?"

"It has potential," said Lance. "How good the book is will depend a lot on how interesting the keys are."

"Yes," said Wayne. "The keys need to be more than worn out clichés like *All is One*, or *Love is all there is*, or something nebulous like that."

"I agree," I said. "These keys need to present some new material, or at least old material in a new light. The first key, for instance, will be the answer to WHO OR WHAT AM I? As you'll remember, Wayne, we've already had a number of discussions on that idea."

Wayne nodded. "And as I remember you did come up with some unusual twists on that one. What's going to be the second and third keys?"

"I don't know yet," I said. "I'll cross that bridge after I start the book. I'm sure you'll be helping me solve them when we have coffee."

"I'll bet Brother Philo could come up with fifty keys," said Lance. "I'll tell you, this guy's well never runs dry. You ought to have him consult with you."

"I don't think that will be necessary," I replied.

"The first key is Love," injected Philo unexpectedly.

There was a short silence.

"You said the first question was WHO OR WHAT AM I?" said Philo. "The answer is Love. God is Love...we are Gods...I am Love and so are you."

As I was contemplating whether or not to give a long answer explaining how love is a part of what we are, but not our core self, Wayne injected his thought on the matter. "That sounds good" he said, "but what part of love creates thought, then? Some thoughts are very unloving. If love were our core ingredient, then love would have to create our thoughts. And I don't believe all our thoughts could be created by love. On the other hand, great thoughts can create the emotion of love."

"That sounds logical," I said, impressed by Wayne's quick thinking.

Philo put his fingertips together and smiled. "Love does not have to be logical," he replied. "It just is. You can't change that."

Then Wayne, who always loves a good argument, countered, "But thought is logical, and if love is our prime cause, then love created logical thought. Therefore, even if you are right, love would have some logic behind it."

"The more you try to explain love, or substitute something

else for it, the more confused you will become," said Philo.

"It's true," said Wayne, "that if you don't think, you won't get confused. I would prefer to continue thinking and allow myself a little confusion now and then."

"Sounds good to me," I added to the jest. "A little confusion is good now and then."

"I have to admit," said Philo, "you are the first people I have ever met who prefer confusion over love, and there's just not one of you, but two."

"You're putting a wrong slant on it," I said, leaning forward. "It's not that we prefer confusion over non-confusion; but we prefer thinking to following platitudes or words from some authority. Thinking reveals the things we don't know, which often brings some confusion. If you just concentrate on emotion and never think, you will not know if you are in a fog or not."

"He who dwells on Love is always in the Light," said Philo, closing his eyes.

"That's exactly the type of platitude that Brother Joe was just talking about," said Wayne. "Before we can even know what you are talking about, we should define what love is. How about it Philo... What is love?"

"You do not understand love by defining it. You understand it by being it," Philo retorted.

"And I suppose you think you are being it?" Wayne asked.

"I am the IT you call love. I cannot be anything else," he replied, smiling.

"You can't define IT, but you think you are IT. Maybe you are the wrong IT. Because if you can't define IT, you don't know what IT is, and you are being a different IT than you think. Maybe the IT you are is blissful ignorance."

"You need help," Philo said after a moment, glaring at Wayne.

"I think he's right there," cracked Lance." I've always thought you needed help Wayne, and I'm not so sure about Joe over there."

"That's funny," I jested, "we always thought it was you who needed help."

"If you guys think you are so smart," Elizabeth injected, looking at Wayne and me, "then why don't you tell us what you think love is."

"I'd say love is an attractive energy," said Wayne, taking the challenge. "If you love someone or some thing you are pulled toward it."

"I would say that is correct," I agreed, "but I would add that there are degrees and types of attraction or love. There is a self-ish attraction - like a fatal attraction type of love - that wants to possess; and then there is a selfless attraction that just seeks sharing."

"I could buy that," said Lance. "But isn't even the selfish lover seeking to fulfill his desire to share?"

"I would say that is true" I said. "The difference between the selfish and unselfish lover is that the selfish looks only at his own desires, and the unselfish looks at the needs of both himself and the object of his desire."

"So the unselfish lover is one who has a little common sense about him," said Wayne.

"I suppose that's true," I said. "True love always brings the mind into play."

Philo rose up from his chair and lifted his hands toward the ceiling, stating in a raised voice, "Must you always attempt to destroy love with your definitions and feeble attempts at thinking?" Then he raised his voice "Love just is! It is a feeling that you have to experience. When you dwell in love, you realize that it is beyond words. If you really desire to know what love is, I am here for you!"

Philo sat back down and bowed his head as we looked on in astonishment for about 30 seconds.

"Well, Brother Joseph," Wayne said, leaning forward to pat my knee. "I guess we don't have to do any more thinking. All we have to do is bask in this guy's presence and we will have blissful love."

"I guess so," I said, laughing. Then after reflection, I thought I would put Philo to the test. "So, you say you are here for us to give us love. If I were to tell you I want this love you have to offer, what do we need to do next."

"You are not ready to experience the Love That Just Is," said Philo in a haughty tone.

I thought that was an ironic statement for me to hear after my experience in the New Jerusalem, where the love was so intense it boggles the mind. "So is Wayne ready for this gift of love?" I asked.

"Both of you are like small rebellious children who want to eat candy and avoid the more nutritious food," he replied flatly.

"But you said you are here for us," I challenged. "If there is nothing you can do for us, then how are you here for us?"

"I am here for you if you are willing to take the correct steps to dwell in the Love."

"And what would those steps be?" I asked.

"It is needless for me to say because you are not ready," Philo replied.

"But if I was ready, what would be the first step?"

Philo looked a little perturbed that I continued with the questions, but finally answered, glancing in the direction of Elizabeth. "The first step is to look in the direction of Love Made Manifest. The love that dwells in me is a starting point. You must blend with that love."

"And how do we do that?" Wayne asked.

"You must subject your thoughts to the feeling of love and keep them under subjection."

"And how do we do that?" I asked.

Philo's eyes brightened slightly, as if he thought he might actually be getting through to me. "To gain the total freedom of love you must put your rebellious thoughts aside and subject yourself to the words of love. If you are willing to do this for a short period, then and only then will you know that what I say is true. You can be one of those who are blended in love. As I have submitted to the Guardian and you submit to me, then we all submit to love and become Love. We then become what is. I AM THAT I AM, and that is Love."

"I have heard that the name of God is I AM BECOMING rather than I AM," I countered.

"How can I become that which I already am?" Philo asked. "If I AM Love, then I cannot become it. Where did you hear such nonsense?"

"It will be in my book," I said.

"That is extremely dangerous doctrine," said Philo. "The core doctrine of the Brotherhood is that we just are. There is nothing to become, for we are gods and one with God, and everything is already present within us. All that needs to be done is to remind us of who we are. If you would but completely submit to my ashram for a few days, you would discover my words to be true."

"I don't think so," I said, shaking my head. "How about you Wayne?"

"I don't submit my will to anyone or anything," Wayne insisted.

"Are you asking them to give up their free will?" Elizabeth asked Philo.

Philo let out a short laugh. "Goodness no! I could not take

away your free will no matter how hard I were to try. Like all other things in your complete self, your free will just IS and cannot be lost. All I ask is to give me a chance to show you a great gift. Let me give you an illustration.

"Let us say you wanted to learn to snow ski and tried to learn on your own, but without success and kept falling down. Finally, you meet a master instructor who agrees to teach you on one condition. That condition is you must obey everything he says until you complete his course. Then after you complete the course you no longer need the instructor and no longer need to submit to his will; you use your own free will to ski with more freedom than before and even become a master instructor if you so desire. Now let me ask you a couple of questions. While taking such a course, have you lost your free will?"

"I guess not," said Elizabeth. "I could withdraw if I was not happy with it."

"That is correct," said Philo. "But then if you complete the course, wouldn't you say that you now have more freedom than before because you can now ski slopes you could not approach before?"

"Yes, I suppose that is true," said Elizabeth.

Philo then looked at Elizabeth closely and said, "Even so, if you were to submit to me as your instructor, I could lead you to a greater love than you have ever experienced. Then after a short time your freedom as well as your enjoyment of life will be enhanced."

"Sounds too good to be true," said Elizabeth, blushing. Then she paused a moment and asked, "Why am I saying that? There is nothing too good to be true."

"That's the spirit!" said Philo. "And let me tell you of a great benefit you will have from completing my course. When you are able to be one with All the Love That Is, you will be impervious to any other negative attack that could bring the spiritual dagger back. Then you could not and would not ever be ill again."

"That sounds tantalizing," she said, smiling.

"It also sounds like it could be a smoke screen for mind control," I injected, not smiling.

"You have too many fears," Philo said to me in a dismissive tone. "You must see a boogieman in every corner. I seek only to give away more freedom, not take it from you. As I indicated, your free will is a gift from God and no one can take it from you. Fearing a loss of free will is as close as you can come to losing it."

"How about you Lance?" asked Elizabeth. "Have you taken his course?"

"I'm not sure," said Lance. He looked at Philo. "You've taught me a lot, but have I taken the course?"

Philo smiled. "You have been taking the course all along since you have known me, my brother. You are like the person learning to ski by being in the presence of and imitating the instructor. This is one way to learn, but then a short intense course will greatly increase the learning time... and that is what I now suggest. I propose giving all that are willing a three-day course of sharing. Then after three days you will know what I know and see what I see."

"So how do we know that you won't turn us into idiots?" asked Wayne.

"Look at Lance," said Philo. "He's still your regular Lance, but a little more enlightened."

"Maybe so," I said, "but I've never known Lance to believe so much on so little evidence."

"Some would think that is good, not bad," said Philo softly.

Maybe some, but not many," I said.

"Whatever," said Philo. "Here is my suggestion. We will be here a few days. Think about it overnight and give me your answer tomorrow. We can begin then if you should so decide, and I decide you are ready."

"I've already decided," I said. "I'll take a rain check."

Philo turned to Elizabeth. "How about you? Have you decided?"

"I'm not sure," said Elizabeth.

"You need to make up your own mind and not look so much to your husband," he said in a serious tone. "Just remember this. Nothing bad can happen from exploring love and great good is always a possibility. I believe we can help you to never experience illness again. Remember, disease is experienced by one who is at *dis-ease*, or not at ease with the love energy."

"I'll think about it," she said, looking down demurely.

"You can't be serious," I said to Elizabeth. "This guy is just blowing smoke. For some reason he wants you under his control."

"You need to chill out," said Lance to me. "Brother Philo only wants to give more freedom, not take it away."

I stood up. "I tell you I can feel it in my bones. This guy is up to something. For some reason he has designs on my wife!"

"Would you calm down?" Elizabeth scolded me. "You're embarrassing me here." I sat down.

"Let us all just relax and take a deep breath," said Philo with his hands outstretched. "We can all make our decisions in calmness tomorrow. By the way, Wayne, you are invited to take my course. Are you willing?"

"I think you're full of BS," Wayne answered, "but you do have me curious about what you have to offer... and I certainly have no fear about losing my will to you. I may come by to see what you're all about."

"Then it is set. We will begin at 8 PM tomorrow," Philo said smiling.

"I thought you were going to wait for a decision from Elizabeth," I said.

"Internally, she has already decided. She will be with us tomorrow and I suspect that you will be there also, keeping an eye on her. You might as well. You will already be here."

I tried to ascertain from Elizabeth's facial expression what she felt, but she wouldn't look at me. I felt as if I was playing chess with this guy and he had called the first check, thinking he was about to mate, but I was not about to yield to him so easily. Somehow, I had to expose him for Elizabeth's sake. I had a sense of danger concerning her.

CHAPTER FOURTEEN
The Confrontation

The rest of the evening we continued to talk about a range of philosophical topics, with Philo always trying to convince us that Love was the answer to everything. He seemed to think that if we just did not ask questions, but experience his brand of love all questions we have about any subject would be taken care of.

After Wayne left, Philo spent about two hours talking to Elizabeth, explaining many of the things he wrote in his journal. Normally this would not have bothered me, but she seemed to be unusually caught up with this guy and hung on his every word. She acted as if Philo's words were greater than John's. I could not, for the life of me, see how Elizabeth could even come close to putting them in the same category. I was confused over her judgment. It was as if she had moved backward in consciousness and had become someone else since Philo had come to visit.

The next day I was glad that Lance decided to visit some friends and took Philo along with him. During their absence I sensed that Elizabeth was looking forward to Philo's class. I decided to attend if Elizabeth did and had to admit to myself that the reason was more out of distrust for Philo than any interest I had in his class.

Lance and Philo returned to our home about six that evening. Lance was again excited about a couple more girls they met at the Ram Pub that they stopped at on their way back. During dinner we tended to talk about standard small talk. The only thing out of the ordinary was Philo's excessive flattery of Elizabeth. She apparently had prepared the best meal he had ever eaten. She looked so beautiful and vibrant since he had taken the dagger out of her back. Her aura was now golden and vibrant whereas before he had arrived, it had dark patches in it. I then felt particularly restless when he warned her not to let anyone close to her allow the dagger to be placed in her again. I knew that was a subtle dig at me but also sensed he would deny it if I brought it up.

About a quarter after eight there was a knock on the door. As expected it was Wayne. "Wow," he mused. "You guys are glowing with enlightenment. I must have missed the class."

"I'm afraid not," I said. "We've been waiting for you."

"I don't know if that's good or bad," he said, "but I guess we'll find out."

After a few minutes we indicated to Philo that we were ready to begin his class. After taking a minute to finish a cup of tea Philo spoke. "Get us five pillows and put them in the middle of the floor."

Elizabeth retrieved five pillows and put them on the carpet in the center of our living room. Philo took one for himself and sat on it with his legs crossed in a loose lotus position. Then he invited us to sit in a circle around him. After we sat down he said, "Come closer and stretch out your hands so you can feel my aura."

We all moved closer and stretched out our hands.

"Closer still," he said. "You must have a part of your body within the circumference of my aura."

We all moved our hands a little closer toward his midsection.

"There," he said. "Now if you remain absolutely still for a moment you will feel a sense of warmth radiating to your hands."

We were all still for a moment. I gave it a fair shake and tried to sense some warmth. I thought I felt a little, but wasn't sure if it was a psychological effect or a real warmth. As I was in the middle of this contemplation Lance blurted out. "Wow! He's not only warm, but I feel like my hands are in front of a fire!"

"How about you?" said Philo to Elizabeth. "Do you feel the warmth?"

"I think so," she said.

"Shut out all distractions and concentrate. You will feel the warmth increase. Now everyone remain silent for another moment and feel the radiation."

I noticed that Wayne was going to say something, but withheld when Philo asked us to remain silent for a time. Again I decided to give Philo a fair shot and concentrated another moment. I still was not sure if I was feeling anything out of the ordinary.

Again Philo spoke. "Now Elizabeth, tell us what you feel."

"I do believe there is an increase in the heat," she said.

"Continue to concentrate and you will feel the fire as Lance has. What Elizabeth and Lance feel is the radiation of pure love that comes from the Guardians though me to all who are open to receive. How about you Joseph? Do you feel the warmth?"

"To be honest I am not sure. I may feel something, but it could be psychological."

"I think it is physical," said Wayne. "I think I feel a little heat radiation from Philo's body. There's nothing mysterious about that."

"You two just need to open up," said Lance. "What I have felt now and at other times is no body heat. No body warmth can feel like a fire. I tell you if the heat were any greater it would burn me. No body heat can do that."

"And it's possible that you have experienced a degree of hypnosis," I said.

"I don't think so," said Elizabeth. "I know I'm not hypnotized and I definitely feel some unusual warmth. I think we ought to give the guy a chance to prove himself."

"Keep tuning into that warmth," said Philo. "And to Joseph and Wayne I admonish to you let go of your blockages and let the warmth into your inner selves so you can be one with the rest of us."

"He's right," said Lance. "I've seen Brother Philo do this with forty people and there was not a single one who did not feel the fire of Philo's love. You guys are just blocking the flow of energy. Now loosen up. Chill out! Do whatever you've got to do."

"I don't care if a million people saw Jesus drive a Volkswagen in a parade," said Wayne. "I wouldn't believe it unless I could confirm it for myself."

"And perhaps with that attitude you would wind up missing the whole Second Coming," said Philo. "Let us continue here. Concentrate on the warmth and keep your negative thoughts in abeyance for a few moments."

We tried again for a for a while. I felt pretty much the same questionable warmth that I did before. Then Philo broke the silence. "Do you feel the warmth increasing, Elizabeth?" he said.

"I believe so," she said.

Then he turned and looked directly at her. "Look me directly in the eyes," he said.

She attempted to do so, blinking several times.

"Do not waiver in your attention. Look steadily at me," he commanded.

As she seemed to be attempting to obey he scooted himself closer to her until his face was less than a foot away from hers. As he continued staring at her he said. "Our auras are now intertwined. As the Guardians send the fire of their love to my aura, even so do I send my love to yours." He stretched out his hand and laid it on her forehead, and said in a loud voice, "Feel the fire of love!" Then he pushed her head back in a way that reminded me of TV faith healers.

Philo then stood up, followed by Lance, and started chanting in a loud voice, "The fire - the fire - the fire is in me burning - burning - burning. Now repeat with me," he said as he repeated it over and over. Lance joined in and so did Elizabeth. Wayne and I sort of watched on with suspicion for a minute. Then Philo stopped and grabbed Elizabeth by the shoulders and looked her in the eyes and said in a voice close to shouting, "Do you feel the heat?"

"Yes," she said softly.

"Do you really feel it? Speak up!"

"Yes, I feel it!" she said.

"Are you willing to do the next step to feel complete love?"

"I think so," she said.

"You must know so!" he said again in a raised voice. He turned his head toward Lance and spoke again, "Lance! Are you willing to commit to a complete love?"

"You know I am," said Lance with enthusiasm.

Then Philo turned toward Elizabeth. "Are you willing to commit to a complete love?"

"Yes, I'm willing," she said finally.

"And when you fulfill your commitment you will then know Love Divine."

During this exchange with Elizabeth I felt very uncomfortable and was tempted to insist that Philo stop this brainwashing technique. Two things made me hesitate. First, I was concerned that Elizabeth would be upset at me for interfering, and secondly, I felt a strong force around this guy that seemed to weaken my will. It was as if there were powers at play that had to be met with a strong opposing spiritual force to neutralize. I somehow sensed that this force around Philo was also keeping Wayne in a state of acquiescence for the time being.

Philo then turned to Wayne and said, "How about you Brother Wayne? Are you willing to commit to a complete love?"

"I guess that's harmless enough," he said "I'll play along."

"It's more than playing along," said Philo. "I need a definite commitment to divine love."

"I said I'd play along."

"OK," said Philo. "But to play along I need a definite yes out of you. Are you willing to commit to complete or divine love?"

"OK, the answer's yes. Now let's get on with this," said Wayne.

"Very good," said Philo with obvious satisfaction in his voice. "Now Joseph are you willing to complete the circle and give your definite commitment?"

"I've already committed," I said.

Philo looked a little startled for the first time, then spoke after a pause, "Have you spoken to the Guardians then?"

"I'm not sure who these Guardians are, but I have committed myself to divine love."

"If you have not committed yourself directly to the Guardians or one of their representatives then you have not yet fully committed to divine love," he said.

"I can't be more committed than all the way committed and I do have a personal commitment to fulfill the purpose of divine love whatever that may involve," I said.

"Then say yes to me!" commanded Philo, "For I am the representative of divine love."

"And if I say yes what or who am I saying yes to? What will you expect from me?"

Philo paused and spoke. "Remember the story I told you about the ski instructor. An experienced instructor does not have to explain everything in advance, but requires a certain amount of trust. What you must do is let go of all the baggage you carry around and trust me. Everyone else has made a commitment. Don't you think it's about time you yielded yourself to love?"

"I keep telling you that I have already committed myself to love."

"But I can see by your aura, my friend, that you have a lot of negative energy that you have carried around for many years. You need to let go and let others help you. You are too fiercely independent. Just release that individualism and merge with the group energy."

"A little independence is a good thing," I said. As I looked in Philo's direction I felt a familiar Presence, the Presence I felt with John and in the New Jerusalem. As I tried to tune into it I began to see Philo's aura and as I looked it occurred to me that his description of me applied to himself. Over his head there appeared to be a dark circulating cloud and around his body was a circulating mass which was red, brown and an off-blue with patches of black. As I attempted to tune into what it meant I immediately registered that this man did truly lack an understanding of spiritual love just as I suspected. Words seemed to form in my heart and mind which said, "Do not doubt that which you receive from the highest part of yourself."

I looked again at Philo and noticed a cord having the appearance of gray and blue hues which seemed to be connected to his middle back and extending upwards towards infinity. I assumed that this was the silver cord I had read about in metaphysical books and also mentioned in the Bible.

After receiving this revelation I said back to him, "I think you are giving me a description of your own condition, my friend."

Philo paused a moment. I got the distinct impression that he felt a strong impulse to lash out at me and would have if it suited his purpose, but held that feeling in check and with controlled calmness replied, "Love knows no darkness, but dispels darkness. Now since you are unwilling to make a definite commitment to one who knows and is able to teach you, do you think you would be so kind as to remove yourself from this class and go into another room so we can continue with oneness?"

"I don't think so," I replied. "Not as long as Elizabeth is here with you. If Elizabeth wants to leave with me then I will leave you alone for a while; otherwise, I am staying with her."

Elizabeth spoke up, "You're being overprotective here Sweetie. I can take care of myself. Brother Philo seems harmless enough."

"I don't care," I said. "If you're staying, I'm staying."

"Then why don't you just make the commitment to love?" said Lance. "Then we can proceed with the class as it was intended."

"If my personal commitment to spiritual love is not good enough for Philo, then that's a problem he has to deal with. This is my definite stand. It's your move Philo."

Philo looked a little ruffled. "Normally I teach in friendly quarters where those who are negative leave before we continue, but since we are in your home I cannot force you to depart. We will continue, but I do ask you to give me respect as a teacher and to participate with an open mind. If you do, you will see the wisdom of my direction."

"I am generally quite a cooperative character," I said.

"We will continue then," he said. "You have disrupted our state of mind so we will start again and move forward." Philo then proceeded to again take us through the program of feeling the heat and ended with recommitting Lance, Wayne and Elizabeth. Finally he looked at me and said, "Now, Joseph, are you willing to make a general commitment to oneness and love?"

"OK," I said. "I guess I can give you that much."

"Very good," he said. "We will proceed on the assumption that you are one hundred percent committed to love and will follow the teacher to new avenues of knowledge and experience."

I decided to remain silent.

Philo paused and continued, "One of the major things that keeps us from experiencing a fullness of love is that there is a veil between us and our true selves. We continue to feed this veil of darkness in many ways on many levels. On subjective levels we keep love away with prejudice, hate, jealousy, possessiveness and other negative feelings. This negativity also has its representation on the physical level. Just as we hide our true selves with negative clothes on the spiritual level, even so do we hide our true physical selves with physical clothing. Clothing is a symbol of mankind's attempt to hide what he or she really is. The truth is this, the physical can be healed by removing spiritual causes and the spiritual can be healed by making a correction on the physical level. True work on the physical level has many prejudices and resistances attached to it, but once they are removed it is much easier and faster to progress on all levels."

I began to see where this was going, but wasn't sure what to do at this point.

Philo continued, "Now to take your first major step the most difficult part will be the setting aside of any prejudice you may have. Once this is done the physical part is extremely easy and leads to a pleasant and unexpected liberation and freedom to explore real love."

Philo then stood up and said, "Now we will begin shedding the physical symbol that hides the true love within." After making this statement Philo began taking off all his clothes and continued until he was completely nude. As he stood before us in the buff Philo spoke again, "See how easy this was for me to do. Because our prejudices are removed the removal of that which hides our true physical selves was very easy. It took only a very small amount of effort and energy. Even so on the spiritual level it takes only a small amount of effort to find a true fullness of love. The reason I asked for a commitment from you to complete love is because we are all reluctant to experience it because of our prejudice. This commitment you made allows you to set aside that illusion and bare your physical self as well as your soul. You have therefore made a promise to follow me toward love and make bare your physical selves. How about you Lance, are you willing to follow your word over your prejudice?"

"Sure," said Lance who stood up and began taking off his clothes without reservation. As he was in the middle of shedding he said, "Come on Wayne. Join in with us. You aren't shy are you?"

Wayne, who was never known to be shy, replied, "I don't see much purpose in it, but if Elizabeth isn't offended I guess I could go along as an experiment."

"Do you see anything to be offended at?" said Philo to Elizabeth.

"I don't suppose so," she said.

Then Wayne started taking off his clothes.

Philo looked intently at Elizabeth. "Now you need to bare your physical as a first step toward releasing real love and freeing yourself from negative energy forever."

Elizabeth looked toward me and I gave her a look that showed my disapproval.

"Don't look outside of yourself for approval," said Philo. "Look within and that which is within will want to go toward the fire of love. Do you feel the fire?"

"Yes," she said.

"Do you seek the love?"

"Yes."

"Then bare your true self."

As Philo proceeded I felt disgusted with this attempt at controlling my wife, but something inside myself told me not to interfere with Elizabeth's free will.

"If my husband does, then I will," she said.

"I see no purpose in doing this," I said. "I think it is an attempt at mind control."

"Don't be silly," said Lance. "I've done this in groups with Brother Philo several times and believe me it's not what you think. This class produces a great liberating experience."

"You can run around naked in the mall if you want," I said. "but I just don't see any benefit in going along with this."

"I think it's kind of silly too," said Wayne. "But I agreed to give this a chance and maybe something interesting will happen. Who knows? Let's get on with it."

I was surprised to hear this from Wayne. He normally is against being controlled more than I am. Perhaps he didn't see the situation from that perspective.

Then Philo spoke again to Elizabeth, "You are paying too much attention to voices outside of yourself. Look within yourself and make your decision. I know you love your husband, but you must not live your life governed by his thoughts."

"I would still feel much more comfortable participating if Joe disrobed too," she replied.

"Yea, what's your problem?" Lance said to me. "Are you shy or something?"

"You have all seen me in the buff except for Philo, so that's not a big deal," I said. "Call me old fashioned, but I think my wife's body is for my male eyes only, and even if she were not involved I do not support any action that seems to be for the sole purpose of control such as this."

Philo let out a laugh that reminded me of a laugh of a professor responding to a stupid remark from a student. Then he said, "My poor deceived friend, you are indeed backward here and not in a good way. In all of creation man is the only animal that clothes himself. This is fine if we are in need of warmth, but it becomes evil when we seek to hide ourselves. The first step to finding who we are in the real world of spirit is to reveal who we are in the physical. When we can let down the barriers represented by clothing and just be whoever we really are in relation to each other, then we can establish a higher relationship on the spiritual level. We seek not to lust after your wife's body or control your mind, but only to take relationship to a higher level. Just let go of your fears and possessiveness and be one with us."

"I choose not to and that comes from my inner self," I said.

"But what's the harm of just trying this once?" said Elizabeth. "If Philo takes us somewhere we will have an interesting experience and if not then what's the loss? I'm sure these guys have seen naked women more beautiful than I am."

"This goes way beyond getting naked," I said. "This guy has a hidden agenda and control through this manipulation is his first step."

Philo laughed again. "Why are you so paranoid about being controlled here? I could not control you if I wanted to. Lance has been with me for some time now and I could not control him if I wanted to. The truth is that you have inhibitions about being nude and you need to face this prejudice you have about being totally honest on the physical level."

"Maybe he's right," said Elizabeth. "When you think about it, what could be wrong with doing this? It's not like we are going to have an orgy."

"Very good thinking," said Philo. "And don't forget that you gave me your personal commitment to follow this course so if you are true to your word you we need to proceed here."

"She didn't give any commitment to getting naked with you," I said.

"Oh, but she did," he commented. "She made a definite commitment to complete love and the first step toward this is complete honesty. To be completely honest we must reveal who we are on the physical level. If she is to fulfill her word she must take this step."

"I guess I did give my word," she said.

"But you didn't give your word on this," I said. "You don't need to do this to discover complete love. This is nonsense."

"Again, I remind you," said Philo, "that this is the first step toward complete love, and if I am right then she would break her word by not following this procedure. I hate to say this, but if you break your word, the dagger will come back along with the negativity and the chances are that your disease will return."

Elizabeth looked shaken, "Why do you say such a thing?"

"Because breaking a commitment to a Master Teacher is breaking a link to your soul, and without this link to your soul your disease will come back. Look at it this way, by proceeding with the course you will insure your health as well as discovering the completeness of love. But if you do not go ahead you could revert to your prior state and disease. Even if you get nothing from the course you have nothing to lose and much to gain."

This was too much for me and I had to speak plainly, "Listen here. I'm not sure what your final goal is, but I'm putting a stop to your mind games on my wife. Elizabeth and I will go into another room and let you guys finish your love seance. Just come get us when you are done."

I grabbed Elizabeth's hand and attempted to pull her along with me, but she pulled back. "Wait a minute!" she said. "You are making a decision for me here. Maybe Philo was right. Maybe you do control me too much."

"But Sweetie, I thought you were beginning to see through

this guy. I felt as if you were looking for a way out."

"But even if I didn't want to participate, I also do not want to take a chance in getting my disease back. I think I should play it safe and go ahead with this. Then when Philo goes back to California we'll never see him again and it'll be as if nothing ever happened." Then she started crying, "Don't you understand! I don't want this disease back."

Philo grabbed her with perfect timing and said, "There, there, I think you need some support here." Then he gave her a long hug.

My first impulse was to physically throw him out of the house, but I resisted, and as I looked upon Philo embracing my wife and Elizabeth almost hypnotically enjoying it I said a prayer within my heart for help. I felt I was in a catch 22. If I tried to force my will I felt as if I may alienate Elizabeth, and if I didn't I felt that I may lose her to some strange hypnotic control that Philo seemed to be gaining over her. As I searched my heart I again felt that wonderful spiritual energy come to me and as this rested upon me my eyes became open in a way I had never experienced before.

What then happened to me could not have taken more than a couple of seconds of real time, but what I beheld had the information of a two-hour movie. Instead of Philo and Elizabeth standing before me I saw myself as a Knight of the Temple in that past as earlier related by Elizabeth. I saw that I was tied down in a torture chamber and in a nearby room was Elizabeth as the young man she was in that life and talking to her was Philo! He was not called Philo then but was Brother Phillippi, one who had great authority in the church. Their conversation was revealed to me as follows:

(Bother Phillippi) "Our last subject was a tough one, but just before he died he told us that this knight we have before us has the secrets we have been looking for."

(Elizabeth in the past) "And how will I know when I find what you are looking for?"

(Bother Phillippi) "He knows what he is supposed to tell you. Just let me know everything he reveals no matter how absurd. Do not take his life until you have inflicted all the pain necessary to obtain everything he knows."

(Elizabeth) "But we have been inflicting so much pain. Do you really think all of this is necessary?"

(Bother Phillippi) "Do not in any way question my authority

again. Just remember this: these knights have stolen invaluable artifacts and writings from the church. These are not normal thieves, but have stolen from God and we must do whatever is necessary to return to God that which is the Church's right to possess. Any pain you cause these knights is a small price to pay to make the church whole again. Spare nothing with this knight. We cannot do enough to punish him for his crimes. Think of it this way. The hot iron we give him will be cool compared to the fire of Hell from Almighty God, which he will endure for eternity."

(Elizabeth) "I do not doubt your authority. I know you speak for the Pope who speaks for God. I will do what you say even though it is distasteful to me."

(Bother Phillippi) "Remember. Reveal only to me the church related information you extract from him. You can give anything else to the King's representatives, but if he mentions anything about bells, writings or a chalice, save this information for me only. Is that understood?"

(Elizabeth) "Yes."

After this dialog passed by me I seemed to have discerned much more information. I saw that Elizabeth in that life was somehow involved in an inner circle that belonged to Brother Phillippi. His inner circle was presented to its members as an inner order commissioned by the Pope, but in reality it was entirely Brother Phillippi's creation. Brother Phillippi taught his students regularly with hypnotic techniques reinforced by many fears such as torture if they betrayed the group and the pain of eternal hell in the Hereafter. I saw that in this life Elizabeth was a basically good person who was deceived by this man's craftiness.

Next it was revealed to me that Wayne was also a Knight who was tortured to death in that life and Lance was also there as an authority among the knights. However, Lance escaped torture and death by cooperating with the King.

After this I was moved backward in time to other lifetimes and saw that both Elizabeth and I had encountered Philo many times and rarely in a good way. Time and time again he had garnered authority to himself and used it to manipulate others. He seemed to repeatedly take a special interest in controlling the entity who is now Elizabeth. Then I was moved forward in time until we arrived at the present and saw that the power of Philo and others like him was diminishing because people, as a whole, were becoming more independent. I perceived that there was not any regular organization in today's world where Philo seemed to fit so he became an authority unto himself and was seeking to establish a power base of his own creation. This thing he sought to create would be of no great significance, but he was in danger of destroying the free will of a few souls, and if one of those was my wife, he would then become a successful agent of the Dark Brothers.

At this realization I was released from the vision. I immediately stepped toward Elizabeth, grabbed her and pulled her toward me and said, "Sweetheart, I know who this is. He was Brother Phillippi who ordered you to torture the Knights of the Temple and now he's trying to control you once again."

Elizabeth backed off from me, "Where did you get such an outrageous idea?"

"Just trust me this one time. This is Brother Phillippi."

"And how would you know anything about Brother Phillippi?" asked Philo, and at that moment I intuitively realized that he possessed a knowledge of who he was.

"I know who you are and what you want to do," I said.

"You know nothing about me and have no understanding of the light that I bring," he said in a voice that was much cooler than any previous tone of voice he used before.   Wayne and Lance just looked on in curious wonder during this exchange.

"If you truly remember me, then you would know the secret of the tree of life," Philo continued. "You would also know the meaning of the bells. Tell me about them and I will release your wife from her commitment."

"I told you nothing then and will tell you nothing now," I said.

This seemed to jar Elizabeth into asking, "Are you really the same entity as Brother Phillippi?"

Philo paused a moment and replied, "I do not know who this Brother Phillippi is, but in past lives I have been the true caretaker of the Tree of Life and the bells, and am supposed to retrieve them again in this life. If your husband knows anything about them he should tell me."

"All you will be allowed to know you can read in the books that I shall write," I said.

"But you will not be able to write all the details," he said. "Tell me what you know and how you know it and I shall release your wife from her commitment."

"I can only tell you this. I know who you are. You did not get what you were looking for from the Knights of the Temple and you shall not get it in this life."

Philo looked impatient, then composed himself and asked, "Tell me what you know about the bells."

"If I did know something I wouldn't tell you. Not in the last life and not in this one."

"You mentioned something about writing a book about a 2000 year old man that you met. You really have met someone, haven't you?"

"I wouldn't tell you if I had."

"That's enough!" he said with a raised voice. "I can tell that you are completely unwilling to cooperate. I am also unwilling to cooperate. Elizabeth! Keep your commitment and disrobe this instant or your disease will return."

She looked back at him with fear in her eyes and said, "You were Brother Phillippi, weren't you?"

Philo looked visibly disturbed, "It doesn't matter who I was. You made a commitment and must keep it or your guilt will punish you by returning the disease to your body!"

I stepped toward Philo and said, "She made no such commitment to undress for you. She made a commitment to love just as she has always been committed to it. All she has to do to fulfill that commitment is to love to the best of her power and I know that is what she will always do."

Philo looked at Elizabeth. "As I told you - you listen too much to your husband. You must make the decision. Are you going to join us in physical honesty or not?"

"I don't think so," she said. "If you want to continue this class then my husband and I will go into another room or you may leave and go elsewhere. I am done with this continuing education for the moment."

"Very well," he said. "There is nothing I can do to help you then. The whole matter is out of my hands. Your disease will come back within days, perhaps hours. I can see that dagger reinserting itself as we speak and when it is in your back again, and you are weak again you will have to come back to me and bare yourself before me if you wish to be restored to health."

"I think it's time you left our home," I said. "You have just sunk to the lowest level of manipulation that I have ever imagined." I then walked over to his pile of clothes and picked them up and threw them out the door. "Now I am going to the bathroom. When I come out I want you and your clothes to be in the same place."

As I started walking down the hall Lance spoke up. "Now

hold on here. Just hold on. I'm not sure what has just happened or what your problem is Joe, but Brother Philo and I are together here. It's obvious that you and him have some bad vibes so I'll tell you what. Just let us stay tonight and we'll get another place to stay tomorrow until we leave. How about it?"

"I'll do that for you Lance because you are my friend, but keep this guy away from my wife."

"It will not be long before she comes to me for help," said Philo. "When her disease returns and she needs my help, how are you going to keep her away from me then?"

"Lance," I said, "take this guy in the guest bedroom, out of my sight, or he has to leave immediately."

"OK," said Lance. He then led Philo down the hall to the bedroom, but as Philo walked down the hall he turned his head and looked at Elizabeth and mouthed two words with a smile. I thought the words were "You're mine," but I wasn't sure. I had never seen a person push his luck so much.

At this point Wayne had his clothes back on, looking a little embarrassed, if that is possible for Wayne. He was the type of character who didn't embarrass that easily.

"I must say this," said Wayne, "this evening has been more interesting than if the whole event turned into an orgy with dancing girls. I must say that Philo is a piece of work. I'd like to know what his whole motive was though."

"I'll tell you one thing," I said, "it's not the teaching of universal love."

"I suppose not," he said. "Most preachers and New Agers are spreading love to the benefit of number one. Some things never change."

"There are a lot of phony teachers out there," I said, "but I also think there are a few good ones."

"Possibly," he said. "I guess I'd better be going. I'll catch you for breakfast this weekend."

"I'll plan on it," I said.

"By the way," Wayne smiled to Elizabeth, "now that you've seen me in the buff I hope your fantasies of me don't hurt your relationship with Joe here."

"I don't think that's going to be a problem," she said, returning the jest.

"Yea, Wayne. That's not going to be a problem," I said allowing him his moment of levity.

"Just thought I'd voice my concern," he said walking out the door.

"At least Wayne is harmless," I said to Elizabeth after he left, "but something about Philo has made my skin crawl ever since I met him."

"Something about him makes my skin crawl now," said Elizabeth. "I just don't know why I didn't sense something earlier."

"You apparently have a history of being controlled by the guy," I said. "Based on what we know now, I can see why you were influenced by him."

"Perhaps," she said, "but I think I should have woke up earlier. I have my modern-day Knight to thank for helping me. Thank you my sweet." She then gave me a long, lingering hug.

CHAPTER FIFTEEN
Temptations

After we retired to bed I laid still for a while reflecting on the events of the evening. I sensed a different atmosphere around Elizabeth, actually a familiar atmosphere - different from what it had been since the time Philo arrived, but similar to the old loving Elizabeth whom I had always loved.

"I'm sorry," she said unexpectedly.

"Sorry for what?" I asked.

"Sorry I have not been the person you married since Philo showed up."

"I have to admit that you have seemed different the past few days," I said.

"I think I know the cause," she said.

"I think I do too," I said. "First tell me what you think."

"I've been laying here thinking about the past life memories that John retrieved for me. Now I see that Philo was Brother Phillippi who ordered me to torture the Knights. I remember that he had a hypnotic effect on me in that life and it seemed to carry over into this present contact. When I met him this time I fell under his spell just as I did when he used a hypnotic influence on me and other followers in secret meetings in that life hundreds of years ago. You were able to help me shake loose from him in that time long ago and now you helped me again. I feel so foolish that I needed your assistance again. I should have seen through him."

"Actually, I may have a better understanding than you think about Philo's influence upon you," I said. "Tonight I had some additional information revealed to me. I was shown that Philo was not only Brother Phillippi, but that we have encountered him numerous times through several lifetimes. He has repeatedly singled you out for domination and in that past life you remember he almost succeeded. You are like a challenge to him and this attitude has carried over with him into this lifetime. I have the feeling that he either wants to conquer you or destroy you. I don't believe we have seen the last of him."

"I hope we have," she said. "Now that I know who he is, he gives me the creeps."

"Me too. I don't feel good about having someone so sinister staying in our home," I agreed.

"Will you forgive me again?" she said, putting her arms around my neck.

"For what?"

"For pulling away from you... For losing our connection for a while."

"There is nothing to forgive," I said. "Here's the way I look at it. Remember that stage hypnotist we saw at the fair? He told a subject that even after he awoke he would be under the power of his planted suggestion, and whenever he would scratch his head the person would crow like a rooster."

"I remember that," Elizabeth chuckled. "Every time the hypnotist scratched his head the guy got up and crowed. It was hilarious."

"But here's what's interesting," I said. "After the guy made a fool of himself the hypnotist asked him why he was crowing. Do you remember his answer?"

"I think so. He said he was just trying to be funny."

"That's right. Now here's what I find interesting about that answer. The guy performed a crazy act because of a subconscious suggestion, but because he couldn't remember the true reason for it he thought that the crowing must have been his own idea. Because people were laughing at him he concluded that he must have been trying to just be funny. The guy was not himself, but he thought he was himself."

"So you are saying that I wasn't responsible for falling under Philo's spell?"

"Well, ultimately we are responsible for all of our actions. For instance, the guy would not have crowed like a chicken, even under hypnosis, if it was totally against a principle he believed in. But a subject can be made to do something fairly crazy if it does not go against his belief system. Philo goes around teaching love, which everyone thinks is a good thing; therefore, his hypnotic techniques do not seem so objectionable. But to your credit you resisted him when you realized that something was amiss."

"Yes. When I realized he may have been Brother Phillippi it was as if a spell was broken. You tried to hypnotize me before and I was not a particularly good subject. This spell or trance from Philo was much more powerful than any hypnosis I have ever seen. It still bothers me. I keep thinking of a dagger returning to my back and getting the disease again." I sensed her shutter.

"You've got to put that thought out of your mind," I warned.

"I know, but the harder I try to not think about it the more it seems to loom before me."

"Maybe you're trying too hard."

"It doesn't seem to matter. If I try to ignore the thought, it is there... and if I don't try, it is also there. It's almost like Philo is still here with me."

"We'll just have to cast him out then," I said.

"I hope so. I certainly hope so," she said as she drifted off into silence.

The next morning I awoke to the sound of footsteps in the hall. At first I thought someone was getting up to use the bathroom and I tried to go back to sleep, but felt an uneasy feeling. After a few minutes I decided I would arise and see if anyone was up. I ambled down the hall into the kitchen and no one was there. Then I noticed a light in the family room and headed that direction. To my surprise there was Philo hacking away at my computer. I couldn't believe my eyes at the gall of this man.

"What the hell are you doing?" I demanded.

Philo looked very startled, then replied, "Nothing. I couldn't sleep and got up and noticed that you had a computer so I thought I'd play around with it." As he arose I noticed he put a floppy disc in his pocket.

"What did you just put in your pocket?" I demanded.

"It's just a disc I brought with me," he said looking downward.

"Let me see it," I said firmly.

"I don't think I need to show you something that belongs to me," he said defiantly.

"I think you need to show me so I can see whether it belongs to you or not," I said.

"I don't think so," he said. "I'm out of here." He then attempted to walk past me as if I was not there.

I grabbed him by the arm and said, "Show me that disc or I

will take it from you."

He pulled his arm away, backing off, and said. "Lay off, will you? I'm getting out of your hair, OK?"

"Not with that disc."

He started to turn around and I knew I had to act now or never so I tackled him. Philo looked surprised and angry as I put a neckhold on him. "What in the hell is your problem?" he demanded.

I tightened my hold and said, "Just give me that disc and I'll let you go."

"You have no right to my property," he said as he struggled fiercely to break my hold.

After a few seconds of struggle Lance showed up in the doorway. "What in the world are you doing to Brother Philo?"

"He has one of my computer discs in his pocket," I said.

"It's my disc," said Philo. "Get him off me!"

Lance grabbed me by the arm and tugged. "Come on. Let him go."

"I'll let him go if he agrees to let me check the disc. I'm sure he's got some of my files."

"I'm sure Brother Philo will let you check it out, won't you?" Lance assured me, looking at Philo.

"OK, OK, I'll let him look at the disc," said Philo.

"There, he's going to let you check the disc. Now let go of him before you hurt him."

I reluctantly let go and said, "Now let me look at that disc."

Philo took a moment adjusting his neck and gradually reached in his pocket and pulled out a disc that had no label on it. I knew I had some new discs that were not labeled and figured it could have been one of them. I reached out my hand and said. "Now give me that disc so I can check it out."

Philo acted like he was going to hand it to me and suddenly snapped the disc in two. "There, I showed it to you," he said.

"Why did you do that?" Lance said with surprise.

"Because he's guilty," I said flatly.

"That disc contained some of my private writings that are not to be revealed to any man," Philo said defensively. "I couldn't allow them to fall into the wrong hands."

"It contained *my* private writings," I said. "But now you've broken the disc I can't prove it."

"If Brother Philo says it's his private writings, then I have to believe him," said Lance.

"What's going on here?" said Elizabeth appearing in the doorway.

"Just some friendly conversation," I said. "Perhaps you'd like to make these boys some breakfast so they can be on their way."

"Sure," she said with curiosity in her voice.

As Elizabeth made breakfast and Lance and Philo were taking showers I checked out the files on my computer. I noticed that the window open on my Mac had my main file containing notes about John. I also saw that the date of the file was the current date proving that Philo had actually opened it. "At least he didn't get a copy," I thought to myself.

At breakfast we treated Lance and Philo with frank cordiality. Lance made arrangements with a friend to stay at his house and I drove them both over there. After Lance got out of the car Philo turned to me and said in a low whisper, "I'm glad to know that John is back. Perhaps we will meet soon," he grinned.

"I knew you opened that file," I said.

"Opened, read and memorized," he said. "I think my path will soon take me back here to Boise."

"Those notes are for a fiction book I'm writing," I said trying to diffuse him.

"I don't think so," he chuckled, getting out of the car. "We will meet again soon. By the way, tell John hello again from his old friend. He'll know who I am." Philo laughed softly in a way that disturbed me.

I felt uneasy again on my drive back home. I thought it was probably because Philo unnerved me, but when I entered the house I was horrified to find Elizabeth sitting in a chair, shaking and crying.

"What is it sweetheart?'

"I'm sick again," she said. "I can't get up."

"It's just temporary. I think Philo just spooked you. That's all."

"But I can't get up. I'm worse than I have ever been!" she shouted. "I feel like I'm going to die."

I knelt beside her. "Tell me exactly what happened."

She wept a moment and dried her eyes. "After you left I went to the bathroom and as I was looking in the mirror I saw the dagger!"

"What do you mean you saw the dagger?"

"There was a dagger in my back!" she shouted at the top of

her voice. "There really is a dagger after all!"

"It's going to be OK," I said as I hugged her, trying to calm her down. "Then what happened?"

"Right after I saw the dagger I collapsed. My strength was just instantly gone... Just gone!"

I looked her directly in the eyes and said. "Remember how we talked about hypnosis and how suggestions can be planted? I think Philo planted this in you. That dagger is not real. You just think it is."

"The dagger is real! I saw it with my own eyes."

"I know you think you saw it."

"But I did see it! How can you not believe me?"

After careful thought I said, "I know this is hard for you, but please listen. You didn't feel sick until you actually saw the dagger, but if the dagger was real it was already in you before you looked in the mirror. Why did you only feel ill after you actually saw it?"

"I don't know. All I know is that I saw it, then I felt it in my back, and afterwards I lost my strength. I know what happened and that is all I can say."

"You've got to think this thing through, Sweetie. This is another case where the mind must rule the feelings. Your mind must convince your feelings that this is illusion. Because you feel this thing is real, it has the power of reality."

"I can't," she cried "Don't you understand? I actually saw the dagger, I feel the dagger and I'm sick again. It doesn't matter what I think, it just won't go away."

"We'll find a way to lick this thing permanently," I said.

"I think I know the way," she said hopefully.

"And what's that?"

"I think that if Philo pulled this dagger out again everything would be OK."

Her statement struck me like a dagger. I knew within myself that any assistance rendered by Philo would only pull her deeper into illusion. "I want you to listen to me," I replied firmly, holding her tightly, "I know this is difficult to face, but here's what I think would happen if we called Philo. He would take this illusionary dagger out and you would have temporary relief. Then your problem would come back and in the end you would have to call upon him again and again until you are totally dependent on him."

"But if I can just get the dagger out I won't have to be dependent on anyone."

"But there is no dagger to take out. Don't you understand? Philo just planted a negative thought in your mind and you're falling for it."

"You don't understand how I feel," she cried." I have had hope revived again and again and now I finally thought I was healed for good. Now look at me. I feel worse than ever. If this is the way it's going to be, I would have been better off dying and getting everything over with. Now that I've gone this far I want my health back and I think getting that dagger out will do it."

"Sweetie. Every bone in my body tells me that we should not call Philo. Think back to your memories of him in that past life. If you remember what he was like, then you will not want to contact him no matter what. Now the day after tomorrow I see John. I think he will be able to help us. I want you to promise me that you will wait until then before you even consider calling Philo."

"But Philo and Lance will be on a plane back to California on Thursday. It may be too late to get help by then."

"But who is it that is more logical to trust? Philo - who has been an enemy of all that is good for many lifetimes - or John, who has been a continuous servant of mankind for two thousand years?"

"It doesn't matter to me. Can't you understand that I am afraid and that if I can just get rid of that dagger I think the fear and the disease will just go away?"

I felt exasperated as I continued, "But look at the choice here. Philo brings nothing but fear, whereas John has brought nothing but peace and love and light. The internal feelings generated by Philo has been only fear generated, but John causes us to feel a spiritual and holy feeling within ourselves. We've got to ask ourselves what are we going to trust here. We can't yield to fear."

"That's easy for you to say." she said defiantly. "You're not sick."

"I think it would be easier for me to say this if I was the one who was sick. You don't realize how much I feel for you when you go through something like this. Even though I want more than anything for you to be permanently well, I don't think we should contact Philo. I believe we should wait until our next contact with John. If he does not have a good answer or offer us hope, I will pay Philo's plane ticket to come back up here if necessary. How's that for a deal?"

"I'll try to hold on, but I feel like I am getting worse by the moment."

"We haven't said the Song for three or four days. Maybe saying it now will help." I grabbed her hand. "Will you say it with me?"

At first I felt some resistance from her to saying the Song, but as we said it I felt a sense of peace come to us and I perceived that Elizabeth was also feeling it. After a pause I spoke to her. "The feeling I get right now is that we must follow the sense of love and peace as it comes to us, and I don't think either of us felt it with Philo. I know that you feel it now just as I do."

"I do feel that saying the Song quieted some of my fears," Elizabeth said softly.

"Let's say it again."

She said it again with me. This time I felt Elizabeth putting her heart into it, having no resistance to the spiritual energy. The energy and sense of peace was greatly amplified. It felt so good that we both said it together a third time. After this I gently picked her up and carried her over to the couch and sat down with her on my lap. We hugged each other for at least ten minutes, just basking in the energy of the peace that passes all understanding.

Elizabeth broke the silence. "You know, when you go a period of time without this wonderful energy you tend to almost forget that it exists, always there waiting for us to tap into."

"Yes. It's like we go away from the Spirit of God, but the Spirit never goes away from us."

"Yes, that's exactly it." She hugged me more tightly, almost like she was seeking energy from me. "Will you say a prayer for me?" she asked.

"Sure. What do you want me to ask for? Your health?"

"Something more important than that. I want you to ask God to help me stay in this true light and love that we feel right now so I don't forget again and become overwhelmed by fear and negativity. Even if I were to die soon, it would not be so bad if I passed away feeling this peaceful."

"That's my old Elizabeth speaking. Now all I ask is that you quit drifting in and out of your normal positive and loving self."

"That's what I want too... Now say the prayer."

I won't repeat the prayer here. Some of it was of a private nature, but I did ask God to keep both of us in His light and love and requested that we have power to stay in consistent tune with this most great peace of His Presence. I also prayed that Elizabeth would receive her health back on a permanent basis and that the way out of fear and illusion would be revealed to us. I felt a spiritual presence with us as I prayed and thought that John may be with us. The words I spoke were inspired and touched the soul of Elizabeth. We both cried together after I finished.

"I think I feel a little stronger," Elizabeth said after several moments.

"Do you think you can walk again?"

"I'm not sure. I can try."

I backed away from her and said, "Try and come to me."

She got up with hope in her eyes and took two steps. At that instant I saw fear and doubt in her eyes and she fell to the floor. "Elizabeth! What is wrong? I thought you were going to make it."

"I thought I was too," she cried. "But as I started to walk the thought of the dagger came back into my mind and I couldn't push it away. The next thing I knew I saw a dagger in your hand. My mind tells me that you would never hurt me, but a part of me is afraid. Suddenly, I love you but am afraid of you at the same time."

The real dagger, I thought to myself, are the thoughts planted in her mind by Philo, but now was not the time to dwell on that idea. I picked her up and sat her on the couch again. "Sweetheart, you are torn here between fear and love. I remember a scripture from the Bible that says perfect love casts out all fear. I think the thing to do right now is to not even think about walking or your illness. Instead, let's just concentrate on our love. In our finer moments I think our love is perfect, and I know that you know deep within yourself that you have nothing to fear from me. Let's just hold each other again and dwell on the loving moments we have had together."

She seemed to think this was a good idea and we held each other and reflected in silence for a good fifteen minutes.

Elizabeth finally spoke softly, "Tell me that John will be able to make me well again permanently."

"I cannot predict what John will tell me on our next meeting, but I do have his word that when I learn the first three keys you will be healed permanently. Now he indicated that you may be healed early, but somehow that is up to you. Remember he spoke of three temptations that you must pass before you see him again?"

"Well, I feel like I have been through a dozen temptations," she said.

"I agree. It looks like temptations of some kind seem to be coming every five minutes. But if we try to narrow them down I would say that the doctor's negativity was your first one. You were weakened but then you saw correctly and got your strength back."

"And I'm sure the second one had a lot to do with Philo," she added.

"Yes," I said. "You were tempted to believe his illusion, but you were able to see through it."

"So, if I am going through the third what could it be?" she asked. "I am no longer deceived by him. I know he was Brother Phillippi in a past life and he wants to control me in this one."

"But you still keep seeing that dagger," I reminded her.

"Yes, but I must concede this is probably some aftereffect of his mind control. The trouble is, even this realization does not seem to help. I don't understand. If this is some big temptation then I should at least know what I am supposed to do to get out of it."

At that moment I wished more than anything I knew what to tell her, but I felt helpless. "I'm sure John will help us," I assured her. "It's just the day after tomorrow and I'll see him again. Do you think you can hang on until then?"

"I think so," she said with moist eyes. "I hope so."

"I know so," I said hugging her tightly.

Unexpectedly the phone rang. "What a time for my clients to start calling," I thought. I answered the phone and there was silence. After about five seconds I said, "Is anyone there?"

"It's me, Brother Joseph. Your new best friend."

"Philo! Is that you? What in the hell do you want?"

"Speaking of hell," he said, "I felt concern that your wife may be experiencing some of it."

"She just needs you to leave her alone!" I almost shouted.

"If I leave her alone with that dagger she will die. I would advise you to let me talk to her. Perhaps I can save her from this dagger you keep throwing at her."

"It's you who is planting the dagger!" I growled.

"Are you sure about that?" he asked. "Are you telling me that your marriage has been perfect and you have never sent her negative thoughts and feelings? I don't think so. You know there is something to what I am saying here."

Suddenly, I felt a wave of memories go through my mind and I became aware of every argument and negative moment we had ever exchanged between us. For a moment I felt fearful that he may be right, but I pushed that fear in the background and said, "I'm hanging up now. Please don't call again."

After I hung up Elizabeth said, "What does he want this time?"

"He knows you're having trouble with the dagger again. Somehow he caused this and he wants to get into our lives and control you for some reason. We can't let him do that Elizabeth. Tell me you won't answer him if he calls when I am gone?"

"How will I know if it's him?"

"The caller ID says he's calling from Bob's house. You need to check the number with every call we get until he leaves town. Please tell me you'll do that."

"I don't think you need to worry. I don't want to see him even if he can heal me."

I hoped she was right, but because of her past life history I now knew she was in a particularly vulnerable area of her life and I was concerned for her. I had to get some work done so I made arrangements for her mother to take her to the doctor again. I figured the doctor probably would not be able to help her much, but that we should still do everything in the normal sense to look after her health.

Dr. Bernstein seemed concerned about her deterioration and suggested Elizabeth be hospitalized, but she refused. That evening, her strength seemed to deteriorate even more. It didn't help matters that the caller ID showed that Philo had called six times. Obviously he was trying to make direct contact with Elizabeth.

The next day was finally Thursday, my scheduled meeting with John. I was so concerned about Philo getting hold of Elizabeth that I rearranged my appointments and took the day off. Lance and Philo were supposed to leave on a flight around 6 PM so I thought if I stayed with her until that time she would be safe.

Around five O'clock as I was making us some dinner she spoke to me. "My strength has been fading terribly since you last spoke to Philo. If you do not get something workable from John I don't know what I'll do. To be honest with you I have been very tempted to call Philo and ask him to take the dagger out. Sometimes I think that if he would just take it out we would have nothing to worry about because he is going back to LA."

"I have a terrible feeling about relying on him for anything. I think if you yield to him in any degree that you will be in danger of being under his total control. Such a thing would bother me more than if you died of that disease."

"My common sense tells me you are right, but my feelings want him to come over and comfort me," she said.

"This must be your third temptation. You do not have long to hold on now before I see John so maybe we can have an answer for you."

"I hope so," she said. "I'm not big on this temptation thing. Right now I would just like to live an ordinary life and have ordinary health and die a happy old age in your arms."

"Sometimes I feel that way too," I said, "but with John entering our lives I think we may have to say good-bye to the ordinary part. I have a feeling that even when you get well, things will never be ordinary again."

She said nothing, but I sensed a sigh within her.

Later that evening I kissed Elizabeth good-bye and got in my car and headed for Denny's in perhaps my most anticipated meeting with John. As I turned on the key my mind reflected back to the time I was teleported to Israel, but as I backed out of the garage I began to think that was some sort of one-time deal. Then about half way to Denny's some words began to form within my mind and I sensed they were from John because I now knew his vibration. The term "vibration" may seem a strange term to many, but I have learned that each soul has a distinctive vibration which is unique to itself, just as are our faces, our voices and our fingerprints. At this point I had become familiar enough with the vibration of John that I could recognize him by this method just as I could if I saw his face.

Then there were other times that the communication was subtler, where I could not tell if the communication was from within myself or from him. This is comparable to seeing a face in a distance in the dark. You think you know who it is but you are not sure. Anyway, on this occasion I was positive it was John speaking to me.

The voice said, "Go to an isolated area and stop your car."

There was a park a few blocks away that did not have much traffic at night so I drove over there and stopped the car in an area that seemed to have little traffic. The next statement I heard startled me beyond belief, especially after what I had gone through with Philo. "Please take off all your clothes so you have nothing artificial touching your body."

My first thought here is that Philo was deceiving me. Even though I was sure this was John's vibration I began to doubt. I thought within myself, "John, is that really you?"

"It is I. If you wish to see me you must follow my instructions."

At this point I considered that it may have been possible for Philo to somehow counterfeit John's vibration and he was somehow pulling a trick on me. Perhaps the real John is over at Denny's waiting for me and I will wind up being the fool. Besides, why in the world would John want me to take off my clothes? It didn't make sense to me so I sent the thought back, "To make sure it is you, John, I will go to Denny's and check out our seat. If you are not there then I will know that it is you who is speaking to me."

The voice returned, "That will not be permitted. There is a window you must take now or you will not see me this week. Contemplate and decide. You have three minutes."

For the first minute my mind fluctuated wildly between the possibility of this voice belonging to John or Philo, and for the life of me, all feeling and logic failed me. I felt like I had spent an eternity in a terrible limbo and also began to fear that I may wind up with a big zero to bring back to Elizabeth. If I can't bring back some hope to her, then I figured she would either die or go to the arms of Philo. Neither prospect was at all desirable.

Then I looked up to the skies and shouted, "John! Tell me again that it is you. Let me feel your essence and vibration one more time so I can be sure!"

There was no answer. Nothing. Nothing at all.

I felt the seconds ticking away and felt tremendous pressure to make a decision. If I am wrong perhaps Philo will assume some type of new control over my wife or me.

As my fear began to grow I reflected back to the time at Denny's that I had to give the key word to John. He went to the bathroom and when he returned I had to give it to him. I remembered that I made the right decision then because I trusted that which I received from the highest part of myself. I concluded that I must do the same again. I reflected back to the vibrations I had received from Philo. They were of a low and disturbing order. I have never felt good or a sense of true peace in his presence. But in John's presence I always felt a wonderful peaceful familiar feeling. Again I decided to go with what I knew for sure. I knew that John could communicate to me through this wonderful spiritual essence, but had no reason to believe that Philo could.

I decided to go with the communication and sent back the thought, "OK, John. I believe it is you. I don't know why you are telling me this but I am taking my clothes off." I couldn't get my pants off in the cramped space and got out of the car and finished the job looking all directions nervously. That's all I needed - to get arrested for being some kind of park pervert. After I got everything off I hopped back into the car and said, "OK John. Here I am in the buff!"

"Now take your watch off," the voice said.

"I guess when he says everything he means everything," I thought as I laid my watch on the seat.

The instant my watch dropped from my fingers I felt that dissolving feeling again and was halfway expecting to land in that apartment in Tel Aviv again, but such was not my fate. This time I felt myself being pulled downward and sensed that I was being pulled right through the earth itself at an amazing speed. The next thing I was aware of was light all around me. It was bright, but not uncomfortable. After my eyes adjusted I saw that I was in a great stone room of some kind with hundreds of pegs on the wall and on each peg was a robe of exquisite whiteness. As I was looking around, John's voice said, "Get your Robe and meet me in the Great Hall."

I felt confused, yet had a sense of knowing at the same time. He did not say *a robe*, but that I was supposed to get *my robe.* Somehow I knew there was a robe here that belonged to me. I walked over to it grabbed it and knew that this was my robe. There was even an inscription on it with what looked like Egyptian hieroglyphics. I did not know why I knew, but I knew that the meaning was *Joseph*.

I put on the robe and immediately felt a very spiritual vibration and feeling, similar to that experienced in the New Jerusalem. Then I had a feeling of deja vu like I had never felt before. I knew I had been here before, but it was like I was not supposed to remember everything. I did know, however, the way to the Great Hall and happily in the outer rim of it found John waiting for me on a crystal bench.

"Have a seat, my old friend," he said smiling.

"You called me your old friend when we first met. Now I finally realize the full meaning of what you said. We are old friends, aren't we?"

"Older than you ever imagined," he agreed.

At that instant a young lady of most wonderful beauty appeared before us with a drink in each hand. "The Ancient of Days sends you a token of his friendship by offering you this essence."

"If you think Gewurztraminer is good, just wait until you try this," said John, taking his glass.

I took the glass handed to me and looked at it. It was like a large crystal wineglass with a liquid in it that was clearer than any water I have ever seen. I held it up against the wall behind me and saw the vessel and liquid was so translucent that I could barely discern that there was a glass full of liquid in my hand. It was like seeing a ghost image of a glass in my hand.

"It tastes even better than it looks," said John as be began a hearty consumption.

I followed his lead and took a drink. The effect was different from anything I have ever imagined. There is no way I can describe it, but the best I can come up with is to say it was like a spiritual Alka Seltzer, but instead of a fizz to the body it produced a fizz to the spirit within me.

"Wow!" I exclaimed. "What is this stuff?

"From this drink," said John, "comes the ancient legends about the Elixir of the Gods."

"I can see why. This drink is amazing! I have never felt so alive. I am sure that if Elizabeth were to drink this she would be instantly cured."

"That is true," he said. "If she were here drinking with us she would be cured instantly."

"Then for God's sake bring her here now and let her have the rest of my glass!" I demanded.

"I'm sorry," he said apologetically. "That is not within my power."

"Sometimes I feel that the powers that be are playing games with Elizabeth and me," I said.

"I feel for you, my friend. Remember - I once lost my wife because she was beyond my power to save. I know exactly how you feel and more. You see, you still have a chance to save your wife, whereas I lost mine to death's door. What's even more difficult for me is that she has been reborn on the earth today and is married to a man with whom she is deeply in love and has three children. She has forgotten me, but I have not forgotten her.

"But you must realize that is the way life is. A greater livingness always requires the sacrifice of many of the things as they were, so to speak. In following the path I have chosen, I have had to leave behind the person who I thought was my soul mate and many friends and acquaintances. In return I have many new friends on a higher level and eventually I will return to earth as an ordinary mortal and pick perhaps a new soul mate."

"You say *perhaps*. Why do you say that?"

"I dream of joining with my previous wife whom I deeply loved, but I am afraid she has attached herself too strongly to this new man in her life. Actually, he is not that new by your measure. She has been with him three lifetimes now. I fear that I must choose again when I assume the regular mortal form. It looks like I will have to let the entity, who I thought was my soul mate, go, but even I have not completely adjusted to this reality yet. So my friend, I hope you can see that I have empathy for you, not because of some spiritual theory, but because of hard experience."

As John told me this I seemed to be in tune with his essence and felt a sadness even beyond that which I have experienced with Elizabeth.

"I'm sorry," I said softly. "I don't think I have ever appreciated what you have gone through."

"As you become one with me as I am one with Christ you will have to take the bad with the good, but there is a richness in becoming one that has its own reward."

"Are you saying that you have gone through an experience with Christ something like I am going through with you?"

"That and more," John smiled. "I am milk toast compared to He whom you call the Christ. His essence has positives and negatives far beyond what you have received from me. The sacrifices He made for the benefit of the world are beyond my ability to communicate with you, but, on the other hand, the joyousness of His Spirit He experiences through His spiritual conquests comprise a fullness that is difficult to hold for more than a few seconds. The time will soon come when you will know Him as I do. After you have merged with my essence then you, through me, will merge with His."

"You make me feel like I am in the first grade," I said.

"You are in the first grade," he said. "Now take the rest of your drink. Even though there are a lot of things in your life to cause worry and concern no matter how hard you try you will not be able to feel anything but a fullness of joy after you finish your glass."

I followed John's lead and drank the rest of the beautiful liquid. I had to admit I felt terrific. As an experiment I thought about Elizabeth's disease, Philo, my financial problems, but nothing seemed to distract from the feeling of joyousness I was experiencing. It was truly an amazing feeling.

"What in the world is in this drink?" I asked.

"Devas," he said.

"Devas?"

"Yes. The liquid deva essence blended with pure water."

"Aren't devas supposed to be some type of metaphysical life form?"

"Yes" said John. "Life as we know it on the earth, such as human, is on the evolutionary arc, but deva life is a descending life rather than ascending. New deva lives are not far from their pure spiritual essence and can bring spiritual renewal and physical strength to old ascending lives such as ourselves. Only the Ancient of Days has access to the pure and holy deva essence. Count yourself privileged for receiving an allotment."

"I never realized that anything like this ever existed," I said. "Yet the effect is familiar. Have I partaken of this before?"

"Did not your robe feel familiar?" he asked.

"Yes. I am sure I have been here before and that this robe I am wearing is one I have worn many times."

"You are correct," he said, "and you have drank of the elixir before just as you suspected."

"There is one more thing I am dying to ask you," I said. "The last time I was transported a great distance I took my clothes with me. This time you made me take all of my clothes off. What was the reason for that, and for that matter - where in the world are we?"

John got up and bid me his hand. "Come. Let me give you a brief tour of our facilities and then I will answer all your questions, or should I say, all that we have time for."

I got up and followed John with the anticipation that this may be our most interesting meeting yet.

CHAPTER SIXTEEN
Shamballa

John explained that the place I had arrived at was a large underground retreat used by the Brotherhood of Light. There are many details that I cannot write, except to say that the retreat was composed of many rooms and corridors. There was one large room in the center called the Great Hall. The Great Hall was large enough to seat 144,000 men and 144,000 women or 288,000 altogether. Linked to the Great Hall were twelve Grand Halls and then linked to them were numerous other smaller rooms that seemed to be classrooms, offices and living quarters of some kind. There were no lights as we know them on the earth, but all the rooms were irradiated with light. The light seemed to come from the walls themselves through some natural process.

Then I saw there were open spaces with wonderful gardens and vegetation that seemed to serve to revitalize the inhabitants when they needed a break from the mysterious work they were doing here. This was indeed a paradise of some kind that would never know night.

At the time of my visit there did not seem to be enough people present to fill the Great Hall, but there were at least several thousand I could account for. On the other hand, I did not tour the whole facility. I also noticed that all residents had on white robes very similar to my own. I was not sure at the time if they were earth residents, such as myself, or permanent residents or a combination. Finally, after a tour that seemed to revive memories more than create new ones, John led me to a small room about twenty foot square with two large crystals in the center and no apparent seating of any kind.

"Have a seat," said John, smiling.

"Surely you're joking," I said.

"Doesn't this room look familiar to you?" he asked. "Contemplate a moment and it will come to you where the seats are."

I looked around the room again and had to admit to myself that it did seem familiar to me. I found myself very curious about the full story here. "This room does seem familiar," I said. "It kind of has the feeling of a study or office that I have spent a whole lifetime in, but the whole knowledge of it seems to be hidden from me."

"You're on the right track here. Now find your seat."

I followed his words, looked around and tried to figure out where the seats were, but saw no indication that there was anything to sit on anywhere. Then the thought occurred to me that maybe there was something I was to remember, so I closed my eyes and tried to tune in to what I was supposed to discover. I had the strongest feeling that I was just supposed to sit down. At first I felt that it was a silly thought, but then it came to my mind again, but with greater familiarity, like a memory, and this time I thought there may be something to it.

"I feel like I am just supposed to sit and a seat will appear or something like that," I said.

"Why don't you just trust yourself and see what happens," John said, somewhat amused.

I started to sit several times and nothing seemed to happen and became nervous that I would fall on my tailbone.

"You won't know if your hunch was right until you sit and let go," he said.

I tried sitting again and this time let go and suddenly found myself caught by some force. I opened my eyes and witnessed myself sitting on what seemed to be thin air. "Hey, this is great!" I said.

"Lay down if you like."

I reclined nervously, and found myself lying down on this invisible force. It felt very relaxing and I found myself wishing I could have a permanent bed this comfortable.

John sat down next to me with no hesitation and said, "Don't get too comfortable. Rise and shine. We have a lot to cover in a short time here."

I rose up and adjusted myself. "Fine by me. Where do we start?"

"First, you wanted to know why you were transported here unclothed. This is a holy retreat for the Brotherhood and, as such, we do not allow any material from the surface, which has been contaminated by astral energy. The robe you wear always resides here, and, when you put it on, all negative energy that surrounds your physical body is neutralized. Thus, within the periphery of this place we maintain a high degree of spiritual energy that makes a comfortable habitation for the Ancient of Days and His associates."

"Is this the legendary Shamballa then?"

"Shamballa exists on several levels. This is one of the lower extensions of the legendary city. My old friend, Shakespeare, wrote the truth when he said that there are more things in heaven and earth than philosophy can dream of. I can reveal little except to tell you that the interior of the earth is an undiscovered country; both the White and Dark Brotherhoods have abodes here. This is a safe area for us where we do not have to worry about being disturbed by mankind for some time to come.

"And you mentioned something about one called the Ancient of Days. I've heard that title before. Isn't He mentioned in the Bible somewhere?"

"Yes, He is mentioned in Daniel chapter seven: *Behold, one like the Son of Man came with the clouds of heaven, and came to the Ancient of Days and was presented before him. And the Son of Man yielded to Him dominion, and glory, and a kingdom, that all people, nations, and languages should serve Him: His dominion is an everlasting dominion, which shall not pass away, and His kingdom that which shall not be destroyed.* You will note that the Christ, or the Son of Man, came to the Ancient of Days and presented his kingdom. The reason for this is that this entity is even higher on the scale of evolution than is the Christ. This high being is the one who is often referred to in Christian terminology as the *Father*.

"The title *Ancient* is a mistranslation. In the original Chaldean language, the term was to imply a person who transfers authority and purpose from one age to the next. The irony is that this mistranslation of *Ancient* is one of his true titles. One of his names has been the Ancient of Days long before any part of the Bible was written. Thus the King James translators rendered the literal translation of His name incorrectly and came up with an alternative title which was still correct.

"So is He called the Ancient of Days because He is so old?" I asked.

"We are all very ancient," said John. "But this person is called thus because he is has been on the earth longer than any other self conscious entity. He was the first Adam on the planet."

"The first Adam? You mean that there has been more than one? I kind of thought the story of Adam and Eve was symbolic."

"Again the answer is yes and no," said John. "The story of Adam and Eve is symbolic, but it also represents real truth. Adam represents the first person or male-female couple in a new era of human evolution. There have been many Adams in the history of the earth. The Ancient of Days, however, was truly the first man who became self aware in a mortal physical body over eighteen million years ago."

"Eighteen million years! Science has not even come close to discovering a human being that old."

"There are many things in the history of man on the earth that is hidden to current science. I will add this, however. Science has discovered that human life is millions of years older than they thought was true a few years ago. As the years pass they will date humanity farther and farther back in time. It may be some time before they find evidence that intelligent beings were here that long ago because man's first habitation is now deep under the ocean waters. The latest Adam of the Adam and Eve story, however, lived in what is now the United States and this entity was actually he who is now called the Christ. Interestingly, Christ is called the *last Adam* in First Corinthians chapter fifteen."

I scratched my head and said, "What you're telling me is a lot different from the religious people I have talked with. A lot of them think the whole earth is less than ten thousand years old. They would flip out to learn that man has been here for over eighteen million years, let alone that Christ was the last in a series of many Adams."

"There are many truths which would upset the devoutly religious, of not only Christian, but most of the other religions also," John replied.

"So when you speak of *many Adams* what do you mean?"

"An Adam is the first being, or set of beings, in a new stage of evolution. In a past life, about 6,000 years ago, the Christ was the firstborn with certain physical attributes. But then He was also an Adam in his life in Jerusalem 2000 years ago. But, in that life, instead of representing a step forward in physical evolution he was an Adam because He was the first man to represent the new spiritual consciousness, which will eventually permeate the earth. Thus He is the last Adam physically and spiritually."

"Is this part of the reason that Christ is called *the Firstborn?*"

"It is the most important reason He is called such," John said. "It is also a reason that some have called Him *the Father and the Son*. The Firstborn, or the first Adam, of a new consciousness or state of evolution must be a being in harmony with divine purpose so he can set the correct example and give new teachings in a pure enough form to guide those who will come after him. Imagine the damage that could occur if someone like Adolph Hitler became the Adam of the next step in evolution. Actually, in connection with the Dark Brothers he was trying to create the next step in physical evolution and by becoming the Father of such beings, he sought to stop the birth of the Christ consciousness from maturing on the earth. Thus he desired to become a physical Adam with power to overthrow the spiritual Adam. This correspondence plays out in our individual lives where the personality tries to thwart the dominance of the soul or spirit." John paused and looked at me curiously. "Why are you smiling?"

"I was just trying to imagine the reaction of a typical congregation if some preacher were to give this material out in a sermon."

John smiled with me. "It would be an interesting reaction indeed. Now I must redirect our thoughts and take care of business. I have perceived that you have met our old enemy. I believe he calls himself Brother Philo now."

I glanced at John, "How did you know that? I thought we had to touch hands for you to tap my memory banks."

"As we become one in the Spirit the touching ceases to be necessary. Does the phrase *nothing is too good to be true* sound familiar to you?"

"So that did come from you! I suspected as much."

"Yes, but I must confess I borrowed that one from Joshua. As the student and teacher become one the tuning in is a little like tuning into a radio station. When the right adjustment is made the reception becomes clear and true."

"I don't quite understand though how the adjustment is made. I am apparently tuning into you with greater accuracy, but I don't have a clue as to how I am doing it," I said.

"Yes, you are tuning into me and do not know how you are doing it and I am tuning into you, but I know how it is done. That is one reason I can perceive you with greater accuracy than you can perceive me." John stood up, "Have you solved the last hint of the first key? This is the power that turns the tuning dial, so to speak."

"It's been a rough week to solve a riddle, but I have thought about it," I said.

"And I perceive that you do not yet have the answer. Can you remember the hint?"

"I believe it goes like this: *Decision plus the new key word equals consciousness and consciousness plus decision equals the key word.*"

"I want you to think on this as we go through our discussion. Since you have drunk of the Elixir and are wearing your spiritual robe in such a spiritual place you should be able to come up with the answer. I'll elaborate a little. What is it that must be applied or added to decision to make decision conscious of itself or you conscious of a decision? Then when you make a decision in a state of consciousness what do you apply to that decision to give it life and power? Think this through in the back of your mind as we continue here."

"I'll do my best," I nodded.

"Now I have tuned in to you over the last week and I am acutely aware of your encounter with Philo. It is unfortunate that he found your computer files and suspects that I am in communication with you. At least you prevented him from getting off with the disc."

"But he said he read my files and knows about you. He even told me to say hello."

"He's partly bluffing," he said. "He just caught a glimpse of your notes about me and is assuming that because we have worked together in past lives we will meet in this one. That is the reason I brought you to this subterranean Shamballa. The Dark Brothers cannot perceive any of our discussions here. This is the safest sanctuary on the earth that is totally shielded from their view and access. Philo will probably figure things out when you publish your book, but until that is successfully accomplished we would like him and his associates to know as little as possible about our plans and discussions."

I stood up and said, "I'll tell you. I felt an instant dislike for the guy the moment I laid eyes on him, and everything that happened during his visit verified my first impression."

John nodded, "The first impression of a person who has soul contact is usually very reliable. We should always pay attention to it."

"What really got me about the guy is that he seemed to be

saying good things. He talked a lot about love and light, removing barriers. The funny thing is that I can remember very little of what he actually said. Nothing struck me as enlightened at all. All his words just seemed to be nebulous feel-good words. Yet, after you teach, I find myself recalling your words again and again and the more I reflect on them, the more I learn."

"That is a good observation," said John. "The Dark Brothers and their representatives cannot gather followers by teaching their true philosophy. If they did all but the most hardened of humanity would immediately reject them. They steal the most popular teachings of the Brotherhood of Light and encapsulate them into catch phrases and then intersperse them with their own teachings. This interspersing of Light with Darkness causes the average person to swallow the illusion with snapshots of the truth. Then when the Dark Ones lead a student to the point where he has digested much falsehood and egotistical thoughtforms, they slowly remove the good to the point that the student receives a clear vision of which side he is on. Unfortunately, once the deceived one has traveled the path this far it becomes difficult for him to back out and start over again on the path of Light.

"Fortunately, much effort is made by the Brotherhood of Light to bring those poor souls back to the correct starting point, and when the choice is made clear most do eventually find their way back. But there are a few who get sucked in to the illusion to the extent that they eventually make a conscious choice to be on the Dark Side. Once this conscious choice is made with full realization, you then have the beginning of the true life of a Dark Brother. Such a true Dark Brother knows who he is and is totally dedicated to self-interest. He completely rejects all light and love from the soul and the power of the Higher Self slowly withdraws from him until there is no light in him. Then is fulfilled the words of Joshua: *If the light that is in thee be darkness, how great is that darkness.*"

"So is Philo a Dark Brother then?" I asked curiously.

"Yes, Philo made his definite decision in that life that he persecuted you and I as Knights. Fortunately for Elizabeth, the two paths were made clear and she made a decision in that life to work herself back into the Light. You, as a Brother of Light, are assisting her in her recovery, but the path is difficult because of the debt she accumulated in that past life while unwittingly working for the Dark Side. She was one of the many who thought she was doing good while doing evil. What has saved Elizabeth so far has been the pure intentions within her heart. If the force of good intent is stronger than the power of ego one will usually find his way back to his true home. The path is always difficult, however."

"So how dangerous is Philo?"

"In the hierarchy of the Dark Brotherhood he is one of the lowest rings. However, he is ever on the lookout for ways to please his Brotherhood, which he calls the Guardians. He is not much to worry about by himself in this age, but if the more powerful brothers see that he has an opportunity to strike a dagger, so to speak, in our work, then they will lend Philo all the power and support at their disposal. Philo by his own power and knowledge was not able to make the dagger real to Elizabeth, but Dark Brothers from the unseen world thought this would be a great opportunity to discredit me and possibly distract you from writing the book. Thus, they lent Philo all their support in an attempt to deceive Elizabeth."

"You mentioned she would go through three temptations before she would see you again."

"That is correct. Which one do you suppose she is working on?"

"I assume she is working on the third. I believe her confrontation with our doctor was the first and Philo's attempt to control her mind was the second. We both concluded that she was working on her third but are unclear about exactly what it is. I would also like to know why she has to go through all of this."

John paused a moment, sitting back down in his invisible chair, and said, "Several times in the past, that is before her current life, she has been deceived temporarily by the Dark Brothers. The reason she must pass these three temptations is that the process will focus her mind on the Light to the extent that she will have a good fighting chance to overcome all the rest of the daggers that the Dark Ones will throw at her in the future."

"But even then I take it that it will not be a sure thing," I injected.

"There are very few sure things in this universe. If the Ancient of Days or the Christ gave me their word on a thing, I would feel like it was a sure thing, but outside of the word of a Brother of Light or confirmation through the Spirit of God, there are very few things that are absolutely certain. Free will and the limitations of the human condition make the game of life difficult to predict with 100% accuracy. We can predict with surety that humanity as a whole will continue to evolve with temporary setbacks."

"So it's not a sure thing that the keys of knowledge will be successfully presented to humanity?" I asked.

"This, my brother, is a sure thing because it has been de-creed by the Ancient of Days. The time frame and the messenger are what is not sure. You have a chance to be the messenger, but there are several things, including your free will, that could sabo-tage the mission. If, for instance, you were to fail in this life, we could either find another messenger or try you again when you are reborn in a future life and are perhaps a little wiser."

"Fascinating," I said as I sat down again in my invisible chair. "Now getting back to Elizabeth. Can you shed some light on what her third temptation is and how she must overcome it?"

"Her third temptation is the most difficult of all," he said while crossing his legs in a lotus position. "In the first two you were able to be of some direct assistance to her. This last one she must pass by looking within herself."

"She and I have both been looking within ourselves like crazy and we are no further ahead. The past couple of days we have been saying the *Song of the 144,000* religiously. It seems to strengthen our spirits but Elizabeth is still deteriorating."

"If you had been saying it just as religiously and focusing on the meaning before Philo came, Elizabeth may have had the strength of spirit to discern the disharmonious vibration of Philo without your help. If you had applied the companion key word to *decisio*n that we are looking for, the three temptations would not have even been temptations. This is another hint about the key word for you. But because you have been saying and concentrat-ing on the Song the past few days Elizabeth will have greater spiri-tual strength to face her last temptation."

I felt the truth of his corrective statements and resolved to be more diligent. "So what is the third temptation then?" I asked.

"The third temptation is twofold. Remember when we were at Denny's and I forced you to give me the key word or our rela-tionship would end?"

"Yes. I have never felt so much pressure in my life."

"What was the turning point for you that made you give it to me?"

"When the key word first came to me I felt an inward witness of it through what I assume is the Spirit of God you just men-tioned. But then after I started using my reasoning mind and feel-ings in examining it, I began to doubt that the word was correct. When I was in the midst of the struggle to give you the word all kinds of things were going through my mind, but then the thought occurred to me. *What do you know and trust for sure?* As I thought of this I knew the only thing that has never let me down is that still small inner voice. It was at that moment I decided to place my trust in it above all else and thus I gave you the correct word."

John smiled, "How much do you think we should trust this spiritual revelation we call the Spirit of God?"

"I'm not sure what you're looking for here. I guess we should trust it all the way," I said.

"Even unto death, if necessary?" John asked.

"I suppose so," I replied.

"This is the true test of a disciple," said John. "He or she is willing to follow the inner voice even if it costs him his life or something else as valuable."

"Is there something else as valuable as life?"

"There are those who would rather die than admit they are wrong," said John. "In some circumstances letting go of our pride is a greater sacrifice than physical life itself."

"So are you saying that Elizabeth may have to sacrifice her life?"

"She must demonstrate a willingness to do so. I'll quote you the words of the Master in relation to this: *For whosoever will save his life shall lose it: and whosoever will lose his life for my sake shall find it. For what is a man profited, if he shall gain the whole world, and lose his soul? Or what shall a man give in exchange for his soul?* (Matt 16:25-26) What do you suppose this means?"

"I don't think Christ was referring to a normal life-threatening situation, but He seemed to be teaching a principle here. It would seem that He implies that if we seek to save our physical lives or put the value of physical life above the value of the soul, then we will lose our souls and our lives. If we are willing to give our life for Christ somehow then we will save our life and our soul. Perhaps we will be born again in a better situation."

"You are very close to the truth," he said. "To lose your life for Christ means to place your faith and trust on following the inner voice of Christ within you, even if it means you will die or that your worst fears may materialize. This is a difficult temptation, but every disciple that is trusted by the Brotherhood must go through it sooner or later."

"Have I gone through such a test?"

"Yes. Elizabeth, put you through it when you were a Knight in that previous life. Then there were other times also."

"So how and when is Elizabeth going to undergo this test?"

"I will show you shortly."

"Is there nothing I can do to help her? You've got to realize that she is in a weakened condition."

"She will have to go through this all alone on the physical plane. The only thing you can do to help is the same as that which I offered to you when you gave me the key word."

"But if I remember correctly you went in the bathroom and gave me no assistance whatsoever."

John replied gently, "You are wrong, my friend. When I was in the bathroom I was in a state of meditation and prayer, sending you a message to trust the inner voice you have received. I was not allowed to send it so your personality could pick up the words. I could only send the message to your soul. Fortunately, you listened to your inner self and responded correctly. Now Elizabeth must do a similar thing and you will be able to help her only as I helped you."

"When will this happen?"

"Sooner than you think. Now I know that you are concerned for Elizabeth, but it is important we continue with this week's lesson. So please try to stay with me, for if you discover the correct answer you will be able to have increased power to help your wife. Now let me repeat the hint: *Decision plus the new key word equals consciousness and consciousness plus decision equals or creates the key word.*"

"It's a very perplexing hint," I said. *"Decision plus or merging with X creates consciousness and consciousness plus or merging with decision creates X.* It seems as if we are creating something that is already created."

"It would seem so," he said.

"There seems to be three items here. Decision, consciousness and X, or the key word. Is it possible that it is an illusion that there are three, that there are really four or more?"

"It is possible."

"OK. I'm going to take that for a yes. I would guess that the livingness you call decision exists on several levels or octaves, like the notes on a musical scale. Is this correct?"

"You are basically correct," said John. "I am impressed. You are getting back to your old self, thanks to your meditation robe and these spiritual facilities. So what was the first decision?"

"I do feel like I am thinking with greater clarity," I said. "I've been thinking a lot about the beginning of all things and it boggles the mind, but the first decision could have only been one thing."

"And that would be..."

"Well, I have been picturing God in an infancy, so to speak, kind of drifting in nothingness. If He is existing outside of time and space, then no decision as we know it would be possible. So before I can understand the principle I would have to know which two or more things were before creation, for before decision can exist there has to be two or more things to decide between."

"Very good reasoning," said John. "But before there was creation as we know it there were two things that have always been before the Decision of God. Decision is eternal because these two things have been, are, and will always be present with God as well as ourselves."

"All I can think of here is Father, Son and Holy Ghost, with God being the Father, but that's probably too simple to be correct."

"It's too nebulous to be correct," he said. "Let me repeat a great truth I gave you earlier. When God created the seeds of all life in the universe he did not divide himself as some of the eastern religions and many New Agers think. Instead He reflected himself infinitely. This makes you and I true reflections in the image of God, and within us are all the attributes, potential and memories of God himself. Right now, on this rare occasion, while visiting this center, you have an opportunity to go back in time as a reflection of God to the time before there was any creation. Would you like to do that?"

"A part of me would," I said, "but I must admit it sounds a little frightening."

"You will not feel any fear," said John. "But if you do, you can stop the process any time you wish."

I felt nervous about proceeding but my curiosity got the best of me. "So how do I accomplish this?"

John walked toward the crystals, "I'm sure you noticed those two crystals in the center of the room?"

"Yes. I've been curious about them."

"They naturally amplify the latent powers within you. All you do is place a hand on each crystal and direct your thoughts. As you feel your thoughts amplified you must then direct the energy to the desired end. Each use of the crystals temporarily weakens your life force, so you must conservatively direct your thoughts."

"And to what end do I direct them?"

"Direct them back to the beginning of existence and then to the time before existence. If you do this, you will retrieve the two things that have always been and will always be before Decision who is God, of whom we are made in the image thereof."

I got up off my invisible chair and walked over to the two crystals. I felt nervous about touching them. "Are you sure I won't be evaporated or something like that?"

"Actually, their spiritual power is so great that one who has not prepared himself through strenuous spiritual endeavor over a period of several lifetimes would be in danger if he touched them. At present, however, you are not in harm's way. If any problem manifests itself I will be aware of it and help you to release yourself from the crystals.

"These crystals are thousand of times more powerful than all the computers in the world. From a lower point of view they could be called giant computers. You have used these crystals before. When you touch them everything will seem familiar and you will know what to do."

As soon as I laid a hand on each crystal I intuitively knew I was supposed to concentrate on the black space between them. When I concentrated on the space I felt a strange sense of oneness with all life everywhere. Suddenly I felt like I was one with all there was and all knowledge was available to me. Even though it seemed as though all things everywhere were before me in my higher consciousness, I somehow knew that I could only take back to my normal consciousness the answer to the question I originated in my standard human awareness.

I put my attention on going back to the beginning and saw all the reflections of God begin to gather into one point in sort of an implosion, the opposite of the Big Bang. In this instant of consciousness all the mysteries of creation from the beginning to the end seemed to be before me, but all I could later remember was the basic experience. I couldn't seem to take the wholeness of it back with me. The one thing I could remember was part of the essence of God before creation. God did exist from eternity as Decision because there were always two things before Him from which to decide. I tried with all my strength to tune into those two things so I could bring them back with me into lower consciousness."

After a few minutes of contemplation John spoke to me, "Are you back yet?"

I removed my hands from the crystals and backed away, "I think so. Wow! All I can say is how great is the mystery of Godliness!"

John smiled, "So did you retrieve the answer?"

"I think so. But what really gets me is what I did not retrieve. I saw endless lives and an eternity of forms and millions of civilizations and solar systems and galaxies, but all that I remember is that I saw them. The only thing I recall about creation for sure is what a small part of it we are on this little planet circling around our little sun in this little galaxy."

"That is always the most impressive recollection after such an experience. What did you discern were the two points that makes decision eternal?"

"It was an amazing feeling, or non-feeling, and even though there was a time that decision existed with no creation, I sensed that there were universes beyond and before creation, as we know it, and I could retrieve no information about them. I did sense that God, or Decision, existed in a point beyond and before time and space. Before this point were two possibilities. They were the possibility of Something, and Nothing, or the possibility of Creation or No Creation.

Suddenly an inspiring phrase came to me. "It was the decision *to be or not to be. That is the question!*" I looked suspiciously at John, "Did you say you knew Shakespeare?"

"I think I did say that."

"Why do I get the feeling that Shakespeare was also here and saw what I just saw?"

"Your feeling may or may not be correct," said John with a knowing look in his eyes. "Now tell me what else you retrieved."

I sensed that John did not want to pursue this line of thought and continued, "The interplay of these two possibilities sustains eternally, without beginning and end, the One Great Decision that interacts between the two. As a reflection of God you and I and all other lives extend the life of God by continually deciding whether to create or not. As offspring of God the main decision before us is always whether *to be or not to be*! Wow," I exclaimed. "This is great stuff."

"It is indeed," said John. "Actually the question is more accurately worded *to become or not to become*, but Shakespeare wisely used a more catchy expression. Now you will have to use your regular human consciousness to obtain the key word. Decision plus the key word equals consciousness. What is that word?"

"Here's the way I see it," I said. "For an eternity the possibility of Creation and No Creation was before the Decision of God. God attained consciousness, as we vaguely understand it, when he focused on the decision of creation."

"That is basically correct," said John, "except the word we are looking for is not focus, but something else similar in meaning."

"God thought about creation."

"No, you're going off track here. Focus was closer than thought."

"God put His *attention* on creation."

"That is the word."

"Attention?"

"Yes. Now fill in the blanks and think about it."

"Decision plus attention equals consciousness. In other words, consciousness was created by putting attention on a decision which had been made. I sense that the power of Decision is eternal and when the Decision TO BE, or TO BECOME, is made then the Trinity of Decision-Consciousness-Attention is instantly made manifest. I perceive that this Trinity is the one great Life we call God."

"Correct. Now apply the word to the second half."

"I'll try. Consciousness plus Decision equals Attention. This didn't make a lot of sense to me until now. I see it this way: In the beginning was the one great Decision, and after the decision was made to create, God reflected himself into an infinite number of duplicates. Each was a unit of latent decision who had to decide whether *to be or not to be*. As each unit focused on an aspect of creation then attention was shifted to a lower order and this attention caused each reflection to differentiate and become unique and separate from every other point. Somehow I know this answer is right. I think I carried enough back with me to be able to see this."

"You must have," said John. "For one time you are very correct. I couldn't have put it better myself. Most disciples are only able to bring back one major piece of information. It looks like you have retained a glimpse of several. Now what you need to do is reflect on this experience regularly over the next few days. It will help you to keep some of the knowledge permanently in your mind."

"I think that one reason I have this information was that as I looked between the crystals I was thinking about the keys. The funny thing is that in a microsecond of time I saw all thirty-six keys and their answers in depth, but for the life of me I cannot now remember any of it, except for the enlightenment about the key word."

"Do you know what that means?"

"What?"

"Because you retrieved this information, it means you are supposed to have it. No great knowledge will ever come to your consciousness that you are not supposed to have. Even if a person is taught forbidden knowledge, as clear as day, he will not be able to hold it until he is ready for that privilege. Even when you write your books and attempt to make these teachings as clear as the noonday sun you will find there will be many that will not be able to hold all the knowledge. All who read with an open mind, however, will receive some benefit, according to what their consciousness and stage of evolution is able to accept."

"I really feel the truth of your words. I'll tell you... there is really something wonderful about being in this place and wearing this robe. All truth seems so obvious here. I cannot imagine two inhabitants here having an argument."

"Actually, there are no arguments here as you understand the term. Truth of normal earthly concerns is perceived so strongly through the soul that *resistance is futile*, if I may coin a phrase from Star Trek."

"So the normal conflicts over subjects like abortion, the death penalty and politics does not exist here?"

"No they do not. There are conflicts on higher levels that are beyond the understanding of the average person, but that is not for the inhabitants of the earth to be concerned with."

I made a mental note to ask John later about the conflicts that exist on higher levels as I said, "So let's pick something like the death penalty. That has been a subject of hot debate for some time. How is it that everyone here would have the same view on that?"

"For one thing," he said, "no one is allowed into any level of Shamballa who is not sensitive to the inner voice of the soul, and in the world of the soul there is only oneness and unity. The one quality those who have soul contact have in common is that they are willing to accept reality or truth no matter what it is. Most of the people on the earth are full of fixed ideas, which are not even their own thoughts, but planted in them by some outside authority. Such a person, if he believes in the death penalty, could not accept a teaching that he is wrong. On the other hand, he who is against the death penalty would have just as difficult a time accepting that he is wrong. To make real progress in spiritual evolution one must be willing to accept change, even if his whole belief system is shattered. Only a true disciple can do this."

"I can see that. I've had a lot of arguments over religion and politics in my life and it is obvious to me that most people are unwilling to change, no matter how clearly the truth is presented."

"This obstacle is the most frustrating human characteristic with which the teachers of the race have to face," he said. "That is one of the reasons I so enjoy visiting Shamballa and the New Jerusalem. Let us suppose two residents of this location and two residents of general humanity were presented with a situation as follows: We have before us a mortal person who has willingly and knowingly killed an innocent person. Because he is caught he seems to feel very sorry for what he did. He pleads for his life. He seems to have potential for good if he can be turned around. Should he be put to death or not? Now the reason two normal people will argue incessantly about the killer's fate is because both have only a snapshot of the cause and effect in the person's life and life in general.

"Here in Shamballa any two people would not just be looking at a snapshot. Instead, they would see the person's whole life, would be aware of the motive of the murder, of the effect of the murder on the victims, and the effect of the various possible punishments on the wayward brother. This awareness would not end with the person being executed as on the earth; they would be aware of the effect of the punishment projected into the future several lifetimes hence. Because of these projections the correct and most beneficial course of action becomes very obvious and any two people who have let go of preconceived notions can accept them. Many people having heated arguments on the earth would be startled if they could come here and see a projection of what would happen if they got their way. They would be extremely relieved that they are limited in power to carry out their little wills when they discover the possible disaster their ignorance can yield."

"So will humanity ever reach the stage where they can tune into the inner voice and become one?" I asked.

"The day when the majority reach that stage is still far away, but the day is near when a few are to achieve it; and that is one of the main purposes in presenting these teachings through you. The next great leap in human evolution is dependent on groups of people being established who are capable of being one through soul contact, that the Will of God is done on earth as it is in heaven, so to speak. People must realize that true oneness is achieved not by giving up individuality, but by expanding the mind and spiritual sensitivity so the truth becomes obvious to all.

John paused and continued, "Let me give you an example of how spiritual evolution brings oneness. A generation ago in the United States it was no big deal to shoot a stray housecat for sport. If a person were to criticize another for such a thing, an individual in a group would argue that it was no big deal, because it was just a stupid cat. Now, in this day, people are sensitive enough that all in an average group would agree that it would be wrong to shoot a stray cat for sport. This latter group did not lose any of their essence or individuality because they are of one mind on the subject. The new generation is just more enlightened about the value of the lessor lives.

One of the greatest barriers to reaching oneness is this fear of losing part of ourselves, but such fear is based on illusion as was demonstrated when the South lost their power to own slaves. Now the nation is unified in the abolishment of that practice and much the better for it. Only a few wretched souls think that the country has lost anything of value.

On the other hand, the Dark Brothers who seek oneness by taking away free will are another matter. Again, they seek to project the image of something good and desirable, yet their method is to be totally avoided. Outward oneness by force does not inward oneness create."

"So, am I finally done with the first key?" I asked in anticipation.

"Yes and no," said John.

"I should have known that was the answer. Let me guess. The answer is yes because I have the key words and no because..."

John smiled at me and said, "Yes, you have the key words and an elementary understanding. You are done to the extent that we will now move on to the second key. But the answer is no as far as you having a complete knowledge of decision and who you are. Even the Ancient of Days still contemplates the full meaning and power of decision. You will find that as you contemplate the teachings we have discussed more light will come. Also, as you complete the rest of the keys your understanding of who you are will be enhanced."

"I sense that what you say is true, especially when I reflect on the feeling I had when I looked through the crystals. I know the depth of who we are is almost an infinite thing... So when do I get the first hints for the second key?" I asked, anxiously thinking I was finally making real progress toward the third key and the promise of Elizabeth's permanent healing.

"We can begin that now if you are ready. Do you want to get up and take a short break first?"

"I wouldn't mind," I said getting up and walking toward the crystals. "Using these crystals was exhilarating, but it made me a little tired physically."

"Yes. High spiritual energy tends to sap physical strength temporarily. You are fortunate you drank the Elixir first or you would really be weak."

"What is the story behind these crystals, anyway?"

"The Biblical name of these crystals is the Urim and Thummim. All Urim and Thummim are linked to each other. This one we see before us is linked to a set that is in the private office of the Ancient of Days. His set is linked to even higher beings in other systems and planets. This universal linkage is what gives them their tremendous power of revelation."

"Didn't the High Priest in the days of Moses have a Urim and Thummim?"

"Yes, but they were much smaller and less potent than the ones here in Shamballa. Nevertheless, it did give them power to receive some revelation for the Israelites. In addition to this, every human being has a tiny duplicate of the Urim and Thummim in their head, which can be activated by the opening of the so-called third eye, or the ajna center. When this is activated correctly a person can become a prophet in his own right, and draw down revelation from the higher realms."

"Very interesting. I have something else I want to see. Can I use the crystals again?"

"Go ahead if you think you are able. I would not ask for anything major, however, for you need to save your strength."

I stepped up to the crystals and placed my hands on them again. The question I had was about the Ancient of Days. I wanted to know all about Him - where He came from, what He looked like and the degree of intelligence He possessed."

As I began to think about this I sensed that I should limit my probe of Him and that I was to be given all I needed to know at the moment. I sensed that the word ancient applied to Him to a greater degree than I thought. Not only was He the first Adam here eighteen million years ago, but that before He became the world's first man, He and several associates lived upon the earth for a long period of time as extraplanetary beings and spent many thousands of years preparing the earth for man and building the city of Shamballa on two levels. A part of their construction was this subterranean dwelling and other centers, under the earth. The other was a city made of refined matter invisible to the human eye on the surface of the earth. Before coming here I saw that He lived over a thousand lifetimes on several other planetary systems in other solar systems until He overcame all regular physical limitations. Then after this He became what is called a Solar Servant and spent over two hundred additional lives as an advanced student and teacher, oscillating between the two.

There are many other things I saw that I will not write at this time, but as I was receiving I felt a desire to see Him as He is now. The instant I sent this desire I saw Him standing with His back toward me next to the crystals in His private office. The first thing that surprised me was His age. For some reason I expected to see an old bearded man, but before me stood a vibrant virile man who appeared to be in His early twenties. His hair seemed to oscillate between a light brown and a rarefied white and He was smooth shaven. His hair was fairly long, but not shoulder length like the pictures that we see of God in various books. He was also quite thin and taller than average. His appearance had a very regal image to it despite his appearance of youth. I got the impression He was a little over six feet, but that could be incorrect as He was the only one in the room and I could not line Him up with anyone else.

I wondered why I was being shown His back and desired to see His face. At this expressed desire I viewed His presence from several angles, both sides, His back, but His face was hidden from me. I became very curious about this and expressed a desire again to see His face. This time a message formed in my mind. *"Even Moses did not see My face. Are you greater than he?"*

Suddenly I fell back startled at what I perceived. I was just curious and had no desire to be greater than Moses. I was hoping that I did not offend this great being.

"What happened?" asked John. "What did you ask to see?"

"I just wanted to see the face of the Ancient of Days," I said getting up off the floor.

"Where did you get the idea to ask for that?"

"I don't know. I just wanted to know what He looks like."

"I had no idea that you would ask for such a thing or I would have warned you."

"Warned me about what?"

"Those who are in mortal physical bodies are not allowed to see His face."

"Why not?" I asked.

"Because, if you saw His face while still in the body you would die," he said.

Images of horrible alien creatures crossed my mind as I said, "I hope you're not going to tell me he has a lizard face or something like that." Then I thought to myself what a horrible thought to think about such a god-like being!

"No, my friend." John said smiling, "He has the most beautiful face in all creation, but if you were to look him in the eye, the spiritual radiation would be too strong for you."

"He did send me an interesting message," I said. "He asked me if I was greater than Moses, because even Moses did not see his face."

John shook his head knowingly, "He was referring to an account correctly recorded in the Book of Exodus chapter thirty-three. God did not let Moses see His face and explained in verse twenty that no one could see His face and live. But if you read over the account you will see that Moses saw the back parts of his body, but not His face."

"Yes, that's what I saw," I said. I saw His back parts and a partial side view. He seemed to be an extremely handsome and amazingly young person."

"One of His names is *The Eternal Youth*," said John. "Even so, for many new inhabitants of Shamballa, He teaches as an older man with a face that is compatible with the energy of the students. Not all the residents here are perfect and many have reservations about accepting the appearance of one so young as their superior. In addition to this, only a true immortal, or a person free from the restrictions of his body, can see this entity as He is face to face."

"You've told me just enough to make me more curious than ever," I said. "Who are the inhabitants here anyway?"

"There are a handful of earth residents who have overcome death to the extent that they change the vibration of their physical body so it is transfigured. These residents such as the Christ and Buddha can look on the face of the Ancient of Days. Other visitors are human disciples who come here in the dream state. Here they attend certain classes to help them correctly fulfill their missions on the earth. Another group are immortals who came here from another planetary system with the Ancient of Days. A final group are temporary visitors from other systems. Shamballa has an exchange program with other planetary systems. A teacher may be sent to Sirius for a period of time and a Sirian may be sent here in exchange. Then when the exchange has ended the returned teacher holds classes revealing how things are being handled on another world. This gives the teachers better ideas as to how to help this one."

"So how are things on Sirius?" I quipped.

"Don't get me started," John shot back. "Remember the second key word. We must focus on the task at hand here or we will run out of time. We need to move on to introducing you to the second key."

John continued, "The second key of knowledge to understand is the Middle Way Principle. The great teacher of the Middle Way was, of course, the Buddha. He realized the Middle Way after experiencing two extremes in life. First, extreme comfort and riches, and later, extreme poverty and deprivation. During the deprivation extreme he was said to have been living on just several grains of rice a day seeking enlightenment when the answer flashed into his mind. The way of enlightenment is neither excess or deprivation, but somewhere between the two points of the pendulum.

"The true teaching of Buddha's middle way has been lost, even in the East, but many of us have the imprint of the knowledge within us... So the question for us to examine is: What is the Middle Way?"

John paused and continued, "There was a major keyword for the first principle and there is another sequential key word for this one. As you contemplate this principle it may be helpful to you to read about the life and teachings of Buddha. They can be an inspiration no matter what your religious foundation may be."

I thought about his words and replied, "I find it interesting that you are a character from the Bible and you often quote the Bible. Now you introduce a non-Biblical person. How does Buddha rate in the scheme of things when compared to Moses or Jesus or the prophets?"

"During the past 6,000 years Moses, Buddha and Christ are the three greatest teachers. They are the greatest because they perceived through revelation and taught the first two aspects

330 of God. The Trinity is of course the Father, Son and

of the Trinity of God. The Trinity is of course the Father, Son and Holy Ghost in Christian language. Together, Moses and Buddha represented the Holy Ghost, and a more accurate description of this quality is Light. Buddha often used the word enlightenment when referring to it.

"Many metaphysical students and teachers have associated Buddha with the aspect of Light but have ignored Moses in the equation. They do not register the fact that Moses paved the way by introducing laws that laid the foundation for civilization as it exists today. These laws forced evolving humanity to use the light within their minds to judge good and evil, right and wrong. In other words, Moses forced humanity toward a more enlightened civilization whereas Buddha directed us toward a more enlightened inner philosophy. Moses represented the outer light whereas Buddha represented the inner.

Our current society corresponds to the influence of these two great men. Western civilization, which corresponds to Moses, demonstrates its light outwardly through its science, technology, business acumen and legal structure. Even if we compare the great cities of the East to western cities such as New York or Paris you will see that the outward physical light of the West is much brighter.

"On the other hand, the intelligence in the East has put its attention more on the Inner Light. Very few in the East have ever believed that God created the world in six 24-hour days and have long saw the earth as an ancient place. Most of the people in the East have also accepted that reincarnation is a true and logical doctrine and have refused to see God as some wrathful entity who takes glee in sending his own children to a burning hell. The devout in the East have received many benefits from meditation and most of the martial arts came from there.

"The time is now coming when the inner and outer lights are merging to create a unified light. The West is taking the benefits to technology and business to the East, and the East is giving back by presenting the West with the best of its inner teachings.

"The Christ, who traveled widely in the East during his missing years, represented the Son aspect and the more precise word for this is Love. Thus did He reveal the true meaning of spiritual Love to the world. This planet still, has a long way to go to understand and apply the teachings of both Christ and Buddha. The world has pretty much learned what it can from Moses and we are approaching a time when practical law will move to a higher level."

"What about the third aspect? Is there more to be revealed about this?" I asked.

"Yes, much more. As the age passes from Pisces to Aquarius this final aspect will be revealed. Many disciples understand this Father aspect to represent power. But there is another key word to be revealed and comprehended. The key word will be revealed soon, but the understanding of it will unfold over a period of a thousand years."

"This first key has taken longer than I expected. Will all of them take this much work?"

"The time it takes you to get the basics of each key will vary. Most will not take as long as the first key. For one thing, you have learned a lot about the intuitive process that you did not know before. That will make future keys easier for you."

"I've got to admit this has been a fascinating session." I said. "You've almost made me forget all the troubles Elizabeth is going through, but not quite. If we are done I probably should be getting back to her. My greatest concern here is that I want to take her back something that will give her hope. Now you said that there is a temptation she must undergo without my physical presence. What can I do to prepare her for this?"

"You've already done all you can do because her hour of temptation has arrived."

"What do you mean?"

"Are you strong enough to use the crystals one more time?"

"I feel kind of weak, but if it involves helping Elizabeth I will make the strength."

"I will approach the crystals from one side and you the other," John instructed. "If you sense through our next experience here that you are losing too much strength, then you must withdraw. I did not plan on you making an attempt to see the face of the Ancient of Days and depleting yourself of so much strength. I was hoping you would have a greater reservoir of life energy for this moment. I will join with you and pour into you all the energy I can."

"I don't understand. What will I need all this energy for?" I asked.

"Touch the crystals with me and you will see."

John and I moved toward the crystals from opposite directions. As I adjusted to the vibration I began to see Elizabeth at home, sitting in her wheelchair. The picture was more real than TV or even a Star Trek-like hologram. It was as if John and I were standing right there watching her. I felt heartbroken as I watched her wheel herself over to the front door and grab the door handle and make a feeble attempt to stand. She pulled herself up a few inches with her shaking hands and fell back into the chair. Then she started sobbing, "Joseph, Joseph, Joseph... When are you coming back and what have you got for me? Has John given you some magical solution to renew my strength? Oh please God, let him find some way to help me!"

I was so moved that I started pulling away from the crystals saying, "I'm here for you, Sweetie..."

"Don't pull away," said John, "or you could sever the connection. Keep touching the crystals."

I continued to secure my hands on the crystals. Elizabeth's presence seemed so real that I felt like I was really there.

"Now you must prepare yourself mentally for what comes next," said John, "and not remove yourself from the crystals. If you wish to lend spiritual strength to Elizabeth in her time of need you must apply the lesson of the last key word and focus your attention on the desired outcome as you never have before."

Just as I found myself wondering what it was I was supposed to prepare for I heard our doorbell ring. The peephole was too high for Elizabeth to see from her wheelchair so she usually wheels herself to the living room window to see who is there before she answers. She headed toward the window, but she was so tired that when the wheels hit the edge of the carpet she muttered, "I'm too tired to check." Then she backed up and opened the door.

It was Philo.

Both Elizabeth and I were totally shocked. We had both assumed he was on a plane back to Los Angeles. Elizabeth moved back in her chair and I just about moved back from the crystals.

"Hold on to the crystals," warned John.

"That son of a bitch!" I shouted to John. "Listen you've got to get me out of here right now! Transport me back home right now so I can protect her."

"This is her temptation," said John "and you cannot be physically there for her. There are certain things she must resolve alone."

"But I just can't be here like a ghost and watch her deal with this guy."

"You've got to," said John. "The only way you can help her now is to focus all your attention and strength in her direction, and for heaven's sake, don't lose contact with the crystals!"

"You're asking too much of me. I just can't stand by and watch this man destroy my wife."

"I'm not asking you to do this. The soul of Elizabeth cries out for your help. Now put all your attention through the energy of the crystal on guiding your wife and just maybe she can come out of this in one piece."

The thought came to me that John had never let me down in this life and possibly others, so I mentally reassured myself that I must trust his words and focus all my attention on the task at hand. I concentrated my attention on the scene in my home and saw Philo push the door open and walk inside. He apparently came alone without Lance.

"I have canceled my flight and came here to remove that dagger and restore your health," he said matter-of-factly to Elizabeth.

My heart sank. I felt so dismayed I didn't feel like I could help a fly out of a cobweb. I wanted so much to just let go of the crystals and demand that John send me back home and so I could throw Philo out. I almost felt that was what I would do if I was a real man, but then my mind remembered that my only real chance to help her was to hold on to the crystals and apply the little knowledge that I had. As I resolved to follow John's advice I realized that I was entering a battle unlike anything I had ever before heard or seen, a battle that Elizabeth and I must win.

CHAPTER SEVENTEEN
The Last Temptation

I watched on in silence as Elizabeth responded to Philo.

"I know who you are," she said to Philo. "In a past life you were Brother Phillippi. You were the one responsible for ordering me to torture and kill the Knights of the Temple. You caused a greater evil to come upon me than the Knights. I have had to bear the cross of this inner guilt and this disease. Why should I trust anything you say now?"

Philo sat down on the couch and softly said, "You should trust me now for the same reason you trusted me then."

"And what reason is that?" she asked.

"Because I can give you power."

Elizabeth paused, stunned at his response, "What do you mean - power?"

"Let me put it this way," said Philo as he flopped down on the couch. "There are two sides to the equation of the life experience. The ignorant call them good and evil, light and dark, but the lines of division are not so pronounced. Before you judge me let me ask you one question. Suppose all that seems good and holy by the regular way of looking at it prevails, yet you as an individual are in poor health as you are now and suffer pain and misery. What benefit would you receive from all this brotherly love when you and the whole universe you know is in Hell?"

"When you choose the right path things don't always work out immediately, but in the end things are better," she said.

"*Eventually* or *at the end of time*, then we shall smell the roses!" he laughed in a raised voice. "The stupid Brotherhood that has the nerve to call themselves *good* always preach to you that good things will happen in some far future that never comes.

Well, we are in the future now. During the past ages your husband, John and others have suffered enormously and still that illusive good they seek eludes them and still they are doomed to suffer more. And now look at you."

"What about me?" Elizabeth asked defensively.

"You were always in vibrant health until you followed your husband. Because you rescued him in that past life and switched over to his side you have brought upon you untold misery. If you would not have switched sides you would have never had any disease at all."

"You're lying!" she shouted.

Philo threw his head back and laughed, "I'm living proof that I'm not lying. Look at me. I'm vital and healthy and haven't suffered more than a cold in several lifetimes. I have done much more of what the world calls *evil* than you have ever thought of. So why are you in that wheelchair when I can run on the beaches of sunny California with the wind in my hair?" He seemed to enjoy rubbing this in.

"I'm not sure," Elizabeth replied weakly.

"It just isn't fair, is it?" he said with such a smirk that I wished I could punch him in the nose. I was starting to get restless listening to this, but felt that I must tune into the general drift of the conversation before I could be of any use.

"Maybe it is fair. I deserve what has happened to me because of the pain I inflicted upon those knights," she said after some thought.

"That's a very stupid statement," he said authoritatively. "You know in the end there are two groups of people. The first is the so-called *Brotherhood of Light* who seek some spiritual world and essence that does not even exist. In seeking after this illusion they suffer life after life and eventually wind up completely dominated by us."

"And who is *us*?'

"We are the second group. Some call us the *Dark Brotherhood*. We call ourselves the Guardians. We are neither dark nor light. We just are. We are the great I AM's who have the destiny to rule the earth. Like I say, at the end of evolution there are two groups; the smart people and the stupid ones. Fortunately, I am with the smart side."

"I wouldn't say you're smart. After all, good always triumphs over evil. Where will you be then?"

"That's just an old wives tale," he said. "That is a statement you hear all the time, but rarely see. For one thing, good and evil are in the eye of the beholder. That which prevails is always what is eventually called good. Do you think Hitler would be called evil today if he had won the war? Of course not. If he had won, Churchill and Roosevelt would be the villains of history for provoking a war and costing millions of German lives." Philo leaned forward, "Now let me give you this important piece of enlightenment Miss Goody Two-Shoes. In the end those who prevail are the ones with the most power. Have you ever raised chickens?"

"My father did when I was a girl."

"The roosters in the henhouse are a good example of what I am saying," he said. "If you have twelve roosters amidst several hundred hens you will see they all desire to be the top guy and they regularly fight for that privilege. Now among those twelve roosters there will be several that will be fairly kind and gentle, but then there are always others who are ruthless and aggressive. Now which ones do you think will wind up ruling the roost?"

"I suppose you are going to say it's the ruthless ones."

"If you raised chickens then you know it's true," he said. "It's not only survival of the fittest, but the fittest and most powerful have a much higher quality of life. Which would you rather be? The mild-mannered loving rooster who is the last to eat and rarely gets a hen, or the aggressive powerful one, that rules the roost and has everything his own way?"

"But you can never have everything your own way. If you did you would trample on the rights of others."

Philo rolled his eyes. "The rights of others have nothing to do with it!" he said in a loud voice. "There is only one right in this universe, and that is your right and duty to take care of yourself and attain the greatest power possible. This is the only means necessary to get the highest quality of life possible for all who are capable of accepting it. If every person takes care of his own interests then the world takes care of itself."

"So you're saying that might makes right."

"Might is right," he said. "Let me tell you the secret guiding principle of the Guardians."

"And what is that?" asked Elizabeth crossing her arms.

"The secret is this: the universe is you and what you perceive. That is all there is or ever will be. This is the principle we live by."

"And how do you live by such a principle?"

"Let me give you an example. Let us say that you had a

chance to save every living person in Australia by the sacrifice of your life, yet in your universe it is as if Australia does not exist. You do not know anyone from there, you receive no money from them - why, you do not even drink Australian beer. If Australia were blown off the map it would make absolutely no difference to the quality of your life or happiness. Everything would continue to go on as it is. In such a circumstance do you think it would be a good thing to give your life for them?"

"If I had the courage, it would be a good thing. Millions of lives are worth much more than mine is."

"That's what your goody-goody brothers want you to believe," he said. "All these stupid beliefs just give them more control over your life so they can extract more sacrifice from you. The reality of the Guardians is this. If Australia has no direct benefit to your life, then it does not even exist in your universe, and it is not in your self-interest to save it. You would only seek to save it if there was a benefit to you."

"But we are all interconnected. Therefore, it is in our best interest to save them," said Elizabeth. I was proud of her for standing up for what was right.

"WRONG!" he shouted as he stood up and then paced back and forth a few times. "This is where the great division comes between the Guardians and the stupid ones. They think we are connected and seek some irrational benefit from that connection. We know that each is his own universe. We are that we are, and I AM THAT I AM. We are not becoming anything more than we already are. We just are and the intelligent ones make the best of it by making their universe a pleasant one. At first this concept is a harsh reality to accept because you sometimes have to seem uncaring to live by this principle, like torturing the Knights, for example. To make my universe better I had to get some important information from the Knights. To enhance my quality of life I had to learn to ignore their cries of anguish. But do you know what the funny thing is?"

"What?" she asked with some disgust on her face.

"I found that when I did the right thing for my universe I actually enjoyed the necessary pain I inflicted."

"I can now remember that time," said Elizabeth. "I was one of the ones who inflicted pain for you, but I was not doing it for myself. I thought I was doing it to help God and the Pope. I never received any enjoyment from the pain I caused. It hurts me to think about it even now," she said, shaking her head at the memory.

"And do you know why that memory hurts you, but not me?" he asked.

"Why?"

"Because I have accepted who I am and you have not. My decision to put the universe I am in, above the universe of all others, puts an end to all inner conflict. After this great decision is made there is no right and wrong and no guilt. There is only one path to take and that is the road that enhances your personal universe, which is all there is."

"It sounds like your path is very selfish."

"Open your eyes lady!" Philo shouted, leaning close to her face. "The universe of self is all there is! Humor me a moment and close your eyes." He noticed her hesitation. "Come on. Close your eyes for a moment. There's no way that will hurt you."

Elizabeth closed her eyes after hesitating.

"Now, do you sense any other universe except where your individual consciousness is?"

"I sense yours."

"You only hear my voice, you don't share my consciousness. Think about it as you sit there with your eyes closed. The other consciousness out there may or may not exist. It doesn't matter. Within your universe you are all there is, and if a thing does not provide some enhancement to your pleasure or quality of consciousness, you are under no obligation to pursue it."

Elizabeth opened here eyes and said, "So if I get no direct benefit I should go ahead and let the whole continent of Australia be destroyed?"

"That's an extreme example, but think of it. If Australia sinks into the sea and you knew nothing about it, or it has no effect on you, it is as if nothing has happened. Consider this: Even as we speak, somewhere in the universe, a star system has gone supernova and billions of lives have been forever destroyed. But do we feel bad for those inhabitants? No. They have no effect on our consciousness so we just continue to live the best we can in the universe of our creation. Forget about the idea that you get some arcane benefit out of sacrificing yourself for the benefit of others when there is no way they can benefit you. If you can't see, feel and use the benefit, there is none. If there is none then why give of yourself? If this seems selfish you are right. It is. But in the end selfishness is the only motivation that can make a better life for you. Nothing else counts."

"That can't possibly be true," said Elizabeth, shaking her head.

"Oh, but it is true, my little acolyte, and you know within yourself that it is. In today's world selfishness has received a bad rap. People love to practice it and need little selling to let the principle of self rule in their own little universe, but they like to pretend they are something they are not. The masses pretend that they care about others whether they benefit or not. For this reason the disciples of the Guardians preach the standard messages of love and helpfulness which the general populace like to hear to assuage their ignorant sense of guilt. We teach them what they want to hear, but give them what they really want. Then after a long period of hypocrisy there are a few who wake up to what is."

"And what *is*?"

"There is only one thing that is, and that is self. When this realization comes to you, the decision to pursue the one path is then easy. Once the decision is made you do what you have to do to move ahead. Everything is simple. No moral judgments are then necessary. The path is simple self-interest. All future decisions are reduced to one easy equation: *Do the thing that benefits you.*"

"So this is the philosophy you live by?"

"Absolutely. And in that lifetime when I was Brother Phillippi, your teacher, you came very close to embracing the One Path. Unfortunately, your current ignorant husband interfered with my plans for you and delayed your entry into the Brotherhood."

"So what difference does it make to you if I come into the Brotherhood or not? It doesn't affect your universe."

Philo grinned widely, "Oh, but it does my sweet Scarlet. It really does."

At this point I was just captivated by the conversation. I felt I was privileged to hear an actual Dark Brother explaining the true workings of their order of things. Through the crystal I sensed this was information that was rarely revealed, and that Elizabeth's life was in danger merely because she was hearing it.

"So what difference does it make in your universe as to whether I join your cult or whatever it is?" Elizabeth continued.

"Good probing on your part. From what I have told you it is obvious that you can be a benefit to me or I would expend no energy in your direction. Here is the way it is. One of the benefits of being a full member of the Brotherhood is that an adept can gain the power to extend his life, health and power indefinitely. Beyond controlling the masses we draw life energy from and through our immediate disciples..."

Elizabeth cut in, "And I suppose Lance is an immediate disciple?"

"Correct. Thanks to him and other do-gooders who are easily deceived I can draw off some of their life energy without them realizing it."

"And where do I fit in?"

"You are different from Lance. Lance has several lifetimes of tutoring coming before he is ready to make the great decision for Self, but you - you've have been hovering between the two paths for some time now. In our past life together you came close, so very close, to embracing the path. Your husband diverted your attention and took you away from me for a time, but you are still hovering at the portal and have not yet chosen your final path. Now the choice is clear. You can choose the path of power, as I have, and have untold longevity, pleasure and vitality, or you can choose the path of illusion which is basically the path of sacrifice for a dream that never becomes real. I like to call it the path of stupidity."

"You never told me what's in it for you if I were to choose your path."

"It's a little like those multi-levels that so many try to sell us on. At the bottom of the chain you have people buying the product and these people are needed. They are the bread and butter of the system. They are like Lance and other casual followers that keep me and other brethren going. But if the business is really going to work you have to replace yourself and get managers under you. A good manager under you can be worth many end-users, and a certain number is necessary to make everything work. I invested several lifetimes in you, preparing you for this work and when you departed from the path you left a vacuum that I have not yet been able to fill. Nevertheless, all the training and preparation I gave you is still intact. If you were to yet choose the path, even at this late date, all the knowledge I have planted in you would return and you would create a springboard for me to move on to a higher level of power."

Philo's words made me uneasy. "This guy is a real-life vampire of some kind," I said to John.

"That he is," John agreed. "The stories and legends that have been passed down through the ages are distortions of the real thing. The Dark Brothers do not drink blood, but they do steal life force of which the blood is a symbol. Now you must concentrate on your wife. Prepare to be the opposite of the vampire and send Elizabeth your soul energy and help her through this crisis. Tune into the situation and you will know when to act."

I tried to follow John's advice. It was difficult, for I did not feel like remaining still. It would have been a lot easier if I could have just been there and thrown Philo out of the house, but I had to acquiesce and continue to listen.

After a pause Elizabeth said, "So I can be of use to you! That's all well and good, but you must be out of your mind if you think I would join your brotherhood just so you can aspire to a greater station of some kind."

"I think no such thing, my dear. If you would be willing to join with us to help put me above helping yourself, it would only illustrate that you are not ready. I expect you to walk the Path because of selfishness just as did all the brothers before you. Once you are definitely on this path, we can predict your usefulness with a high degree of accuracy."

"I'm sorry to disappoint you, but I see no reason to join you even if I was the most selfish person on earth. Now I think our conversation is over. Would you please leave?" she asked flatly.

"I don't think you want me to leave," he said with confidence in his voice.

"And why don't I know what I want?" she demanded.

"Because I know how you feel."

"And how do I feel?"

"You're feeling very tired. You are so tired and depleted of energy that you feel like you may die."

"We all have to die sometime."

"But you're not ready to die, are you? You have hopes and dreams you haven't even shared with your husband. It crushed you to be incapacitated and useless to God and man. It feels terrible, doesn't it?"

"Of course it feels bad, but my husband will help me and I will soon be healed again."

"You think this John will help you, don't you?"

"It's possible."

"He's just playing with you," he laughed. "That's what the stupid ones do. Oh, excuse me, I mean the *Brothers of Light*. I don't want to be rude here. These light-headed ones dream and dream and dream and never deliver the goods. That's one real basic difference between us. We really deliver the goods and they don't. By the way, the only reason you got sick again is because of your husband's negativity. That's why the dagger returned to you and if I might say so, it is planted more firmly than before and is quickly killing you."

"You've just played with my imagination. I will ignore it and it will soon go away, then I will be well again," Elizabeth said firmly.

"You are indeed mislead." He grabbed a mirror from the coffee table, walked to her side and held it up. "Here. Take a look."

She put her hands to her eyes. "Just go away!"

"I said take a look," he demanded in a loud voice.

"I don't have to look. The dagger is not real!"

"If it is not real then why are you afraid? Now take a look!"

Elizabeth slowly pulled her hands down from her eyes and quickly glanced in the mirror.

She screamed.

"Look again," Philo shouted, grabbing her hair forcing her eyes toward the mirror. "If you want the damned thing removed you have to be aware of the problem. Now take a good look!"

I felt tremendous empathy for Elizabeth as I saw that she could not resist taking another look. She was visibly shaken as she said, "The dagger... It's larger than it was before."

"Of course it is and even as we speak it is getting larger and deeper. I'm sure you feel even weaker now than you did even five minutes ago - like your life is fleeing away from you and there is nothing you can do about it."

"What are you trying to do to me?" she cried, pushing the mirror away. "Do you get some warped pleasure out of destroying me?"

"I am here to help you, and remove the dagger that your mislead husband put there."

"I don't believe you!" she screamed.

"Do you believe you're dying then?" he said.

"And what if I am? What can you do about it?"

"I can give you your life back. Here, let me grab the dagger and pull it out for you."

"Just go - please!" she pleaded.

"You don't really want me to go, do you? I know you want me to take it out and make everything better."

"No. No! I don't want anything to do with you!"

"Yes, you do." After saying that he forcibly grabbed her neck with one hand and seemed to pull the dagger out with the other. "There," he said. "Now you will feel your strength return to you."

"You're just playing with my feelings. Now leave or I will call the police!"

"Why don't you see if you can get out of the chair and walk to the phone?"

"I wouldn't give you the satisfaction even if I could!"

"You will give me the satisfaction," he said. He then shoved her wheelchair over and Elizabeth toppled to the floor. On seeing this I had difficulty remaining still enough to stay focused through the crystal, but I reluctantly gave in to my limitation and continued to watch. But then I found myself surprised to see Elizabeth rise up and give Philo a hefty shove.

"Now get out of here!" she shouted.

"Look at you!" said Philo. "You're standing."

Elizabeth did not seem to realize what she did until that moment and said, "Yes. Yes, I suppose I am standing, aren't I?"

"You certainly are. Now why don't you see if you can take a few steps?"

She seemed to forget about her anger at Philo as she managed to take a couple of shaky steps. "You must have done something right," she said. "I do feel strength coming back."

"Walk around some more. You'll feel stronger by the moment."

She did as he said and walked around the living room and seemed to increase in strength. "OK," she said. "Maybe you have helped me here. Now you can go."

"It isn't quite that simple," he said. "You forget that I am not a member of the stupid brotherhood that does good deeds and expects nothing in return. I have given you your strength back and now I want something in return. That's the code we live by."

Elizabeth stopped walking and sat back down and asked, "So what do you expect?"

"Here's the deal," he said. "I want you back in the fold. I lost you temporarily back in the days of the knights, but now I've come to get back that which is mine."

"I'm not yours, but I am curious as to what your deal is."

"Quite simple. All you do is dedicate your life to the pure benefit of self. Part of that dedication is a commitment to me, for without me you will have no self; therefore, as you help me you help yourself."

"What do you mean by that?" she asked with suspicion in her eyes.

"I mean that I have the power of life and death over you. You commit to me and I will allow you to have a long healthy life. If you refuse, you will die."

"Like I said, we all have to die sometime," Elizabeth replied.

"Not the way you will. If you do not make a commitment I will allow the dagger to return and within hours you will turn into a living vegetable. You will probably linger on in a painful immobile state for several months before you die."

"Even if you do your worst, Joseph will be able to help me. He is getting information right now that may heal me."

"You don't sound very confident."

"I have faith in my husband."

He laughed in a surly way, "I don't know why. You might have felt a little better a couple of times, but your disease always came back. That's because the so-called Light Brothers live in a dream world. Things will always get better tomorrow, but today you're sick, poor and sacrificing. It never ends. This is why the path of the Guardians is so much better. With us you get instant results. You are healed now and you can stay well. Not only can you live a long, successful, healthy life with our path, but the foundation has been laid to extend our lives for perhaps hundreds of years."

"You're dreaming."

"Is it a dream that you have received your strength back? I think you know the answer."

"I will admit that it is possible you represent some type of superhuman power and I may be selfish from time to time, but I don't think I could be purely selfish and I don't want to be on any dark side."

"Dark, light, they are nebulous terms. Whatever you want to call my choice, it is the side of common sense. If there is a side of light, this must be it because I can certainly see with greater clarity of vision than the dreamers. I see immediate benefit and satisfaction."

"You overlook one more thing," she said. "My husband would never go along with supporting you. I would lose him and then I would feel like dying."

"It's you who are overlooking, my dear. Your sweet husband loves you dearly. If he really loves you don't you think he would stand by you no matter what? Isn't that what normal people in love do? I believe that he will not only stay with you, but that he will eventually come over to our side."

"You don't know Joe," she said softly.

"Oh, but I do," Philo responded. "I have dealt with him in

more than one lifetime and I have the advantage. I remember them and he does not. I know his weaknesses better than he knows himself and the plan of attack with him is simple. We don't spring this on him all at once, but we make it a gradual thing. If we do it right, you will not lose him but we will have a great chance to bring him into the fold. If we succeed, his essence may very well add an extra hundred years to each of our lives."

"I don't understand."

"You don't have to understand. All you need to know is that we have a very great and real opportunity here and if we pull it off no one gets hurt. You get your health back for life, I get my disciple back, and Joseph gets to keep the love of his dreams. I call that win-win."

"Even if I wanted my health so badly that I was willing to be completely selfish, I don't think I could take the chance of losing Joseph."

"So are you saying you're refusing my offer?"

"I guess that is what I am saying. I'll just have to take my chances here. Now, will you please leave?"

"I don't think so and I don't think you're refusing me. Let me remind you. If you deny me this day you will begin your march toward a horrible death. By the time you see your husband again you will be a vegetable in torment. Now neither one of us wants that to happen do we?"

"You're just trying to frighten me. Now go."

"Frighten you? You do not know what frighten is. Have you ever thought about what the true key to power is?"

"I don't care."

"I'll tell you anyway since we are having our little moment of truth here. The true key to power is fear. Once a person understands how to use fear to control and manipulate people, then he can virtually get anything he wants out of them."

"But you failed with my husband and others. When he was a Knight he resisted the fear of death and you had no power over him."

At that instant Philo slapped Elizabeth in the face with great force. "That is the last time you will challenge me. Do you hear me? The last time!"

I was so unsettled by this that I just about lost contact with the crystal, but John motioned to me. "Getting upset will not help her. Just hang on and focus and the moment of opportunity will come."

"But I can't wait any longer. I've got to do something!"

"You will - trust me," John replied.

"But how will I know when and what to do?" I asked.

"If she either vocally or in her heart cries out for help from God, then at that moment, you can help her and it will be given you what to do."

"But look how distracted she is. What if she does not think to ask God for help?"

John glanced downward and said, "Then we must let her go."

"Let her go? Are you crazy? I will never let her go!"

"Whatever a person's decision is, good or bad, we must not interfere as far as it affects his own life. If a person decides on the Dark Path, the best thing to do is withdraw. If you do not he, or she, will drag you down with him."

"Then she must make the right decision because I don't know if I could just let her go. I think I'd rather have a dagger in my back," I said with a lump in my throat.

"I know how you feel," he said sadly. "It would be difficult for you, but I have faith you will do the right thing no matter what happens here. Now if you really want to help your wife you must focus on the situation at hand."

I turned back to the scene and was amazed that we seemed to have that interchange of conversation with little or no time passing. It was a little like watching a recorded movie, freezing the tape, and then resuming.

Philo composed himself and said, "The true path to power is not without obstacles, but I will tell you this. Obstacles in our path are removed with much greater ease than the so-called path of Light and Love. Your husband and others are merely a mild irritation to us with no ultimate consequence."

Elizabeth got up, shaking her head, trying to regain composure and said, "But from the way you just reacted, he must have been more than a mild irritation to you."

Philo's face turned red with an inner rage that was dangerously surfacing and he nearly shouted, "All those who have opposed the Guardians have had their day. The time has come when all will be forced into submission or die! The will of those who oppose us will be crushed under a mighty weight!" Philo paused, composing himself and added, "Perhaps a little demonstration is in order here. It is your time to make a decision. You must either be for or against me. If you choose to be with me you will live, but if you side against me you will die a horrible death. It's that simple."

Elizabeth seemed shaken, but gathered her forces and replied, "What if I don't want to decide?"

"You must decide. Now go ahead. I dare you. Try to decide against me and I will first-handedly demonstrate how fear controls and wills are crushed, and why our side is the only side that has a chance of ultimate triumph."

"I refuse to cooperate with you by making any decision," Elizabeth answered resolutely. I felt proud of her for her courage.

"Then let me put it to you this way. Any answer you give me that is not a *yes* is a *no*. Now let me ask you one more time. Are you for or against me?"

Elizabeth looked very strained but managed to reply, "I refuse to give you any answer." She started walking toward the phone and said, "I'm calling the police."

Philo ran over to the phone, grabbed it and ripped it out of the wall, "It looks to me that you are giving me a *no*. I expected such for your first response. But this is good. It gives me an opportunity to demonstrate the true power of fear and terror."

He then forcibly grabbed Elizabeth, put his left arm around her and applied heavy pressure to two points in her throat just below the chin. As he applied the pressure he whispered something to her as she drifted out of consciousness.

"What has he done to my wife?" I exclaimed to John. "We have to do something here!"

"He's applying a forcible hypnotic technique that is one of the favorites of the Dark Ones."

"Well, that's not fair then. If Elizabeth goes along with him because she is hypnotized, that shouldn't count against her."

"But hypnosis has its limitations," said John. "It can amplify the power of our fears or desires, but its power cannot force a person to knowingly decide for or against something that is contrary to his internal principles. It is a universal law that the choice between the two paths cannot be forced. Circumstances may be forced upon us as is now the case with Elizabeth, but the choice cannot be forced. Both sides of the Brotherhood know this."

"It just looks to me as if Elizabeth is a victim of unfair circumstances," I said.

"As were you and I at one time," John replied. "But on the bright side, if she passes this test, circumstances will be in her favor with her next choice."

"I hope so," I said as I looked on. "I certainly hope so."

For a moment Elizabeth continued to lie motionless on the floor as Philo continued to whisper in her ear. He released the pressure and she slowly regained consciousness. "And what do you think of the little torture chamber I have prepared for you my dear?"

Elizabeth let out a blood-curdling scream.

"Now what's going on here?" I demanded to John.

"Philo has created a very real illusion for Elizabeth," he said. "You can see it by making a mental request through the crystal."

I did so and began to see phantom images appear around Elizabeth. I saw that the poor woman thought she was in some ancient torture chamber stretched out on a rack.

"You poor thing," said Philo sarcastically. "Despite all your efforts you have not been able to rid yourself from all your guilt that was caused by your horrible past. That's the trouble with the stupid unselfish ones - their guilt brings them untold pain and suffering. I have a big advantage over you, my dear. I feel good about what I have done and have no guilt; therefore I have no punishment." He laughed in a way that made me cringe.

Elizabeth looked around her in horror. "Take me out of this torture chamber - please."

"Please? What a silly word." He turned the phantom wheel of the phantom rack and Elizabeth screamed in pain. To my surprise and horror her body seemed to respond as if it was on a real torture rack. "Is that tight enough for you, or perhaps a little more pressure?" He then turned the wheel again. She screamed again.

"John!" I shouted. "We've got to do something here! Please let me help her!"

"The only way to help her is to be patient and wait for your window. Now get a grip on yourself or we'll lose contact completely and all will be lost," he replied impatiently.

This was the most difficult event of my life. I felt I was in more torture than was Elizabeth; I couldn't let her die at the hands of this devil. Nevertheless, I tried my best to bide my time.

Philo spoke again to Elizabeth. "Before you torture anyone else in the future you must be aware of one important thing. If you continue on the path of Self and commit to it, you have nothing to worry about. The pain you inflicted cannot be used against you. But if you get weak in the knees and follow the delusion of redemption, then sooner or later karma does work and everything will come back to haunt you. But it won't be God that is doing it to you. It is used as a useful tool in the hands of the disciples of the Guardians."

At this point my curiosity got the best of me. "Is it true John that a man as wicked as Philo can escape karma while people trying to redeem themselves suffer? That doesn't seem right."

"On that point he is deceived," said John. He does not escape karma, as he supposes but delays the payment with interest. His correction will eventually take a different, more drastic form. Now you must pay attention."

I looked toward Elizabeth and heard her plead, "Please make all this go away!"

"Sure. I can make it go away," Philo laughed. "All you have to do is make a simple commitment to me that you will be my eternal disciple."

"If I did that it would just be a lie. I would change my mind later."

"Not so, my dear. Not so. You must make an oath to me in the name of the Most High God. When you make this oath in God's name you then swear allegiance to me and the Guardians and this creates a binding power between us that cannot be severed. On the other hand, if you do not cooperate, you will not only be put to death physically, but you will lose your soul. Perhaps a little hot iron on your feet will help you make up your mind."

I saw that Philo placed a phantom red-hot iron on the sole of Elizabeth's foot. She screamed and grimaced in pain just as much as if it were real. He released the iron and said, "Because of your past selfishness there is no way out for you. From here on out I have power to bring you great pain, even from a distance. If you do not commit to me, all that awaits you is a short time of pain and suffering. Then you will die, but that's the fun part. If you think there is not a hell you ought to think again. If you reject me, then an eternal hell awaits you where you will suffer forever in a state that makes your current situation look like paradise."

"You're trying to frighten me again," she cried.

"Of course I'm trying to frighten you, but you are only frightened because a part of you deep inside believes me. You see, the Guardians are the caretakers of Hell. We take souls in the next world who are wracked with guilt and play with them. It's a great source of entertainment for us and prepares them to be our puppets in a future life."

"You're horrible!"

"What's horrible to one is delicious to another," he laughed.

"Now, have we reached a decision yet?"

"NO!" she shouted.

"Perhaps this boiling oil will help you decide." He raised a phantom vase of hot oil and proceeded to pour it over her stomach.

My poor wife screamed again. I didn't know how much longer I could take this.

Philo stopped pouring and said, "Just tell me you have a decision for me and I will make this all go away and you will feel fine again."

Elizabeth said nothing and Philo started pouring again.

"OK, OK, I'll make a decision. Please stop!"

"And what is that decision?"

"I need a moment to think without pain. Make it go away and I will give you a decision."

"I will give you several moments to think about it, but if I take away the pain you may make the wrong decision. Here, let me help you make up your mind." A large phantom saber then appeared in his hand. Elizabeth saw it and screamed, but Philo merely smiled and shoved it through Elizabeth's upper thigh. The poor thing withered in even greater pain. Philo then took another sword and did the same with the other thigh. Finally he took a third one and shoved it into her abdomen. I think I felt more pain than she did as I forced myself to wait for the window John promised.

"Are we nice and comfortable now?" he asked Elizabeth in a mocking tone. "Now you just take a couple of minutes to think about your little decision while I go in your kitchen and make me a sandwich. Oh, by the way, if your decision is *no* I have another saber that I will shove into your heart. That will begin a long and painful death process for you."

As he walked laughing toward the kitchen she shouted toward him. "How can you do this to me?"

"You'll find out soon enough. Now don't disturb me while I eat." He then went to the refrigerator and began making himself a sandwich.

I somehow sensed the window of opportunity that John talked about was approaching and I used all my energy to send Elizabeth comforting thoughts. I began to realize how drained I was because of my encounter with the Ancient of Days and wasn't sure if my thoughts were of any use.

As I paid full attention to Elizabeth I did begin to sense her thoughts and feelings. I felt she was going through tremendous fear, pain and stress and that she was feeling that God himself had betrayed her and had left her out to dry, so to speak. "I feel the window is approaching," I said to John. "What should I do?"

"Before you can help her she must call out to God for help. The best thing you can do for now is to send her all the love you can."

I tried to follow his advice. I thought it may help to amplify my feelings to think back on our most loving and stimulating moments. As I did this my feelings of love seemed amplified. I sensed it had something to do with the power of the crystal. It seemed to have some effect on her as I sensed her thoughts drifting toward God, but not necessarily in a good way. "Why God?" she said within herself, "are you allowing this to happen to me? Haven't I suffered enough? Now there seems to be no way out. It looks like I may have to play along with him to save myself."

"No!" I tried to shout at her. "You can't go along with him in any way or I will lose you forever!"

Elizabeth's thoughts seemed to still a moment and I wondered if she registered my plea. Then I felt her thoughts again, "It seems like I must make a choice, but I'm damned if I do and damned if I don't. If I choose the Dark Side I may get my health back, but I couldn't live with myself if I became like Philo. If I tell Philo no then I will die a horrible death and may go to that hell he talked about. I don't want to make either choice!" she exclaimed within herself. Then her thought continued, "According to the parable that John gave us those who go to the true hell are those who cannot make a choice. I must make a choice because Philo said no choice would be the same as a *no* answer. The problem is that neither choice seems desirable."

There was a silence for a moment that greatly disturbed me. I thought she had given up. Then I felt her thoughts again, thoughts that pierced me to the very soul. "O God! Please tell me what to do! There has to be a way out. Please, please show me what to do!"

"This is the window!" John shouted. "Tune in to the crystal and you will know what to project to her."

I tuned in and somehow the words I was supposed to send her formed in my mind, and I knew that I was to send them to her with all my power. I tried to gather the spiritual energy to convey the message, but contact with the crystal was a constant drain on me and I couldn't hold on any longer and collapsed to the floor.

John released himself from the crystal and came to my aid. "I was afraid of this," he said. "I thought you were too drained to do this, but we had to try."

I forced myself up and staggered toward the crystal, but John held me back. "No!" he shouted. "You are too weak. If you touch it again before you recover you will die."

"It's better to die trying to help Elizabeth than to live with her as Philo's disciple." I headed toward the crystal again.

"NO!" shouted John pulling me back again. "Don't you understand? Even if we lose Elizabeth it's important that you stay on and do the work you were born for!"

"But don't you understand?" I cried. "I will be of no use to you or anyone else if I do not make every possible effort to save her!"

I started toward the crystal again and just before I touched it John tackled me with a decisive force that surprised me. To my amazement I found myself in a life and death struggle with the man I admired most in all the world, but something within me - with even greater authority than John told me I had to make every effort to save Elizabeth at any cost.

I found that John was no weakling for his age but I finally got a little leverage on him and shoved him backward. This gave me just the time I needed to lay my hands on the crystals again. At the moment of contact I realized that John knew what he was talking about. It felt like a lightening bolt passed through me and I had a strong feeling that certain death awaited me. Then the thought occurred to me that if I must die then I will die trying; and at that moment I drew strength within myself that I never realized I had... and again Elizabeth appeared before me. I sensed that she was waiting for an answer and that I was supposed to give it to her. I had the message for her with crystal clarity in my mind, but even with superhuman will I had no strength to deliver it and felt my life beginning to leave me.

At that instant I saw John's face. He had a look of disappointment I will never forget. Not only did he look like he was losing his best friend, but he had the look of a person who was watching 50 years of labor going up in flames, the look of a person who was losing everything. I sensed that I had about two seconds of thinking time left in this world and during that short eternity I thought about how I was failing not only the love of my life but also my best friend. I couldn't go this way. I just couldn't. I had time to release one sentence and one sentence only.

I shouted with all the energy I had left, "O Lord, my God give me strength!"

Suddenly I felt a Presence. At first I thought it was some angel sent to escort me to the next world, but then I realized that I was still standing with both hands touching the crystals. Again, Elizabeth was clearly in my view and my strength seemed to return. I sensed the power of a great being to my right and a glance revealed a vague outline of a human form. John's eyes widened as he quickly got up and also put his hands on the crystals and shouted. "Don't you see what's happened here?" He spoke reverently, "The Ancient of Days has come to assist us. He has given you the strength to continue. You must act now!"

Without hesitation I tuned into Elizabeth's thoughts. I realized that she had reached the limitation of her endurance and was about to give up on any answer from God. I immediately poured out with all my soul the words I knew she needed to hear. "He that will seek to save his life shall lose it, but he that will lose his life for my sake shall save it." I repeated this over and over with all my strength, hoping beyond hope that it would help. Then I ended it with the saying we both loved. "There is nothing too good to be true."

Even with the help of the Ancient of Days my power seemed to be limited and I only had strength enough to observe and pray from that point on.

Philo came back into the living room where Elizabeth was lying on the floor. He was just finishing off a sandwich as if he had no care in the world as he said flippantly, "Well, my dear, I assume that ten minutes of this agony is much more than you want to ever put up with again, let alone the rest of your life and eternity. So what is your decision?"

Elizabeth rose up on one elbow and spoke with a strained voice. "I asked God what to do and I received an answer."

"You're delusional my dear, but I'm curious. What is the answer?"

"The words of Jesus came into my mind. *He that will seek to save his life shall lose it, but he that will lose his life for my sake shall save it.*"

"That's the stupidest statement anyone has ever made," Philo shouted angrily. "The best thing to do with things that make no sense is to ignore them."

"But it does make sense," she insisted. "It makes more sense right now than anything has ever made to me. If I seek to save my life by going along with you I will lose it, but if I am prepared to do the right thing even at the cost of my life, only then will I have a chance to save it; and somehow I believe that Joseph will deliver me from whatever you can dish out."

"So what is your decision in plain English?" he demanded.

"The answer is no! I will not go along with you in this life, in my next life or any other life. Is that clear enough?"

He kicked over the coffee table with great force and shouted. "You poor stupid ignorant devil! You have no idea what you have just done. You have not only consigned yourself to unimaginable terror and suffering, but you have just made yourself my sworn enemy and the enemy of all Guardians from henceforth and forever! You have delayed my next step forward, but you won't deny my a final pleasure of putting an end to you once and for all!"

Suddenly he produced another phantom sword of great length and instantly shoved it into her heart. "How much pain does this poor woman have to go through?" I thought within myself as I watched her scream with pain.

"You are privileged my dear to be a recipient of my trade mark, my lethal death blow. It's the perfect crime. No one will be able to prove that you did not die of natural causes." He then pulled out the other three swords from her thighs and stomach and made the illusion of the torture chamber disappear. "There," he said. "Now you just have one good instrument of death as your final companion."

"You can't leave me this way!" she exclaimed.

"Oh. Does this mean you have second thoughts?" he asked.

She paused a moment. I couldn't blame her for being tempted for an instant, but then she replied firmly. "I've made my decision. I will never desert or betray my husband, and I will never follow you or the Dark Brothers with you."

"Well, you made your bed. Now you must lie in it. This last saber will take all your strength from you in less than an hour. After that you will be too far gone for anyone to save." Philo headed toward the front door. As he reached for the handle he turned and said, "But not to worry. If no one removes the sword, your life will linger on for about three months. You will be just conscious enough to enjoy a slow death while I sap your remaining life energy. Now I must bid you adieu."

As Philo opened the door and started to leave Elizabeth called out to him. "Philo," she said.

"Yes?"

"There is nothing too good to be true."

He stopped a moment as if he was considering the phrase and said, "Whatever." Then he closed the door and was gone.

All my strength was gone. As Philo closed the door I had to let go of the crystals. As I did I felt the Presence of the Ancient of Days depart. John came to me, offered his hand and lifted me up. Instead of his usual calmness he had great excitement in his voice. "Do you realize what just happened?"

"Yes, I think I do. It seems that we have saved the soul of Elizabeth and now I must save her life."

"Yes, that is true, but something even more important has happened. Don't you realize?"

"I'm not sure."

"The Ancient of Days was here and personally assisted you."

"Is something unusual about that? I would assume he helps a lot of people."

"Oh, he does, he does, but not personally. He just about always works through others. That's what I and other members of the Brotherhood are for. This time He made an exception and came to personally assist you. Do you know what that means?"

"What does it mean?"

"It means that the success of our mission is even more important than I realized. The Ancient of Days has a personal interest in you and this means that we are going to see some great things happen in the days ahead. This may be the cycle of opportunity the Brotherhood has so long awaited," he said with great emotion in his eyes.

"That's great," I said, "but meanwhile I have less than an hour to get home wherever it is from here and save my wife. You've got to get me back there right away."

"I must say that I admire you for not even letting the Ancient of Days distract you from your goal. Maybe it's because you don't see the big picture the way I do, but whatever the case, my hat is off to you."

"Thanks, but I'm against a deadline here. You've got to send me back home."

"And once there, how do you plan on saving her?"

I had to admit I had not thought about that. I was just following my impulse to get back to her, thinking there had to be something I could do. I paused a moment and looked at John. "You have to go with me. I know that you can restore her to health again."

"The teacher does not do for the disciple what the disciple can do for himself," he said softly.

"What are you saying? That I should heal her?"

"Yes. That's exactly what I am saying."

"But I'm not a miracle-worker like you are. I don't know what to do."

"You don't? If I read you correctly you have already restored her to health once before. What makes you think you can't do it again?"

"But the last time I simply followed what I saw you do. I'm not sure what to do this time."

"All great works are done by people of good intent who merely learned what needed to be done and then had the courage to go ahead and do it," he said.

"So what am I supposed to do to heal her?"

"You have to pull out the sword Philo left in her."

"But the sword is an imaginary one produced by hypnosis."

"That doesn't matter. By using mind control Philo was able to insert a phantom sword that is just as deadly to her as a real one. An important lesson for all healers to learn is that a thing imagined, yet sustained by the power of belief, is just as real as reality itself."

"So I am just supposed to go up to her and pretend I am pulling something out?"

"You will not be pretending. In the illusion she is experiencing you will be doing something real."

"Well, I guess I will do whatever it will take. Just pulling out a sword does not seem to be enough though."

"There is one more thing you must do."

"What is that?"

"Before you withdraw the sword you must tell her that I told you to do it."

"Why? Will that help with the healing?"

"The key word here is authority," said John. "Many doctors are not particularly good healers, but if a patient trusts their authority, even a sugar pill can bring them great relief. Now that Philo is overcome I am the greatest living authority in Elizabeth's mind. You must use this key to your advantage."

"I think I understand. Now can you get me back home?"

"Yes. It is about time for you to go. We must go back to the receiving room and return your robe. Then you can return home."

We rushed back to the receiving room and I seemed to know

exactly where my robe belonged and hung it up again. I wondered in my mind how long it had been since my last visit. For some reason that was hidden from me. I also wondered how long it would be until I would return to this place and also what other surprises were in store for me. "OK. What do we do now?" I asked anxiously. "Is there a Scotty here to beam me back?"

"No. It is not like that, but it is a scientific process. I concentrate and draw from the knowledge and power of the Masters above me and focus on your location. In order to transport someone besides myself I must take advantage of certain windows and one is approaching in about ten minutes."

"Ten minutes! There isn't much time. Can't you send me now?"

"Because of the nature of this location we have to rely on windows of energy. My hands are tied until one arrives in about ten minutes. We should be able to get you back in plenty of time to save Elizabeth, however."

"I hope so," I said. "After all she has gone through I don't want to fail her now."

"I understand your concern," said John, putting his hand on my shoulder.

We both waited in silence for a couple minutes. For some reason I had reservations about the healing power of removing the phantom sword. Finally I asked, "What if I pull the sword out and nothing happens? Is there anything else I can do?"

"That should be sufficient," said John. "The only real danger would be if you did not arrive in time and I have calculated that should be no problem."

Being acutely aware of Murphy's law prevailing in my life I asked, "But let us just say that by some fluke the pulling out of the sword was not enough... Then what?"

"Every disciple must face a crisis like this several times in his life," said John. "Hopefully, this is not one of those times. But just in case let me offer you the words of the Master. *With God all things are possible.* You have been a great example of this teaching even here tonight. Even I thought you were in a situation where it was impossible to save Elizabeth, but you risked your life, put everything on the line and called out to God for help.

"After you did all in your power a Brother came forward with more power and knowledge than yourself and helped you. Then a similar thing happened to Elizabeth. She did everything within her power to do the right thing and called out to God for help. At that point you came forward and assisted her."

"That's true, but I'm certainly not God in the sense that anyone prays to me."

"Maybe not, but you are in touch with the One Great Universal Spirit of God that connects all the Workers of Light. As you notice from our experience here the assistance that God offers comes through lives such as ourselves, great and small. We are like the appendages of God just as the Apostle Paul taught. Without the help of spiritual beings responding to the Spirit of God most prayers would go unanswered."

"So, if I do all I can do within my own power and still get in a jam, the final step is to ask God for help?"

"Yes, and if you ask in faith and selflessness a member of the Brotherhood will register the need and respond. Then there is one more thing you must do."

"And what is that?" I asked.

"You must listen with the inner ear for the answer. This is perhaps the most overlooked step in the process."

There was another short period of painful silence. Finally, I said, "You know Philo made some compelling arguments for selfishness. I have to admit that somewhere in the universe, even at this moment, a star system is going nova and billions of lives are destroyed as we speak. If we were to be concerned about all lives in the universe it would be enough to drive us crazy."

"To follow the path of selflessness and love does not mean that you scatter your energy all over the universe. It does mean, however, that you seek to help others within your sphere of influence. Another star system is way out of your influence, but if all the Brothers of Light in all parts of the universe do their job, however small that may be, then eventually the spiritual hopes and dreams of all the lives in all parts of the universe will come true. If everyone were selfish like Philo, no one would have their prayers answered and the God of Love would be rejected. The universe of Self must be expanded to the universe of All. The evolving soul is not alone in his consciousness as the Dark Brothers suppose. As you continue to experience the joining of souls and learn this from experience you will find a fullness of joy."

"Even at this moment of tension I find myself enjoying your words," I said. "How much longer?"

"The window is now approaching," he said, looking up with his eyes closed. "Now do not disturb my concentration or you may wind up in California rather than Boise, Idaho."

"OK," I said. "Let's go for it! Just don't beam me to San Franciso."

"Beaming is not the right word. Now be quiet and let me concentrate. It is safest to return you to the spot where we picked you up. Just be careful you don't get arrested."

"Arrested. Why would I get arrested?" Then I looked down and remembered that my clothes were back in the car. "OK. I'll be careful."

After a moment of silence I felt that tingling feeling again and the next instant I found myself about ten feet away from my car. I quickly looked around. Fortunately no one was in immediate sight. It was nighttime so that helped. I ran over to my car and grabbed the door. To my horror it was locked. I went around to the other side and that was locked also. Either some do-gooder, thief or heaven-only-knows who locked my doors for some reason that even John did not foresee. Then a thought came to my mind that bothered me almost as much as anything that Philo could have come up with. I had to somehow make it home through several miles of highly populated city streets in the nude and in the process avoid being arrested before time ran out on my beloved wife.

I immediately took off running at top speed through the park and figured that the safest route would be to hit as many back alleys as possible. Maybe I could find a clothesline on the way and steal something to wear. The first five minutes seemed to go all right. I made it across the park and through several alleys. It wasn't like the movies though where the hero always finds some clothes after a moment or so in this situation. After this experience I concluded that there is not a single outdoor clothesline in the whole city of Boise. Then after about the third alley I had to cross a major street and almost caused a wreck. As I darted into another alley I heard honking and shouting behind me. I ignored it and continued on at full speed.

The next thing I became aware of was that I seemed to enter an area of the city with a high density of dogs. Each alley I ran down seemed to have about a hundred of them. Fortunately, up to this moment they were all tied up or in dog runs, but then I encountered a loose one that started chasing me. I grabbed a stick and tried to fend him off, but it seemed to make the creature more determined than ever. He bit me twice on the leg before I finally got away from him.

As if that were not bad enough, in the next alley I stepped on a broken bottle and put a sizable gash in my foot. This slowed me down considerably. I hobbled along the best I could as I looked through several trashcans for something to put on my foot. The best I could come up with was several pieces of cardboard and a trash liner. As I was working to tie the cardboard on my foot with pieces of the plastic liner I heard a boy shout. "Dad. There's a naked man going through our trash." Then as soon as I heard "Honey, get my gun!" I was on my way, bad foot or not. My makeshift shoe kept coming off and finally I found a place with no barking dogs where I could take a moment and fasten it more securely.

That helped a little, but now I had another major hurtle. I had to cross at least three blocks of high traffic area where there were no alleys. If this was what it is like to be an exhibitionist, no one has to worry about me becoming one. Nevertheless, I took a deep breath, hoped for the best and ran down the sidewalk. I must have been quite a sight. There I was with a piece of cardboard tied on one foot and streaks of blood from a dogbite on my other leg.

The first three or four people I passed seemed to be somewhat entertained by me, but as luck would have it I bumped into some guy who looked like a football player with his date. He seemed to want to impress his girlfriend by running me down and teaching me a lesson.

As I turned around I saw that he was not far behind me. I ignored the pain in my foot and ran ahead at full speed and finally came to another alley and ran into it. I found some bushes and hid behind them. The guy was in hot pursuit but seemed to not notice me as he walked by the bushes. Then to my horror some more dogs started barking and he spotted me and jumped on me.

At that time I found myself in a life and death struggle with a much younger and probably stronger man. It was not my life that was at stake, but my wife's and perhaps that gave me extra strength, for I had a much greater motivation to win than my opponent did. I freed myself of him for a moment but then he tackled me again and I found I had no choice but to deck him a good one. Fortunately, the blow stunned him for a moment and this gave me the extra few seconds I needed to get away.

I was getting close to home now and hoped I could make it the rest of the distance without incident. As I reached the end of the next alley I saw three police cars whiz by with lights flashing. I hoped they were not looking for me, but feared they could be. Now I had three blocks left to go. The good news was that there was not much traffic in those three blocks; but the bad news was that the alleys were in the in the wrong direction for me to use.

I took another deep breath and headed up the hill toward our home. A car appeared out of the blue and drove by, stopped and started backing up. I darted into another alley even though it headed the wrong direction for me. After reaching the next street I headed toward my house again, going around the block in the other direction. After I finally got there I concluded it was too dangerous to try to enter through the front door. Besides it may be locked and I had no key. I went to the back door and it was locked tight. I banged on the door but realized that Elizabeth was incapacitated and could not answer.

I had only one choice and that was to break in. I found a cement duck we had on the patio and broke our den window with it and crawled through it as quickly as possible. I ran into the living room and found Elizabeth barely conscious on the floor.

"My sweetheart. Can you hear me?"

She looked at me with tired eyes, "My dear husband, I knew you would come. My faith in you was never broken. Oh, I feel so weak, so tired. I think you may lose me. Maybe we can be together in a future life."

"We'll be together in this one. Now look at me," I demanded, holding up her head.

"I'm too tired to go on," she sighed.

"No you aren't. I've put too much investment in you to lose you now. Now open your eyes."

After a pause she managed to force them open. I looked deeply into them and said, "Sweetheart, I am going to pull the sword out of your heart and then your strength will return and everything will be OK. Do you hear me?"

"Yes. How did you know about the sword?"

"It's a long story, but I know all about it."

"You've got to get Philo to pull it out. I don't know if you can do it."

"Listen to me very carefully. John knows all about the sword and he sent me back to pull it out so you can be well again."

"John sent you?" she asked hopefully.

"Yes. John sent me and gave me instructions to pull the sword out."

"If John told you then you must have the power to pull it out."

"Yes. I do have the power to pull it out. I am going to pull the sword out now and you will be restored to health. Just tell me when you are ready."

"Are you sure this will work?"

"Yes. I am sure. John hasn't been wrong yet has he?"

"No I guess he hasn't. It's just that I feel so weak. I hope you are not too late." She paused a moment and said courageously, "OK. Go ahead. Pull the damn thing out!"

I couldn't see the sword the way I could from the crystal, but I did remember the approximate location and placed my hand there as if I were grabbing the handle and said, "There. Are you ready for me to pull it out?"

"Get a good grip and do it in one pull."

I did my best to imagine that I was pulling out a real sword. I acted like it was in so deep that it took a major effort on my part to yank it out, but finally got the job done with an academy award performance. "There. I've got it!"

"Yes, yes, I think you have. I felt it leave. The pain and discomfort is leaving, but my strength is gone. I think you may be too late. Hold me my darling, at least I will die in peace."

"Elizabeth! You must stay with me. After all that has happened I cannot lose you now," I cried.

She bravely forced her eyes open. "You'll just miss me for a short time. We will be together again soon. I want to tell you how much I love you and that thinking of you gave me the strength to resist Philo. I am finally free of him and feel at peace. I want you to know that."

As she closed her eyes I felt tears stream down my face. This could not be the end. It just couldn't be. "Elizabeth!" I cried. "The sword is gone! You don't have to go! You don't have to go..."

I held her lifeless body for a moment before I realized that she was indeed gone. I felt her pulse to make sure and there was none. I wet my hand and put it under her nose and mouth and felt no breathing.

"Was this it?" I thought. "Is she really gone?" If she is really dead, then there seemed to be nothing else I could do. As I held her another moment in silence the words of John came back to :

Then I remembered that I was supposed to ask God after I did all I could do. Well, I reached a dead end. There was nothing further that I could do to help Elizabeth so I cried out, "Oh God, My Father, My Mother, my Brother, my Sister! Whatever form You take and wherever You are, I know that with You all things are possible even to the bringing my beloved back from the land of the dead. I ask in the name of Christ and all that is holy and good, return Elizabeth to me."

I was silent for a moment as I watched Elizabeth's face, hoping that she would open her eyes. But then one moment turned into two and nothing seemed to happen and I began to become disheartened. "Who am I to think that God would perform this impossible feat for me?" I thought. Then, as I was about to give up I again remembered John's words that the most important part of this process was to listen.

It occurred to me that I was perhaps too emotional to listen as I should, so I calmed myself down, held Elizabeth tight and tuned in to my inner self. At first nothing happened, but then after a period of time a thought came to my mind with great force. The thought went something like this: "Speak aloud the name of God and the power, glory and life thereof will be manifest."

I pondered upon this thought with great perplexity. John had taught me that the words of God to Moses revealed that He had no name. Instead, He merely told Moses that *I AM becoming that which I decide to become.* If He has no name, as we know it, then how am I to speak it? After another moment's contemplation I decided to ask for more knowledge. I cried out again, "What name am I to speak?"

Again nothing came and I had to force myself to listen. After a short reflection the phrase from the gospel of John came to me, "In the beginning was the Word and the Word was with God, and the Word was God... Speak the Word."

"But how can I speak the Word when I am not sure what the Word is?" I thought to myself. I was aware that standard theology interprets the Word as Christ, but somehow I felt that this was not the Word I was guided toward.

Another period of silence passed and another impression came: "Remember the chairs."

The chairs, the chairs. Yes. In Shamballa I was told to sit and there seemed to be no chair upon which to sit, but when I trusted, there was an invisible chair to hold me. Did this mean I was to attempt to speak the name of God or some mysterious Word, and the Word would just come or be there? I concluded that this was the direction I must take.

I laid Elizabeth on the couch, held her hand and prayed within my heart, "Please God, let me say the right Word." Then I looked at her lifeless, yet beautiful and angelic face and opened my mouth and a strange sound came out. I knew intuitively that it was the wrong sound, but I was on the right path and I attempted to say the Word again. This time it felt better, but still wrong so I tried a third time. Suddenly, I felt within every fiber of my being that I had the correct Word. The Word reverberated within my soul and seemed so familiar that I wondered why every living thing in the universe did not sing it out.

I looked at Elizabeth and repeated the Word, fully expecting her to rise, but nothing seemed to happen again. I began to feel sorry for myself when I shook myself and realized that maybe there was one more thing I needed to listen for. I asked, "What final thing must I do?"

Again the answer came, "As you say the Word, see the Word creating Life, bringing glory to God."

My heart took courage and I again grabbed Elizabeth's hand and visualized her life returning as I said the Word. I felt an additional energy surround both of us and sensed a slight glow around her body. I continued saying the Word as I thought about the Glory of God. Then I visualized Elizabeth living a life that would bring glory and honor to the name of God and that I would also dedicate myself to this goal. This thought seemed the most powerful of all, and in the midst of this thought I felt a bolt of spiritual energy go through me into my wife. It made me feel so weak I fell to the floor. Immediately I struggled to lift myself and as I raised myself to Elizabeth's eye level I saw her eyes open. looking at me with that curious look of hers, "Am I in some dream or are you naked as a jay bird?"

I laughed with nervous joy, "Yes. I guess I am. It's a long story."

"This better be good," she said, lifting herself up, smiling, showing off that mysterious inner glow that I have always loved. "And look at you! You're hurt. Your foot is bleeding on the floor and the other leg looks like you have dog bites and you've got scratches on your body. I think I want to hear your story before I tell you mine."

"Do you realize what just happened?" I exclaimed.

"I'm not sure," she said. "I thought I was going to die and it seemed like I went to sleep, but it was so real, not like a dream. I went to the New Jerusalem and saw many wonderful things."

"You'll have to tell me what you saw, but first let me hold you close"

We embraced sweetly for several moments, but then she pushed me away and said, "Let's get you cleaned and doctored up." She led me toward the shower.

"Look!" I exclaimed. "You have your strength back."

She twirled around and said, "I do and I feel great! This is the best day of my life."

"And this is the best day of my life," I affirmed as I headed toward the shower looking forward to being cared for by the love of my life.